Praise for *The Book of Malchus*

"*The Robe* meets *Pirates of the Caribbean*. Mythology, adventure, irresistible romance, and a refreshing plunge into life's deepest dilemmas, all masterfully intermixed.

"In all, a punishing read—no sleep, no food, no breaks, constantly fabricating excuses to explain why I couldn't leave my recliner.

"It'll cost me something to redeem these thirty hours of domesti Flowers. An overnighter at our favorite resort. A gift card to N

"'Honey, you gotta read this,' I say.

"Chill silence. She's got me. She knows it.

"Can't leave the book, so I'll have to pay.

"Fantastic. Truly well done. A joy to read."

— Frank Richardson, author of *Where the*

"The authors of *The Book of Malchus* weave an interesting tale of a hard-eyed Roman businessman whose life is changed by a chance encounter with a Judean teacher crucified under the authority of Rome as a rebel. The intricate plot gives the protagonist both a plausible reason to cross paths with one Jesus of Galilee and a plausible tie to a new world across the ocean where the coming of a Savior has been foretold. The tale illustrates how a mighty change in one man's heart can influence generations yet unborn. If you enjoy historical fiction, you will find this story intriguing."

— Don Searle, editor and author of *Light in the Harbor,*
 Two Works, and *Double Image*

"Fascinating historical events with equally fascinating characters are woven together to create a compelling historical novel which is both educational and exciting. A great plot with substance and style!"

— Harold Brown, former commissioner of LDS Family Services
 and past managing director of Welfare Services

"Weaving history and faith into a vivid tapestry of startlingly rich textured storytelling, Newell and Hamblin create a sweeping tale as profound as it is captivating. Characters, crafted with insight and compassion, draw you into their deepest yearnings and fears as they move with passionate determination and courage through the epic arc of their lives. *The Book of Malchus* delivers an action-packed, character-driven story that takes us into the fascinating world of ancient Carthage, Jerusalem, and America and illuminates a fresh and thought-provoking perspective on belief, courage, and faith."

—Peter Johnson, motion picture writer and director

"Written with both riveting skill and a deft grasp of history, *The Book of Malchus* draws readers into a rich and lively tale of wealth and intrigue, of profound questions about life's meaning, that exhales a fresh breeze across the worn paths that crisscross the ancient world, enlivening them, marking them anew. In this intriguing story that bridges two hemispheres, the Christ moves steadily to center stage, stepping from the darkness of superstition and ignorance as men and events collide and the Roman empire breathes out its last breaths. A superb read."

—S. Kent Brown, former professor of ancient scripture
Brigham Young University

"I found the book a delightful and pleasant read with a plot that kept me intrigued and anxious to return to the text. One of the strong points of the book was the authors' understanding of the period and their mastery of not only one time period but two, and not one culture but three.

"It was also a pleasure to be able to relate to the book's primary characters, men who, though imperfect, were yet true to themselves and to the women they loved. This quality, with others, made their later acts of courage, daring, and self-sacrifice very believable."

—Richard D. Draper, professor of ancient scripture
Brigham Young University

"This fast-paced and engaging narrative brings to life events from the ancient ministry of Jesus Christ on two continents. As the characters in the novel experience these events and wonder at their significance, the reader can contemplate anew the reality of the Savior's life and the powerful and revolutionary truths that he taught."

—David R. Seely, professor of ancient scripture
Brigham Young University

The Book of Malchus

The Book of Malchus

A novel by
Neil K. Newell
with William J. Hamblin

DESERET
BOOK
SALT LAKE CITY, UTAH

Visit us at DeseretBook.com

Library of Congress Cataloging-in-Publication Data
Newell, Neil K.
  The book of Malchus / Neil K. Newell, with William J. Hamblin.
    p. cm.
  ISBN 978-1-60641-833-8 (pbk.)
    1. Philosophers, Ancient—Fiction. 2. Christian inscriptions—Fiction. 3. Carthage (Extinct city)—Fiction. 4. Church history—Primitive and early church, ca. 30–600—Fiction.
I. Hamblin, William James. II. Title.
  PS3564.E89B66 2010
  813'.54—dc22   2010022029

Printed in the United States of America
Malloy Lithographing Incorporated, Ann Arbor, MI
10 9 8 7 6 5 4 3 2 1

For my beloved mother, Verna Lloyd Newell,
who, in spite of compelling evidence and logical argument
to the contrary, always believed in me
and who, from the time I was a toddler, urged me to
"Say it with feeling!"

—NEIL NEWELL

To the cutest grandkids in the world:
Alyssa, Tyler, Megan and Will

—WILLIAM HAMBLIN

Acknowledgments

For the most part a writer's work is a solitary one. Every line on the page represents time away from other, often more important, things. I am grateful to all who indulged me in that effort, principally my family, whose patient and generous support has made this possible.

While Bill and I have gone to great pains to keep the history pure, where there are historical mistakes or inconsistencies, they are mine. Consider it a storyteller's prerogative to warp the iron of historical truth just a little around the story in order to reveal a greater human and hopefully more universal truth. We hope the notes at the end of the chapters are informative and illuminating.

—Neil Newell

Chapter 1

A hot desert wind stroked the city and pressed Lucius Fidelis Crescentius' robes against his skin as he walked. It was hot for August—even for this time of night—and it suited him well. It should be hot. Sweltering hot. Better to match his own mood.

How had it happened that a citizen of Rome could be pulled from his bed in the middle of the night and summoned to appear before a dim-witted priest of the dead Galilean? How had it happened that a son of Rome could be reduced to this—leaping at the wag of a finger attached to the hand of the insufferable Bishop Aurelius?

Lucius' pace quickened to the point that his servant—or to be more accurate, his slave—could not keep pace.

"Master, not there. You must not enter!" Gunderic said, stress rising in his voice.

Lucius grabbed his slave's arm and dragged him to the left. "This way."

"It's not safe."

"It won't do to be late to an *official* summons, Gunderic," he said, rancor dripping from every syllable.

"This area of the city . . . and at night. You are not a young man . . ."

"And yet," the scholar replied, "we continue."

A few steps more and they entered the narrow streets of the insula, the cesspool of the city. It smelled of fish heads and rancid fruit, and the

1

stench stuck to the skin and burrowed into the brain. Lucius stepped over a man whose sprawled legs twitched in restless spasms.

"Give us some light," the man muttered.

Did these people never bathe?

Gunderic held the lamp aloft and, with difficulty, kept pace. "I only trust your will is in order."

And if there was trouble, what of that? Lucius wouldn't shy from a fight. Why not? His seventieth birthday already lay behind him.

He was old, and Rome seemed even more feeble than he. Even now, the greatest city in the world stood surrounded and besieged by an army of unschooled, uncivilized Visigoth barbarians. Its citizens were without bread, hoping in vain for the arrival of its emperor—Honorius, that imperial coward—who had abandoned his own capital city while he summered in safety in distant Ravenna, protected by his army.

The memory of glorious Rome was already fading into legend. Would the empire fight? Or merely cower in fear?

Decades ago, Julian—the last great hope of the pagan religion—had once likened Rome to a massive bull. Powerful and feared, the world knelt before its name and revered its might. How had it happened that in so short a time the Galileans had clamped a golden ring into the nose of that great bull? Now, whenever the church tugged, the head, neck, and body of Rome whirled in response.

Even if others had not seen it, the Emperor Julian had. He had known instinctively the threat this new religion posed. He refused to call them by the name they gave themselves and, instead, referred to them merely as "Galileans." He had done his best to turn back the tide—perhaps had he lived another thirty years, he could have done so—but it was not to be. After Julian's death, the empire once again fell under the influence of the Galileans, and today, a mere forty-seven years later, it was as though Julian had never reigned at all.

Today, the mighty empire of Rome followed the summons of charlatans.

Was that what had deepened Lucius' choler so much? His own, similar plight? Was it because he, himself, had to obey the summons of Aurelius?

With each step, Lucius' rage deepened and the spirit of Bellona consumed him more. What was it this time, Aurelius? Discovery of the finger bone of some thick-headed, shriveled beggar who had stupidly managed to impale himself on a barbarian spear? Was there an eclipse on the day St. Vitus ate venison, foreshadowing the penitent's entrance into paradise? Had moisture condensed to form a tear on a piece of clumsily carved beech wood?

It was all insufferable. All of it.

From across the street, a dog growled menacingly at him. Normally, Lucius would have sent his slave to remove the nuisance, but not tonight. Lucius changed directions and quickened his pace, leaving his surprised slave behind as he charged at the canine. He wasn't sure what he would do once he reached the snarling beast—kick him, he supposed. But with sandaled feet and bare lower legs, he was vaguely aware that the idea was as foolish as it was unworthy.

Luckily, the confrontation never materialized as the astonished beast repented of his challenge; he retreated and disappeared into the dark, saving the old philosopher the indignity of a gladiatorial battle that, more than likely, would have ended inelegantly.

Why had Bishop Aurelius called an emergency meeting of the city senate in the dead of night? Lucius did not have the patience for this sort of theater—endlessly calling together the elders of the city for special, urgent meetings which nearly always were nine parts thunder, one part rain. The Galileans despised the theater, of course, calling it evil and enticing, not to mention that it glorified pagan gods and heroes. And so they substituted this—the insufferable, endless councils, meetings, and masses—processions winding through city streets, statues lofted on heaving shoulders, and celebrations of martyrdom.

If they weren't so terribly serious about it all, it would be funny. No—perhaps it was funny precisely because they were so terribly serious about it all. But, in the end, Lucius merely felt drained, overwhelmed with the sense of loss of the magnificence and power that once had been Rome.

The Galilean influence had done this. They were the ones who had brought the once great empire to its knees.

They would be the end of Rome.

That knowledge, perhaps more than anything else, filled Lucius' heart and mind with a nearly ungovernable wrath.

He passed the magnificent Antonine Baths and emerged into the purer air of the Decumanus. They had successfully traversed the squalor of the slum and were now only a quick walk from the Great Basilica. "You see, Gunderic, none the worse for wear," he said. "And all without loss of limb."

"I trust this will be the last time?"

Lucius laughed. "And all this time I thought you and your kind had the faith to face lions."

"I don't ask God to pull me out of a pit I have dug for myself."

By the time the two men entered the Great Basilica, they discovered the meeting already convened. Aurelius, a pious-looking man in bishops' robes, stood on a dais overlooking the hurriedly assembled group. Beside the bishop stood another man also dressed in bishops' robes with a gray beard and a large nose; Lucius had the feeling he had seen the man before.

"I know the hour is inconvenient," the cleric said in a voice that, Lucius begrudgingly admitted, sounded profound. Aurelius was the kind of man who had spent hours perfecting tones: the tone of holiness, the tone of understanding, and, of course, the ever-useful tone of righteous anger. To give him his due, the man had learned well his lessons of rhetoric.

The bishop continued, "I assembled this body tonight because you must be informed of certain terrible events. News that cannot wait. By the time the city awakens, it will be on the lips of every Carthaginian. I wanted you, the leaders of this great city, to hear it firsthand before the fires of gossip begin to distort the facts."

Aurelius nodded to an elderly man who stood behind him. "Some of you know Liberius Flavius of the senate of Rome."

The man looked oddly familiar and Lucius struggled to place him. The man had the marks of aristocracy, but whoever he was, he seemed a broken man. His hands and bottom lip trembled. His eyes darted from side to side as though searching the room for unseen assassins.

The man stepped forward, slowly and unsteadily. There was something in his eyes. It was not timidity. Nor confusion.

Lucius would have said fear, but fear was too weak a word.

What Lucius saw in the face of the senator from Rome was unmistakable.

Horror. A distinct hint of madness.

"It grieves me . . ." The senator stumbled through his words as though each were a boulder that could be sidestepped only with great concentration and care. "It grieves me deeply . . . I regret . . . that I must inform you . . ."

Lucius looked into the eyes of the senator. Was he searching for something? Striving to recognize someone? At last, the man let out a sound that seemed to emerge from deep within his chest. Not quite a sob, not quite a groan. Whatever it was, it chilled Lucius to the bone. Would the man never speak?

After a terrible pause, Flavius straightened and stood, regaining at least a portion of the dignity he might have once possessed as an aristocrat of a great empire.

"Rome," he whispered in a voice only just audible, "has fallen."

From that moment, all sound blurred.

Shapes and colors moved about Lucius, but he could not distinguish them.

Three words pounded at his temples. Three words hammered again and again. Three words took his breath and withered his soul.

"Rome has fallen!"

The words roared like deep drums rolling a dreadful doom. From the depths of an ocean, Lucius heard their saturnine lament. Over and over the tidal words swelled and receded. Smothered and left him bare.

"Rome has fallen!"

"Rome has fallen!"

Too stunned to think, too dazed to speak, Lucius stood lifeless—a statue powerless to do anything but stand as silent witness to crises he could not control and catastrophes he could not comprehend.

"The Goths . . . Alaric . . ." The words came in patches. Pieces of syllables. Snatches of comprehension.

"Surrounded the city."

"The people inside . . . starving."

"Survived by . . . eating human flesh."

"The slaves . . . betrayed us . . . opened the gates . . . turned on their masters."

"Bodies . . . blood . . . so much blood . . ."

Lucius looked about him. No one protested or called the man a liar. No one shouted. No one cursed.

"There is no stopping them." Flavius' words seemed to come quicker now. "Alaric has vowed to conquer every city in every province of Rome. Without doubt, he will march south. He is coming this way. It is only a matter of time before he will be at your gates. At Carthage!"

The eyes of the men in the room darkened, and they looked into the distance, the way a sacrificial ox looks at some unknown paradise before a knife cuts across its throat, bringing endless darkness.

Time did not exist. Whether an hour or a night had passed, Lucius could not tell. He slowly turned and allowed his feet to lead him from the Great Basilica.

He heard voices behind him but could not understand the words.

All was muffled and dense, and the sounds of outrage blended with sounds of fright until Lucius fled from the hall and all grew quiet in the welcoming darkness of a sweltering Carthage night.

NOTES

Carthage: *The Book of Malchus* begins in the city of Carthage in late August, A.D. 410. The legendary founding of the city occurred in 814 B.C. by Phoenicians from Tyre who wanted to establish a colony for their western Mediterranean trade, especially tin from Spain and England. The founding was attributed to Queen Elissa of Tyre, whom the Romans knew as Dido—the famous Carthaginian queen from Virgil's *Aeneid.*

In the eighth century B.C., the Assyrian empire began a series of invasions and conquests, including that of the Phoenician city of Tyre. Once Tyre fell, many of her richest merchants fled to Carthage (bringing with them their wealth and trading connections). With this influx of wealth, Carthage became the new center of Phoenician trade, and one of the wealthiest and largest cities in the world, renowned for its merchants, mariners, and explorers.

In the middle of the third century B.C., Carthage became a rival of Rome, with which it unsuccessfully fought three wars, including Hannibal's famous campaigns—in which Hannibal won every battle but his last. After the Romans' final victory in 146 B.C., Carthage was destroyed. It was refounded as a Roman city in 30 B.C. by Augustus, and by the second century, it was again a wealthy and thriving center based on supplying grain from the fertile fields of Tunisia (the Roman province of Africa).

It also became an early center of Christianity, home to such notables as Tertullian and Cyprian. The official canon of the Bible had been formally established at the Council of Carthage in A.D. 397, thirteen years prior to the beginning of this story. (S. Lancel, *Carthage: A History* [1994].)

Galilean: Lucius (pronounced Luk-EE-us), a zealous pagan philosopher, follows the practice of many of his contemporary non-Christians by deprecatingly calling Jesus "the Galilean" and his followers "Galileans." From the perspective of the sophisticated urban Roman philosophers, this would be similar to calling him "the hick."

Paganism—in this context, the polytheistic worship of the ancient Greek and

Roman gods—had once been the official religion of the Roman Empire, but, with the visionary conversion of Emperor Constantine in A.D. 312, Christianity became the court religion, eventually overwhelming the pagans, closing their temples or converting them into churches. By the early fifth century, paganism had lost the sectarian struggle with Christianity and been transformed from a persecuting majority to a persecuted minority. (For an example of fourth century anti-Christian polemics, see J. Hoffmann, *Julian's against the Galileans* [Prometheus, 2004]. In general, see R. Wilken, *The Christians As Romans Saw Them* [2003]; A. Lee, *Pagans and Christians in Late Antiquity: A Sourcebook* [2000]; R. MacMullen, *Paganism and Christianity* [Augsburg, 1992]; and *Christianity and Paganism* [Yale, 1999].)

St. Aurelius: St. Aurelius, a correspondent of St. Augustine, was bishop of Carthage from A.D. 391 to A.D. 430. Little is known of his life, though some of Augustine's letters to Aurelius survive. Though based on historical attitudes and actions not uncommon in fifth-century Christian leaders, the character of Bishop Aurelius portrayed in *The Book of Malchus* is fictionalized.

Slavery: Slavery was ubiquitous in the ancient world. Paul discusses slavery (KJV, "servant") in some of his letters, especially Philemon. The lot of many slaves was often deplorable and involved a life of hard labor in agriculture, mining, or building, which often led to numerous slave rebellions, most famously, by Spartacus (73–71 B.C.). However, household slaves were often treated as members of the family, becoming friends and confidants to their masters. Slaves could, with their master's permission, own property, conduct business transactions, and marry. Some were given freedom and an inheritance upon the death of their masters. Many were freed by grateful masters, and yet chose to remain in service as "freedmen." (T. Wiedemann, *Greek and Roman Slavery* [Routledge, 1989]; B. Shaw, *Spartacus and the Slave Wars* [Bedford, 2001].)

Insula: Insula was a term for a block or large, multistoried tenement building, where the urban poor lived. In modern terms they would be considered dangerous ghettos, rife with crime.

Julian: Julian "the Apostate" (r. A.D. 360–363) was the nephew of Constantine the Great. Although raised a Christian, he secretly converted to paganism under the influence of his pagan tutors. Julian's conversion was in part caused because his Christian cousin—the Emperor Constantius II—had massacred Julian's family whom he saw as potential rivals to the throne. Julian himself, who was seven at the time, was merely tortured. "If this is Christianity," he undoubtedly thought, "I'll have none of it." After Julian was proclaimed emperor in 360, he attempted to restore paganism as the official state religion of the Roman Empire. A passionate and literate man, he wrote a number of orations against the Christians.

The Jews, however, had a different attitude toward Julian, many calling him a new Cyrus because he ordered the rebuilding of the Jewish temple in Jerusalem. It is likely that Julian's motivation for this, however, had little to do with his deference toward the Jews and everything to do with wanting to discredit Jesus who had prophesied that "there shall not be left here [upon this temple] one stone upon another, that shall not be thrown down" (Matthew 24:2). (W. Hamblin and D. Seely, *Solomon's Temple: Myth and History* [Thames and Hudson, 2007], 77.)

St. Vitus: St. Vitus (d. 303) was martyred under Diocletian and was later invoked by both those seeking healing and those seeking to prevent demonic possession. In the early fifth century, the cult of the saints was spreading rapidly among Christians. Fundamentally, the cult believed that extraordinarily holy people would be sanctified at their deaths. This meant they would be brought eternally into the presence of God, where they could intervene with God on behalf of mortals who petitioned them. (P. Brown, *The Cult of the Saints* [1982].)

Theater: Tertullian (died c. A.D. 235), who lived at Carthage, was a Christian theologian who wrote a tract on the evils of the theater and Roman games (*On Spectacles*). He viewed them, probably correctly, as encouraging sexual promiscuity, drunkenness, and violent behavior. Nonetheless, Roman theater continued throughout the sixth century; Theodora, the wife of the Emperor Justinian (r. A.D. 527–565), was reputedly a theater actress (and prostitute) before marrying Justinian—a matter that was rather impolitic to discuss openly at court.

Antonine Baths: These were large public baths built by Antonius Pius in the mid-second century. Roman baths were similar to civic gymnasiums, with sport and exercise facilities, swimming pools, saunas, and massages. Their descendants are the "Turkish Baths" of the modern Middle East. The buildings were often huge and ornately decorated with statues and mosaics. A great deal of business—as well as scandalous gossip—was discussed at the baths.

Decumanus: The main east–west oriented street of Roman cities. In February 2010, part of the Decumanus was discovered in the plaza by the Jaffa Gate of Jerusalem.

Rhetoric: Rhetoric (the study of the effective use of language) in the Roman Empire was based on rather unsuccessful derivations of Ciceronean eloquence and sophistry. The ideal textbook was Quintillians' *Institutes of Oratory*. Rhetorical posturing and gesturing had become highly formalized by the early fifth century. The familiar Papal gesture using the thumb and two fingers to bless ultimately derives from such stylized Roman oratorical gestures. (M. Clarke, *Rhetoric at Rome: A Historical Survey* [New York: Routledge, 1996].)

Alaric: King of the Visigoths (a Germanic tribe) from 395 to 410, Alaric led several successful campaigns against Rome, culminating in the sack of the city on 20 August 410. The city fell without a fight when the Salarian Gate was left open.

During the sieges, the city faced famine, and there were rumors of cannibalism in the face of starvation. Eventually the Visigoths migrated into Spain, where they established a kingdom that lasted until the Arab conquests of Spain in A.D. 711. (M. Kulikowski, *Rome's Gothic Wars* [Cambridge, 2008]; P. Heather, *The Goths* [1998].)

Ironically, the Goths were Christians, although of the Arian sect which was considered heretical by the Catholic denomination of the empire. The Goths, while plundering the city in general, respected the sanctity of Christian churches, designating the two great basilicas of St. Peter and St. Paul as sanctuaries. The Senate house was burned, but few other buildings were destroyed.

For contemporary Romans, the psychological impact of the fall of Rome would have been similar to the psychological impact that the 9/11 catastrophe had on many Americans. A supposedly unbreachable barrier had been shattered, leaving an overwhelming sense of confusion and ultimate insecurity. (For background see Peter Heather, *Goths and Romans, 332–489* [Oxford, 1991], 213–18; and Peter Heather, *The Fall of the Roman Empire* [Oxford, 2006], 227–32.)

Alaric planned to march on Carthage to secure the vital grain supply from Tunisia. However, he died en route and the invasion never materialized. It was another German tribe, the Vandals, who sacked Carthage thirty years later in A.D. 439.

Chapter 2

Lucius' villa was not only his home but also his sanctuary, his library, his place of contemplation and reflection. It was where he had received his students and where he had confounded pretenders.

In the nearly four decades he had lived here, how many hundreds of students had passed through the hallway, across the atrium, and into the columned peristylium that surrounded the garden at the back of the villa?

The rich and powerful of Carthage—of Rome itself—had dined with him here. And they had all come in search of something. An endorsement. Advice. Vindication.

They all pretended to come for knowledge and intelligent discourse. They alleged to be seekers of light. Yet, so very few had anything on their minds but their own advancement. They came to take, to pry something away from him that would fill some insatiable void—satisfy some crying hunger that they hoped would slake some deep, unquenchable, self-absorbed thirst.

Greed was the devourer of the age, and in its path lay the ruin of the beautiful, the true, and the good.

Lucius had often felt relief when the door closed, separating himself from their pretense. He cherished the quiet—the aloneness—of being here. He embraced the silence that left him alone with his thoughts in his sanctuary.

The sweetest memories of his life had happened within the walls of his beloved villa.

His deepest sorrows as well.

He passed into the garden, the words of the senator from Rome still echoing in the empty hollow of his soul. He needed time to grasp the impossibility of it. It was absurd, really. The very thought of Rome being sacked. Absurd! The man must be delusional. Possessed by madness.

Lucius stepped into the inner courtyard that opened into the heavens, allowing the light from stars, moon, and sun to dapple through olive trees and vines onto a marble floor. A small stream of water followed a cutaway trench that passed through the center of the cloister and encircled a mosaic of Prometheus, bringer of fire and light, who extended a torch to an unseen mortal.

The perimeter was lined with magnificent statues, each piece carefully and personally selected. He had added them one at a time until the courtyard was populated by a host of deities—a veritable Olympus.

Here, Demeter, mother of fertility and mistress of the Eleusian mysteries, stood clasping a sheaf of life-giving grain. Next to her, wing-footed Mercury, messenger of the gods, and heroic Hercules. Neptune, Jupiter, and the Fates—each looked inward toward the center of the courtyard. How often had he drawn strength and energy here? How often had he quoted Homer, Virgil, and Plato within this space?

How many hundreds had come to Carthage to sit at his feet? He had long ago accepted the celebrity laurels of Africa. And they all came here: Christians, Jews, even atheists. All had come to Carthage to sit at the feet of Lucius the orator, Lucius the philosopher, Lucius the sage.

Had he not befriended the great Emperor Julian himself? Had he not stood at his side at the crest of Mount Pion, witness to the rising glory of the eternal sun? Had he not shared with the emperor of all the world the hallowed Eleusian mysteries of Demeter, Pluto, and Persephone? Had he not, with Julian, learned the secret rites of Mithras, god of light, and Sol Invictus, the all-powerful ruler of heaven and earth?

He moved from one statue to the next, a heaviness in his step.

More than a millennia ago, Rome had stretched a hand out of the mud of obscurity and reached into the heavens, grasping eternal fire and rising until it stood glorious and triumphant as sovereign of the world. For more than seven centuries, the city of Rome had stood unassailable. Majestic and supreme. Ruler of nations. Proud and defiant. Terror and order of the earth.

And now?

Gates breached, city defiled, fire and ruin.

And all it took was five decades.

In the forty-seven years since the death of Emperor Julian, the Galileans had brought the greatest empire in the history of the world to its knees. These priestly pretenders had infiltrated the government. Their influence now determined policy and law. They cut off funding for the pagan temples, and the holy edifices had begun to wear away. Robbed of its religion, the empire became weak and corrupt. And as the once-bright buildings fell into disrepair, the empire crumbled as well.

Crumbled to dust.

Lucius looked blankly into the painted, stone eyes of Diana, goddess of the hunt. Fortuna, goddess of fortune. Juno, queen of the gods. Mars. Apollo. Ceres. Minerva. Jove.

"Where are you?" he whispered.

When the barbarian army surrounded the walls of the city that had for a thousand years sung hymns of praise to the immortals of Olympus— where were they?

For a thousand years, a great nation had offered prayers and bathed the feet of the gods with their tears. They had faithfully offered libations, erected sacred temples, stood sentry at shrines. The devotion of a thousand years—did it mean nothing?

Was the coin of a thousand years of worship of so little value to the gods that they abandoned their people at the moment of greatest need?

A people who had ushered the entire world to their feet and caused every nation to speak the name of Jupiter Optimus Maximus?

Were the gods spoiled children? Selfish? Interested only in what mortals could do for them? Was there no reciprocation?

Could they not see that if Rome died, their names would fade from the lips of man?

Had they all fled? Ceased to care? Had they, like a petulant child, simply turned their backs when Rome flirted with the Galilean god?

Or had they become powerless? Old men and women. Toothless. Bileless. Afraid and cowering before younger, more powerful gods?

"Where are you?" Lucius shouted, his voice lifting into the night, piercing the heavens.

Had the gods abandoned this world and fled to some distant corner of the universe?

Had they never existed at all?

Was it all a hoax? An illusion? Superstition by desperate mortals trying to grasp something—anything—that could grant meaning to a life otherwise too terrible to comprehend?

"Where are you?" he demanded. His voice carried out into the open air and shattered the solemn night. Others would hear him. Would be awakened from ignorant slumber.

What of it?

Should they not awake? Should they not rouse from their stupor?

They had been unconscious all these many years.

Unthinking.

Herded like sheep from first gasp of breath until they entered the grave.

The sorrow in his heart began to evaporate, replaced by a growing rage that shook him and made him tremble.

"Where are you?"

He strode toward the statue of winged Mercury and cupped the statue's face between his hands. "Where were you?" he whispered. "When Alaric's armies starved the people of Rome and forced them to eat human flesh to survive? Where were you? Are you not the messenger of the gods? Their herald? And yet you stood by speechless, motionless. You did nothing. You stood—scepter in hand, unbeating wings at your feet—and did *nothing*."

What use did Rome have for such gods?

If they did not care for Rome, why should Rome care for them?

"Are you listening?" His voice rose along with his rage, and he began rocking the marble form back and forth, each swing widening the arc. "Do you hear me? Do you hear?"

But the god did not hear.

And if he did not—could not—hear, of what possible use could he be?

Lucius rocked the stone more violently.

"Take *this* word to Jove, messenger. If the gods do not care for the people of Rome—"

He pushed and the statue tipped past the point of balance and fell to the stone below, shattering arms, a leg, and severing its head.

"Listen to me, you gods of Rome," he whispered as he grasped the head of helmed Minerva. "Listen to Lucius, your defender, advocate, and citizen of Rome. Listen to the words of he who upheld you day and night against the Galilean blasphemies. If you do not care for Rome, I will not nursemaid you in senility!"

He tipped the marble image over until it, too, smashed against the stone.

From Demeter to Juno to Diana, he pulled them all down, shattering stone against stone, each defiled image fueling his rage.

"Rome will not remember you! And if Rome does not remember you, then you will be forgotten in the world. Laughed at. Ridiculed. You will become a child's story. A fairy tale. A phantom."

He strode toward the statue of Mars.

"You, most of all, are to blame," he said between clenched teeth. "God of war. Bringer of death. Terror of wives, lovers, and children. Where were you when the barbarian hordes flooded into the city? Strike me down if you have any power!" he shouted. "I lift my hand to destroy you, god of vengeance. Terrible warrior, will you not defend yourself?"

He pushed the statute until it, too, cracked against stone.

He looked wildly around him. Only one statue remained. Jupiter himself. King of the gods. Vengeful lawgiver. Master of lightning. Feared and obeyed. Lord of Olympus.

"There are three possibilities," Lucius said, his chest heaving, his lungs constricting around his words. "Three possibilities. Either you are powerless to help, you do not wish to help, or"—he pushed his face close against the marble—"you do not exist."

Which is it, Jove? he wondered. *Are you a lie?*

Is it all a lie?

But he knew the answer before he had finished asking the question.

He pulled the head toward him and then pushed as hard as he could, watching as the stone tipped backward.

He turned without looking at the effect of the impact as the statue collided with the mosaic floor.

He looked about the peristylium and frowned at the destruction, the mangled corpses and severed limbs.

Although the statues had fallen, there was one last monument yet standing—the family shrine. Four marbled columns stood on a base of ancient stone. On the surfaces were carved sculptures of exotic trees, gods appearing to man, and a snake at the top of a four-sided pyramid. The family lararium. The shrine of the household gods that had protected his family for generations. He remembered the day his aged grandfather had told him its history.

"This shrine is most sacred and ancient," he had said. "Long ago, our ancestors were great explorers who were known throughout the world for their daring and skill. They crafted this monument from stone they discovered in a faraway land. The gods who inhabit this shrine have watched over our family for centuries. If you honor them with your devotion, prayers, and sacrifices, they will prosper you. Ignore them at your peril."

"What does it mean?" Lucius had asked.

The meaning of many of the raised images had been lost in antiquity, but his grandfather had offered his own opinion about their meaning. "The carved image of a boat," his grandfather said, "refers to the occupation of our fathers as merchants and explorers."

He pointed to an image of a tree with branches that stretched across the back of the shrine. "This is an image of prosperity. A promise that as long as we honor the family gods, we will grow and prosper."

"And this here?" Lucius asked, pointing to the image of a bearded snake.

"I can only guess," he replied. "But I believe this is a symbol of our family Genius, the family god that gives us inspiration and watches over our household."

Lucius ran a trembling hand across the words that were inscribed across the top of the shrine: *"Veritas Intum Latitat."*

The truth lies within.

"This refers to the true devotion of the gods," his grandfather said. "As we worship them, we discover the truth inside ourselves."

All his life, Lucius had honored the ancient shrine. Very few days had he passed into sleep without honoring the lararium with a prayer or libation. If he had been anything in his life, he had been dutiful to the devotion of the gods—particularly the gods of his own family.

But if Neptune, Pluto, and Saturn were dead, then so were the gods of his family. If Jupiter could not save Rome, then why should these small gods of his family have any power?

Superstition all.

Ignorance and lies.

From this night forward, he would be free of foolish faith. Free of belief.

From this night forward, he would believe only in that which he could prove with his own senses.

It was a night of liberation.

Rome had fallen, and so too had its gods.

There were no gods.

The philosopher Lucretius had been right after all. No hand of fate watched over a nation, much less over one man's insignificant life.

At that moment, Lucius knew that he would destroy the shrine that had been treasured by his family for hundreds of years. And the understanding of what he was about to do did not cause him distress so much as deep feelings of relief and peace.

"Forgive me, grandfather," he whispered. "But for too long, we have worshipped lies. The dishonesty ends tonight. There is no such thing as the sacred or holy. It is all a lie. And lies must be exposed."

He pushed at the altar, but it was too heavy to tilt.

He searched frantically for a tool, something he could use to work destruction upon it—perhaps fearing that if he did not act quickly, he would not be able to carry out his intent.

At the side of a nearby wall, he found what he was looking for, the broken forearm from the statue of Jupiter. He knew it would be heavy, perhaps too heavy for him to use, but as he hefted it, he was astonished at his own strength. Before this night, he would have credited his strength to the intervention or blessing of the gods. But now, he credited it to emotion and coincidence. Like everything else that happened in the world.

It was all coincidence.

He stood for a moment in front of the shrine, lost in nostalgia. How many times had he stood in this very place, his heart filled with joy? How many times had he wept?

The balance of the opposites brought clarity to his thinking and he hefted the carved forearm upon his shoulder and swung.

He would tear down the last symbol of faith and destroy it by the hand of Jupiter.

A pillar cracked. Another blow sent shards of stone flying. And finally, the structure began to crumble.

As it fell, Lucius threw more of his strength into the blows.

He began to weep. Each time he heard the crack of the marble, new sobs wrenched at his heart. He felt as though the grief would crush him and snuff out the life of him, leaving him lying beside the other casualties of that night.

He swung and the altar caved.

He swung and another pillar fell.

He swung and the pyramid cracked into a dozen pieces.

He lifted the weapon again but stopped. In the light of the moon, something gleamed from within the shrine.

He let his stone weapon fall to the ground as he moved closer.

Something was inside.

Within the pyramid.

Gold?

He gently took a piece of stone and pushed it aside. And then another.

Metal. Could it be some ancient treasure?

Lucius pulled a lamp from its stand and peered into the crevice.

He removed another piece of stone. More frantically, Lucius worked to clear away the debris.

Then it became clear.

Inside the pyramid was a gleaming, metallic object half again as tall as his hand and as wide as the spread between his outstretched thumb and little finger. The left side of the object had been pierced and two heavy rings of the same material had been inserted into the holes.

His rage momentarily forgotten, he lodged the lamp between two pieces of stone so he could examine the object more closely. His hands trembled as he pulled it from its niche, still bright and gleaming in the lamplight.

Bronze. It was definitely bronze.

What mystery is this? he wondered.

Who had placed this object in the family shrine? And why?

He ran a hand over the smooth surface and down the edge.

Something lifted.

The object was not solid, but composed of thin sheets.

Slowly, he lifted the first sheet and folded it over. He pulled the lamp closer to allow a better view.

What he saw struck him as deeply as if he himself had been toppled by the blow.

The bronze sheets were not blank, but covered with intricate markings.

Someone had filled these pages . . . with writing.

And the letters formed words—words he could read.

The words were in Latin.

NOTES

Eleusian mysteries: A "mystery" religion centered at Eleusis, a city near Athens. The initiates were inducted into a secret ceremony in which they were given the promise of eternal life through the revelation of the secret meaning of the story of Demeter. (C. Kerenyi, *Eleusis* [1991].)

Mithras: A Persian celestial god whose male-only secret rituals promised the ability for the soul to ascend to the heavens upon death. For more than a century, Mithraism was a major rival to Christianity, but declined with the demise of paganism. (R. Beck, *The Religion of the Mithras Cult in the Roman Empire* [Oxford, 2006]; M. Clauss, *The Roman Cult of Mithras* [Routledge, 2000].)

Libations: When Romans would drink wine they would often pour a small amount onto the ground as an offering to the gods. (Jacob offers a libation in Genesis 35:14.) The Bible describes drink offerings (Hebrew, *nesek*) being offered in the tabernacle (e.g. Exodus 29:40–41; Numbers 15, 28–29).

Genius: To the ancients, a person was not a genius, he *had* a genius—a special, protective, guiding spirit. The Greeks called them *daimon* (from which our word "demon" derives), and Socrates claimed that his guided him and sometimes gave oral instructions.

Chapter 3

The mystery of the strange object momentarily displaced Lucius' anger. The anguish, still a dull ache that hovered and swelled at the back of his throat, was ever there. But he welcomed this new enigma and latched onto it with the ferocity of a man adrift in an endless ocean, clinging to any bit of flotsam that could keep him afloat.

He carried the plates to his bibliotheca and set them upon his desk. Using metal plates for writing was not unheard of—the twelve bronze Tablets of the Law that hung in the Roman forum attested to that—but it was rare. And painstaking. The only reasons anyone would go to such a masochistic effort to scratch a message into sheets of metal was if he was extremely paranoid, exceptionally vain, or determined that his record would endure through time. Someone with a lot of time on his hands had taken great pains to do this. Whatever the reason, the author had gone to great trouble to ensure that these words lasted beyond the transitory life of parchment.

The bronze sheets were discolored, tinted green, but not corroded. Lucius wetted a cloth and gently applied it to the surface of the plates. By doing so, he was able to remove the thin patina that covered the metal.

The tiny letters had been painstakingly etched with a sure hand. He could not begin to comprehend the amount of time it must have taken to write this. It appeared as though each small symbol had been engraved several times—each time more deeply until the words emerged from grooves in the metal.

Lucius caressed the plates, feeling a whirlpool of emotions. He hungered to pull the mystery from them and discover their secret. Yet he was loathe to discover too soon what was written inside. Once he began reading, the mystery would likely give way to something as mundane as an accounting record of pork or pottery. And, as fascinating as that might be to a historian or economist, it had no appeal to him. He did not want this record to be filled with the banalities of the bartering of grain or the fluctuations in the value of cloth. The undiscovered mystery of unopened pages was much more intriguing than the tedium of inventory or disposition of estates.

But at last, he could no longer withstand the curiosity, and he gently pulled the plates toward him.

And began to read.

The Book of Malchus, son of Mago, of the house of Hanno

Two things you must know at the start. First: I am not a man of letters. From my youth, I have ever been more interested in studying the set of a sail than in analyzing the skill of Sophocles.

Second: You will not believe what I am about to write. Perhaps you will think me a liar, or mad. Possessed. Intoxicated. Perhaps even evil. My assurances to the contrary will do nothing to change that opinion—perhaps I would think the same myself were our roles reversed.

Believe what you will. What I write, I have seen with my own eyes. I have sailed strange waters and walked upon soil that few have even dreamed about. My eyes have seen beasts and birds whose description would astound, frighten, and amuse. My ears have heard unearthly languages. My tongue has tasted food so strange that had I the vocabulary of Cicero, I could not find words to describe them.

Yet, in spite of the fact that you will not believe me, I feel compelled to etch upon this metal the story of my life.

Were we together in person, you would hear in my voice and see in my eyes absolute and unwavering conviction. Perhaps then I could convince you; I believe I could convince the Emperor Tiberius himself had I the opportunity. But I am not able to speak to you in person and so the words I write must carry the weight of my experience, as weak as those words might be. I only plead that you hear me out. Consider that perhaps there was a man such as Malchus, son of Mago, of the house of Hanno. For truly I have witnessed remarkable things.

My story, like these plates, begins with bronze.

Bronze is the key to wealth.

As a young man, I knew this and, being possessed with a measure of ambition, I came to the understanding that if I could supply the ingredients to make this precious metal, I could pave the floors of my villa with gold.

As everyone knows, bronze is superior to iron. Stronger, it does not rust and is less brittle, but most important, bronze can be liquefied and cast into any shape.

Iron is the poor man's bronze and inferior in nearly every way.

Why, then, is iron used so commonly?

The answer is simple: bronze is rare. The main ingredient of bronze is copper—a metal common enough and readily found. But copper, by itself, is nearly useless—it is too soft and doesn't hold an edge; good only for decorative art and jewelry. However, add molten tin to copper and you have something remarkable.

Bronze!

Fortunately for someone like myself, tin is nearly impossible to find near Carthage—the city of my birth—or Rome for that matter. In fact, the world's greatest supply of tin lies in the Cassiterides—the Tin Islands—that barbaric northern land of the Britons. There, it is pulled from the earth in abundance. Because it is no easy feat to travel to that distant place and bring the tin back to civilization, there is money for anyone intrepid enough to successfully make the attempt.

The risks of securing tin from that dangerous land are formidable, for the land lies beyond the laws and civilization of Rome. In order to acquire tin, you must possess a ship large enough to make the journey worthwhile, and seaworthy enough not to end up at the bottom of the ocean. In addition, you must be shrewd enough to outmaneuver the pirates that hover about the coasts, ready to pounce upon ripe merchant ships. Many a pirate has become wealthy by taking the lives and property of those who come within their sight.

Britain itself is dangerous, inhabited by a savage and unpredictable people, who, though they know it is in their best interest to establish trust with traders, at times will be taken with a murderous whim and decide to accept a trader's money, ship, and, indeed, the lives of his crew, as a donation to the common good of their tribe.

In short, becoming a tin merchant is not something for those lacking courage, nor is it a profession for those whose primary goal in living is to continue drawing breath.

But, being a foolhardy youth and coming from a long line of impulsive adventurers, mariners, and explorers—I am, after all, of the house of Hanno—I decided to make the attempt. For his part, my father—a rather timid man—had been satisfied with the marginal profits he gained from the grain trade between Africa and Rome. I sought for greater wealth and adventure. Using a ship I inherited from my father, I made the first trip to Britain with the loss of only a few men. The second, without any loss.

By the time I was thirty, I had not only made a name for myself but I had become modestly wealthy in the process. In fact, I was invited on one occasion to dine with Emperor Tiberius himself, who, as everyone knows, is entirely distrustful of strangers and allows precious few outsiders into his chambers.

But even an emperor needs tin. How else can he provide armor for his troops and decorations for his palaces? And the merchant who can provide it becomes a person of importance—even to an emperor.

That visit to the regal halls of the stepson of Augustus created within me an even greater thirst for wealth and honor. And that thirst could not be slaked with the ordinary income of a merchant—not even that of a wealthy merchant.

I wanted more.

The key to wealth was possessing the proper ship. It needed to be fast, of course. Strong enough to carry a rich cargo of heavy metal in the potentially rough seas beyond the Pillars of Heracles. But what I coveted—and the thing that was so desperately hard to find—was a deep-keeled ship. Roman vessels were built with flat bottoms, best designed for the shallow waters of the Mediterranean and sailing close to land. But they were notoriously unstable in heavy seas, which forced them to hug the shore. I needed a ship that could leave sight of shore—away from the marauding pirates and competing merchants. With a deep keel I could sail in the less-traveled waters of the deep ocean.

But with every plan comes its attendant problems. And mine lay with the Lusitanians. For over a century the people of Lussa had resisted conquest by the Romans and had only been marginally subdued a few decades ago by the Emperor Augustus himself. I was loathe to deal with the Lusitanians because their coast was still frequented by pirates—probably the Lusitanians themselves. But they were renowned ship builders and had mastered the art of building ships designed to sail in the deep waters of stormy Oceanus.

I coveted such a ship, but to obtain one meant dealing with Audax, a Lusitanian lord well-known as the greatest shipbuilder in the province. Unfortunately, Audax was as unpredictable and capricious as the Britons. After several meetings, we came to an agreement: a shipment of tin in return for a vessel patterned after his own great ship.

I soon realized why Audax had such a reputation for shrewdness. After the tin was deposited in his warehouse in Conimbriga, he led me to a room where, upon a table, sat a miniature ship—a toy—with a red ribbon draped over the mainmast.

"There is your ship," he said.

The agreement had been for a deep-keeled, two-masted ship built after the design of Audax's *Runesocesius*, the pride of his fleet. And there before me stood the literal realization of that agreement. In miniature!

An amused Audax stood surrounded by his laughing guards. I remember still that nettling grin. I remember still the laugh of the man—a full-bellied, mocking laugh.

And in that instant I knew two things: the first was that I had been taken for a fool; the second was that someday, I would get even.

It was more than a personal grudge. This sort of thing would spread among merchants and traders. I would gain a reputation as a gullible fool who could easily be taken advantage of.

Of course, once a trader's reputation is tarnished, his work and headaches triple. If someone has taken advantage of you, others feel they can do the same. Kings, cooks, and galley slaves all look upon you differently from that point on.

Obviously, I had to respond. And quickly.

I waited until the feast of their patron ancestor Lusus, son of the god of wine, Bacchus. The feast was a raucous event, the general object being to become so drunk with wine that to remain standing was an insult to the deity himself. The Lusitanians had a fondness for this celebration and surrendered themselves to their revelry with an abandon that would astound even the most self-indulgent Roman.

After Audax and his men had saturated their livers with wine, I sent three men to the lord's warehouse where they set fire to the building and everything inside—his entire store of inventory. Once their besotted attention was focused on putting out the blaze, I slipped into the harbor with the remainder of my men, boarded the now-undermanned *Runesocesius*, and pirated it away into the open sea before anyone knew we had been there.

One final touch—something that to this day fills me with a strange mixture of pride and regret.

I left the *Runesocesius'* crew on a raft in the harbor—each man naked, bound, and with a large red bow wrapped around his neck.

"You're absolutely certain about this, are you?" Glaucus was my right-hand man and had been with me on every voyage since the first. I trusted him with my life. He was, in fact, the only man I knew whom I could count on to speak the truth no matter the consequence.

"You don't think it punctuates the whole affair?" I placed a final red bow around the neck of the last Lusitanian sailor.

"Think of it this way," Glaucus said. "You've set fire to his warehouse, causing him untold loss of wealth."

"Quite correct."

"You've stolen his best ship."

"So I have."

"Everyone who hears of this will know you have had your revenge."

"That is my earnest desire."

"That being said, this last bit with the bows—don't you think it's a little much?"

"I'm making a point."

"You're making an enemy."

Audax was my enemy from the moment he presented me the miniature ship. There was no point in pretending otherwise, and I said as much to Glaucus.

"There are enemies, and then there are bitter, sworn enemies," was his reply.

But the memory of Audax's laughter yet stung, and this would, I thought, settle the score. Perhaps there were those in the world who still chuckled when they heard of how Audax had swindled a merchant, but now they would howl with laughter when they heard of how the merchant had exacted his revenge.

"It won't stop, you know," Glaucus persisted. "Not after this."

I knew he was right, but at the time I was too impressed and satisfied with myself to consider any other option. As a final gesture, I fastened a board onto the chest of the deposed captain of the *Runesocesius*. Written on the board were the words, "This receipt in acknowledgment of prior agreement. Paid in full. Malchus."

Glaucus shook his head and said, "I was going to suggest that you might as well sign your name to the whole business, but I see you are, once again, ahead of me."

I didn't care. I wanted Audax to know. I wanted the world to know.

And with that, we launched the raft with Audax's men, turned our new ship away from land, and let the wind fill its sails.

It was a magnificent vessel, far exceeding my expectations. It bit into the water and handled the waves with balance and grace unlike any ship I had ever known. As I tested and tried her in the face of wind and storm, I became increasingly impressed with the Lusitanian shipwrights. This wonderful vessel was exactly what I needed to become the greatest tin merchant in all the world and one of my first acts as its captain was to christen it with a new name: the *Morning Star.* I was quite fond of the name because it gave homage to that bright star that often heralded the coming of a delicate and hopeful dawn.

Now, with my newly christened ship and possessed of a crew emboldened with a new sense of pride, and our prospects for riches brighter than ever, we set our course to our purpose. All seemed bright in the world.

Except for one thing.

Audax.

Glaucus was right, of course. It is one thing to be hated. It is another thing altogether to be relentlessly hated by someone whose reputation depends on his exacting revenge. Worse, my enemy had the financial means to indulge himself in the excessive—no, let me say *fanatical*—pursuit of that animosity.

Audax, after surveying the damage to his warehouse, after learning of the disappearance of his flagship, and after finding the ship's crew adorned with the bows and carrying my message, vowed with a solemn oath that, though it might cost him his entire fortune, he would have my head on a stake.

In spite of his fury, I felt I had come out ahead in the affair. After all, although I had an eternal enemy, I also possessed something that I treasured above all else: a magnificent deep-keeled ship. And that was something I could use to full advantage.

Of course everything comes with a price and the price of the ship was heavy and one I continued to pay every day thereafter. Whenever I passed the coast of Lusitania on my way to or from the Tin Islands, I always did so at night, far away from shore. I was careful and canny and, thus, confident that neither Audax nor all his sailors, spies, or priests could ever find, let alone apprehend, me.

After that, it was a simple matter of watching for assassins at every port and ensuring that I hired men I could trust without reservation. A man of means can protect himself most of the time from attempts of poison, sabotage, and sword. And I was certainly a man of means. The problem was that my nemesis was a man of even greater means and, as I learned again and again, he was a man consumed with a solitary obsession: to have my head.

Because of Audax's zealous devotion for revenge, I gradually came to the realization that no matter how careful I was, Audax must ultimately succeed if for no other reason than that luck would eventually favor him. I had to be perfectly successful every time; Audax needed to find success only once. As that realization grew upon me, I began to realize that the cost of obtaining the *Morning Star* was heavier than I had ever imagined, and I began regretting my foolhardy act. The suspense of not knowing when or where the next attempt on my life might happen began to weigh heavily upon me.

Eventually, I started to wonder if the only way out was to disappear. Perhaps leave the tin trade for more "eastward" pursuits—perhaps spices. Something that would take me away from the northern seas and far away from Audax.

But I was established in the tin business and, with only a few more shipments, I would have enough wealth to retire. I could purchase a mansion—perhaps in Cyprus or Crete—somewhere distant and half a world removed from Lusitania. I could even marry a pretty daughter of a local nobleman, have children, and live in anonymous ease for the remainder of my life.

Ultimately, I decided I would risk the last few shipments I needed to make my dreams come true. I had always been blessed with a measure of luck and had developed a reputation for cheating death and danger.

My efforts had brought coin into my coffers and made all who sailed with me rich as well. In fact, everything was going according to my well-laid plans until that day.

That fateful day.

Even now, I have no idea how Audax managed it. Perhaps it was Fortune—that unpredictable goddess who favors the brave. Perhaps I had offended one of the gods who protected the Lusitanians. Or perhaps the pirate lord had gone to the expense of spreading out a spider's web of spies so vast and so thorough that ultimately, he had to succeed. No matter the cause, on one early morning in late August, on returning from my final trip to Britain with a hold filled with tin, I awoke to discover a vessel trailing me from the north.

By itself, this was no cause for great concern. It was not uncommon to be trailed by another vessel. But after tacking to the west, then south, then east, it soon became apparent that the ship following us was mirroring my every move.

I was being followed.

Even so, I was not particularly worried, for we had a large enough

32

lead. I could stay ahead of whomever was behind—at least until dark when I could certainly elude them. And, of course, I had a deep-keeled ship that enabled me to sail out into the deep ocean. No one would follow me there—unless they were terribly foolish or utterly desperate. Either way, it would only be a matter of time before I lost them.

But then, something strange happened. The single mast I saw on the horizon became two. Then two gave way to three.

There was no longer a single ship following me, but three. And they were spreading out. One veered to the north in a circling maneuver, the other to the south. My curiosity gave way to concern. The way back to Britain was blocked. I could not flee east to Gaul. Venturing west into untamed Oceanus was madness. There was only one available route: south.

I had a fast ship but, burdened with my cargo, I would certainly not be able to outrun the other ships. I contemplated dumping my precious tin—that would give me a better chance of losing my pursuers. However, I reasoned that if I could only keep ahead of them until we were clothed in the cloak of night, it would be impossible for them to track me.

I had every confidence that I would escape. Of course, I had no choice: the consequences of failure would be unspeakable. If I could not outrun Audax—for I was certain that these ships belonged to him—I would be faced with only two alternatives: surrender or fight. I was badly outnumbered. If it came to a fight, I could not win.

But surrender? Was Audax the kind of man who would kill me and my crew for the embarrassment I had caused him? Or was he the kind of man who would take his full measure of revenge through torture or some other form of humiliation?

If I didn't escape, I would certainly not live to enjoy the wealth I had accumulated.

My crew sensed the same and they worked tirelessly, following my every command. Yet, because of the added weight of my cargo, Audax's ships continued to gain ground. I prayed for the shadow of evening and hoped we could elude our pursuers until we were embraced by the comforting caress of the goddess Night.

I should have jettisoned the cargo immediately; I know that now.

It was foolish to think I could both escape Audax and keep the tin. Unfortunately, my greed exceeded my wisdom and I made the choice to retain my riches rather than ensure my escape.

I was actually beginning to believe that we would make it. That we would be able to travel south until night, then circle to the east and outrun my pursuers. But then something happened that took me completely by surprise.

It was at dusk, just before the sun dipped into that great water Oceanus, when two new sails appeared—both coming from the south.

The fool must have devoted his entire fleet to pursuing me.

I could not turn south. The north and east were still blocked. This left only one option.

Without hesitation, I ordered my ship to veer into the path of Apollo's chariot and head west—out into the depths of the unknown Oceanus. It was suicide, of course, but I had no other choice.

My crew understood as well as I what was happening, and I saw fear growing in their eyes. The fear of the bloodthirsty Lusitanians balanced against the unknown ocean. Whether they were more afraid of Audax or Neptune, I could not determine. The dangers of the sword versus the terrors of the deep—both were real, both certain. All I knew was that, in a world of very limited options, this was my only chance for survival.

In a few minutes it would be dark and, with a cloud-filled sky, it would be completely black. With the protection of the goddess Night, I told my crew, we could escape our pursuers and soon head back toward familiar seas and welcome lands. Continuing our course into the uncharted waters to the west was our only hope for salvation.

NOTES

Bronze: An alloy of roughly 10% tin and 90% copper widely used in the ancient world, bronze was especially valuable because it could be liquefied and cast, something that could not be done with iron at the time.

Cassiterides: Cassiterides ("Tin Islands") refers to the British Islands, where mines in Corwall were a major source of tin for the Romans. In later Christian legends, Joseph of Arimathea was said to have been a tin merchant and to have settled, with the Holy Grail, at Glastonbury in southwest England.

Grain trade: As the city of Rome expanded during the first century A.D., the agriculture of the Italian peninsula proved unable to support its huge population, so huge supplies of grain were imported each year from Sicily, Tunisia, and Egypt.

Augustus: Augustus (r. 27 B.C.–A.D. 14) was the first Roman emperor and nephew of Julius Caesar. He was patron of Herod the Great and emperor at the time of the birth of Jesus.

Lusitania: Roughly modern Portugal.

Oceanus: The source for our term *ocean*. Greeks and Romans believed that the inhabited world was completely surrounded by a huge sea. Oceanus is the Atlantic Ocean.

Runesocesius: The Lusitanian god of the javelin and war.

The Morning Star: The planet Venus was worshiped as a god by the pagans. Christ is described metaphorically as the morning or day star (2 Peter 1:19; Revelation 2:28; 22:16).

Chapter 4

The Book of Malchus, son of Mago, of the house of Hanno

There are those who believe that spots on a liver portend ill luck. When I was seven, Ecebolius Gracus, a wealthy builder of Carthage, brought a bull to the temple of Apollo for sacrifice. Unfortunately, the priest misspoke a word of the ritual and the ceremony had to start again. Worse, the bull trembled and tried to escape before he was killed (a ruinous omen). Finally—as though any other catastrophic presage was necessary—the bull's liver appeared streaked with yellow pus.

Ecebolius did not speak; he did not ask for an explanation. The look on the priest's face was language enough.

The very next day, Ecebolius was dead. Of what cause, no one is certain. But there was little doubt that his fate had been foretold and was, therefore, inevitable. It was another reminder that the Fates hold a man's life by a thread and that, in an instant, life can be extinguished.

I have known many who staked their fortune on the flight of a crow or who paled at a badly-timed strike of lightning.

Not I. Perhaps as a child such things troubled me, but as a merchant I had the wind and water and unscrupulous lenders enough to worry about without adding witchery and the meddling of unseen powers to the list. If the gods did exist—I know it is heretical of me to say, but I did not entirely believe that they did—if the gods did exist and should turn against me, then why worry? If a god has a knife at your throat, what is there to do but lean back so he can get a clean cut? Can a man triumph over a god?

My concerns ran more to the mundane and less to the supernatural. To be honest, I would have to say that my lack of attention in making sacrifices to the gods had not hindered business in the slightest. In fact, many claimed that I lived a charmed life or that some deity had placed an unseen but watchful hand upon my shoulder.

Now, it seemed all my previous good luck had been called in on the day that those five sails appeared on the horizon. I was certain, however, that after a dark and moonless night, rosy-fingered Dawn would light the sky and reveal a vast and empty sea. But to my horror, when we searched the horizon at first light for signs of pursuit, five sails were visible behind, to the north, and to the south. I had absolutely no explanation as to how Audax could follow me in the dead of night in a vast and open sea. It was as though he could read the tracks my ship left as it plowed through the waves.

The sea was not so calm that the splash of an oar or the whisper of a watchman could be heard from a distance. I had assumed that Audax would guess that I would tack east and south to avoid sailing too far away from land. So I did the unexpected: I turned west and north.

How had he known? How could he have followed?

Was it sorcery? Was he aided by the gods?

I ordered a report from sharp-eyed Antonius who had volunteered to spend the night at the top of the center mast looking for any signs of our pursuers.

"Nothing, sir," he said. "The night was pitch-black. Couldn't see past my nose."

I looked back at my pursuers. They were still gaining ground—I knew it and my men knew it. I had to act or we all would be on our knees in front of Audax pleading that our heads remain attached to our bodies.

"I do hope you have a plan." It was Glaucus again.

"I have a plan."

"Of course you do," he replied without a hint of sarcasm. "Just wanted you to know that although the crew is loyal, they would be perfectly willing to hand you over to the Lusitanian in order to save their own skin."

"Thank you for lifting my spirits in a time of need."

"Sometimes the hardest words are the kindest."

"If you would be so kind to ask the crew to delay thoughts of mutiny, I would be most appreciative."

"They will be comforted to know you have a plan," Glaucus murmured as he turned to walk away.

"Would you please stop worrying?" I said. "I have a plan!"

I had no plan.

At least none that had any chance of success. However, since I wasn't willing to risk my life on any other option, and knowing that I could not outrun five ships with a hold bursting with tin, with bad grace I gave orders to dump half of my cargo into Oceanus and set every inch of sail.

"They're still coming," Mus shouted. Mus was my attendant, a young man of nineteen whom I loved dearly though he had the mental capacity of a five-year-old child. "There they are! One, two, three, four, five."

"Very good, Mus. Excellent counting."

He beamed as he always did when I praised him.

"But we must be quiet from now until the time we can no longer see them. We don't want them to hear us, especially at night."

"Especially at night!" Mus shouted with feeling. But Mus said everything with feeling and often in a shout. Perhaps it was this trait that endeared him most to the crew. He rarely thought before he spoke; nevertheless, he rarely said anything without absolute conviction—no matter how absurd. He had come by his nickname, Mouse, due to the fact that he was weak of mind and timid around the crew. Mouse eventually evolved to Mus, which means the same thing, and it stuck. He was our Mus. Our good-luck charm, our little brother.

But what about Audax? What could I do but lighten my ship yet again and attempt to outrun him? Though my cargo was precious to me, I gave the order and watched as half of the remaining tin was cast overboard.

And still they gained.

And with every passing minute my ship—and the five who followed—slipped ever further from the safety of shore. It was insanity traveling this far from land. I knew it and Audax knew it. Every mariner's child could recite tales of unknown terrors of the deep. Monstrous creatures, storms, lightning. Waves so large and deadly that, should Neptune desire, he could transform even a ship as large as the *Morning Star* into splinters and jetsam.

Every sailor possesses a deep-seated fear of both the gods and the dangers of the ocean—even hardened mariners who doubt the existence of the gods would never tempt fate by showing such arrogance or disrespect as sailing into the open sea. In fact, one of the first lessons every merchant learned was that Neptune was impatient with those who had the temerity to trespass too far into his domain.

Yet, Audax had left me with no other choice: I could not turn back. Better to risk all by fleeing west than to embrace certain death by allowing capture.

And so we sailed on.

Although the Lusitanians had drawn closer, they had not yet overtaken us. Not yet. We were still ahead of them and, if we could once more stay ahead until nightfall, I was confident we could elude them.

Once again, Fortune favored us with another black night. This night, however, cloud-shrouded seas began to swell. All signs pointed to a storm—Audax must have known that. Why did he not turn back?

I sent Antonius back up the mast to keep watch lest Audax come upon us while we slept. After another tense night, we peered attentively at the horizon for signs of our pursuers. Three sails stuck out behind me like splinters sprouting from the ocean. Was this sorcery? Would nothing discourage the man?

Knowing that I was in a fight for my life, I again gave orders to dump overboard another half of the remaining tin—leaving only a fraction of our original supply—and gave orders to sail directly with the breath of Zephyr, no matter where it might take us. And the direction the wind blew was to the southwest—ever away from precious land.

It was at this time that I began to see something in the eyes of my men I had never seen before: panic. Mind you, these men were accustomed to the uncertainties and dangers of a perilous profession. They were calm in the face of storm or flight. Nevertheless, I knew what they were thinking: precious few had ever sailed more than three days into the heart of Oceanus and returned alive. The further we sailed into the west, the greater the risk and the greater the terror. Only a fool could fail to see it.

My men knew well the capriciousness of Neptune. What they could not understand, however, was the resolve of Audax.

I had to do something to steer them from thoughts of mutiny. I had to say something that would inspire courage and hope. But any words I spoke were merely a mask that covered an unthinkable reality. They knew it. I knew it. There was only one certainty—one truth everyone knew but no one had the nerve to speak: If we didn't lose our pursuers and turn back toward shore very soon, we would never see our homes again.

My crew stood before me. Men I had personally picked for their skill and bravery. And yet they could not look at me. They did not speak.

"Are you afraid?" I nearly shouted the words.

"I'm not afraid!" It was my little Mus. And I knew that perhaps he was the only one of my crew who could say it with honesty. How I loved that innocent soul.

"Anyone else?"

No one responded.

"Very well then, let me be the first to confess. I am as frightened as a little girl."

At last, a smile appeared on the lips of a few of them. Glaucus gave a supportive chuckle that seemed more forced than genuine.

I reviewed the details of our situation. Reminded them of Audax's sworn oath to have our heads. Impressed upon them the importance of losing him without delay. I explained that I did not know how he was following us so closely, but that we had no choice except to evade him.

"It's magic," said one.

"It's the dark arts, surely. Otherwise, we would have lost them long ago," said another.

I could see it in their faces—despair and defeat. Contagious as a wildfire and growing as fast.

"I will ask only one thing more of you," I said at last. "Work with me this night. Do everything I say. If we have not lost them by morning light, I will turn about and surrender."

While the words seemed to pacify them, they filled me with unspeakable apprehension. I had no doubt whatsoever that if I did not shake my pursuers this night, the next morning would be my last.

At dusk, I reduced my cargo yet again, leaving only a trace of the precious tin, and, with that weight lifted from the belly of the *Morning Star,* we tacked toward the setting sun.

One thought brought me comfort: If my men were terrified, then Audax's men must be feeling the same. If my loyal men were troubled with thoughts of mutiny, what must Audax's men be feeling? He had to be facing the same danger aboard his own vessels. Was his anger so great that he would risk almost certain death in order to capture one man?

For the third night, I sent Antonius to the top of the mainmast to watch for signs of pursuit.

"Yes, sir," he said.

And that is when I caught it. Perhaps it was something in the tone of his voice. A look in his eye.

He was hiding something.

The city of Gades, I think, was where I had found him. After a run-in with a turbulent north wind, my sails were butchered, and I had put in to port for repairs. Antonius was on the docks with a fine cloth and an even better proposition. He offered, free of charge, two sets of new sail; the only price he demanded was that I rescue him from his master and allow him to work as a seaman on my vessel. I couldn't remember many of the particulars of his story—a typical tale of brutality, predictable beatings, and wages withheld. He showed me the scars on his back. He parted his tunic to show me ribs that protruded from malnourished flesh.

At the time I remembered feeling only moderate compassion for the young man. So fate had dealt him the role of a slave. What of that? There were slaves in the world and there were masters. Although I personally had never cared for the practice of slavery, it was the way of the world. And I never let that get in the way of business.

And this particular business—procuring fine sails at no cost and with only moderate risk—suited my purposes well.

For two years, Antonius had been invaluable to me. I discovered that he could write and allowed him access to my accounts. He was an eager pupil, and so I taught him how to be a seaman—even to the point where he could pilot the ship and track our position by the stars.

Because he owed me his freedom as well as his life, I had never questioned his loyalty.

But now, lost in the depths of Oceanus and fleeing for my life, something troubled me.

I watched as Antonius climbed the mast to search for signs of our pursuers. I went to the stern and pretended to occupy myself with steering the ship but I watched him carefully.

It was some two hours later that I caught a glint of light from the top of the mast—a brief spark, like the light of a falling star.

I had solved the mystery of how Audax was able to track me.

A few minutes later, Antonius knelt before me, weeping and pleading for his life. At his side was a rectangular box, open on one end, but concealed on all the others. Inside, the surface was coated with soot, and hidden inside, a lamp.

"I had no choice," Antonius said. "He has my mother. He said he would kill her if I did not do it."

Whether he was lying or not, I could not tell, nor did I care. Because of him, the life of every man on my ship was in jeopardy.

"Were you in his hire before I rescued you from your master, or after?"

"After, I swear."

That also could easily have been a lie. Audax was rich enough and clever enough to have set the bait I had hungrily devoured. Whether before or after, the fact was I had been betrayed by a man whom I trusted. For the last three nights, Antonius had, with a lamp hidden in the back of a box, revealed our position to Audax and his ships.

I had little choice as to what to do with him. Had I kept him on board, the others would have torn him limb from limb and thrown him into the sea. But I had a better, more productive, idea.

I rigged a couple of planks to create a small raft and tied Antonius to it.

He screamed, of course, and pleaded with me to be merciful. He swore his love for me. Ah, if only all men were knitted of such loyal stuff as those who are about to perish.

I handed him his lamp and the materials to light it. "Your only hope," I shouted to him as his raft separated from me, "is to bring the ships to you."

"Don't leave me, I beg you!" he screamed.

But of all options, this was both the most practical as well as the most merciful. And one that would allow me to make my escape.

"If you do not perish this night," I shouted, "may the gods protect you if we ever meet again."

In a few minutes, the raft fell away from view, and I applied every resource toward making good my escape.

But if I had any illusions that the gods had finally decided I had been punished enough, I couldn't have been more mistaken. West winds whipped at my sails, growing stronger by the minute. In the distance, rumbles of thunder and sheets of angry lightning flashed between black clouds, slashing the night with deadly fire as though Jupiter were at war with Neptune.

I could not turn around without moving directly into the storm, directly toward Audax. And turning east was suicide.

I shouted orders and soon the rudder bit deep into the roiling waves, turning my ship grudgingly toward the southwest. If the gods would only smile upon me for a short while, there might be a chance I could outrun the storm and circle my way back to land.

NOTES

Liver divination: Technically known as hepatoscopy or hepatomancy, divination by examining the livers of sacrificed animals was practiced throughout the ancient world, dating back to at least the third millennium B.C. in ancient Mesopotamia. The liver was chosen because it was believed to be the source of blood, and hence life force. The "Liver of Piacenza," in Italy, is a bronze model of a sheep's liver that provided a guide to priests for "reading" livers.

The Fates and the thread of life: The Three Fates (Greek *Moirai,* the "apportioners") are described as weaving the threads of each individual's life into the tapestry of the world. When a thread is cut by the Fates, that life is ended. Belief in fate and predestination was widespread in the ancient world, as exemplified by the Stoics. This ancient debate about fate and predestination has spilled over into Christian theological disputes in various ways, most notably among the Calvinists.

Zephyr: The winds were described as the breath of the mighty wind gods; Zehpyr was the classical god of the west wind.

Gades: An ancient Carthaginian colony; modern Cádiz in southern Spain.

Chapter 5

Lucius looked up from the page and dabbed a cloth against his forehead. What had he discovered? The bronze plates certainly had the appearance of authenticity. The tarnished metal gave every indication of being centuries old. The script, though written in Latin, was different enough from the vulgar corruptions of contemporary language that it could be authentic.

Who was this Malchus? Was it possible Lucius was reading an actual account of someone who lived centuries earlier? Or was it only a fanciful tale fabricated from whole cloth, an imaginative story intended to entertain and amuse?

There was nothing like a good mystery for taking one's mind away from the troubles of the day, and today had certainly had its share of troubles. As far as mysteries went, this was, indeed, a compelling one. The fires that had burned within Lucius earlier that night had dwindled. His rage had transformed into a lingering and deep sorrow. But he did not want to revisit his grief of earlier—not yet. Instead, he turned his attention to this new puzzle.

Lucius' grandfather had often told him of his navigator ancestor—foremost among them, Hanno. The legendary Hanno was a brilliant and intrepid navigator who, a millennia ago, had sailed from Carthage west and south down the coast of Africa. His grandfather claimed that a record of those voyages still existed, although Lucius had never seen evidence of it.

But try as he might, he could recall no mention of any "Malchus." He cursed himself for not paying better attention. Why had he not written down the names his grandfather recited so easily?

If this Malchus was an ancestor of his, why had he chosen to record the events of his life on metal plates? And how had those plates ended up in the family lararium? These were secrets Lucius longed to know and ones he hoped the record would reveal.

A coughing sound pulled Lucius from his thoughts, and he turned, startled to see Gunderic standing outside his study. Beads of sweat dimpled his forehead.

"Forgive me," the servant said.

"It's late. Shouldn't you be asleep?"

Gunderic whispered, "No one is asleep."

A brief and painful smile appeared and faded from Lucius' face. "I suppose you are right."

Gunderic glanced behind him. "I waited for the anger to pass before disturbing you."

Lucius stood and gestured for Gunderic to enter the room. "Come. Sit with me."

Gunderic took an unsteady step forward and then stopped. Lucius could read the emotions on his servant's face and, in spite of his earlier wrath, he could not suppress a chuckle. What a spectacle he must have presented—an old man in the grip of passion, throwing down statues and railing at the stars. Gunderic must have thought him mad. Capable of any sort of violence.

There truly was no fool like an old fool.

He beckoned Gunderic once again to approach. "You are wondering if I am in possession of my wits?"

"I was concerned . . ."

Lucius took a cloth and draped it over the plates in a movement that he hoped would be unnoticeable. "It is behind me now, my friend. See for yourself. I am no longer a danger to anyone. I am safe. You are safe. Your wife and child are safe. All of Carthage is safe—at least from me."

There was something in Gunderic's eyes—not fear exactly. Was it distrust? Sorrow?

A flush of guilt spread through Lucius as he considered the distress he had caused the man. The poor fellow had enough troubles of his own.

"Tell me, Gunderic. How is your daughter?"

"She is the same."

"I have asked Cyril Marcellus Andronicus to come this morning. He is the finest physician in Carthage. I would trust my life to him."

"Thank you."

"Do her symptoms improve?"

Gunderic replied that his daughter was still very ill but they were hopeful a cure would be found. He offered a few words of thanks to Lucius for providing the services of his personal physician. He was grateful for Lucius' offer to pay for a sacrifice of a goat to Asclepius but said that it would not be necessary.

It was a consoling conversation. A comforting argument that perhaps the world had not tilted and transformed as much as he had thought. It provided a desperate hold onto normality. And Lucius needed that.

"Please, come in for a moment, Gunderic. Sit."

Gunderic hesitantly sat next to his master.

Lucius' eyes were searching and sorrowful. "Go ahead, ask," he prodded.

"What do you mean?"

"The obvious question. The one compelling question you must have on your mind."

"It is only that you have spent a fortune acquiring the statues. The Venus came from Tuscany. I unloaded it myself from the merchant ship. I paid the manifest for the Apollo from Corinth and the Jupiter from Sicily."

"You have a fine memory, Gunderic. Alas, it matters not. Not anymore. After you have rested and your daughter is returned to health, please dispose of them." He gestured to the scattered fragments of statues.

"Yet still the question remains."

"Why?" Lucius shook his head and laughed softly. "Are you familiar with the name Lucretius?"

Gunderic did not respond.

"Why should you be?" Lucius continued. He stood and walked to the other side of the room to a wall covered with shelves filled with dozens of scrolls, some of them cased in leather, others bare with exposed papyrus.

"Your church fathers would applaud your ignorance," he continued. "You see, they did not care for Lucretius. Your Jerome claims he was a madman and that he wrote his treatise in the throes of an inner torment so great that, shortly after completing the work, he took his own life."

Lucius selected a leather sheath, brought it to his table. "Lucretius was Greek. He lived four and a half centuries ago—at the time of Julius Caesar. He was an observer—a philosopher. He wrote of the wonders of the universe. How everything works perfectly. The motion of the stars and moon. The regular rise and fall of the ocean tides. The seasons. All perfect, cold, and, above all, predictable."

Gunderic raised an eyebrow. "Evidence of supreme creation."

"Not to Lucretius."

Lucius pulled from the casing a scroll written on leather parchment. The ink had faded, leaving the text readable, but only with difficulty. "When an earthquake destroyed a city, the people surrounding it attributed the disaster to an offense against one of the many gods. Lucretius disagreed. He claimed it had nothing to do with supernatural passion. Rather, it had everything to do with rock shifting against rock deep inside the earth—not because some god was offended or that the sacrifices to him had not been satisfactory—but because that is what rock does from time to time. It shifts. Lightning strikes and sets an edifice ablaze—to what do you attribute that?"

"I know some consider it a sign of disapproval."

"Exactly. Lucretius, however, did not. He claimed it had nothing to do with the displeasure of Jove. Rather, it was lightning doing what lightning does—striking the earth during a storm. A result of cold, uncaring, conscienceless, and conscious-less natural law."

Gunderic shifted uncomfortably.

Lucius continued, "Therefore, if everything operates without emotion, without variance—if the universe is mechanical—where are the gods?"

"Who created it?"

Lucius shrugged. "Perhaps in eons past some being formed the universe. But Lucretius believed that the passionless working of the universe was evidence that, if the gods ever did exist, they have long since moved to a more agreeable location. You see, if everything operates perfectly and predictably, what need is there for a capricious deity?"

"There is always need of God."

"Be careful of what you wish, Gunderic. Do you really want to be at the mercy—at the whim—of an impulsive deity possessed with supreme power? Do you really wish to be subject to a god who, merely to amuse himself, could snuff out the life of a man, a village, the entire world?"

"We have very different ideas of the personality of God."

"Do we?"

"In my religion," Gunderic said, "God is love."

"Ah, yes, the Christian paradox."

"I'm not sure what you mean."

"Your god of *love*. Tell me, Gunderic, is this god of yours not responsible for more deaths and more suffering than from any other source? Is he not responsible for more misery than anything that has been inflicted upon the world from all the tyrants who have ever lived since the beginning of recorded time?"

"That is absurd."

"The flood of Decalion—what name does your holy book give him . . . ah, yes, Noah. Was not your god responsible for that flood? Or was it, instead, one of Lucretius' acts of random nature?"

"But the earth was filled with iniquity—"

"So we are to excuse your god for wiping out countless lives because they didn't measure up to his standards?"

"It was the only way to cleanse the earth."

"There is always justification, is there not? Isn't the same true for the pickpocket, the embezzler, the murderer? There is always a reason, a rationalization. Even when the vilest of criminals commits unspeakable acts, does he not, at least in his own mind, make perfect sense of his actions?"

"You're twisting the facts. The flood was an exception. God loves His children and wants what is best for them."

"Do you really believe that?"

"With all my heart."

"Is not your god the same who destroyed cities by fire, murdered the firstborn sons of Egypt, commanded genocide of sovereign nations?"

"I fear you have me at a disadvantage."

"It is your religion, not mine."

Gunderic frowned. "What I mean is that you are famous throughout the world for your ability to form arguments and defend them. I am a slave who does not have the benefit of your training in rhetoric."

"Let us set aside rhetoric, then. Tell me simply, Gunderic. Why do you believe? Why do you follow the Christ?"

The slave was silent for a moment. "My reasons will hardly satisfy a scholar. Nevertheless, you ask what I know about Jesus Christ. He was the only perfect and sinless man. He taught His followers to love God and to love one another. He was the Son of God and atoned for the sins of all who believe in Him. I believe in the Christ because He was pure, innocent, and without blemish. And for that, He was never forgiven."

Gunderic rose to his feet and continued, his voice quiet but firm. There was no hint of dissemblance in it. Only conviction. Only certainty. "Evil men conspired against Him, nailed Him to a cross, and shed His noble blood. Although His lifeless body was wrapped in linens and placed in a tomb, He broke the eternal chains of darkness and burst asunder the insensate doors of death. Three days after He died, He rose, glorified and resurrected with an incorruptible and eternal body of flesh and bone. He conquered death not only for Himself but for all who have ever lived— the just as well as the unjust. I believe in immortality. That is why I believe in the Savior of all mankind."

Lucius examined the eyes of his servant, looked for clues of deception in his posture. But the man believed what he said. Had Lucius himself ever been as certain about his own religion? Even in the days of the Emperor Julian, had he ever truly believed in Mithras with the kind of certainty his slave believed in the Galilean?

But belief was not enough. He had learned that lesson once and for all earlier that evening.

"Ah, yes, the eternal optimism of the true believer," he said.

Once again, Lucius was reminded of the reason he avoided debate with fanatical believers of any sort. What was the point? Arguments, facts, evidence—what were they to them? How could the candle of truth stand against the conflagration of impassioned yet ignorant belief?

"Have you ever considered," Lucius said in a kind voice, a tender voice, "the possibility that it is all a lie? What if there is no soul? No life after death? What if, after we close our eyes for the final time, there is nothing more?"

Over the years, Lucius had watched many men squirm. He was famous for turning politicians, clerics, and sophists into silent, gaping-mouthed statues. When he made Maximus the Thracian enraged to the point of spittle, profanity, and purple-veined rabidity—had he not enjoyed that? When, through force of argument, he had humiliated that pompous Galerian and reduced him to actual tears—had he not enjoyed that?

But he felt no pleasure in challenging his slave. For one thing, he was fond of Gunderic. For another, he respected him. The man had no training and little education. He didn't have the slightest understanding of the tenets of philosophy.

But should any man, even though he be a slave, remain in ignorance?

And because Lucius loved him, did not he have some obligation to enlighten him?

"Would you agree," Lucius pressed, "that for an argument to have weight, it must be accompanied by proof?"

Gunderic did not respond.

"Very well then, we must have evidence for that of which you speak. What you do not realize is that you actually are in a strong position with your argument. I claim there is no life after death. All you must do to win the argument is show simple proof. You don't have to prove that all men have souls and live after death, you merely need to supply one example. Just one. Without that proof, however, one must come to certain cold and unpleasant conclusions. I am sorry, Gunderic, but there is no Hades, no heaven, no spirit." He brushed his fingers over the scroll with the words of Lucretius inscribed upon them. "There is nothing beyond what we see in this life.

"Believe me, Gunderic, I take no joy in speaking to you of these things. But there is too much delusion in the world. Too many lies. And they must be confronted. It may be distressing to abandon the faith of your childhood. But do we not have an obligation to adhere to the truth—even if it takes all our courage to recognize it?"

Gunderic's thumb traced an uncertain pattern across the palm of his hand. After a long pause he looked up and said, "One thing I know."

"What is that?"

"Merely because a man says something does not make it true. And because a man disbelieves, that does not make it false."

Lucius laughed appreciatively. "Exactly my point."

"Respectfully," Gunderic interrupted, "respectfully, master, not even when *you* say them."

Lucius chuckled and nodded. "Very good, Gunderic. That is the spirit. Let us speak again of evidence. Prove me wrong. You could do it quite easily. My proposition is that the cornerstone of Christianity is a fable. The man Jesus did not rise from the tomb. No man has. No one will. Death is cold, final, and absolute. There is no consciousness after we close our eyes for the last time. There is not even an eternal sleep. There is . . . nothing."

It surprised Lucius how quickly he had come to this conclusion. All his life he had defended the gods. He had spoken the words of a believer. He had, with Julian himself, been initiated into the mysteries of Eleusis—those sacred rites that lifted the curtain on the fate of man and promised a new existence after this mortal one. Had he, at one time, truly believed? Or was it only a role he had played?

"Deliver one man," Lucius continued, "only one—who truly died and who now walks the earth. It does not even need to be your Christ. Let it be any man, woman, or child. In all the world, show me one such person and you silence me, Lucretius, and all other disbelievers instantly once and forever."

Lucius had spent his life convinced of the fantasy that his mind, his personality, his essence would live on. In the sunset years of his life, he had clung even more tightly to the flotsam of belief that promised he would not simply vanish from existence after he ceased to breathe.

It had been a consoling thought. A necessary thought. Without it, chaos pressed upon him, smothered him, took away breath and life and hope. Even now—now that his eyes had been opened, now that he at last had recognized the truth—he wanted to return to the innocence and faith of his cherished childhood. In that safe refuge, good was rewarded, evil punished. In that world, he would never die, only change to a purer and more celestial substance. In that world, one could depart from this life with hope knowing that the world to come would be more wondrous, more fascinating than could be grasped by the mortal mind. Perhaps more tempting than any other thought was that he would once again embrace his beloved Livia and press her close to him and never be parted from her ever again.

But the child he had once been had matured into a philosopher. A lover of wisdom, a seeker of truth. And the truth—even when cold and monstrous—must be his guiding light, no matter how desperately he wanted and needed the fable.

"Man believes what he desperately needs to be true," Lucius continued. "No matter how preposterous. That, unfortunately, is the stock and trade of religion. And as you said, wanting something does not make it so. Believe all you want, it does not change what is."

Gunderic remained silent.

"Can you deliver what I ask?" Lucius pressed. "Can you provide evidence of this resurrection?" Lucius asked the question not as a prosecutor, not with a hammer, but with an empty cup in want of filling. "Show me this evidence, and I will believe."

Gunderic still did not respond. Was the man frightened? Too consumed by his own sorrow? Or was it that he had nothing to say? No proof. No facts. Only baseless belief?

It surprised Lucius how terribly he mourned the silence. Why could there not be hope in this universe? Why could there not be evidence that life was more than a brief, quivering flame fighting against the irresistible wind, growing ever more faint until its last, desperate flicker?

His own light would dim, and all too soon that terrible darkness would envelop him.

He would follow those countless others who had preceded him into the grave. The thought both terrified and embarrassed him. That his life should amount to this—from flame to ember to nothing—humiliated him as much as it terrified him.

Shame and rage took hold of him and grew like a consuming fire within him. The terrible reality was that no matter how valiantly he fought, no matter who he was or what he had achieved, the final outcome was as certain as cold, unfeeling stone.

"Are you feeling well?" Gunderic asked.

A smile crossed Lucius' lips and he shook his head. "I am well enough. But I have taken advantage of you. Please, return to your wife and daughter. They need you far more than I."

Gunderic stood, bowed, and silently walked out of the room, leaving Lucius alone once again.

He stared at the flickering light of the lamp for several minutes before shaking himself from his stupor. He turned his attention from the scroll of Lucretius to the other object in front of him. He removed the cloth from the bronze sheets and ran his fingers over the letters. Perhaps there was nothing he could do about the inevitability of the coming darkness. But, while he was alive, there were mysteries to investigate.

And that, for him, was reason enough for living.

And so he turned back to the metal plates and allowed himself to sink once again into the story as the sounds of slumbering night fell around him.

NOTES

Latin: Much like differences between the English of modern times and the English of Shakespearean and Jacobean times, in the four hundred years between the first and fifth centuries spoken Latin had changed a great deal, along with the script. A scholar like Lucius would have been able to recognize the differences.

Asclepius: A god of medicine and healing. There were a number of Asclepions, or healing sanctuaries, in the ancient world. Those seeking healing would pray or offer sacrifice to Asclepius, and would often visit or sleep in one of his sanctuaries, hoping for a miraculous cure. Cures were commemorated by placing votive offerings in the shrines depicting the part of the body that had been healed, a practice still associated with healing icons in Greek Orthodox churches in the Middle East.

Scrolls and books: The late antique world was a period of transition in bookmaking. The earlier practice of writing books on rolled scrolls was giving way to the codex, a bound book. Codices allowed writing on both sides of the page, hence making a book half as expensive. (Hence the difference between the Dead Sea Scrolls of the first centuries A.D. and B.C. and the Nag Hammadi Codices of the fourth century A.D.) Codices, or bound books, also allowed the reader to quickly flip through the pages to find a particular passage, rather than laboriously unrolling and rerolling a scroll. Pages were generally made from leather parchment, or from papyrus paper imported from Egypt. Books were preferred by Christians for writing scriptures because they allowed rapid flipping between passages for quick reference and comparison.

Jerome: Jerome (A.D. 347–420) was a monk at Bethlehem and one of the great Christian scholars of late antiquity. He is especially noted for his translation of the Bible into Latin (known as the Vulgate), which for Roman Catholics remains the canonical version of the Bible. His monastic cell survives in the grottos under the Church of the Nativity in Bethlehem.

Deucalion: An ancient Greek hero who, with his wife, survived the flood sent by Zeus who was angered by human sacrifice. In Sumerian mythology, the survivor of the great deluge was Utnapishtim. Lucius would have obtained his knowledge from reading the Septuagint, a Greek translation of the Bible from the second century B.C., which was the main Christian Bible used during this period.

Hades: The Greek name for the underworld, as well as the name of the god of the underworld, who was known to the Romans as Pluto. Hades was the common term for "hell" among Christians. In the Greek of Matthew 16:18, the "gates of hell" are the gates of Hades.

Chapter 6

The Book of Malchus, son of Mago, of the house of Hanno

I cannot write the hundredth part of what happened that night. In truth, even now I cannot think of it without terror clutching at my heart. To this day, it haunts my sleep and burrows into my soul, leaving wounds that refuse to mend or fade.

But, in order for my story to be understood, I am compelled to write a few words.

I have spent my life on the sea, and I have survived winds and waves that have taken the lives of others less skilled or less fortunate.

But the storm of that night was a cataclysm beyond imagination and beyond my poor ability to describe. From the depths of watery canyons, massive waves towered above my ship. I can yet feel the sickening motion of being thrust up toward the stars, high into the sky, with death roiling below. From terrible heights we tottered upon the crests of mountainous waves, only to plunge terrible depths down and down into black, roiling valleys. Water crashed against us and engulfed us, tossing us about with the violence of a wolf shaking a rodent in its teeth.

It seemed as though Aeolus had unleashed the might of every wind against us. Rank after rank of wave assaulted us and would have crushed my ship to splinters had I not struck sails and steered with all my might into the waves. In truth, there was nothing else I could have done to resist the merciless forces that hurled us ever forward.

I still feel it.

Even now.

Even now I feel the despair and the horror of that night.

Culleo and Crassus were picked up by a wind that, with the ease of a child tossing a rag doll, threw them over the side.

Massive waves slapped at my ship, carrying away Lurco and Varrus.

I shouted for everyone to lash themselves to the deck but, for poor Tullus, that was an act that cost him his life. Tullus bound himself to the forward mast which broke into splinters, one of which pierced him through the heart. He was dead before the water swept him away.

Bassus, despite anchoring himself to the side of the ship, was washed overboard; we dragged his lifeless body behind us for more than an hour before anyone realized he was missing.

When morning arrived, the wind still howled fiercely, pushing us ever westward, farther away from safety and away from home. The waves of the following days, although still sometimes as high as the sides of my ship, were miniature in comparison to those from the night of the storm.

For the moment, we would survive.

Of the seventeen men who sailed with me during that terrible storm, only ten remained the following day.

Of those, only four were healthy enough to lash a sail or hold the rudder.

To my relief, little Mus had survived. Slow of wit, clumsy, and awkward of speech, Mus was as dear to me as though he were my brother.

His father, a fishmonger of Carthage, had begged that I take him. I protested, of course. I explained the dangers of the sea and of my profession. But his father persisted in his pleadings to the point that I, eventually, relented. But from the moment I hired the boy, my fortunes picked up to the point where I began considering him more than a faithful and loyal friend. He was my good luck charm.

Mus never questioned an order; when I told him to wash the deck, he flew instantly to the task and worked at it until it was complete. When I told him to unload cargo, he put his back into it.

During the night of the storm when all seemed lost, Mus refused to leave my side but lashed himself to the ship and threw his muscle into helping me and Glaucus hold the rudder. Without his strength, we may not have had the strength to keep the ship turned into the waves.

I repeatedly ordered him to go below deck, but he would not abandon me. It was the first time he had ever disobeyed me.

When others cowered, he remained courageous.

Every order I shouted, he echoed in a voice twice as loud as mine. He was a hero that night. He, as much as any other man, was responsible for our survival.

No, I cannot speak of that terrible night without thinking of my brave and valiant Mus.

The day following the storm, we took inventory of our casualties. Not a man remained unchanged. The nightmare of the storm had transformed us all.

All except for little Mus, who moved from man to man, patting heads, praising each for surviving the night, reassuring them.

"You did a good job," he told them. "Time to go home. Going home now."

But in spite of Mus's reassurances, we all knew the reality of our situation.

In the eyes of my tattered crew was a look that asked the same question: "Will we ever find our way home?"

What could I answer? What possible hope could I give?

Nor did our luck change for the better. The wind blew relentlessly to the west. It was a sailors' dream, that wind—strong, steady, and irresistible—but it drove us farther from home with each passing minute. If only it had blown in the opposite direction we could have made it back.

Within a week we would have been safe in our beds, free of fear, free of drowning despair.

But the wind did not change, nor did it lessen. If anything, it raged all the harder. I knew that I had to keep my wits about me. I had to do something. I had to come up with a plan. Invent a reason for hope. My men needed that. I needed that.

My days and nights were consumed with finding a solution. I briefly considered ignoring the wind and turning into it. Was it possible to sail against the wind and travel east?

No matter how desperately I wanted that to be true—needed it to be true—I knew the attempt was impossible.

If the wind quieted and reversed direction, perhaps then. If luck turned in my favor, perhaps then. But I wasn't willing to risk my life and the lives of my crew on the chance that luck would favor me—not any-more. The wind had to quiet down eventually, perhaps even reverse itself. But when? And how long would it take?

And even if it did, what of the current? The waters of the deep seemed to have a will of their own, pulling us west. Ever and ever to the west, ever and ever away from the safety of home.

I spent my days recording the winds, speed, and the direction of our daily course, but it was difficult to calculate with any degree of certainty the distance we had traveled. One thing was clear, turning about and fighting wind and wave was certain death.

While I concentrated on distance, direction, and time, my men set about the work of repairing our craft and making it seaworthy. The storm had battered us badly and my once-proud ship was but a shadow of its former self. I set those of my men who were able to work to patching up the tears in the sides, bailing water from the hold, and reinforcing the rudder. All that remained of my forward mast was a splintered shard, but the back mast had survived, although the wood was cracked. We lashed it tightly so it could bear the weight of a sail and prayed to our various gods that it would withstand the force of the wind.

After another five days of repairs, the waves quieted and the ship was finally strong enough to test a course of sail on the masts. They held.

But where were we?

Lost in an endless landscape of blue. An impossible distance from home. With the west wind of Zephyr still pushing us away from land, and with our supply of food dwindling, I forced myself again and again to accept the truth: We had come too far. We would never make it if we tried to sail against the wind and return the way we came.

Fresh water was not my highest concern, for we had stretched our sails to collect rain and funneled it into amphorae. We would not die of thirst. But even with our diminished crew eating half-rations, how long could our supply of food last? Two weeks? Three? Perhaps longer if we were fortunate enough to supplement our meager rations with fish from the ocean. But was there life in the sea this far from land? Were the fish edible? And what of the legends of monsters that terrorized those foolish enough to defy Oceanus and stray this far from shore?

Hopeless. And with that unrelenting, cursed west wind perpetually pushing us farther away from home, even had I been possessed of the wit of Ulysses I could not think of an answer to our dilemma. It was as though the only decision left was to choose how we were to die.

And my men knew that as well.

The thing about storms is that they do not lend themselves to the comfort of neutrality. For the most part, we retain our sanity by walking through our lives as though asleep, ignoring the terrible realities of life. Storms do not permit that luxury. Storms open our eyes. Storms demand that we face terrifying truths that rip us from our hiding places and summon us to stand before the judge of our consciences.

Each member of my crew discovered something about the gods during those fateful days. Each man made his own choice. Some clung to the beliefs of their childhood, finding a renewed and passionate faith. Others became hateful and cursed the gods. Some discovered faith while others embraced bitterness and despair.

However, in spite of our entreaties to Neptune, Venus, Castor, and Pollux, our circumstance remained unchanged, driven ever onward toward the setting sun and away from our beloved homeland. For my part, I appealed to Juno who, according to ancient legend, loved the city of Carthage above all others in the world. But my devotion was an outward show intended largely to give courage to my men. Secretly, I did not have much hope that my prayers would be heeded. After all, if Juno could not save her beloved Carthage from the Roman general Scipio and the destroying might of his army, what hope did we have that she would be mindful of the plight of a small ship in the far reaches of Oceanus?

The wind continued to push us westward, and the gods continued to turn a deaf ear to our prayers. Indeed, it seemed the only god with any interest in us was death's harborer, Pluto, and his was merely a patient curiosity—waiting for the moment we would enter his domain and forever vanish from the world of mortals.

It was during this dark time that a thought began to occur to me—a thought born of madness, surely brought about by the most desperate of conditions—but the further west the winds pushed us, the more I forced myself to consider it.

What came to my mind was a story my father had told me when I was a boy. A legend of the beginning of our family—the story of two brothers who founded a merchant dynasty that would ultimately become the house of Hanno.

The story went something like this: A century and a half before the time of Hanno, two brothers lived in Phoenicia, on the eastern Mediterranean coastal city of Tyre. They were merchant seamen who with hard work and fortune had won for themselves modest success. With their wealth, they built a small fleet of merchant vessels that sailed the

Mediterranean trading purple, jewelry, and images of deities that they represented as Aphrodite to the Greeks, Isis to the Egyptians, and Asherah to their own people at Tyre.

They established a wide reputation partly because of their fearlessness, but mostly because their ships were larger than most merchant vessels and built to withstand the capricious moods of an unpredictable sea.

They had wisely managed to stay clear of political entanglements, surviving both the Assyrian as well as the Egyptian occupation of Phoenicia. Through shrewdness and tenacity, they increased the reach and scope of their business each year.

But then something happened that changed the fate of both the brothers as well as the entire world: Babylon. That once terrible empire rose again from the ashes and, for a second time, lifted its scepter over the nations of the world.

The Babylonian king Nebuchadnezzar marched west, sweeping the nations before him. Assyria was destroyed; Egypt trembled and fled at his approach. The only nations who outlived the Babylonian invasion were those who surrendered, offered their wealth, and pleaded for mercy before the invaders arrived at their walls.

Judah, a small, presumptuous kingdom that neighbored Tyre to the south, made a foolish decision. After an initial submission to Nebuchadnezzar, they switched sides and made a futile alliance with Egypt—a disastrous choice that angered Nebuchadnezzar who decided to make an example of the rebellious upstart.

As it happened, the simple-minded king of Judah, though incompetent as a ruler, was quite successful at one thing—breeding sons. When the Babylonian conqueror smashed the gates of Jerusalem, his first order of business was destroying and plundering the temple of Jerusalem. His second was to gather the heirs to the throne of Judah and assemble them in front of their father. There he murdered them, one by one, while their father watched.

That the death of his sons might be the last thing he ever saw, Nebuchadnezzar then put out the eyes of the king of Judah. Then he bound the blind king and carried him away to Babylon along with all those of the younger generation who showed intellectual promise, skill, or physical beauty.

But as terrible as that day was for the unfortunate Jewish king, there was one lambent hope—not all of his sons had been apprehended and murdered. The youngest, a young man, had been spirited away by the king's servants and had escaped the fate of his brothers.

And it was that son—I cannot remember the name—who fled to Tyre where he landed at the doorstep of my ancestors. The two brothers were promised a fortune to ferry the young prince far away from Babylon's outstretched hand.

The brothers may not have known the details of who the stranger was, but certainly, they understood the dangers of risking the ire of Babylon. The brothers knew that the decision before them would change their lives. If they agreed to take the young prince of Judah, the long reach of the king of Babylon would never allow them to return. If they took this commission, they would have to leave Tyre forever.

Nevertheless, the shrewd brothers were convinced that Tyre would soon be added to the conquests of Nebuchadnezzar. Thus, the best future for free merchants lay to the west.

The Fates have a curious way of opening doors and kicking mortals through them. And that was what had happened to the two brothers of Tyre.

They accepted the Jewish commission, packed up the prince, and sailed with their entire fleet away from Tyre and toward Carthage, a city founded by Phoenician merchants and known for its martial spirit and boundless enterprise. Once there, energized by the influx of new capital, the brothers established a new base of operations for their trade through-out the western Mediterranean, careful never to stray too far to the east and into the reach of angry Babylon.

But peace was not to be their lot. Less than a year after their depar-ture from Tyre, the servants of the exiled king of Judah appeared a second time. Nebuchadnezzar had learned of the defection and had dispatched agents to Carthage to find the young Jew and assassinate him along with those who had helped him escape. The Babylon agents were also instructed (and perhaps this was what truly drove the decision) to find the remnant of the royal treasure of Judah and bring it back to Babylon.

Once again, the boy king appealed to the two brothers. This time, their desperation was even more evident. They had to preserve the royal blood of their tribe, they said, no matter the cost. No matter the danger. They begged the brothers to take them so far away that the hand of Nebuchadnezzar could never reach them.

The brothers consulted with each other and, at long last, offered a proposal.

There was a legend, they said, of a land beyond Oceanus to the west—far beyond the reach of Babylon. An unspeakable distance away.

The risks, however, were too terrible to attempt. Not only was it re-mote and beyond the reach of any mortal, but the voyage itself was next to impossible. Dangerous; if the terrible monsters of the ocean did not swallow the ship, the gods would, in their wrath, crush all who made the attempt.

The Jews, in response, made two preposterous claims: the first, that their god would save them from the wrath of other deities who might be offended by the attempt.

And second—and this the greedy brothers could not resist—they promised to lay at the brothers' feet a treasure that would make them as wealthy as the king of Carthage.

In the end, the gold convinced the brothers to make the attempt.

Three ships were specially built—large enough to carry provisions for a long sea voyage and deep-keeled enough to venture into the untamed waters of the unknown ocean.

The brothers drew lots. The first brother was to guide the Jewish prince into the unknown western sea. The second was to remain in Carthage and enjoy the treasure. If the first brother ever returned, he would be given three-fourths of the treasure.

The three ships sailed west and were never heard from again.

With the wealth of the boy king of Judah, the second brother founded the merchant dynasty that was to become the house of Hanno.

That man was my ancestor, and the ancestor of Hanno the Navigator.

The question that filled my mind in those dark days of sailing the endless ocean was, what had happened to that first brother?

Had he perished at the hands of vengeful gods or been swallowed up by the cold ocean? Or was there a land far to the west, beyond the great Oceanus? Was it merely fable? Or could it be true?

I agonized over the dilemma before me.

Turn about and try to return to the east against enemy, wind, and wave? Or, instead, follow the course of my ancient ancestor and continue into the unknown, hoping to find a land of myth and legend?

Ultimately, the winds made the decision for me. Our only chance for survival was to sail west as swiftly as possible before we perished of starvation. To turn east and attempt to sail into a strong wind with our food nearly gone would guarantee that we would never see our beloved homeland again.

I had no other choice.

My proposal met with surprisingly little resistance from my men. Perhaps they knew that the homes and lives we had known before the storm were gone forever. Perhaps they believed they were doomed as well.

Thus, with the plod of men marching to their doom, we added all the sails we could and watched as the wind filled them.

Glaucus made an ingenious fishing net from pieces of rope and debris, but though we dragged it alongside our ship, we gathered with it nothing but dark seaweed that floated about us in surprising quantities.

I rationed the remaining food to last another six days, and then I set about making my vessel sail as fast as it possibly could.

During this time, two more of my men died of injuries and lack of proper care. I now had only eight men, including myself.

The surprising thing to me was how little my men complained. Those who could work did so with their might. We managed to salvage some old cloth and rigged a second sail that added to our speed. We all knew we were in a race with death and, just as we had fled before Audax, we now raced before an even more merciless and unforgiving antagonist.

I think all of us were pretending in those days. Unable to accept the face of Death, we played our parts like characters on a stage, unwilling to believe that life could end so quickly.

I stopped counting the days from the time we left and began counting the days that remained until our food supply would be gone.

At three days remaining, we spotted a bird far away in the distance. It appeared briefly and then disappeared. I changed course slightly so that we would travel in its direction, but we saw nothing else that day.

Later that day, the sky grew dark with clouds. We could have passed within a mile of land without being able to see it. Winds swelled, and once again, my ship was taken out of my control and we were pulled by the elements in ways I could not change.

On the second day, two remarkable events happened. The first was that we saw several peculiar birds circling overhead. One of them perched on our mainmast. Every sailor knows that where birds are, land must be close by as well, but, no matter how intensely we looked, we could only see water.

The second thing that happened was that Glaucus' net filled with so many fish that I feared it would break. The crew eagerly pulled two score large fish into our boat. We dared not make a fire, so we cut into the flesh and ate it raw, not knowing if the creatures were poisonous. To our relief, we did not perish. In fact, the meat was delicious to the taste—whether because the flesh was actually good or because we were starving, I do not know. But that meal fed our spirits as well as our bodies.

We set out the rest of the flesh, hoping the sun would dry it, but that was an unnecessary precaution, as Glaucus' nets were soon replenished with more life-sustaining meat.

And then one day, just as the rosy-fingered Dawn began turning the black sky to pink, Mus shouted the words we had so longed to hear.

"Land! Up ahead! Land!"

I ran to the bow of my ship and peered in the direction Mus was pointing. There, on the far western horizon, a faint haze lined the blue of the water.

Land!

And where there was land, there would be food and water. And where there was food and water, there was hope and life.

We each of us gave thanks to those deities to whom we had offered our allegiances. Those who had cursed the gods in their hearts wept for forgiveness.

We all wept that day.

And with renewed energy, we steered our valiant ship toward blessed land.

NOTES

Current: In the novel, Malchus follows the southwest Canaries current that merges into the Caribbean current to reach the Americas.

Sailing into the wind: Before the development of the lateen sail in the fourth century A.D., sailing into the wind was very difficult, thus Malchus' problem of trying to return eastward against the strong, prevailing winds of a hurricane.

Amphorae: Large ceramic jars used on ships to transport liquids.

Scipio: The Roman general who defeated Hannibal at the battle of Zama in 202 B.C. and forced the surrender of Carthage to Rome.

Phoenicia: Roughly the region of modern Lebanon, Phoenicia was anciently renowned for its merchants, craftsmen, and wealth. Phoenician merchants and explorers from Tyre and Sidon founded Carthage as a colony.

Tyre: The greatest city of Phoenicia. In the Bible it is noted for its wealth and for the participation of the Phoenician king and craftsmen in the building of Solomon's Temple (1 Kings 5–7).

Purple: Royal or Tyrian purple was a special dye said to be worth its weight in silver. It was secreted by shellfish indigenous to the coasts of Phoenicia. Phoenicians harvested the dye, selling it throughout the Mediterranean region. Dyed cloth was highly prized by Romans for imperial ceremonial robes, thus to "take the purple" meant to ascend the imperial throne.

Aphrodite, Isis, and Asherah: The Greek, Egyptian, and Canaanite goddesses of love and fertility. Asherah was sometimes worshipped by Israelites; Jeremiah calls her the "Queen of Heaven" and blames her worship for the Lord's anger against Judah (Jeremiah 7:17–18; 44:17).

Nebuchadnezzar: Nebuchadnezzar (605–562 B.C.) was the greatest and most powerful of the Babylonian emperors. He defeated the Egyptians at Carchemish (605 B.C.) and conquered Syria, Phoenicia, and Judah. Nebuchadnezzar's siege of Tyre is described in Ezekiel 26–28. He is most famous in the Bible for sacking Jerusalem and destroying the temple in 586 B.C.

King of Judah: The reign of Zedekiah and the sack of Jerusalem are described in 2 Kings 24–25; 2 Chronicles 36; and Jeremiah 52. The massacre of Zedekiah's sons is reported in 2 Kings 25:7.

Youngest son: This is Mulek of the Book of Mormon (Mosiah 25:2; Helaman 6:10; 8:21), probably to be identified with "Malchiah, the king's son," in Jeremiah 38:6. The seal of Malkiyahu has been discovered in Jerusalem (see J. Chadwick, "Has the Seal of Mulek Been Found?" *Journal of Book of Mormon Studies* 12, no. 2 [2003].)

Land beyond Oceanus: This idea refers to the ancient understanding that the earth was spherical (as demonstrated by Eratosthenes in the third century B.C.) and to legends of the *antipodes,* people who lived in lands opposite on the sphere to the Mediterranean.

Chapter 7

"Forgive me for interrupting," a voice said from behind Lucius.

Lucius looked up to discover Gunderic once again standing at the doorway to the study.

"What is it? Your child—has something happened?"

"You have visitors."

"At this hour?"

"It is the bishop, master. Here with three armed officers. There is a second man with him, also a priest."

"What does the esteemed bishop want?"

Gunderic shook his head. "He wouldn't say. Only that he had come to speak with you. He said if you were asleep, I should awaken you."

"Invite them to wait in the *aula*," Lucius said. "Oh, and tell Aurelius that I do not allow weapons in this house. His men can guard against stray dogs in the street while we converse. That task should be equal to their abilities."

Gunderic bowed and disappeared.

What could the old bishop want, and why could he not wait until dawn to deliver his message? Had he come asking counsel? No, that would be out of character. The man had exhausted half a million words already, publicly insisting that the Greeks and Romans had nothing of value to offer a Church already possessed of light and truth.

Had he come to ask for support?

An alliance?

Well, there was little point in wondering. The old bishop was in the *aula* waiting for him. The quickest way to unravel the mystery was to give the man an opportunity to speak.

Lucius placed a feather on the plates where he had left off reading, closed them, and walked over to the wall where he made an opening between an avalanche of scrolls. After satisfying himself that the plates were invisible, he left the room and proceeded to the *aula*.

The torches in the greeting room were already burning when Lucius appeared. Aurelius was there, dour-faced and almost imperceptibly shaking his head at the frescoes on the walls of a nude Neptune and the mosaics on the floor of Apollo pulling back his bow. Beside him stood the man Lucius had seen earlier that evening—the man in bishops' robes who had stood at Aurelius' side. The man he thought he knew.

Then, as now, Lucius felt there was something about him that seemed so familiar. Perhaps an old student? But the face he was trying to place was so much younger than the one before him now. He focused his memory and concentrated on the face.

And then he knew.

The man had changed a great deal but Lucius recognized the eyes and the nose of his old student. What was his name?

Augustine.

That was it. It had been at least thirty years. Perhaps longer. He had been a young man. Full of promise. Alive with the flush of new knowledge and new thought. The man who stood before him now seemed too old. Was it possible that it was the same man?

It had to be.

The man had inherited his dark skin from his Berber father. His face was framed by thick, graying hair that was thinning at the temples, and a curling, full beard that fell to his chest. But it was his over-large hawk nose, however, that provided the unmistakable clue to his identity. A nose that stole whatever beauty the man might have had a chance of possessing.

Lucius remembered it on the face of a much younger man who, along with Aurelius, had sat at his feet, focused on his every word. A good student, much more promising than Aurelius. Although the man was now already in his fifties, he appeared distinguished, despite being dressed in the humiliating robes of the Galilean sect.

"An unexpected pleasure," Lucius said with the same tonality he would have used had he been commenting on a loaf of bread.

"Thank you for accommodating us, Lucius," Aurelius said. "I believe you know the bishop of Hippo?"

Lucius locked eyes with the visitor. There was no hint of guilt in Augustine's eyes, no embarrassment, no retreat. Perhaps it was true what others had said of him. Perhaps the man truly believed. That such a promising mind could have converted to the cult of the Galilean was something that had caused Lucius no small distress when he first learned of it. He had assumed the conversion had been motivated by desire for advancement or position, but there was no hint of that in the face of his former pupil.

"I am surprised to see you here again, Augustine," Lucius said. "People still call you that, don't they? Or have you taken a quaint Galilean name as ornament to your conversion?"

The man smiled. "The last time I was in this room, I was but a child seeking for truth."

"Whereas now," Lucius interrupted, "you are old, wise, and no longer have a need to seek for the truth. Is that the case?"

Augustine looked at the walls. "I remember well these paintings and this mosaic. The color is growing faint, Lucius. Fading with time. An intriguing symbol, don't you agree?"

Now Lucius remembered why he had been relieved when the young Augustine had departed decades ago. In spite of the young man's promise, he was frankly annoying. When young, Augustine had been an accomplished and persuasive rhetorician. But he had developed an arrogance, an eagerness to lock horns with his intellectual superiors. And it did not matter what side of the argument he argued. Black, white, true, false, winning the argument was the thing he cherished above all.

Potential. The boy had indeed possessed potential. If only he had applied himself, he could have perhaps made a name for himself—perhaps even a name as great as Lucius' own.

"Tell me, Augustine, how is your son?" Lucius tossed the phrase at his guest as though he were conversing about the migratory patterns of geese. "Adeodatus, I believe is his name? And the mother? Is she well?"

Lucius regretted the words as soon as he had spoken them. It was beneath him to bring up Augustine's relationship with his concubine and the son born of that relationship.

Augustine, for the briefest moment, looked as though someone had struck him. He recovered quickly, smiled, and said, "Always on the attack, Lucius. It's good to see that you still follow the techniques you taught your students."

It was true. Attack, attack, attack. Always keep your opponent unsure of where the next blow would land.

"I wonder, Augustine, if you know what I was thinking before you came," Lucius said. "I was thinking that the world had gone mad—or perhaps it has always been mad and I only realized it tonight."

What a night this had been. Surrounded by evidence that the gods had abandoned the realms of mortals, each new revelation deadened him to the life he had known before. First, the fall of Rome and now, Augustine, one of his most promising pupils, stood in front of him, dressed in the robes of the Galilean priesthood. A bishop, no less.

The world had indeed gone mad.

"I once knew a man who mourned the lack of civility in the world," Augustine said. "He complained that everyone he met seemed uncommonly rude, mean, and unfriendly. I suggested to him that there might be a much simpler explanation: the man himself might be at fault rather than the whole of the world. He was not amused, of course, but yet . . ."

"And now it is you on the attack, Augustine."

"Sometimes it is the simplest of explanations," he said, "that provides the most revealing of answers."

It angered Lucius that he allowed his old pupil to annoy him. And yet, could it be that the man was right? Was it possible that he himself was mad? Was he like one of those poor elderly souls who drifted into senility, unable to grasp his own dementia?

But still, the arrogance of the man before him could not go unchallenged. Well, why not twist the blade?

"You were about to tell me of your son—"

"That was long ago, Lucius. I am not the same man I was when I last stood here in this *aula*."

"Pity," Lucius answered. "I rather admired that young man. He showed tremendous promise, if sadly unfulfilled."

Aurelius stepped between the two rhetorical gladiators. "We have not come here tonight to reminisce about old times, Lucius. We have not come to be taught, but to teach."

Lucius tried to focus on the pompous words but found himself instead fascinated and repulsed by two bits of white saliva that formed at the corners of the bishop's mouth as he talked.

"Did you hear me, Lucius? We have come to teach."

"An intriguing thought. And what will be the subject of our instruction? Mathematics? Philosophy? Ethics? Rhetoric? What about literacy? That should be entertaining."

"Self-preservation, I think," Aurelius said tautly.

"You have no influence here, Aurelius. You may have control over those you have baptized, but you will find that your threats of eternal fire and torment have little effect within these walls."

"I am not here to speak of *spiritual* fire and torment," he said ominously.

"How remarkable. Have you also become a barbarian, Aurelius? Are you here to threaten torture and destruction?" Lucius laughed when he said it, expecting the two men before him to laugh as well. But they did not laugh. Nor did they smile.

"Tonight, the whole world changed," Aurelius said.

"On that we can agree." Lucius waved an arm. "Rome is no more. Thanks to you and your religion, the great city is in ruin."

"It is the punishment of a just God," Aurelius said.

Lucius felt the blood in his veins pulse against his temples and his anger rising within him. Why did he allow these Galileans to provoke him?

"The punishment of Rome was sent by God as a result of sin," Aurelius repeated, speaking to Lucius as though lecturing a child.

Once again, Lucius attempted to repress the inner fire.

"The whole world lies in sin," the bishop continued. "And for this, the Lord is purging the wicked."

"May I remind you that Rome is under the influence of *your* religion?" Lucius interrupted. "The worship of the Roman pantheon is no longer supported by the state. May I also remind you that the entire Roman world has departed from venerating those beings who inhabit Olympus in favor of your own theology? So, it therefore follows, if God is punishing Rome . . ."

"The world lies in sin, and until that sin is purged—"

"Have you actually deluded yourself into thinking that the reason Rome fell was because it wasn't *Christian* enough? For a thousand years, the Roman Empire worshiped Jove, Juno, and Apollo. For a thousand years, the Roman Empire was ever victorious. It thrived! It was blessed beyond imagination. It was the marvel of the world, prosperous and peaceful beyond hope."

"Like a child, Rome has put away childish things—"

"For a thousand years, Rome stood triumphant and glorious. No other kingdom in the history of the world is worthy to carry its wine cup. A thousand years, it stood undefiled and undefeated. And then something peculiar happened. A new religion gained favor. The pagan gods were abandoned in favor of your Galilean myth. And then what happened? In the space of five short decades, the indestructible empire crumbled. Its glorious temples now lie in rubble. The world that once praised Rome as the glory of man now laughs at her weakness and corruption. The responsibility for this lies at your feet, Aurelius—you and your fellow Galileans. In the space of a single generation you have driven Rome from universal dominion to dust!"

"I have already explained to you, we are not here to be taught of you—"

"So I remember. You are here to teach. Why should you listen to anyone who disagrees with you? Truth, after all, would only muddle things up. Heaven forbid that anyone think for themselves. Heaven forbid that anyone use reason and logic to determine the truth."

"You will not speak to me this way, Lucius. I will not permit it."

"What will you do about it, Aurelius? Bring in your guards? Arrest me for speaking the truth? Tie me to a post and set me aflame?"

The men in front of him looked down.

The silence bled on.

"You can't possibly be serious," Lucius finally said.

Aurelius pursed his lips, making the bubbles of saliva expand. He stared at Lucius.

Was the man attempting to intimidate him?

Still, the silence remained.

Finally, Augustine spoke. "The infidel Alaric will not stop at Rome. He will turn south. He must secure the grain of Africa. Make no mistake, he will come here. He will appear at the gates of Carthage and Hippo. We must take action now."

Lucius could not believe what he was hearing. The whole world had indeed gone mad.

Augustine continued, "We will begin immediately to reinforce walls, store up food and water in case of siege."

"Rome could not withstand a siege. What makes you think Hippo or Carthage could?"

"I don't," Augustine replied. "For that reason, we must rely upon our faith and upon our God."

"Are you actually contemplating purging the city of all those who do not believe as you?"

Aurelius spoke solemnly. "Since we cannot withstand the heretics by force, we must rely upon higher powers. To show our devotion, the land must be purified."

"And how will you do that? The first light of morning is even now descending on the city and with it, the news of what has happened to Rome. What do you suppose will happen when this city arises and learns that the capital has fallen? I should think if anyone or anything should be purged, it would be those who caused it. Look to yourselves, my friends. You do not realize the wrath that will come upon you."

"No, Lucius," Aurelius said in a serious tone. "It is you who does not understand."

Lucius bristled. Enough of threats. Enough of self-righteous blindness. Aurelius was beyond hope, but perhaps he could still reach his old pupil Augustine.

"Listen to me, Augustine. You once loved truth. You once held the pursuit of truth and beauty as central to a fulfilled life."

"I still do, Lucius. While my thoughts do not conform with yours, that does not mean I have abandoned the pursuit of truth."

"Do you realize what you are saying? Do you realize what you are about to do?"

"It is our only hope. Sometimes reason must give way to faith."

"You are like drunken men who believe the reason they stumble is because they are not drunk enough. Instead of throwing off this Galilean superstition, you attempt to save yourselves by immersing yourselves more in the very thing that caused the problem in the first place. Do you not know that the barbarian Alaric—the man who sacked Rome—is one of you? He is Christian! It is the *Christians* who are destroying the empire."

"Do not call him by the name Christian," Aurelius shouted. "He is an Arian heretic."

"He venerates the Galilean as do you. Augustine, you must understand. Open your eyes! Your religion is not the solution; it is the problem."

Aurelius held his hands out, palm down, and patted the air in front of him. When he spoke, it was with a bluster, the words coming out in a sputter, broken and unhinged. "Alaric follows the heretic Arius. He is thoroughly given over to the Evil One."

"But that's the point. You turn on everyone! Unless they conform to your set of preposterous dogmas—derived not from God but from a majority vote—they are heretics and must be destroyed. You once understood logic. I remember. You were both able to divide nonsense from clarity. Can you not see the madness?"

"Listen to me, Lucius," Aurelius said with finality. "Your life is in peril. Within ninety days you must leave the city."

"By what authority—"

"By the authority that comes from my office as bishop of the Holy Apostolic Church. Ninety days, Lucius. You will leave with the other heretics: Arians, Jews, and pagans. I will do my best to protect you between now and then, but if you defy me and refuse to leave, I will not be responsible for your safety nor your property. Do you understand?"

Lucius felt as though he had been struck by a blow.

Madness. Monstrous.

He looked at Augustine, but his face remained calm and serene.

"You are banishing me from my home? From my city? I refuse! I will not leave!"

Aurelius spoke again, emphasizing each word. "Ninety days. Do you understand, Lucius?"

Lucius turned to Augustine. "Rome was your city. The capital city of your religion. It was the city of your God. If Christianity is God's truth, why? Why did it fall? Tell me, Augustine, why did the city of God fall?"

Augustine looked deeply into Lucius' eyes as though searching for an answer. "I don't know," he said at last.

"Until you have an answer for that question, my old friend, your religion is nothing more than a sham. A pretty story. A fable. Tell me why God allowed his own city to fall! Explain it, Augustine! And if you cannot, then as a seeker of truth, you must abandon your false beliefs!"

"Ninety days, Lucius," Aurelius said, taking the other bishop by the arm and leading him toward the door. "Do not try me."

And with that, the two men opened the door and disappeared.

NOTES

Aula: Similar to an atrium, an *aula* is the open central court in large Roman houses.

Apollo pulling back his bow: The mosaic pavements of Roman Tunisia, many now in the Bardo Museum, are rightly world famous (A. Ben Abed, *Tunisian Mosaics* [Getty, 2006]).

Augustine: The greatest theologian of late antiquity, Augustine (A.D. 354–430) was bishop of Hippo, a city some 150 miles west of Carthage. He died there during the siege of Hippo by the Vandals. His most famous works are the *Confessions* (Oxford, 1998) and the *City of God* (Penguin, 2003). A pagan in his youth, Augustine was enamored of Neoplatonism, which greatly influenced his understanding of Christian theology. He converted to Christianity in 386 and was baptized in 387, becoming the greatest Christian spokesman of his age (P. Brown, *Augustine of Hippo,* 2d ed. [2002]; P. Remes, *Neoplatonism* [2008]; J. Rist, *Augustine: Ancient Thought Baptized* [Cambridge, 1996]; R. Wallis, *Neoplatonism,* 2d ed. [2007].)

Berber: Pre-Islamic Tunisian North Africa was a multiethnic society with Phoenicians, Romans, Greeks, and Jews. Berbers (often called Moors), however, were the indigenous population of the region, and were a majority in the countryside. Augustine's mother was a Roman Christian, while his father was a Romanized pagan Berber.

Arius and the Arian heresy: Arius (A.D. 260–336) was a Christian theologian in Egypt whose interpretations of Christology were rejected by the council of Nicaea in A.D. 325. For the next half century, the Arian controversy plagued the empire. Many Arians, followers of Arius' theology, were persecuted, and many fled. Ulfias (A.D. 310–383), an Arian bishop, translated the Bible into Gothic and began the conversion of the Goths to Arian Christianity. By the time Alaric sacked Rome in 410, most of his Gothic warriors were Arian Christians. (R. MacMullen, *Voting About God in Early Church Councils* [2006]; L. Ayres, *Nicaea and Its Legacy* [2006]; R. Williams, *Arius: Heresy and Tradition* [2002]; R. Hanson, *The Search for the Christian Doctrine of God: The Arian Controversy, 318–381* [2006].)

***City of God*:** The questions raised by Lucius are precisely those Augustine attempted to answer in his *City of God* in the years following the Gothic sack of Rome.

Chapter 8

As Lucius walked through the atrium the light of dawn crept gently through the sky. How the world had changed in the last few hours. How *he* had changed. He wondered if he was a better man now than he was a day before.

No. He did not think so.

In truth, he liked who he was yesterday more than who he was today. Imagining Helios driving his chariot through the skies and Atlas turning the world to face it toward the stars—those beliefs had flooded his life with magic and wonder.

He mourned the loss of mystery and awe—the feelings that once had brimmed and overflowed his soul as he stood at Emperor Julian's side during that wondrous night of initiation into the Eleusian mysteries.

Now, he faced in the first light of dawn the consequences of his disbelief.

Upon reaching the peristylium, he stopped and fell back a step as though struck by a blow. In the light of a new day, his battle with the immortals of the night before wrenched his stomach and brought a surprising sense of remorse. Limbs, heads, and torsos lay strewn about the courtyard.

Had someone else done this, Lucius would have been consumed with righteous anger. He would have eloquently raised his voice in a passionate defense of the gods and in condemnation of the blasphemy.

Momentarily, he felt fear. What wrath had he brought upon his own head? Was it possible that the gods, seeing this desecration, could send destruction his way?

He fought against the feeling.

It was superstition, he repeated to himself. Only myth. What power did a story, a fiction, have to hurt him?

Might as well fear stepping on a crack or withering at the sight of an eclipse. Did the ancients truly believe that if they did not appease the sun with sacrifices at the December solstice that the days would continue to shorten? Did they actually believe that their actions made a difference, or was it simply an exercise in consensual delusion? Did they truly believe that the massive, cold, unthinking machine of the universe would care one whit if they sacrificed a hundred doves, a thousand bulls, or even a human life? That the sun would lengthen its course one millionth of a degree as a consequence of their prayers?

Insanity.

And he had worried for a moment that the gods might exercise their wrath against him for destroying these images? What irony! That they would descend from Olympus to punish an old and powerless philosopher while ignoring the barbarians streaming through the gates of their own Eternal City—what an ambrosial absurdity that would be!

These scraps of statues before him—carved faces, limbs, and torsos—these were not gods. They were not earthly images of reality. They were merely the handiwork of some humble craftsman trying to feed himself and his family.

These broken images were simply cold marble and as unfeeling.

These were not gods.

There were no gods.

Still, he mourned the loss of belief. He preferred the fantasy of river nymphs and prancing satyrs. He remembered the wonder he felt believing that the prayers and libations offered in temples actually lofted up into the halls of Elysium and were truly acknowledged, welcomed, and considered by immortals who, should the fancy take them, could bend the universe in response.

What a terrible catastrophe, the loss of mystery. Perhaps Augustine was right. Perhaps men needed faith to give meaning to life. Perhaps they needed it so desperately, they were driven to invent it.

"Will you be retiring now?" Gunderic asked. The faithful slave had been at his side the whole while, had witnessed the conversation with Aurelius and Augustine.

"In a while," Lucius said. "You must not worry about me, Gunderic. Your wife and child need you today. What is the state of your daughter?"

"Worse, I'm afraid."

"What can be done?"

"Only have faith. God is our final hope."

Lucius resisted the temptation to say anything that would diminish Gunderic's hope. If that was all the poor fool had, let him hang onto it. It could not possibly help the child, of course, but what harm could come of it? Perhaps in the end that was the purpose of faith—to help mortals make sense of the incomprehensible ache of life.

"Before you leave, Gunderic, tell me. What did you think of your fellow Christians Aurelius and Augustine? Do you not find any conflict in belonging to a religion that would persecute those who do not believe as they do?"

Gunderic picked up an empty water vase and tucked it under his arm. "You must understand—not all Christians are the same."

"Perhaps not." Lucius took Gunderic by the arm and turned toward his study. "Perhaps not. But answer this: Can the body move on its own accord, or does it take direction from the head?"

"The mind controls the body."

"You are wise, Gunderic. And in the body of the Galilean sect, Aurelius and Augustine are the head. What the head wills, the body performs."

Gunderic nodded and asked if there was anything else Lucius needed.

"Attend to your child, Gunderic. I have required too much of you already."

The servant departed, leaving Lucius once again alone with the ancient record of his ancestor.

The Book of Malchus, son of Mago, of the house of Hanno

The beauty and wonder of this new land continually surprised us. It seemed, at times, as though we had wandered into an earthly Elysium. Plentiful water refreshed our throats and cooled our skin. We discovered exotic and mouth-watering fruit on trees and in the forest. For meat we discovered strange boar-like creatures and a curious sort of small deer. In short, it was a place of recovery and rest. And with a little time and work, the eight of us who had survived the long voyage soon recovered from our ailments. Since the temperature never became unpleasantly cold, we did not have to worry about keeping ourselves warm. The only fires we needed were for cooking.

It wasn't long before we had constructed several shelters made of branches and covered them with sail cloth that effectively kept us dry during the frequent rains.

We had many discussions underneath the canopies of cloth and broadleaf, listening as hot rain splashed against our little shelter and rivered away into the forest. The primary topic—and the one that caused the greatest controversy—was how to return home.

There was plenty of wood, and although we had only a few tools, it was conceivable that we could repair our ship. It would take time, but we had that in abundance. The burning question we all asked was could we make the vessel strong enough to survive the return voyage? But to even attempt that journey—would it be madness to try? What if there was no season when Eurus blew east? What if, failing a favorable wind, the voyage took twice as long? Three times? It was possible. Would we starve or die of thirst on a crystal sea, floundering in the middle of an infinite blue wilderness? We had been swept here by the gale of a great storm; could we weather another one? What hidden dangers lurked deep within the currents and waters of the vast sea? Would the gods favor the attempt, or would they marshal wind and wave and throw us back or pull us into Hades?

Or should we submit ourselves to the will of Olympus and remain? Build a city here—a new Carthage? But the one thing that defeated this argument was that in this paradise of a world—a place possessed of everything one could desire—the one thing we did not have was women. What would be the point of building a city if it would perish with the last man?

Ultimately, we resolved to a man to focus our every effort in achieving the goal of returning to Carthage.

We knew we were gambling with our lives, yet we were all willing to do so. Consequently, I divided the men into two crews. The first gathered food and experimented with means of preserving it so that it could last throughout a long voyage. The second went to work repairing and strengthening our ship and rebuilding the masts. Once that task was completed, we would build a second ship—as large as our original. This second ship would be towed behind our first ship and would have a double purpose: first, it would be a floating storehouse, doubling our supplies of food and water. Additionally, it could be used in case of misfortune, doubling our chances of survival.

Whether we had a fighting chance at successfully making the return voyage, I did not know. What I did know—and with clarity—was that my men needed work to keep them from fighting among themselves and to keep them from succumbing to swings of depression and rage. And so we worked, baring our backs to the heat of the sun, making tools, framing timber, and fashioning rope.

Our greatest challenge was what to do for sailcloth. Drusus attempted to make a substitute using various fibers from plants and leaves, but these experiments were either too heavy or too fragile and became impossibly unyielding when wet. In an equally valiant effort, he attempted making sails both from animal skins and woven plant mats. Neither proved viable.

Nevertheless, we continued our labors, trusting that eventually we would find a solution.

We had settled into a comfortable routine: rising with the sun and working until night. The progress we made was slow; I knew it would take months before we could make the attempt of returning. But we worked happily knowing that, although we stretched our bodies to their limits, each day brought us closer toward our goal.

It was on the thirty-second day after our landing, on a windless morning with a cloudless sky, that we discovered something that would change our lives completely and forever.

Mus was the first to notice it off in the distance: a dark plume of red smoke, a narrow string of crimson cloud that tied heaven to earth. We climbed to the top of an outcropping of rock that allowed us to see over the forest foliage.

Glaucus said the words we all were thinking, "That could not be caused by natural means."

I agreed. One tendril of blood streaked into the sky, dividing the horizon.

This was a controlled fire. And that could mean only one thing.

We were not alone.

"Man," I said.

"Perhaps," Glaucus said, the tone of his voice implying something sinister. "Or perhaps something else."

"Do we approach them? Or do we stay hidden? Perhaps they are men like us—"

"Or beasts."

"—and they could help us."

"Or kill us."

"We need cloth for sails."

"Or it could be a demon."

I frowned at Glaucus. The last thing I needed was for him to put fear in the minds of my men by telling them of supernatural creatures and devouring beasts.

"Some intelligent creature has created that fire," I continued.

"That's obvious," he replied. "But why red? What kind of magic makes fire bleed red vapor into the sky?"

"We have to investigate."

"I don't think we do."

"Ulysses would investigate."

"May I remind you that Ulysses, in his obsession to investigate, nearly became roast flesh for a Cyclops?"

"He survived, if I remember correctly."

"True, but most of his crew did not."

Why must Glaucus always argue? Why did he have to contradict me at every turn?

"We can't return without a sail. We have to discover who made that smoke."

"And what will you do once you find them? Sit down and have a little chat? Just the two of you?"

"I don't see why not."

"And what language would you speak?"

He had a point. There was a possibility that they spoke Latin—the language of the gods—this far from Rome, but the likelihood was slim. Yet, in spite of the danger, in spite of all the reasons not to go, I turned to Glaucus and said, "We're going."

"This is what I like about you, Malchus," he replied in a tone not devoid of sarcasm. "Consistency."

"And you are coming along."

"Perfect."

Mus insisted that he come along as well and, regrettably, I agreed.

Back at the ship, I hurriedly searched the belongings of old Varrus—a retired legionnaire who had been swept overboard in the storm—and found his sword and helm. I strapped on the helmet, regretting that I did not have more to share with the rest of my men, and wrapped the scabbard around my waist. I found a second sword for Glaucus and handed Mus a small dagger.

And with those meager preparations, the three of us set out to find the source of the mysterious red smoke.

NOTES

Solstice: In Latin, the word derives from *Sol Sistere,* which means "Sun stands." The winter solstice (between December 20 and 23) is the longest night of the year. It was widely celebrated in antiquity as the rebirth of the sun, as the following days grow increasingly longer.

Eternal City: Another name for Rome, reflecting the belief that the city was divinely protected by the gods and would endure forever.

New Land: While the geography of Malchus's "new land" is intentionally vague in this novel, we are assuming a Mesoamerican setting for the Book of Mormon. For many articles and books linked with this "limited geography" interpretation, see the web page of the Maxwell Institute at BYU (http://maxwellinstitute.byu.edu/) and the Foundation for Apologetic Research and Information (http://www.fairlds.org/apol/ai178.html).

The best introduction to the topic are two books by John Sorenson: *An Ancient American Setting for the Book of Mormon* [1996] and *Images of Ancient America: Visualizing the Book of Mormon* [1997]. Brant Gardner's *Second Witness: Analytical and Contextual Commentary on the Book of Mormon* [2007] is an amazingly detailed analysis of the Mesoamerican context for the Book of Mormon.

Elysium: The land of paradisiacal afterlife of the pagans, broadly similar in concept to the biblical Eden.

Eurus: God of the east wind.

Chapter 9

The Book of Malchus, son of Mago, of the house of Hanno

We clawed our way through the branches and thick undergrowth. Arduous work. Few paths, myriad branches and leaves. Strange flashes of things dark and sudden that flitted from shade to shadow before evaporating into darkness. We saw few of these creatures but heard many— strange guttural calls that came from throats both small and large. My imagination attached terrifying forms to those throats.

Perhaps most menacing of all were the serpents. I did not know which I feared more: the large, ponderous things that appeared as though they could swallow a child or the smaller, quicker, more unpredictable ones colorfully decorated with red, yellow, and black bands. We saw some small ants, and Mus began playing with them until one stung him and he began shrieking that his foot was on fire.

Living in a forest such as this could drive a man mad. You would never know when something would drop from the trees or wrap about your throat. Death was here. And I could feel in advance the piercing sting of the fangs and the growing paralysis of the poison.

This forest was alive. And with it came a low, groaning terror, an aching anticipation. Every sound, rustle of leaves, and uncertain smell snapped our nerves, quickening our efforts to push through such inhospitable terrain.

From time to time, we took turns climbing high into the trees to get our bearings and ensure that we were still moving toward the mysterious plume of red smoke.

Although the distance was not great, we moved slowly through that dark and strange wilderness. Finally, as the sun sank toward the horizon and the shadows began to lengthen, we heard them.

Voices.

Unearthly voices.

Chanting an eldritch melody that sounded only partially human.

I questioned more than a few times my decision to pursue the smoke, and for the hundredth time I wondered what kind of creatures we would find. My imagination actively set to work in an attempt to attach bodies to those voices.

Were they human or god? Man or beast?

Were we, like Ulysses, walking toward unimaginable danger? Were we destined to die at the hands of fiendish creatures, or be thrust into the underworld by the shades of Tartarus?

As we neared, the voices grew louder. Low voices. Men's voices. Chanting.

Always chanting.

Over and over, the same two or three syllables.

We reached the edge of a clearing and peered through the foliage.

Men.

Will I ever forget my first sight of them?

Twenty or so men stood in a circle. Three beat drums with heavy clubs, while another shook an immense gourd that rattled in time with the beat of the drums. Several of the men were dressed in strange costumes: one had the hands and head of a crab; others the head of a lion or a dragon or some other unnamable beast. One of them rattled a tortoise shell while the man next to him played a flute made from what appeared to be a human leg bone. A mournful tone emerged from a conch shell that one man held to his lips.

All chanted that soulless strain, their feet shuffling in slow rhythmic steps.

Except for a skin that covered their loins, the men were completely naked—all but one who was clearly the leader. He wore an additional skin on his shoulders that looked something like an African leopard I had once seen in the Colosseum. He wore large pendants on his chest carved from huge pieces of a clear green crystal that appeared to be emerald. On his head rested a large, jewel-studded crown from which flowed stunningly bright blue and green feathers resembling those of a peacock.

And, most ghoulish of all, they were all drenched in blood. The red gore dripped and spattered as they stepped. When they turned their heads, it sprayed from their hair. It seeped into the earth, making the ground slippery. The stench of it filled the air with the foulness of death.

I looked over at my little Mus who, pale and in shock, looked as though he would vomit. I pulled my tunic over mouth and nose to filter out the smell and instructed him to do the same. Mus obeyed.

He always obeyed.

My valiant Mus.

The light began to soften and fade, and I knew it would soon be impossible to see clearly. Without the benefit of sight, we could not protect against surprise, and I had no desire to be discovered by these barbaric creatures.

I looked around and saw a small cave opening away to the left. We could circle around and, in that elevated terrain, get closer while remaining hidden behind the cover of several large rocks that littered the ground before it.

We moved into the forest once again in an effort to flank the men and reach that strategic point. We moved as carefully and silently as we could. I did not see guards posted; either these men were unaccustomed to war or they had no fear of enemies. But their mistake was our advantage, and we pressed forward until we arrived behind the cover of the rocks.

The savages appeared to be wrapped in a bacchanalian frenzy now—the drumming growing faster. They seemed unaware of anything but their ceremony. I was strangely transfixed by the blood. Had the men cut themselves? Was it a sacrifice of some kind—similar to a Roman *taurobolium* where the priest is baptized in the blood of a sacrificial bull?

I watched as an older man pulled from his waist a dagger with a black blade that appeared to be nothing more than a sharpened stone. Were these men so primitive that they used weapons made from chipped rock? But my disdain for their weapons wavered when the old man approached a tethered dog and effortlessly slipped the knife across its throat. Instantly, blood poured from the wound, drenching the ground below.

My feelings of condescension faded in that instant. How sharp must that knife be to cut through hair and hide and so easily let out the life of that poor creature? I could not think of an equal in my world.

The man placed a large bowl underneath the dying animal to collect the blood. Raising the bowl above his head, he chanted while those around him repeated the syllables. He dipped a branch in the bowl and moved from man to man, splattering them with fresh blood. The liquid ran down their foreheads and into their mouths and they reveled in that blood, growing even more animated as it covered their faces and ran down their chests.

Ah, this was a bloody race.

I have seen many horrific things during the course of my days. I have witnessed crucifixions and executions of every kind. I have witnessed gladiators drop to their knees as their lives slipped away from them and their eyes cloud in death. I have seen desperate men grapple with beasts and watched as their blood saturated the sands of the Colosseum. In short, I have not been sheltered from the barbarities of the world or the hatred of men.

But these people—they reveled in the taking of life, in the slip of the knife, the flowing of blood. They gloried in death and celebrated as the life spirit ebbed from their victims. It was a society of death. Of compassion, they had none.

Then I heard something that jarred me from my thoughts. It was a voice unlike those I had heard before.

It belonged to a woman. And she was singing.

I searched the group for the source of the voice and eventually saw her standing alone at the edge of the forest. Although the scene was becoming cloaked in the shadow of a descending sun, I could still make out her features. Despite her ragged hair and her blood-spattered face, the woman was beautiful.

But what intrigued me most was her voice. Clear and without trembling, it pierced the dark and sounded its mournful and searching keen.

I could not look away but felt as entranced as those men who encircled her and chanted softly.

Why would this solitary woman be part of this bloody group? Were they worshipping her? Was she a queen? A priestess?

What was the purpose of this ceremony? What would happen next?

I did not have long to wait for answers. The woman looked toward the cave—toward us—and began moving in our direction. As she moved, the men moved with her.

There was no time to return to the forest. We could not escape notice if we tried. There was only one option—retreat into the darkness of the unknown cavern. I gave the sign, and the three of us crept from our hiding places and entered.

If the light was dim outside, it was black inside. Faint shadows of rock and pillar emerged from the left and right. From the cave opening, the chanting grew stronger.

They were coming.

We had no choice but to plunge ahead into the dark and pray that our feet would find earth beneath them and not empty air. The cavern was surprisingly large. Although I could not see its dimensions, I could tell from the echoes that we were in no small space. As the chanting grew in volume, we pressed toward the back, hoping to find a place of concealment.

Was I afraid?

Only to the point of shaking.

Briefly, I wondered if the cave itself was safe. Did it contain another group of blood-spattered savages? Was it inhabited by some ravenous creature? Did slithering reptiles curl in the dark crevices, waiting for the right moment to strike?

I cursed the lack of light but pressed forward, fearing the certainty of the human threat behind me more than the unknown ones in front of me.

Back and back, we moved into darkness.

At last, we reached rock and, by running our hands over the surface, discovered an alcove that would offer cover.

Soon after, the cavern began to fill with torchlight. The sounds of chanting echoed from the walls, creating an eerie and frightening dirge.

As the cavern slowly illuminated, the sight of it filled me with surprise and wonder. Instead of rough and raw rock, the walls were covered with a sort of plaster that created a flat surface upon which magnificent, heroic-sized images had been painted. Men, monsters, and animals in strange, exotic designs looked down from the sides of the cavern into the space below. Swirling whirlpools of color sprang from headdresses and plants. The colors were bright and vibrant. Reds, yellows, greens, and blues. As I had suspected, the cavern was large, tall enough to encase a small temple. Indeed, I began to wonder if this underground space wasn't, indeed, a temple.

In the center of the flat cavern floor, several intricately carved stone pillars encircled what I could only assume was an altar. And like the ground outside, the floor, columns, and altar inside were covered with dried blood. The ceremonies we had witnessed outside must continue in here. I looked carefully for signs of bones, but the ground inside the cavern was clean. Not so much as a loose stone cluttered the floor.

I wanted desperately to study the images on the walls. Perhaps in the art, I could discern the history and customs of this barbaric race. In spite of my interest, I forced my attention away from the drawings and focused on the activity in the center of the cavern. Although the paintings were fascinating, they did not have the immediate ability to take my life as did the men before us.

One thing was certain: we were trapped. There was no way out except the way we had come. I had decided, perhaps too late, that there could be no alliance with this band of men. Our best hope was to wait things out and, after they had left, make our way back to camp.

But remaining undiscovered was more difficult than I had imagined. The acoustics of the cavern were such that the slightest tumble of a rock echoed throughout. I whispered to Mus to remain quiet, unmoving and unspeaking.

I moved to get a better look at the group in front of me, careful not to make a sound. We were close—not thirty feet away.

What I saw next filled me with horror.

The woman stood in the center, encircled by the men. She continued to sing, and the men chanted with her. Although her eyes were open, it appeared as though she could not see. The old man who had cut the throat of the dog walked toward her, knife in hand.

Closer and closer he walked toward her. And the woman stood unmoving.

He was going to kill her!

Was it possible that human sacrifice—the ultimate blasphemy that Rome had extricated from among the Celtic Druids—was practiced here?

The woman appeared so helpless. So beautiful.

Could I remain hidden and allow murder?

Could I force myself to remain silent and watch as the man with the knife pulled it across her throat?

I looked at Glaucus who shook his head solemnly. I slowly pulled my sword from my belt. He shook his head and mouthed the word, "No!"

To this day, I am not sure why I did what I did.

Although I have a guess: it was because of the poet Virgil. Yes, perhaps that was it. When I was a child, my mother read many stories to me—heroic tales of mortals and gods. But it was Aeneas, I think, that caused me to unsheathe my sword.

Aeneas, who searched through an enemy-infested, burning Troy to look for his beloved wife. Aeneas, who escaped the Cyclops and who descended into the very depths of Tartarus and lived to tell the tale. Aeneas, who slew the mighty Turnis in single combat.

Yes, I lay my actions at the feet of Virgil.

No matter the cause, I could not allow that girl to die, even if it meant the forfeiture of my own life.

I turned to Mus and whispered in his ear, "Will you do as I command?"

"I'm a good soldier," he replied.

"Stay here. No matter what happens. Stay until all have left. When it is safe, work your way back to the ship and tell the men to make their preparations as quickly as they can and leave as soon as possible. Will you do that?"

"I'll come with you," he said.

I shook my head and ordered him to remain. "Will you do it?" I demanded.

"I'm a good soldier," he replied.

I smiled at Mus and nodded at Glaucus. He shook his head but still drew his own short sword.

"I hate you," he said.

"You're not alone."

I launched from my hiding place with a shout and barreled full speed toward the old man raising the knife. The blade was close to the girl now—terribly close.

Our presence stunned them all, and the surprise froze them in place as we flew. With a stroke, I cut down the man with the knife. Another few strokes and two more men fell to the ground.

In the midst of this I was thinking that perhaps we could fight our way through the throng and deliver the girl to freedom. Now, of course, with the benefit of years of recollection, I understand how utterly foolish the plan was.

Could I have left Mus behind? No.

Even had I rescued the girl, would she have been safe? What would I have done with her once I had rescued her? Where would she go?

In the perfect logic of hindsight, it was the worst of decisions. Perhaps it was at this point where the realization dawned upon me that, in order for us to survive, some dozen others would have to surrender their lives. And that thought sickened me.

Could I kill a dozen to save one?

Perhaps in the back of my mind, this reality began to dawn on me. With Glaucus' help, four of their men were on the ground before they realized what had happened, but the others quickly began to surround us. Many of them with daggers and clubs edged with black blades in hand. Two of the men had axes, the heads of which were also made of that sharp stone.

I had hoped that, with the advantage of surprise and superiority in weapons and armor, the men in front of us—they were practically naked, after all—would either be wise and run or be cowards and do the same. In short, driving them to flight with our first assault was the essence of my plan.

Like many of my other thoughts that day, however, it was a foolish and hopeless one. The men had no sign of fear in their eyes. Only outrage and cold-blooded purpose. I could tell from their expression that these were not the type of men who would flee from battle. Instead of rushing to the attack, they surrounded us in a circle.

I stood back-to-back with Glaucus as the circle tightened around us.

"This is as good an opportunity as any," Glaucus said, "to thank you for a brilliant military strategy."

"It's not over yet."

"I assume you have something in mind?"

"You mean at this moment?" I replied.

"One could hope."

"Nothing comes to mind."

Glaucus growled, "I have a thought."

"I'm listening."

"I truly do hate you."

"Considering the circumstances, there might be better objects for your hatred."

"I just thought you should know it before I die."

"We'll get out of this. There's always a way," I said.

We stood facing the slowly shrinking circle of enemies. Soon, the men would be within an arm's length, and it was apparent that the next conflict would be short and decisive. The barbarians brandished their weapons and shouted at us in their incomprehensible tongue.

I was beginning to think the only option remaining was to throw down our weapons and surrender when, out of the shadows, came a bloody shout.

Mus!

He charged the group from behind, giving us an instant of opportunity. The men fell back briefly, not knowing how many men were coming at them. In that moment, Glaucus and I struck with all our might. Another three of the barbarians fell to the earth before I heard a scream that chilled my bones.

I whirled around to see Mus pinioned and disarmed, a black dagger at his throat.

I shouted to Glaucus to stop and threw my weapon to the ground, ordering Glaucus to do the same.

"Are you insane?" Glaucus shouted.

"They'll kill him if we don't surrender."

"We're dead already."

"Do it!" I commanded, and heard the clangor of iron rattling against stone as Glaucus released his weapon.

The barbarians shouted in triumph, and soon we all had daggers at our throats. I could feel the cold stone against my skin and the sharpness of the blade as a trickle of blood began to wet my neck.

"I have to say," Glaucus said, "that I never truly understood the extent of your genius until now. My only regret is that I won't have the time to thank you in an appropriate way."

Perhaps I have made better decisions than I did on that day. I have thought often of what I could have done differently. But every life is filled with regrets, and what is the use of spending your days immersed in regret and guilt?

Unfortunately, in this case, my decisions affected not only my own life but that of my two friends as well.

The barbarians spoke for awhile in their bizarre language. What surprised me most was the reaction of the girl. The woman for whom I had sacrificed my life stood looking at me with such hatred and contempt that I could not meet her eyes.

Surely, I must be misunderstanding her intent. Surely, it was merely the way of Her culture. I had been expecting her to rush forward and throw her arms around the brave souls who had risked their lives to save her. But there was no sign of that.

In fact, she stepped toward me and spit at me.

No misunderstanding that.

"Again, congratulations," Glaucus said through clenched teeth.

"Doesn't she know I saved her life?"

"I'm at a loss for words."

Had the world gone mad? Had Aeneas been despised for avenging Pallas? Hercules hated for conquering the hydra? Were heroes of so little worth in this new world that the women they attempted to save despised them for their efforts? Did saving a life have so little value that instead of praise, it drew scorn?

As the men talked, they examined our swords and pointed at my bronze helm. They seemed intrigued by our arms; could it be that they were unfamiliar with iron like those strange barbarians who inhabited Ultima Thule?

If that were the case, we had the advantage of technology, although I could not think of a way to use it in our favor now—something Glaucus continued to remind me of.

At last, the discussion was over. One of the men pointed at Mus, and they pulled him away from us and pushed him near the altar.

He looked at me as a child looks to his father. To my shame, I smiled and told him all would be well.

What transpired next happened so quickly that I had no time to react.

One of the older men dipped his hand in a bowl and drew it out. His hand was covered with what looked like blue paint. He dabbed a circle on Mus' forehead.

And then a large man with a broken nose and scar across his cheek stepped forward, a heavy axe in his hands.

I did not have time to shout before the axe rose.

Mus did not see it coming—for that I am grateful. His eyes were on the blue paint.

"Pretty color," were his last words before the axe fell.

I screamed and reached for my weapon, wrenching it from the yielding grasp of the man who had taken it and resumed the battle. I killed the man who had Glaucus' weapon, ripping the blade from his fingers and tossing it to Glaucus.

It was futile.

I knew it. Glaucus knew it.

But dying in battle seemed preferable to waiting for the head of an axe to descend upon our necks. We fought like lions, littering the floor with the bodies of those who opposed us.

Glaucus shouted and I wheeled around, but too late. The man with the axe—the man who had taken the life of my friend—was behind me, the axe already descending. Instinctively, I turned my head toward the weapon in the hopes that my helm would deflect the blow.

I staggered under the hammer force of the axe, feeling a deadening sensation, a metallic taste filling my mouth.

From what seemed a distance, the sound of shattering stone scattered across rock. I told myself not to fall, but I could not keep my balance. I reeled and fell, stunned.

Cheering.

Wild cheering.

By sheer force of will, I demanded my body to rise.

It did not.

Mustering all my strength, I demanded my eyes to open.

One did.

The walls spun around me. Somewhere in the turning, I made out Glaucus, backing away from five men who were quickly closing.

To remain on the ground would mean death. I had to stand. I had to face them.

I prayed to the gods of my youth and felt a little strength return to my limbs.

I pulled myself to my knees and, mustering all my will and all my strength, I arose, sword in hand, and shouted defiantly, "Come here, you savage sons of a goat! Come and face me!"

But they did not come.

They stared at me in awe and terror, backing away.

Every one of them.

And then something happened that astounded me. One by one, they dropped their weapons and fell to the earth.

I looked at Glaucus and he at me.

Amidst the carnage of that battle, eight barbarians knelt before me, heads face down to the earth. They began biting their fingers and then held their hands in front of their bowed heads so the blood from the bite wounds dribbled down their hands and dripped to the floor.

There could be no mistaking those gestures.

These men who were trying to kill us only a moment before were now on their knees in front of us.

Worshipping us!

NOTES

Tartarus: The "deep place," a pit or abyss in the underworld, reserved for the torture of the monstrous Titans and the wicked.

Heads of beasts: These descriptions are based on the masks worn by people depicted in the painting of an eighth-century Mayan procession found at Bonampak (M. Miller, *The Murals of Bonampak* [Princeton, 1986]).

Animal sacrifice: The Maya often sacrificed turkeys, dogs, quail, iguana, and jaguars.

Murals on the cave wall: This is based on the exemplar of the Maya San Bartolo murals that date to the first century B.C. (see http://en.wikipedia.org/wiki/San_Bartolo_%28Maya_site%29#Murals).

Human sacrifice: Human sacrifice was practiced among the Maya, though not as extensively as it was among the later Aztecs (D. Carrasco, *Religions of Mesoamerica* [1998]; V. Tiesler, ed., *New Perspectives on Human Sacrifice and Ritual Body Treatments in Ancient Maya Society* [2008];, J. McBrewster, ed., *Human Sacrifice in Aztec Culture* [2009]; S. Sugiyama, *Human Sacrifice, Militarism and Rulership*

[2005]). The Carthaginians and the Druid priests of the Celts were renowned among the Romans for their human sacrifice, a practice suppressed by the Romans.

Virgil's *Aeneid:* The national epic of the Romans was widely read as part of the education of elite Romans during Malchus' life. Much of the story in that poem takes place in ancient Carthage.

Thule: The farthest northern regions known to the Romans, probably northern Scandinavia and Iceland.

Biting the fingers: This ritual offering of blood was an act of submission among the Maya, as depicted on the temple of the murals at Bonampak.

Chapter 10

Lucius' head jerked down and then up. He opened his eyes, momentarily surprised to find himself clothed and in his study. He tried to focus, grasping for an anchor—something to make sense of time and place.

Had the events of the night before been only fantasy? A consequence of a late-night glass of wine?

He forced himself to remember, and his thoughts began to settle. And as they did, the events of the night before began to emerge, ghostlike, from the haze of forgetfulness to horrifying, cold memory.

Was it possible that Rome had been sacked?

Monstrous night.

Had he truly blasphemed against the gods?

Was it possible that he had destroyed his cherished statues?

Aurelius and Augustine—had they come to his villa? Ordered him to leave? Threatened him?

He stretched out his hand and felt . . . cold metal.

The plates.

And instantly, his mind snapped into clarity.

Why could it not have been a dream?

Why could not his entire life have been a little fantasy—a pleasant flight of fancy?

Must bitter sorrow, like water seeking the deepest crevice, always find him? Must grief always settle so heavily? From the day his Livia had ceased breathing the air of this world until this dreadful day, he had experienced neither peace nor joy. From that moment, his steps had led irrevocably to last night. To his great sacrilege. To his final despair.

No sweet comfort. No reconciliation.

Only bitter truth.

Others, in their old age, settled in pleasant pastures. Others lived out the remainder of their days in peaceful study and solitary meditation.

His was a fate of a different kind.

Discord. Panic. Rage.

As the pieces of the previous hours began to fit together in an intricate and terrible mosaic, something began to intrude upon his consciousness. A sound—a commotion coming from outside the villa.

Shouting. Raised voices. Angry cries. Wood pounding on heavy wood.

Where was his servant? Why had Gunderic not silenced the noise?

He shook his head and pushed himself away from his table. The pounding grew louder as he, once again, stowed the plates away and out of sight.

As he strode toward the front of the villa, he passed his servant's quarters. Where was Gunderic? He should have been at the door at the first sound. The more he thought about it, the more annoyed he became. And, as this new irritation grew, the anger from the night before filled him again.

He may not have the power to halt the barbarians at the walls of Rome, but, by Tartarus' gates, he had the power to command his servant and mete out punishment for this dereliction of duty.

Lucius entered Gunderic's quarters and stopped short. Gunderic was lying on the bed against the wall, a feverish child in his arms. They were asleep. His wife, too, had slumped over in exhaustion. Her cheek glistened with tears.

Gunderic's brow, though relaxed in sleep, still looked weighted with concern. The little girl's face appeared flushed and burning.

And, instantly, Lucius understood. And, with understanding, he found yet another reason to hate himself.

He backed out of the room and stood for a moment in the hallway. Was he to be robbed even of the right to be angry at his servant?

In a brief moment of insight, he glimpsed the true source of his anger, but he was in no mood for self-recrimination—certainly not today. He thrust the thought out of his mind and made his way toward the source of the commotion.

As he approached the door, the pounding grew louder. Angry voices snapped and whipped and grew in intensity.

"Lucius!"

"Open!"

What insanity was this? He flung open the door, and, for a second time, his anger vanished. A dozen or so familiar faces greeted him, their boldness instantly replaced with a sheepish, apologetic deference.

Publius and Festus, Longinus and Crescentius—students of his. Other familiar faces peppered the crowd.

"What is the meaning of this?" Lucius demanded.

The crowd quieted.

"Have you lost your tongues?"

At last Faustus, a promising student who had abandoned the study of philosophy for a job collecting coins for municipal officials, spoke up. "Have you not heard?"

"Based on the scale of the commotion, I should hope that you bring news of Achilles and Hector striding arm in arm through the streets of Carthage. Tell me that is what you have seen and all is forgiven. We'll invite them both inside—Homer along with them if he is here. I have a few questions that have been nagging at me for decades; perhaps they can enlighten us."

"Then you don't know," the young man said.

Lucius had no desire to play the game any longer. "Are you referring to the news that Alaric and his army have penetrated the walls of Rome and sacked the city?"

"All Carthage is in the streets."

"As it should be."

"The Galileans are blaming us."

"And this surprises you?"

"Aurelius is laying the blame at the feet of the old believers."

"You might as well be astonished that rain falls from clouds or that the carcasses of dead animals attract maggots."

The people in the crowd all began speaking at once until Publius managed to shout louder than the others. "Aurelius is claiming that unless Carthage is purged, Rome's fate will be ours."

"Wood burns. Fish swim. What next? Stars appear at night?"

"You don't understand. He's calling for action. Today! They're going to purge the city, starting at the temple of Caelestis."

Why should that surprise him? After all, the Galileans were famous the empire over for suppressing and silencing those who believed differently from themselves.

And then his thoughts drifted to Hypatia—a pagan philosopher and mathematician whom Lucius had known while studying in Alexandria, Egypt, during his student days. Hypatia had a wonderful mind, but she was possessed of one unfortunate and fatal flaw: she believed in the old gods and valiantly defended Platonic philosophy. Because of this unforgiveable offense, Cyril, the bishop of Alexandria, incited a mob against her. The crowd raged out of control—monks and priests among them—and assaulted her in the streets, beating her to death.

The Galileans were no kinder to their own when it came to disagreements over dogma. The Donatist Christians, for example—those who railed against Christian priests who had lapsed during Roman persecutions and offered pagan sacrifices to the old gods—were among the most unforgiving. Of course, the rich irony was that the Donatists themselves were later forbidden to perform priestly activities because they were named "heretics" by other, more enlightened, Galileans.

It was always about *enlightenment*, wasn't it?

And holiness.

And moral superiority.

In Carthage and around the countryside, gangs of armed "holy men" called Circumcellions—Galileans who lived as hermits around the martyrs' shrines—roamed the streets, terrorizing the "unfaithful" and shouting their watchword *"deo laudes"*—praise God. Armed with clubs they called "Israels," these "athletes of Christ" were fearless. They had assaulted and even murdered orthodox clergy and Donatists whose conversion to Catholicism, they presumed, was motivated by their desire to escape persecution. The Circumcellions were so passionate about their beliefs that they actually sought martyrdom; one fanatic even threw himself on the fire at a pagan altar to stop the sacrifice.

Whether or not these stories were embellished, underestimated, or fabricated, Lucius did not know.

He did know Aurelius, however—knew him well.

Was Aurelius so completely consumed by the Galilean sect that he could forsake the love he had once possessed for Jupiter and Hera?

"Did you hear me, Lucius?" Publius insisted. "Aurelius is going to purge the city."

"Where is he?" Lucius said at last.

"Already at the temple of Caelestis. He's tearing down the statues of the gods. He's going to convert it—make it a Christian sanctuary."

The news stunned Lucius. If he had any doubt about the bishops' intents, now he was certain.

It was a shrewd strategy by Aurelius—beginning at the temple where once he, himself, had served as a pagan priest.

"Well then," Lucius said. "Let us go and see what the bishop is up to."

The little band seemed reinvigorated as they left Lucius' villa and walked purposefully toward the temple.

On a small rise in the city of Carthage, not far away from Lucius' villa, was the temple of Dea Caelestis, a rather obscure goddess in the Roman pantheon. She had once been known as Tanit, the patron goddess of Carthage, the Queen of Heaven. When Carthage was rebuilt on orders from Augustus, the goddess was Romanized and *adopted* into the Roman pantheon as Juno Caelestis.

While this representation of Juno was obscure, the temple was not. Set on the slopes of Juno's Hill, in its prime it had been a magnificent structure, the pride of Carthage. Nearly a thousand paces deep, it was surrounded with small shrines and statues of gods great and small. So numerous and lifelike were these images that many who visited the temple remarked that it seemed as though they had entered upon a second Olympus.

The temple had been built long after the glory of Hannibal and had been dedicated two centuries ago by none other than the great Marcus Aurelius who, as emperor, priest, and philosopher, was a true believer in the gods of Olympus. The structure had been sacred to the city of Carthage and a source of great pride. Few visitors set foot upon Carthage soil without making pilgrimage to the great temple of Caelestis and making an offering of bull, ram, doves, or wine.

But that was before the Galileans came to power.

That was before Theodosius, the Christian emperor, who, twenty years earlier, had discontinued funding for pagan temples throughout the Roman Empire. Without money, pagan priests were forced to find other means of employment. They couldn't even pay for the upkeep of their own buildings.

Worse, priests who persisted in sacrificing to the old gods could be fined the enormous sum of fifteen pounds of gold. It was an effective move on Theodosius' part, for without priests to maintain the temples, the buildings inevitably fell into disuse.

Some temples were destroyed, while others were repurposed to become places for Galilean sacraments. Others, including the Temple of Caelestis in Carthage, were simply abandoned to the elements. In time, the temple sunk beneath the brambles and weeds, leaving an empty, haunted place that local believers claimed was inhabited by all manner of deadly serpents—the only living creatures that remained within the ancient and hallowed walls. Predictably, the pagans saw these serpents as evidence of divine protection while the Galileans saw them as symbols of Satan.

As Lucius approached the temple, the rattle of shouting grew.

"Enter into every corner!" The voice belonged to Aurelius. "In the name of Christ, I banish you vile serpents! Cower! Flee! Depart! You creatures of the pit cannot abide the light!"

Lucius arrived to see the temple scoured. He winced when he saw the once-great image of Juno Caelestis toppled and shattered. Hundreds of Galileans milled about, some removing the remaining brambles, others singing hymns.

The Galileans eventually noticed Lucius, and the singing softened and stopped.

Whispers rippled through the crowd until the sound reached Aurelius, who stood at the place of the statue of the goddess.

Lucius stepped toward Aurelius, the solid mass of people giving way before him. He, himself, had not been to the abandoned temple in over a year, yet, despite his epiphany of the night before, he couldn't help but feel anger at the state of disrepair of this once-beautiful place.

It was inevitable, of course. Once the temple of Caelestis had lost its state funding, most of the priests faded away, attending to other occupations. Some of them, Aurelius among them, not knowing what else to do with their specific and limited skills, traded their togas for robes of the

Galilean priesthood—the new state-sponsored religion. While conversions of this sort delighted the Galileans (who saw in them a manifestation of God's power and grace), they inflamed and saddened those who remained faithful to the pantheon of Jove.

Lucius looked into Aurelius' eyes, more curious than angry. How could the man do such a thing and not blush?

How could a priest of Juno become a priest of the Galilean?

Lucius looked around the temple at the broken images and repressed a surge of anger. Here, there was a toppled image of Mars. There, Pallas Minerva. Each defaced image brought grief and rage to his soul. Such disrespect and blasphemy. Truly, these Galileans were bereft of civility, tolerance, and charity. They were hard souls. Blinded by the plague of their beliefs. How had the mighty empire of Caesar, Augustus, and Julian been conquered by men such as this?

As his anger grew, he glimpsed in his mind the events of the night before when he, himself, had done the same work the Galileans had done.

How could he condemn these Galileans for the very acts he had committed himself? The thought annoyed him.

Must he be robbed of every opportunity for righteous anger?

"You see, Lucius," Aurelius continued to speak with boldness. "You see what has happened at this shrine of false worship? This is what will happen in all of Carthage! In all the world!"

His words emboldened the gathered hundreds, who cheered and echoed his words.

"What you see is the power of truth! Evil vanquished! False beliefs rooted out! Satan banished! God Himself will fight the battles of a purified Carthage against the wrath of Alaric!"

Aurelius, if nothing else, knew how to make a speech. Perhaps it was his training in rhetoric, or his days as an actor in the theater, or his years of performing pagan rites. The man had the voice of holiness. The inflection of the words held just the right amount of humility and righteous outrage. He looked the part of a cleric. Confident eye, strong stance; broad, sweeping gestures. He was a man who had found his place and been supported in it by those unable to distinguish facade from fact.

"Today, all here are witnesses," Aurelius blustered. "This day the Serpent is cast out, blasphemous idolatry torn down, true worship consecrated."

The man did have a cherubic face. A handsome, kindly face.

As Lucius watched the man pontificate, he was surprised at how cold and unemotional he felt. In prior years, he would have thrown words at him like a man throwing scraps of gristle at a hated pet.

But after the previous night, there was little fire left in him. There was little anger.

Merely regret. Regret and sorrow. Profound sorrow.

"You are witnesses this day," Aurelius shouted. Lucius frowned; would the man never stop talking? "You are witnesses that not only are the serpents banished, but the mouths of the pagans are stopped. Righteousness prevails."

The last comment roused Lucius and brought him out of his reverie.

"What is that you say?" Lucius asked.

"Evil cannot stand before the light."

"So thought I, and yet you refute it by remaining here."

A few of Lucius' students chuckled.

Aurelius reddened and spoke, "It is you who are evil. You and your false gods. They shall all be ground into dust and forgotten."

"I assume you are prophesying?"

"It is the will of God."

"Very well then, perhaps I will prophesy as well," Lucius replied, noting with satisfaction the silence of all who were at the temple. They were hanging on his every word. Listening. Memorizing every inflection, every syllable. The tale of this day would be retold for years to come.

"But first, would you enlighten me on an issue I have been pondering?"

Aurelius nodded.

"There once was a prince who considered himself just and fair. He punished evil and encouraged all in the true and proper worship of heaven. When he saw impiety and blasphemy, he set his hand against the hypocrites who made pretense of holiness but inside were rotting with greed and lust. He threw down those who worshipped falsely. He avenged those who ground the faces of the poor. Here then, Aurelius, is the question: Was this prince justified in righting those wrongs and cleansing the people of evil?"

Aurelius considered the question for a moment and then smiled. "You do me great honor, Lucius. I am that prince. What I do here today pleases the ruler of heaven. It is the will of God. In answer to your question, friend, I tell you not only was this prince justified, he was required by the hand of heaven to purge that wickedness."

Lucius smiled and nodded. "But I wasn't speaking of you, Aurelius."

Aurelius' face hardened. "Then who?"

"Alaric, of course. The Visigoth prince who set his hand against those who, in his mind, worshipped falsely and who embraced iniquity. Alaric, after all, is a Christian—the same as you. It was Alaric the Christian who destroyed Rome. He did it to cleanse the city—cleanse it of those hypocrites who, with the name of deity on their lips, defile the sacred and pillage the poor. Alaric the Christian is that prince."

"Blasphemy!" shouted someone in the crowd. But Aurelius did not respond.

"Here is *my* prophecy, Aurelius. There will ever be a prince. From now until the end of time, there will ever be someone who justifies his work of persecution, hatred, and destruction as the will of the gods. At Rome, it was Alaric. In Carthage, Aurelius. After you, there shall be another and another until the sun no longer makes its rounds. It is easy to destroy,

Aurelius. It is the easiest thing in the world. And always, *always*, he who destroys proclaims that what he does, he does in the name of heaven. As you do this day; as Alaric did in Rome. As you do here, so it will be done again. *Sicut erat in principio et nunc et semper et in secula seculorum:* Thus it was in the beginning, and is now, and shall always be, even in this age and all ages to come."

Silence settled upon the crowd. Aurelius seemed confused and unable to respond. Lucius suspected he recognized the words—they came from a Christian hymn, after all.

Aurelius glowered, the cherubic features of his face turning demonic. He searched for words. His tongue tapped the top of his mouth, as though the words were nearly there but still out of reach.

Lucius smiled; it had been a nice touch quoting a Galilean hymn in blasphemous parody. But there would be time for gloating later. Now, tired and weary, he turned and made his way through the crowd. What was the point of staying? Aurelius would not stop. Alaric would not stop. And other men like Aurelius and Alaric would not stop. The world was doomed to repeat this senseless drama time and again, one eternal round to the end of time.

As he turned his back to the bishop and passed through the crowd, the low murmur began to shift.

"Look at the inscription!" a voice rang out.

Lucius looked back, recognizing a young man, Quodvultdeus, who, like Augustine and Aurelius, had left the gentle serenity of pagan philosophy, art, and music for the inelegant worship of the Galilean.

All eyes turned toward to where the young man pointed—the bronze inlaid inscription on the façade of the temple.

"Aurelius pontifex dedicavit!" he shouted. "Do you see it?"

Lucius saw the inscription. It was there in bold, bronze letters over the pillars: "Aurelius, the chief priest dedicated this."

As the voices grew, a sense of wonder and awe overtook the Galileans, and they fell to their knees and began uttering prayers of rejoicing.

How could they possibly think this inscription referred to this day? To this Aurelius? Had they lost their minds and forgotten that Marcus Aurelius the emperor and chief priest of Rome had dedicated this temple two hundred years earlier?

"A prophecy!" cried one.

"A miracle!" shouted another.

"Rejoice in the mercies of God! This day was foretold!"

Lucius shook his head.

What good could come from arguing with such insanity?

And, in the midst of this ebullience, Lucius turned and left the crowd. His steps took him further away from the temple of Caelestis and toward the silent sanctuary of his villa.

There, perhaps, he would find refuge from the madness of the world.

There, the strange, ancient plates awaited him, their centuries-old mysteries locked between stiff sheets of molded bronze. There, indeed, perhaps only there, would he find solace and respite from the madness of the world.

NOTES

Christian persecution: Christian persecution of the pagans and Jews became fairly common after the conversion of Constantine and the establishment of the Imperial Church (M. Gaddis, *There Is No Crime for Those Who Have Christ: Religious Violence in the Christian Roman Empire* [2005]; J. Carroll, *Constantine's Sword* [2001]; T. Sizgorish, *Violence and Belief in Late Antiquity* [2008]).

Hypatia: A famous female philosopher and mathematician of Alexandria who was murdered by a Christian mob in 415, five years after our story (M. Dzielska, *Hypatia of Alexandria* [1996]).

Donatists: Donatists were puritans who believed that sacraments offered by sinful clergy were not efficacious. Their branch of Christianity was dominant in Tunisia during the fourth century, but was persecuted by the Imperial Church because they rejected the authority of many of the Orthodox bishops because of moral and theological lapses (W. Frend, *The Donatist Church* [2000]; G. Willis, *Augustine and the Donatists* [2005]).

Circumcellions: Violent, radical peasants and monks of ancient Tunisia whose behavior, as described here, was scandalous to many Christians (See "Circumcellions," in F. Cross, ed. *The Oxford Dictionary of the Christian Church* [2005]).

Marcus Aurelius: Marcus Aurelius (r. A.D. 161–180) was the last of the "Good Emperors." He was noted both for his successful campaigns against the Germans and the Parthian Persians and for his profound philosophical thought and life, which was reflected in his book *The Meditations* (Oxford, 2008). Renowned as a true philosopher-king, he was praised by Christians such as Justin Martyr (F. McLynn, *Marcus Aurelius: Warrior, Philosopher, Emperor* [2009]; A. Birley, *Marcus Aurelius: A Biography,* 2d ed. [1987]).

Theodosius: For his Christianization policies regarding the closure of the temples, see S. Williams and G. Friell, *Theodosius: Empire at Bay* (1998). For his fines on priests, see Theodosian Code 16.10.10.

Aurelius at the temple of Caelestis: This incident is based on actual events described by an eyewitness Quodvultdeus, *The Book of the Promises and Prophecies of God* 3.38 (translated in A. Lee, *Pagans and Christians in Late Antiquity* [Routledge, 2000], 138–39). However, the event actually occurred in 407; we have moved the event to 410. Quodvultdeus eventually succeeded Aurelius as bishop of Carthage (437–450).

Sicut erat: Lucius mocks Aurelius by citing the Christian "minor doxology": "Glory be to the Father, and to the Son, and to the Holy Ghost. As it was in the beginning and is now, and shall always be, even in this age and all ages to come."

Chapter 11

The Book of Malchus, son of Mago, of the house of Hanno

And so began a strange, new era of my life: the time when I became a god.

As a Roman citizen, I had been taught from my earliest years that certain emperors were divine. The whole world believed that Julius Caesar ascended to heaven after his death and took his place among the other exalted beings in the pantheon.

Few argued that Caesar's nephew and successor, the divine Augustus—*pontifex maximus,* high priest of the *collegium* of priests, ruler of all things temporal and spiritual in the Roman Empire—had undergone apotheosis and was himself deified. The question was not *whether* he was a god, but *when* he had become one. While mortal? Or did some eternal power transform him after his death?

There even were those who advocated deifying Tiberius, Augustus' son-in-law and successor, who was still very much alive and, coincidentally, very much human.

Even Tiberius!

Timid as a youth (perhaps from his paranoia of being murdered like so many others), he became debauched and cruel as an adult. After assuming power, he ruthlessly cut down any who posed a threat, ordering his henchman, Sejanus, to massacre men, women, and children and throw their corpses into the Tiber. He even went so far as to put to death an old friend who had insulted the emperor by keeping from him (and his well-known lecheries) his attractive daughter. Tiberius rewarded this act of paternal concern by charging his friend with incest as justification for his actions.

But even Tiberius had redeeming qualities. To his credit, he had refused a petition to rename the month of September after himself, and he did not allow statues of his image to be placed amidst the gods in Rome. He did, however, authorize a temple in Smyrna to be built honoring himself and his mother—perhaps it was a precursor of his secret desires and a foreshadowing of what was to come.

In spite of his flaws, in spite of the murders and slanders and sexual license, in spite of the fact that Tiberius had deserted Rome completely and retired in seclusion to the island of Capri, far removed from the capital, in spite of the rumors that surfaced, claiming that, because of his excesses, the gods had afflicted him with festering sores that covered his skin—even then, there were those who spoke of him as divine.

While I had never been much interested in theology, I must confess I have wondered what life must be like for an emperor. Power to raise or condemn. To spare or to destroy. Every desire fulfilled in a moment.

In the end, I knew that it was too great a temptation. To live in a world where every whim was satisfied, where every uttered word was taken as the will of heaven. To be studied, scrutinized, measured, worshipped, recorded.

Not for me.

Better to be the ruler of a stately ship than to rule the ship of state. The feel and gentle roll of deep water was enough for me. Standing on the deck of the *Morning Star,* its belly heavy with cargo, and feeling the surge of the wind catching taut sails as the prow of my ship lurches into the crest of gushing waves—that was enough for me. My daily measure of risk, danger, and the pleasures that accompanied modest wealth were more than enough.

No, I did not wish to become a god.

But regardless of my wishes, the Fates had determined another destiny for me.

After the incident in the cave and the murder of Mus, the strange men pleaded with us to follow them. At least that is what we assumed they wanted; their language—if it could be called language—was completely incomprehensible to us.

But should we go?

In my defense I must fall back on the old saw that power does strange things to a man. A few moments before, I would have fought to the death to escape these barbarians. Now, however—now that they were on their knees before us, now that they worshipped us—curiosity once again took hold. Though still dazed from the blow to my head, I was not unaware of some of the possibilities of this newfound opportunity.

I was a god, after all. And what a god wills, he transforms into reality. With the help of a new source of labor, I could build a third boat, stock it with enough food for the voyage home, and fill its hold with goods to trade.

With hundreds of men, I could command a navy. Command an army. Could this be the beginning of Malchus the Great? Malchus the Emperor? As Caesar was to Rome, could Malchus be to this land?

"You can't possibly be considering going with them," Glaucus interrupted my thoughts.

"Aren't you curious?"

He shook his head. "You actually are thinking about going with them."

I glanced again at the girl. Still, she glared at me with such hatred that I could only look into her eyes for a few seconds. What was it about her that was so strangely fascinating? Whether for her beauty, her unpredictability, or perhaps even the fact that she hated me, I felt a strange and powerful attraction to her.

Glaucus, prescient as ever, shook his head. "In case you hadn't quite grasped it, the girl despises you."

"Do you think I can't see that?"

"I would think given the number of astoundingly bad decisions you've made of late, you'd be satisfied with your score and call it a day."

"Doesn't mean things can't pick up."

"Going for a record, then?"

Why was he always right?

Was there anything more annoying than arguing with someone who was right? A nearly unforgivable trait in a friend, but one I needed in an advisor. Looking back, I know that, had I followed his counsel, my life would have been very different. But if I had listened to him, I would not have experienced the tale I am writing now.

Perhaps I had made some poor decisions, but ultimately, it was those decisions that led me to where I am now. And, though the cost was great, I would not change those decisions for the world.

"In case there is any part of your brain that is interested in my opinion, now would be a good time for us to turn around and go back to the ship," he said.

I looked at Glaucus, then at the men kneeling before me. Finally, I looked at the girl. She had not fallen to her knees but stood to the side, glaring at me, dried blood covering her skin, hate filling her eyes.

What *was* it about her that made her so appealing?

I turned to Glaucus. "I'm going with them."

"Of course you are," he said.

"Don't ask me to explain."

"Wouldn't dream of it."

"I understand if you want to return to the ship. You're free to do what you will, but I have to go."

"You *have* to go."

"I don't know why."

"Makes absolute sense."

But I did know.

Greed.

I confess it. Greed was the reason I consented to follow them. I pictured in my mind glorious wealth and power. And that image was sweet and irresistible.

Greed, and curiosity. Who were these people? Could I become their leader? Their god?

And what of the girl? The cold, distant, disturbingly beautiful girl? Could I leave her? Could I live without knowing the mystery of her?

"I have to go," I said again.

"Fantastic," Glaucus replied.

Should I have thought it through?

Yes.

But I was curious and greedy.

And I chose to follow them.

It is strange, as I look back upon the events of my life, to see how my steps have been ordered. It is as though there was a preordained plan for my life that I was powerless to avoid.

Yes, I am certain that I have indeed been directed and driven by an unseen hand. From my first decisions as a dewy-eyed youth to my last of old age—even when I made the wrong choices, they turned out to be the only choices that would bring me to here, to this table, holding this stylus in my hand, inscribing on these sheets of metal the story of my life.

I am water.

I have spent most of my days on the deep blue foam and have always felt a kinship with that element. Free to travel wherever my will desired. Chaotic and spontaneous, capricious and shapeless.

Water, however unpredictable it may seem at times, eternally follows nature's law. It leans with the moon and sways with the wind. And it ever flows downward. Always down. And while it can break its bounds for a pace, while it can wear away new paths, ultimately, its nature will win out.

I have gone where, inevitably, I must have gone.

I am water.

And though I was free, a higher power determined for me the path that led me inexorably to here. And no matter my decisions, no matter the diversions, ever I returned to the path that brought me to here.

Whether all men are so driven, I do not know. But this I do know—even when I thought I was alone, abandoned, and forgotten, my destiny led me to here.

So in that dark cave, I consented to follow. I agreed to accompany the strange men to wherever they led me. Whether toward fortune or death, I did not know. And Glaucus, dear and faithful friend that he was, followed me.

I refused to leave the cave, however, without first burying Mus. Every Roman knows that the souls of those who are not properly buried cannot enter the world of the dead but are doomed to walk the world for a pace, searching for peace. I had a duty to my friend who had saved my life. I had a duty to the boy's father. And, although my head hurt terribly where I had taken the blow of the axe, I was able to work alongside the others in digging a solitary grave for my faithful Mus, who, because of me, no longer breathed the air of this earth.

While we were placing his body in the ground, several of the strangers made stretchers to carry their own dead. They wrapped the bodies in shrouds after placing strange grain and emerald-like beads in the mouths of the fallen.

Strange business. Awkward business, working shoulder to shoulder with the friends and family of those you had recently killed. I can only assume that brothers, sons, and fathers were among the dead. Strangely, there seemed to be no rancor, no anger—at least from the men.

Finally, Mus lay under the ground, and I was satisfied that he would, at last, be able to cross the river Styx and find peace among the dead.

By the time we finished, it was the middle of the night. In spite of the late hour, we set off into the forest. At dawn, we arrived in a small town populated perhaps by a hundred dwellings, most of them sitting on cleared ground.

They were farmers and craftsmen, these people. Their diet consisted of berries, beans, and *Kuum*—a delicious food that grows on stalks and has a long, oval head upon which grows a wonderful yellow-white fruit. They eat this raw or cooked, or they dry it and make a flour paste from which they make delicious breads.

Their skill as craftsmen is impressive. They work in stone, pottery, and gems. Especially valuable is a green, jade-like stone they call *k'an*. Their craftsmanship is different from anything in my experience, and I believed their curious jewelry and ornaments would be highly prized in Rome, if for nothing more than their exotic nature. Already, I was working out how to profit by bringing a cargo of this exotic material to the emperor.

As a people, they seemed peaceful enough.

More importantly, they revered Glaucus and me.

When we entered the village for the first time, we drew the curiosity of everyone. Hundreds of men, women, and children rushed toward the center of town and surrounded us, chattering constantly.

The man who killed Mus lifted my battered helmet above his head and, as he spoke, a look of awe came over those who surrounded us.

Within a few minutes, the entire group was on its knees, heads bowed, hands upraised in gestures of what could only be veneration.

Had I known then what I know now, I could have used those first days after our capture to leverage an empire. It was within reach. Had I wanted it, I could have commanded the moon, and my captors would have provided it or died in the attempt.

In that early period all who surrounded us competed with each other to ensure our comfort and pleasure. For his part, Glaucus nearly forgave me for my rash behavior that cost Mus his life. "You always thought of yourself as something special," he said on more than one occasion. "You've finally found an audience that agrees with you."

But although celebrity had its advantages, it was impossible to find comfort in a barbaric society that paradoxically appeared pastoral in daily routine but that reveled in blood and took the lives of innocents for sacrifice.

I marked the man who killed my little Mus. He was a quick-tempered and unforgiving man. He seemed to be the leader of this community. Younger than I, and stronger. I rarely saw him smile. I memorized his face and kept it before me, vowing to ever be wary. This was a man who could not be trusted. He was dangerous, and I had the unsettling feeling that he was already plotting our murders.

I saw the singing girl often as well. In fact, she came to us daily, though surely not of her own will, for her eyes were piercingly cold and filled with animosity.

The day following our capture, and after several frustrating attempts to communicate with the elders of the tribe, she appeared. Washed of blood, her skin appeared soft, smooth, and glistening. Her dark hair fell straight and caught the light as it fell over her shoulders like water. Her perfect eyes were endlessly dark and infinitely deep, and I wanted nothing more than merely to take her in my arms and speak to her hour after hour and shield her from every concern until there were no worries or cares left, until time ceased to exist. How I longed to feel the press of her hand in mine. How I hungered to feel the eternal and tender embrace of her arms.

But it was not to be. If I thought she hated me in the cave, it seemed as though her anger had multiplied in the time since.

I could not understand why I felt a compelling need to speak with her. To learn her language. To understand her and for her to understand me.

"Malchus," I said, holding a hand to my chest.

"Xen," she replied coldly, putting a hand on her breast.

And so began our training in the language of this strange people. I was an eager student and paid attention to every word. We learned simple nouns at first: bowl, food, hair. Eventually we learned verbs: eat, run, talk.

As a merchant, I understood the importance of language in making a profit. Glaucus and I knew that our lives might very well depend on learning how to communicate. But I had other motives in mind as well. I had to speak with this woman. I had to understand her.

Within a few months, I could understand simple words and sentences. Within six months, we were both able to hold conversations. Several times, another man or woman would offer to teach us our lessons, but I turned my back to them and insisted that Glaucus do the same. I was worried that Xen would not return. And so, I insisted that she and only she would be our teacher.

Did she hate me for that as well?

Perhaps. But I could not risk the chance of never seeing her again. And so our lessons continued. Several times, I attempted to draw her into conversation about herself, about what had happened in the cave, but each time she stopped me with a cold stare. When I continued to press, she would leave.

Once, after I had persisted in questioning her, she did not return for three days. During that time, I felt as though the world would close in and crush me.

How I could have been so foolish, you ask?

I have no answer other than to plead with you to remember what it is like to be in love. In the first blush of love, you yearn to hear her voice; you look into a crowd of people caring only to catch the merest glimpse of your beloved's face; your mood changes from desperation to elation simply by looking into her eyes.

"You do realize," Glaucus said on one occasion, "that it is becoming increasingly difficult for me to have any sort of respect for you."

"Noted."

"And just so that on the day when she does this I want to be able to say that I warned you, I'm telling you the truth—she would sooner put a knife in your heart than be in your presence."

"I would take the knife gladly."

"This is a day to remember," he said. "On the scale of pathetic, you may have just exceeded the highest mark anyone in the history of mankind has ever had the ineptitude to reach."

"I can't help it," I said. "I can't get her out of my mind."

"The simple truth is that you're only obsessed with her because you can't have her."

What was the point of arguing with a man who could only see shades of gray instead of all the beautiful colors? Consequently, I shrugged off his incessant barbs, focused on learning her language, and devoured every precious minute I had when she was near me.

Kix-Kohor—that was the name of the man who killed Mus—was the leader of a group of several hundred people roughly associated through family. They had taken upon themselves the name of an ancestor and were known as the clan Atanahlka.

It surprised me to learn both that Kix-Kohor and Xen were brother and sister and that Kix-Kohor had only recently assumed power. I supposed that made Xen some sort of princess in her culture, although she needed no official title for me to know that.

Although my ability to comprehend the language came haltingly, I tried to learn as much about the culture as I could. There were numerous other tribes of people that lived relatively close by. Some of them were larger, some smaller than ours. There was no central government that I could see, but each tribe lived together in an uneasy peace.

Before Kix-Kohor knew how quickly I was learning to understand his language, he invited me into his war councils. The only purpose for this was that I served as an ornament, a symbol of divine approval. There, I learned of the Laanchus and Almani tribes and of the Githioni and Palenti clans. Each of these groups had little trust for the other but, in spite of their mutual hatred, none dared attack one without first amassing sufficient power to conquer all.

It was there that I learned the other name Kix-Kohor had taken upon himself: K'u-nak—"god conqueror." He had taken that title after his triumph of murdering Mus. As a result of defeating the demigod, he claimed to have the stature of a hero and strutted about like Achilles.

He held out his hands to those in the council saying that his were the hands that defeated a god. But all I saw were the hands of a barbarian stained with the precious blood of a defenseless innocent.

He had plans, this god conqueror. Plans to overcome the other tribes and create an empire under his dominion. It didn't take long before I understood the role he wanted me to play in those plans.

As he spoke to his war council, he described the power of the gods and how Glaucus and I had descended from heaven to aid him in his quest.

He used us.

We knew it at the time, but that was his way. Kix-Kohor used others without remorse or conscience. I suppose I could forgive his hatred of me, but I could not forget the way he treated a young man in the village by the name of Be'nach. In a way, the boy reminded me of Mus; he was slow and awkward like Mus, but unlike Mus, he was also given to seizures. The poor boy jerked about when nervous and choked on his words, unable to get them out of his mouth without tremendous difficulty. Kix-Kohor dressed the boy in outlandish apparel and brought him into his meetings to provide comedy for his guests.

The boy, although slow, understood that he was being used. I could see it in his eyes. He looked both humiliated and afraid.

I wondered if Kix-Kohor had been threatening him. Perhaps beaten him. Forced him to perform like a trained monkey for the amusement of his guests. I needed no new reasons to hate Kix-Kohor, but this renewed my dislike for the man. I could not get out of my mind a recurring thought: I would somehow take revenge for his brutality. Somehow, I would get even.

But as I was thinking of the many tantalizing ways I could avenge my Mus, I began to realize that Kix-Kohor knew the truth about me and Glaucus. He knew that we were not divine, but merely men with superior armor and weapons. Nevertheless, it served his purpose to parade us about from time to time as emissaries of the gods; it elevated his own stature and brought him awe and respect.

But he knew.

And the fact that he knew made him dangerous in the extreme. From the moment of that realization, I did not sleep easy, imagining in every whisper and rustle the sounds of an assassin.

It was no surprise that as we began to learn the language, he limited our "appearances" among the people and kept us under increasing scrutiny—always watched. Had we seen an opportunity, we would have taken it and escaped. But Kix-Kohor was meticulous and watched us as carefully as though his life depended on it.

I did not fully understand how shrewd he was until later. Until the day he brought us into his private chamber and displayed my helm that still bore the mark of the obsidian ax.

"Where are you from?"

"You wouldn't understand," I replied.

"You will find that you will live longer if you do not insult me,"

Kix-Kohor said coldly. "Your lives hinge not only on your cooperation but also on your manners."

It was a time of risk and decision. If we accepted his power over us, we would be slaves until the day he no longer needed us. And, on that day, our heads would be separated from our bodies—I had no doubt of that. But challenging the man directly could bring instant death.

In the end it was my pride that drove my decision. As the captain of a ship, I was accustomed to command and bristled at this insolence.

"Kix-Kohor," I said in a measured voice, "you are a man of ambition. I can work with a man of ambition. Those who have ambition have great desires. That is where you and I have something in common. We both have something that drives us and for which we would sacrifice all to obtain. Is this not so?"

The man did not speak.

"But we are both different. While I desire simply to make a profit, your desire is an all-consuming one. You desire power. And the only way you can get it is if I place it in your hands. I am the only one in all the world who can give you what you want."

"You think highly of yourself."

"We can dance around the truth for days on end, but we both know what you seek. You want the armor that caused your deadliest weapon to shatter. With that, you would have a strategic advantage that would allow you to expand your domain. You might, perhaps, even become a king of kings."

I watched as the words sunk in. I had him. I could see it. "The truth of the matter is that you need me far more than I need you."

I watched his face redden and admired the man for managing to keep his temper under control.

"Your lives are in my hand. You live at my pleasure," he said at last.

"True," I replied coldly. "But if you kill us, you will remain forever what you are today: an insignificant, weak vassal always living in terror. Always wondering if today will be the last day of your power. Your ambition will not permit that. You want more. You want what only I can provide."

I watched his face carefully, wondering if I had pushed too hard. But I would not live in terror of this man. I would not live as a slave to the man who murdered my Mus. This was the moment that would decide all. If Kix-Kohor agreed to my terms, there was yet a possibility of escape—even of profiting from the venture. If he refused, then Glaucus and I would return to our ancestors, and we would no longer have the cares of this world to trouble our sleep.

The man sat before us for a long while. He did not speak but only stared into my eyes. That he wanted to kill me, I had no doubt. The only question was whether he wanted power more than my death.

I repressed the nearly irresistible temptation to speak—to sound the man out. But to speak would have been a sign of weakness.

And so I waited for Kix-Kohor, the tyrant, to decide whether to murder us or make us his partner.

At long last, he shifted position and laughed a full laugh that rose from deep in his belly and filled the room.

"What is your offer?" he asked.

NOTES

Deification of Roman emperors: Based in part on Hellenistic models, Roman emperors were widely venerated as gods, both during and after their lives (I. Gradel, *Emperor Worship and Roman Religion* [2004]). Seneca's satirical essay *Pumkinification of Claudius* mocked this belief, using the Latinized *apocolocyntosis* ("being made into a gourd") as a play on words for the Greek *apotheosis,* "being made a god."

Pontifex Maximus: Literally "the greatest bridge-builder," this was the high priest of the ancient Roman priesthood; Julius Caesar and his nephew and successor Augustus both held the office. It was later adopted by the Roman Catholic popes as a title for their role as the new high priests of Christian Rome.

Collegium of priests: Roman priests were organized into *collegium,* or "orders," to perform their duties. The concept of modern university colleges ultimately derives from this practice. For more information on Roman religion, see V. Warrior, *Roman Religion* (2006) and *Roman Religion: A Sourcebook* (2002).

Tiberius: The scandalous behavior of Tiberius is recounted in detail by Suetonius, *Lives of the Caesars* (Oxford, 2009); for a general account of his reign, see R. Seager, *Tiberias* (2005). See also R. Graves's marvelous novels, *I Claudius* and *Claudius the God.*

September: The plan to name September after Tiberius floundered (see Suetonius, *Life of Tiberius,* 26); July, on the other hand, was renamed after Julius Caesar, and August after Augustus, Tiberius's predecessors.

Tiberius' temple: Temples to the emperors were built throughout the empire. Herod the Great, most famous for building the magnificent Jewish temple on the Temple Mount in Jerusalem, also built temples in Caesarea, Samaria, and Banias to his Roman patron, the Divine Augustus (E. Netzer, *The Architecture of Herod the Great Builder* [2008]).

Capri: Capri is a spectacular island located off the coast of Italy in the Gulf of Naples, where Tiberius resided in his decadent semiretirement. The remains of his pleasure palace on the island can be visited today.

Divinity and human power: Humans exhibiting extraordinary power were often equated with gods by ancient peoples; for example, Barnabas was called Zeus, and Paul was called Hermes (Mercury) by some of the pagans who were amazed by their miracles and teachings (Acts 14:12).

Kuum and k'an: We are using Mayan terms since that is the oldest well-attested language in ancient Mesoamerica. *Kuum* is Mayan for maize; *k'an* is classic Mayan for *jewel,* used here for jade.

Chapter 12

The Book of Malchus, son of Mago, of the house of Hanno

From the moment of agreement with Kix-Kohor I became what I had always been—a merchant. Instantly, I felt comfortable and confident. This I could do.

That other occupation of being a god—standing before a hundred adoring worshippers—that was awkward work.

Exchanging one cargo for another and making a handsome profit in the process, this was work I had done a thousand times. This was power I was accustomed to.

At last, my destiny rested in my own hands.

The deal was a simple one. Kix-Kohor would provide us with all the supplies we needed to make the armor. The rate of exchange was set at one measure of bronze for an identical measure of gems or other materials Glaucus and I felt we could sell in Rome. Knowing that a one-time exchange would have been too great a temptation for Kix-Kohor, I ensured that the trade of goods would happen over time—receiving payment for each helm as it was produced.

The greatest difficulty we faced was the lack of tin. Copper was available, though only used in a limited fashion. Tin, on the other hand, was unknown in this land. In one way, it was a great stroke of luck for me in that it made my cargo priceless. The problem was, of course, that the only source of tin in all this world lay in the hold of my ship. And getting that tin without Kix-Kohor discovering the source was critical to my success.

In order to keep the process of bronze-making a secret, I demanded various bizarre and sundry supplies. In addition to copper, I requested the bark of barren palm trees, a mandrake-like root, various dyes, and obsidian. But mainly, I sought the beautiful jade-like gems (these I appropriated and put into our treasury—there was no need for anyone to know that they were not an integral part of the creation process). I also collected *kukul,* a type of brilliant blue and green feather highly prized by the people. These would ride lightly in my hold and could be sold in the Roman marketplace as an exotic and rare alternative to peacock and ostrich feathers. I knew wealthy, fashionable Roman ladies would pay well for such unique accessories. Finally, I demanded yards and yards of a suitable cloth stitched to my specifications—perfectly fitted for the masts of my ships.

Through all of this, Kix-Kohor's greed became the one constant. Whatever we asked, he provided with an ever-increasing urgency.

I expected that my greatest challenge would be getting the tin from my ship, but in the end, this task proved surprisingly simple. I explained that I needed to journey to the sacred cave and, through a special ceremony, seek the aid of the Great Spirit in finding the final ingredients. Once there, I offered a strong wine to my escorts—drinking at the cave appeared to be something of a habit, if not an obligation—and, within an hour, they were fast asleep. I slipped into the forest desperately trying to remember the way back to my ship. It had been six months since my disappearance. Was the ship still there? Were my men still alive? What would I do if I did not have the tin required to make the bronze?

All my fears soon faded when I discovered my camp and reunited with my men. It was a happy reunion. My men, without sails and without a pilot, had resigned themselves to being stranded and were setting about making themselves as comfortable as they could.

After our disappearance, they had waited two days for our return, then set out on their own in an effort to discover what had befallen us. It hadn't been difficult following our path through the forest since we had cut our way through a great deal of it.

Ultimately, they arrived at the cave, saw the blood on the ground and the mounds of fresh earth covering a fresh grave, and assumed the worst.

I was saddened to learn that while I had been gone, another of my men had died from the bite of a poisonous serpent. And with Mus' death, only six remained now, including myself and Glaucus.

Ah, it was good to be among my men once again. But, as much as I wanted to stay with them, time was of the essence. I quickly explained the situation and what was at stake, and my men, renewed with hope after my arrival, agreed to follow my every instruction.

I inventoried what little remained of my cargo of tin. Most of it had been dumped into the ocean in our desperate race to evade Audax and survive the storm. I had scarcely more than what three men could carry. This was a great disappointment for, had I a hold filled with the metal, I could have been rich beyond my wildest dreams.

Nevertheless, the supply was sufficient to make all of us wealthy. I urged my men to work as quickly as possible to make the ships seaworthy as soon as possible for, with any kind of luck, within six months we would all be sailing back to Rome as rich as senators.

I told them that I might return at any time and that they should have the ships well-provisioned, seaworthy, and ready to launch at a moment's notice, day or night.

I had little time for talk as the guards back at the sacred cave would surely be awakening soon. And so I loaded a portion of tin into a sack and made my way back to the cave, pleased to find the guards still asleep in their drunken comas.

Glaucus, for his part, was immensely relieved when I returned to the village. He had been held as ransom against my return and, apparently, had every reason to believe that I would never return, leaving him both friendless and headless.

"I discovered something I didn't think was entirely possible while you were gone," he said. "An entirely new level of dislike for you."

"Really, Glaucus, your lack of faith astounds me."

"Here's an idea. Next time, let's have you be the one who stays while I go out adventuring."

"Soon," I replied, "we'll leave together. And we'll both be rich."

We immediately began the process of creating the armor, demanding more and more exotic ingredients to hide the secret of the process. The blood of a red-maned monkey, scales from a blue fish, buckets of pure rainwater, and furious prayers and chants that could be heard from a distance. All of our activities were designed to create an aura of complexity and magic.

I made an additional demand of Kix-Kohor: an apprentice. He, of course, wanted his own man in that position—a spy. I flatly refused. I told him that the apprentice had already been selected by means of sorcery and that any deviation would jeopardize the entire enterprise. I wanted Be'nach, the stuttering boy Kix-Kohor had used for entertainment.

Reluctantly, Kix-Kohor agreed, and so the three of us began our great adventure as bronze makers. Whereas Be'nach had been the object of jokes and abuse, now he was an apprentice to the gods. We dressed him in royal attire and made him chief chanter. This association was a good thing for him, as it elevated him to a position of celebrity, and for the first time in his life, people sought him out and desired his company.

Of course, we kept the process of making bronze a mystery—a difficult task. We were watched continuously; Kix-Kohor was desperate to learn our secret. But we understood that, at the instant our secret was known, we would cease to breathe the air of this world. And so we made a great show of chanting incantations and combining ingredients, rejecting many of our concoctions as not being the right color, lacking the correct texture, or having the wrong magical aura.

It was all a sham, but if theater is what they wanted, theater is what we would give them. Trying to cast an entire bronze helmet would require more time, a hotter furnace, and special mold makers. Of course, we lacked all these things. Instead, after we had complicated the process beyond anyone's ability to remember the steps, we melted down the copper and tin and poured the metal into a series of molds we had carved in rock to make small, thin bronze plates about the size of two or three fingers, with a small hole in one end. These we sewed onto a leather cap, creating a helmet of metal scales such as are used by the Scythians and Parthians.

The following day, when I produced the new helmet, Kix-Kohor seemed radiant. After examining and testing it, he measured out an equal weight of jade gems and handed them to me.

And so my career as an armorer began. The more we made, the more efficient we became. With ten pounds of tin I could produce roughly ninety pounds of bronze, enough for half a dozen jackets and helmets of bronze scales. I even made a dozen short swords patterned after my own weapon.

The question that plagued me—the one unsolved mystery that remained—was how to get out alive. This was a task that I realized was becoming more and more doubtful. And even if we did manage to escape with our lives, I refused to think about the difficulties of the return voyage: finding the right winds and currents that would enable us to make the long, perilous journey across an infinite ocean.

But I could not stay here. I could not stay among barbarians who murdered my Mus in cold blood. What is more, I desperately wanted to avenge his death before I left this land. How I would accomplish that and escape with my riches, I had no idea. But I vowed that if application and will accounted for anything, I would find a way.

Though my days were spent in armor-making, I made it a point to watch for Xen. She was altogether remarkable—a mystery and a siren.

Regal in bearing, she seemed forever cloaked in a deep, unspeakable sadness. But even through that sorrow, she smiled—always, she smiled. At others though, never at me.

Her smile, unlike so many others I had known, was not born of indulgence and pleasure, but one birthed from the womb of some unspoken grief. She smiled with her eyes, and it was a smile without pretense. Other people smiled out of politeness or social obligation. But her smile—it was as though she saw what others could not see. It was as though her appreciation, her amusement, could not be contained in her earthly form. Like the sun breaking through clouds, it shone from her features and broke through in unexpected and unpredictable moments.

I would have given anything to know what was in her thoughts.

She often spent her time teaching the children of the village. And I often heard her voice singing unbearably sweet melodies that the children echoed with delight.

One day, a wild dog entered the city, sending men, women, and children flying in fright. But when the creature came at the children, Xen, with amazing calm and quickness, took the beast's mouth in her hands and clamped its jaws shut tight.

While the men ran to fetch their weapons, Xen sat beside the dog, speaking softly and calmly until the animal relaxed and began wagging its tail. From that time on, the dog was always at her side.

It wasn't that she did not fear, only that her past, secret grief had overwhelmed her fear and left her with a calm resolve and willingness to accept whatever the Fates had in store for her.

If I loved her before, how can I explain what I felt now? Now, after watching her grace, her kindness, her beauty?

Glaucus, I'm afraid, persecuted me dreadfully for what he called a schoolboy crush, but I knew better. This was a woman unlike any other

I had ever known. And I cursed my fate that I had fallen in love with a woman whose depth of hatred for me seemed as limitless as my love for her.

I frequently approached her and attempted to start a conversation, but, unless it advanced my learning of the language, she would not speak with me.

"Why do you hate me?" I asked her.

"You think highly of yourself." Her tone of voice made it clear that I was insignificant to the point that my comment was unworthy of eliciting the smallest reaction from her, let alone an emotion.

"Why do you hate me?" I repeated in exasperation. "I risked my life to save yours. In my land, when someone saves the life of another person, the customary reaction is one of gratitude, not loathing. I don't expect you to write poetry or bring gifts, but I did hope for something more than consuming hatred."

"You saved my life?" It was a question rather than a statement.

"Of course. In the cave. The old man was coming toward you with a knife. Have you forgotten?"

She stared at me, unblinking.

Why would she not speak? Why would she not tell me why she despised me?

Slowly, she raised her arms, palms up.

I looked at her skin. I noticed several small scars all the way from her wrists to her shoulders. Cuts that had long since healed but still left thin streaks that marked the trail of a forgotten blade.

What could she mean by this?

Were they self-inflicted? Were they wounds she had received as a child?

"I don't understand." I struggled to understand her meaning. "I saved you . . . from the old man."

Ever, her eyes stared into mine. And the sorrow and hatred within them cut my soul.

What had I done?

Why would she not speak?

"The old man was not going to *kill* me," she said.

And the scene at the cave returned. I saw the man with the obsidian knife approaching. I saw Xen singing, innocent, holding her arms outstretched . . .

As the gravity of the revelation began to sink into my mind, a mounting horror filled me with agony.

I could not take my eyes away from her arms. The small scars. The lines contained a history as surely as though they had been written in script.

Was it possible that the old man wasn't going to kill her? Only cut her a little? Draw a little blood? A drop or two? Only prick her flesh and allow her blood to mingle with that of the sacrificed animals?

I remembered rushing out from the darkness. Sword in hand. Dealing death at every turn.

How many of them had I slain?

In the girl's eyes I saw a reflection of myself. What must I look like to her? The embodiment of some demon?

Mus! Was it possible that *I* was responsible for the murder of my faithful friend?

Had it all been a mistake?

"I am a descendant of queens who are descended from goddesses," she said in a cold and serene tone. "We were offering the sacrifice of renewal. Those of the royal house must offer their blood as a sacrifice in imitation of the sacrifice of the gods at the creation of the world. Without blood, there is no life. It is the life force of the universe."

My heart pounded inside my chest. Thoughts stalled without taking form. I could not speak. Could not form the words of a sentence.

"The old man you speak of," she said at last.

"Yes?" I said, scarcely hearing the sound of my own voice, scarcely possessing the breath to speak the word.

"The old man that you killed . . ."

"Yes?"

"He was my grandfather."

I felt the strength of my limbs give way as my body slipped to the ground. A hollow thunder pulsed in my ears, drowning out thought. Drowning out sound except for the noise of rushing waters that overtook my senses and weakened my knees.

I tried to speak. Tried to form words.

But I had no voice. My throat was empty and dry.

And in my ears the ever-pounding rush of a world torn from its foundation.

Was it possible?

The sound of a word echoed deep within my breast. Over and over, pounding and pounding, mounting in intensity. Increasing in horror.

A word filled with terror.

A word filled with judgment.

A word filled with infinite shame.

Murderer.

NOTES

Kukul feathers: The Kukul or Quetzal birds look somewhat like parrots, and their strikingly bright feathers were highly prized and widely traded in ancient Mesoamerica.

Bloodletting rituals: Mayan bloodletting rituals were widely practiced in ancient Mesoamerica. The idea was that blood was the most valuable source of power and was needed to sustain the gods. Human sacrifice was the ultimate bloodletting, but forms of cutting and bleeding as sacrifice were also widespread (L. Schele and M. Miller, *The Blood of Kings,* 2d ed. [1992]).

Chapter 13

Lucius stretched the muscles in his neck and lifted his head to the ceiling. After reading so long, everything further away than arms' reach seemed out of focus. More, things seemed darker, as though in shadow. A troubling occurrence that seemed to happen more frequently of late. Could he be losing his vision?

Was this merely the latest in a long list of unsought and unexpected "discoveries" of old age? Another pain, another body part that would no longer bend, lift, rotate, or function as it had during youth? These "discoveries" normally appeared from the shadows, dark and distant and scarcely recognized until they were nose to nose. The pain in his knee, the constant ache in his throat, the ringing in his right ear.

And now this? The world turning dark?

It had happened so gradually that he hadn't noticed until recently the dimming of candles and the shadow falling over the light from the sun.

But he confronted this new realization with the same calm he had used to confront every other awareness of physical infirmity: he resolutely denied its existence. If it continued to the point where he could no longer ignore the unfortunate reality, he would proceed to the second strategy: downplay its significance.

"It's a good thing it is the elderly who suffer old age," he muttered. "The young would not survive it."

He looked into the hallway and noticed the light of the sun streaking into the villa. Perhaps with a new day's light, things would appear more hopeful. Perhaps with the coming of Helios, despair would vanish with the shadows.

But what was he talking about? Helios? Old habits would be hard to leave behind.

A rustle startled him, and he turned to see a figure in the doorway. He forced his eyes to focus and made out the form of an old friend.

"Ah, Cyril," he said as he rose to take the doctor's hand. "Thank you for coming so early. You've seen the girl?"

The physician nodded.

"Tell me your diagnosis and what you have prescribed."

Cyril Marcellus Andronicus was perhaps the most respected physician in Carthage and one who charged enough to ratify and amplify his reputation. He had established his fame by healing Drusus, the son of a well-known Carthaginian sculptor. The boy had been afflicted by a plague that had turned the whites of his eyes yellow and caused him extreme pain in his stomach. The malady had been pronounced fatal by three other physicians, but after two weeks of drinking one of Cyril's medicinal elixirs, the boy began improving and, within a short time, was back on his feet, completely healed.

Lucius invited the physician into his study and showed him to a chair. "What can be done for her?"

Cyril shook his head. "Nothing."

"Surely there must be something. A poultice? A potion? Some exotic herb? Whatever the cost, it matters not."

"She has too much black bile."

"What does that mean?"

"The child has fevers and night sweats. Her head pounds with pain. She can scarcely move her joints; she aches in her bones. Bruising. Her gums bleed. Her stomach is swollen."

"I say again: surely something can be done?"

The physician looked into Lucius' eyes and slowly shook his head. "I have seen three other similar cases. In all three, the patients died quickly and painfully."

"Perhaps there is something new you can try?"

"Make the child comfortable, Lucius. That is all. I have given instructions to her father to acquire an herb from the apothecary. It will take away some of the pain, but it will not cure her. In cases such as this, it is better to know what you are facing than to hope for that which will never be."

"So you have told her parents?"

Cyril nodded. "There is nothing left but to prepare for the end. They have decisions to make, and it is better for them to say their good-byes while there is still time. I am sorry, Lucius. I regret that I do not have something more agreeable to tell you."

Lucius nodded, engaging his old friend with other obligatory pleasantries until custom dictated he could show the physician to the door without causing offense.

He was relieved when the door finally closed.

What a tragedy this sorry life was. Filled with disappointment and death. An endless string of bitter events. What good were the few brief moments of happiness? They were simply glimmers of promise inevitably swatted away by unavoidable tragedy of one form or another.

Life, love, longing. They all ended the same. In death and in darkness. Despair and defeat. In shadow and forgetfulness.

If there was a god, he was cruel.

That a supreme being would create mortals, bursting with love and lust, with poetry coursing through their veins, only for it to end like this was monstrous.

Although everyone faced their day of disappearance, Lucius knew his day was particularly close. And he burned with crimson heat at the thought. That he should cease to exist! That his body should be lowered into a dark and cold grave. That he should be cast off and forgotten. That the ground should cover him and that he should be lost to the world. As though it had never mattered that once there had existed a Lucius Fidelis Crescentius.

But such was the destiny of mortals. All of them creatures of a cruel, merciless destiny.

As he made his way back to his study, he noticed Gunderic walking among the broken stone statues in the peristylium. He knew he should try to comfort him; say a few words; give him hope. But what words did he have that could comfort a man about to lose his only child?

Nevertheless, something must be said, and it would be better to do it now rather than delay as the weight of it pressed ever more heavily upon his mind.

"I have spoken with Cyril," Lucius said at last.

Gunderic appeared to have aged ten years overnight. A deep, sorrowful smile appeared on his face as he turned to his master. "Thank you for calling for the physician. I am sorry for the cost."

"Nonsense. You must promise not to give it another thought. You will be certain to purchase the medicine he has prescribed?"

Gunderic nodded.

Lucius surveyed the broken stone that littered the ground in front of him. It was the first time he had looked closely at the battlefield in daylight. Wounded, mutilated statues lay littered about, witnesses to his grim temper.

A terrible silence fell. Why didn't he know what to say on occasions such as this? But what was there to say? What could he say that would ease the pain of this moment?

"Speaking of cost, what do you suppose is the tally of my little indulgence of last night?"

"You did a thorough job."

"In retrospect, perhaps not the smartest of economic decisions."

Gunderic looked about the yard and smiled. "May I ask why you did it?"

Lucius laughed softly and stooped to examine the head of Pallas Minerva. A deep crack had severed the face from chin to forehead. "A momentary madness, I suppose."

"It's only that I don't understand," Gunderic replied. "These images were sacred to you."

Lucius lifted the head of Jupiter and felt the stone split in his hands, leaving two halves. "Perhaps if I asked a question of you, I could better explain. Why do you follow the Galilean?"

"My mother and father were Christians."

"So you were indoctrinated as a child into the belief?"

"You could say that, I suppose. My parents were devout believers and taught me to be the same."

"So you have never truly examined what you believe? You have never objectively weighed the evidence to determine whether or not your faith is genuine? Have you ever questioned the behavior of those who also believe as you do? Earlier this morning, I confronted your Bishop Aurelius at the temple of Caelestis. To be blunt, he was stealing the building. What do you think of that?"

Lucius admired his servant's steady demeanor. He could not remember a time when Gunderic had raised his voice in anger or frustration. The man was simply who he was and no amount of provocation seemed to affect him.

"As I said last night, not all Christians are the same," he said.

"Forgive me for questioning your faith, Gunderic, but if that is the case, why does no one of your faith stand up to leaders who do wrong? Why does no one stand up and decry their madness? As we speak, the fruits of your religion are apparent: unlawful seizure of a temple, persecuting those who disagree, purging citizens from their homes merely because they do not conform to their theology. Until Christians themselves stand up and condemn this abuse of power, why should anyone consider the notion that some Christians are different than others?"

Lucius could sense how his questions weighed heavily on Gunderic, and it troubled him that he had added to the man's burdens. The poor man had much more pressing things to worry about now than debating theological tenets with an old philosopher. He decided to change the subject.

"Tell me about your mother and father, Gunderic. I don't believe I know much about them."

"I do not remember much," he said at last. "I can scarcely remember what they looked like. I had an older brother and a younger sister. We lived in a country of snow and frost. One terrible winter, we migrated southward, hungry for a warmer climate and prosperity of Rome."

"What country are you from?"

"I don't remember. All I know is that when we came south, my father, along with many others, crossed the great river and enlisted in the Roman army to fight against the enemies of Rome."

It was one of those terrible ironies of the world, Lucius thought, that the son of a man who risked his life in the service of Rome could end up a slave. But why should this injustice be any more absurd than those that saturated the rest of humanity? There were a million unexplainable wrongs in the world, each terrible in its own right, each linked together in one great chain of chaos.

"We had scarcely established a home," Gunderic continued, "when a new threat arose from the east."

"What threat?"

"A warlike people. They destroyed everything before them. Those of my village panicked. The invaders were merciless animals. Locusts. Those whom they permitted to live were used so cruelly that they often sought relief through suicide."

What could be expected of a godless mob of barbarians led only by an unquenchable thirst for plunder?

"What did you do?"

Gunderic pursed his lips. "We could not stay on the frontier; to do so would have meant annihilation. The leaders of my people petitioned Rome to allow us to cross into their lands. Without the protection of Rome, we couldn't stand against the hordes of barbarians. The negotiations did not go smoothly."

"What happened?"

Gunderic grimaced. "Rome granted the petition to enter their lands, but only upon their terms. We had to surrender our arms."

"It is understandable that Rome would fear an outside body of armed men coming into their territory."

"Unfortunately, there was not enough food for both the Roman soldiers and us, so the Romans offered an option. Parents could purchase the food that would save their lives by selling their children into slavery."

"Surely the parents refused?"

"It was either that or watch them die. By capitulating to the request, they saved their children and themselves. An added benefit—at least from the perspective of Rome—was that the children would become assimilated into Roman culture and be properly educated and civilized."

Gunderic shrugged. "Faced with death on the one side and humiliation on the other, my people reacted in predictable ways. Within six months after the treaty, they had armed themselves and were ready for war. But now, having lost their children and their dignity, they carried an eternal hatred against the nation that allowed them 'safe' passage at the cost of their dignity."

"What happened to you?"

"In my case, my father was poor. And so I was put on a ship with a hundred others and transported to Alexandria. Once there, I was assigned to a proper Roman family, who, upon seeing that I was quick-witted, taught me to read and write. Eventually, I became an assistant to the household steward until they found an opportunity for profit. They sold me to the slave-trader Plautus, who eventually sold me to you."

So that was the story. That it was true, Lucius did not doubt. Gunderic had never lied, had never shown bitterness, had never been resentful. But why? How could the man not be bitter with a past like that? Not be consumed with hate?

"Are you unhappy, Gunderic?"

Lucius took pride in being an enlightened master. He had, after all, given Gunderic great responsibility, allowed him to marry and have a child. He was well-fed and lived in a beautiful villa. There were ten thousand free men in Carthage alone who would give anything to trade places. But yet the thought nagged at him.

"Are you unhappy?" he repeated.

"I am content."

The man seemed sincere in his response, and Lucius allowed it to pass. But there was something else in his servant's story. Something he could not put his finger on.

"You say you lived in a country of snow and cold. Surely you remember more than that."

"Not much," he replied.

"What about legends? History?"

"My people were warriors. That is, until we embraced the light of the Lamb of God."

Something nagged at Lucius. Something about this story that didn't seem right.

"You said you were forced into Roman territory. Who were these barbarian invaders? Was it the Goths? Did the cursed tribe that sacked Rome also drive you from your home?"

He could see why Gunderic's people would need protection from the Goths. They were a savage people who had swept across Rome committing atrocity, murder, sacrilege. Alaric—may he be forever damned—was a Goth. And it was he who had led his bloodthirsty hordes against the world's only hope of civilization: Rome.

"Was it the degenerate, depraved Goths you were fleeing?" Lucius repeated.

Gunderic shook his head.

"Then who?"

"We fled from the Huns. My father . . ."

"Yes?"

"My family . . ." Gunderic smiled sadly. "*I* am Goth."

NOTES

Roman medicine: In many ways, Roman medicine was highly advanced for antiquity, but it often only treated symptoms rather than causes and was often powerless in the face of many diseases (I. Dawson, *Greek and Roman Medicine* [2005]). The works of the most famous physician of antiquity, Galen (A.D. 129–216), remained standard medical texts until the sixteenth century (R. Hankinson, *Cambridge Companion to Galen* [2008]).

The Goths: Gunderic's story of his family and the migrations of the Goths into Rome can be found in M. Kulikowski, *Rome's Gothic Wars* (Cambridge, 2008) and P. Heather, *The Goths* (1998). For information about the Huns, see E. Thompson, *The Huns* (1999) and C. Kelly, *The End of Empire* (2009). For information about the Gothic conversion to Christianity, see R. Fletcher, *The Barbarian Conversion: From Paganism to Christianity* (1999). For information about Arianism, see R. Williams, *Arius: Heresy and Tradition* (2002).

Chapter 14

The revelation that Gunderic was a member of the race that had sacked Rome was more than Lucius could bear. That one of Alaric's hated race lived in his own villa! That he had provided him with shelter and food! Lucius could not stay in the presence of his servant. He could not speak with him, could not smile at him, could not support nor comfort him.

Lucius could not decide which he detested more: that he had not known before this moment that his own slave was a member of that accursed tribe that had raped the Eternal City, or that Gunderic, a man he admired and respected—a man of probity and control—could come from that barbaric clan.

Some truths are unforgivable. Others, unthinkable.

How could he not have known?

Everyone knew that the Goths were drunken, uncontrollable savages.

How could Gunderic, who would without hesitation sacrifice his own life to save that of his master, be part of that race?

Could it be that his servant was merely an exception? A product of Roman culture and education? No, the boy had been mistreated and abused by Romans. Separated from those he loved at a young age. Forced into slavery and menial labor.

If anything, the man should be even more savage and bitter. He should despise Rome. He should despise his master!

Had their roles been reversed, Lucius wondered if he wouldn't have risen in the night, murdered his master, and tried to escape.

How could the cankerous, diseased tree of the depraved Goths produce such fruit as Gunderic?

Gunderic was civilized. Temperate. Educated, eloquent, capable.

Impossible. Impossible!

Lucius could not even allow the thought to form.

Was it conceivable that other Goths were similar to Gunderic? That they were in bearing and ability inherently as capable as a Roman?

No.

They were a lawless, brutish, uncivilized people. What had they contributed to the world?

Art? Invention? Philosophy? None!

No! Aristotle had known it from the beginning. Barbarians were by nature who they would forever be: half animal, instinctively bestial, driven by base desire.

And yet, there was Gunderic. Surely he was no animal. The man was literate, an invaluable aid.

Was it possible that Aristotle had erred?

That was a subject Lucius could not bear to think about at the moment.

Besides, he had other things to occupy his time and his thoughts.

Yes, he would push it out of his mind. Deal with the information another day. There was work yet for him to do, a mystery yet to uncover. And, gradually, his thoughts returned to another time—to Malchus, Xen, and Kix-Kohor. The thought of them softened the pain of Gunderic's revelation.

Yes. He would return to his study.

Enough of the present. Better to push all thoughts of Aurelius, Rome, Goths, and Gunderic from his mind.

He would immerse himself in another man's story. Yes, that was exactly what he would do.

And so, he took a seat at his table and opened the metal pages in front of him. And, once again, he allowed himself to drift far away into the distant world of his forgotten ancestor.

The Book of Malchus, son of Mago, of the house of Hanno

A successful merchant understands this principle: value is based on perception. When the Sidonese bead merchants discovered a way to make low-cost, lightweight beads by blowing glass, they became wealthy beyond imagination. Not because the glass beads they created were costly, but because they were new and unique. And women desired them. The Sidonese were smart; they limited the supply of beads, which caused the price to rise until their profit was obscenely high. They became rich.

The Sidonese bead merchants understood this principle.

I understood it as well.

Consequently, I made sure that the process of creating bronze helmets, breastplates, and swords was slow. Painfully slow, complicated, and risky.

Kix-Kohor demanded more. Demanded faster.

But I refused to hasten my work. His response was to offer more in exchange. Ten percent more, twenty percent. Yet I maintained my schedule. The process needed to appear to be complex and arduous, else our lives were forfeit. I understood with clarity that the day Kix-Kohor could produce the armor himself would be the day Glaucus and I would cease to breathe.

It wasn't that he hadn't tried to imitate my efforts. I was not blind to his spies who hovered around our small foundry. I knew they were reporting to him our every move. And I knew that in another part of the village, Kix-Kohor had set up a second shop where he laboriously attempted to duplicate my process.

Of course, without access to my tin, they failed at every opportunity, creating only copper with remnants of spider webs, palm husks, and goat's blood.

With each finished helm, I demanded immediate payment. Whenever we had acquired some forty pounds of precious jade, Glaucus slipped away into the night with the gems on his back. Once he had evaded Kix-Kohor's spies, he made his way to our ships, where he handed over the treasure and brought back another portion of tin. And so we worked, our supply of tin growing smaller with every week. I could not escape the realization that soon, I would not be able to make more, and my work as a metallurgist would end. The only plan we could think of for escape was to make a run during the night. Not a very good plan since there were guards at the door who kept constant watch over us day and night. Still, no better plan had emerged and so that simple plan would have to do. At least for now.

When Kix-Kohor demanded an explanation of Glaucus' night journeys, I explained it was a necessary part of the process.

"There is an essential ingredient that is very rare," I explained.

"Tell me what it is and I will supply it. Is it a stone?"

"It is the rarest of elements," I explained. "Available only in nearly invisible veins of rock and impossible to distinguish from ordinary rock except by those who have spent a lifetime learning to recognize it. It can only be seen in the glimmer of moonlight which complicates things terribly—and why my man sometimes must journey at night from time to time. Those who have the capacity to learn to see this element are so rare that they can command any price for their services."

"Substitute another ingredient."

"It cannot be done. Already, my supply is running dangerously low. As rare as it is in my own country, it is a hundredfold more rare in yours. If we do not find more, I will have no other recourse but to return to my homeland to procure more."

It is here that I must write of how I misjudged Kix-Kohor. I assumed that his greed for bronze would guarantee our safety. I assumed that we would be free from harm because, of all the people in the world, only we could provide what he most desperately needed.

But I was wrong.

I also misjudged his shrewdness. Tired of his guards losing Glaucus in the dead of night, the time came when he decided to act. He simply waited for Glaucus to return and confiscated his inventory of precious tin.

This was a matter of life and death because once Kix-Kohor had tin, he had the power to create bronze on his own. He had cut off our supply once; and if he did it once, he could do it again. This would not do.

I ran to his quarters and brushed past his guards. He was eating, surrounded by his war council. On a table in front of him rested the tin he had taken from Glaucus.

"Return it!" I shouted.

And then Kix-Kohor did something that surprised me and turned my rage into fear.

He smiled. And though he smiled, something in his expression told me everything had changed. He no longer cared if I remained alive. More, the seeping hatred that spread from his malignant eyes suggested that he wanted me dead.

I was no longer merchant, but prey. And he was deadly and dangerous.

"If you want more bronze, you will hand that back to me."

"Now that I have this, what need do I have of you?"

"You are a fool. You no more understand how to make bronze than a child understands the complexities of your calendar."

"I think I will manage."

"What you have in front of you is a precious metal called tin. It is as rare in your land as dragon's teeth. Take that and you will never find more."

"Now that we know what it looks like, we will find it. How hard can it be? After all, you found this."

"Don't be a fool, Kix-Kohor. Only I know the secrets of making bronze."

"Then the time has come for you to teach me." His voice was menacing. Deadly.

There are times when you simply know that there is no more need for talk. This was such a time. He had made up his mind. He would take out the middle man.

"Harm me and the secret dies."

"I believe you will tell me every secret you know," he said smiling.

And then he nodded to his guards, who pinned my arms and led me away.

We learn too slowly lessons that could save us great heartache. We deny terrible truths. "Of course that could happen," we tell ourselves. "But to others. Not to me."

We cannot believe that tragedy will knock on our door, that disaster will strike our lives.

We learn too late that unhappy chance can choose us. That in mere seconds our lives can shift from dream to nightmare.

This was one of those moments.

And that was what I thought about while he tortured us.

I will not speak of the pain. The terrible agony. The screams of my friends Glaucus and Be'nach. The merciful blackness that came when I lost consciousness.

Perhaps as terrifying as the physical pain was the mental anticipation of greater pain to come. He threatened to put our hands into molten ore. He threatened to place us in coffins filled with serpents and deadly spiders. He placed devouring worms over our open wounds and told us if we did not talk, he would allow the worms to burrow inside our flesh and eat us from the inside out. He cut our bodies with blades coated with poison that twisted our limbs in agonizing contortions.

And throughout this torture, his war council watched. Kix-Kohor wanted them to watch. He wanted them to witness the power he had over the gods.

But if his purpose was to make us talk, he was disappointed. Glaucus and I had long since come to the conclusion that we would die here. And knowing that, we understood that pleading for our lives could have no chance of improving our circumstances. And so we remained silent. We did not speak but held our tongues as he took burning embers and pressed them into our flesh.

When it was clear that we would not talk—at least not on that day—he directed his men to savage us with wooden clubs.

The three of us wished to die before it was finished. And when it finally ended—when they had scorned, scourged, and spit at us and degraded us in every imaginable way—when they finally abandoned us to our solitude—we three huddled together and tried hard to remain unmoving.

But after a time, Glaucus and I made the mistake of opening our swollen eyes and looking at each other. I am not sure to this day what it was, but there was something astonishingly funny in our current situation. Glaucus' bruised body and swollen face looked unearthly and monstrous. I must have looked the same.

And that is when we looked into each other's eyes . . . and laughed.

We had survived after all. How long we would remain alive, we did not know, but there was something about our pathetic appearance that seemed absurd and impossible. Perhaps, after being so certain that this hour was our final one, the impossibility of remaining alive struck us as something comical. And worse, every time we laughed, the pain spiked and wrenched at us, which, for some unknown reason, made us laugh even more.

Even Be'nach, poor child, laughed with us.

And then Xen appeared.

She must have thought us mad to be laughing at such a time as this. Nevertheless, we could not stop. Though it hurt beyond belief, we could not stop.

Xen tended to our wounds, and her tender touch healed me. I watched a different kind of anger rise within her—particularly when she tended to Be'nach—and the delightful, ambrosial thing about this new anger was that it was directed toward someone else. The pain in my body seemed to fade away as I watched her concern for Be'nach, Glaucus—and yes—for me!

And something else happened. As we continued to laugh, the stern expression on her face began to transform until she looked at me . . . and smiled.

And the smile grew. She did her best to hold back a laugh of her own. But her eyes laughed. They laughed and they smiled and they looked at me for the first time since I had known her, and within her beautiful eyes, the coldness had melted. She seemed a different person. A tenderness crept into her eyes that I had seen in her relationships with others but never with me.

She spent the evening cleansing our wounds and stanching the blood. In the end, after the final cut had been closed and the last drop of blood had been wiped away, she sat on the floor with us, and we closed our eyes and let the warmth of the soothing night envelop us.

And I reflected on the sound of her laughter—a purifying sound that removed the physical pain and cleansed the emotional pain.

Through suffering, I had become a new man. And through our suffering, Xen had become changed as well. Through suffering, we had all become transformed and whole and healed.

NOTES

Barbarians: Most Greeks and Romans followed Aristotle's belief that barbarians—that is, non-Greeks and non-Romans—were inherently inferior and therefore justly susceptible to enslavement (*Politics* 1.2–7, 3.14; *Nicomachean Ethics*, 7).

Chapter 15

Lucius closed his eyes and remembered.

How it felt to be in love.

One would think that after seventy years memories would be like bones: brittle and weak—but no. He had always been a foolish lover, an embarrassing lover. Writing maudlin notes and composing sentimental songs and laughing and gushing in such a transparent manner that he advertised to the whole world of his infatuation.

How could he—someone so meticulous in logic, study, and rhetoric—be such a love-struck child when it came to falling in love? Even after seven decades, he marveled at how he had changed when overcome with the effects of Cupid's barb.

And Livia. His dear, beloved Livia.

It was not love at first sight with her. In fact it took time for him to even see her as anything more than a . . . cipher. There are those striking personalities that you notice instantly—rare individuals who are unforgettable from the first moment you meet them—but Livia was not of that sort.

Beautiful, yes. But modest and quiet. She more or less blended in with the world. She was like a tree in the forest—beautiful in its own right, but, among so many other trees, how does one stand out from any other?

He met her when he was young and beginning to develop a reputation as a promising sophist and defender of the old gods. She was one of the many pupils who surrounded him. She was one of the many ornaments that gave credence to the fantasy of what he thought he represented. But whereas other students came and moved on, Livia simply came.

And she did not move on.

And she did not demand attention. Did not demand anything of him. She merely was.

And was. And was.

Until the day—years after her first appearance—when Lucius looked down at an auburn-haired pupil and saw not a student, but a woman.

And the more he thought about the girl, the more intrigued he became. Why had he not noticed her nose? It was perfect and pretty; he felt quite infatuated with her nose.

And her forehead that rounded at the top. Why had he not noticed that? And her feminine voice, and the elegance of her walk.

And her eyes. Particularly the way they took fire when she looked at him. Why had he not noticed that?

And the more he noticed, the more obsessed he became until one day, he asked that she stay awhile after the others had left.

"You have been with me now, is it two years?"

"Four."

Lucius was developing a reputation for having a silver tongue, for being able to string words and syllables together in such a way that listeners—even those who disagreed—marveled at his art.

But this conversation with Livia, could it have been more awkward?

"Four years, you say?"

"Four and a half, actually."

"Four years. And a half?"

She nodded, and then a terrible silence fell between them.

How did one approach this subject? A man of his eloquence and reputation couldn't simply ask outright, "Do you like me?"

He couldn't sound like a schoolboy infatuate with his first crush. But that was all that came into his head. That was the point of the conversation, after all—to assess whether or not she felt anything for him.

But, "Do you like me?"

How could he?

He would die of embarrassment. He had gone to great pains to establish himself as a sophisticate. He was supposed to have words for any occasion. He was supposed to know what to say under any pressure. But all he could think of was that one piece of information he most wanted to know: Did she like him?

He had to know.

"I was wondering," he said at last, breaking the awkwardness of the moment, "if you could ever see yourself in a relationship with someone like me."

There, he had said it. And he blushed as he said it, knowing how absurd and clumsy the words sounded. And oh, if he could only take them back, erase them from the record of the world. He was already searching for a way to turn the query into a philosophical lecture—anything to mask his vulnerability—when she spoke.

"Yes, I believe I could," she replied.

But then he hated himself even more because of the lack of clarity of his question. This was torture. Why had he simply not asked her directly?

But he could not bear to be in doubt, and, worse, he knew he would not have the courage to have another, similar, conversation in the future. So he pressed on.

"When you say, 'Yes, I believe I could . . .'" It was agony, but he could not help himself. He could not bear to proceed, but the thought of not knowing weighed more heavily on him than the almost certainty of humiliation.

"When you said that," he continued, "did you mean someone *like* me? Or could you possibly mean *me* specifically?"

And then she looked at him for the first time not as his student but as something more. She looked at him the way a woman looks at her beloved. And Lucius looked at her eyes, her beautiful eyes.

And that was the beginning.

He loved her so desperately and so awkwardly.

She gave him everything—every thought and dream and hope.

And after the infatuation had calmed and he was able to see her with clearer eyes, he realized that he still loved her—a remarkable thing!

Yes, he loved her. But not with the perfection that she loved him.

Whereas she was a swan in her love, he was a camel.

Whereas her love was effortless and elegant, his was awkward, stumbling, and littered with clumsiness.

How she remained in love with him, he did not know.

She was a remarkable soul. And Lucius knew it. The women of his life had always been better people at heart than he was. Lucius' mother, case in point, was kind and gentle. Encouraging.

It was she who urged him to sit up straight and look the part of a nobleman. When, at eight years of age, he practiced reciting from Homer, it was his mother who encouraged him to do better.

"Do it again, Lucius," she had said. "But this time, say it with feeling."

That phrase had remained with him throughout his life, and he had always, in everything he had done, tried to say what he said with feeling.

He had always been an awkward and gangly child who often hid from schoolmates who teased and tormented him, but his mother believed in him and it was because of her faith and hope that he perceived that he might have hope of a future for himself.

Yes, the women of his life had all loved more purely, their motives transparent and open, their concern unselfish. They had always been better than he.

His mother and his Livia were of a different world than he.

He was not worthy of them. Not worthy of their love. Not worthy of their devotion. And though he never vocalized that fact, he knew it in his heart.

And on that terrible day when Livia lay dying in his arms, when she looked up at him for the last time and breathed her final breaths, he knew it then more profoundly than he had ever known anything.

How could he make up for his many mistakes? His habitual forgetfulness? His selfishness? His inattention?

It was too late to do anything but kiss her gently and tell her over and again how desperately he loved her. How desperately he needed her. How happy she had made him.

This seemed to soothe her pain, at least for a moment.

And her last words to him were words that burned.

She smiled a beautiful smile and looked into his eyes.

"Lucius," she said, "remember me."

And with that, she took her final breath and departed.

The sorrow of that day and the sorrow of the years he had had with her where he had not cherished her more—where he had not made it his life's work to fill her life with joy and adventure and love—the sorrow of those hours, days, and years accompanied him from that day to this.

But mercifully, those memories faded with time until what remained was her sweetness, her goodness, and her love. And that he could not forget.

And that was with him every day of his life.

He had fulfilled her final wish.

He remembered her.

Chapter 16

The Book of Malchus, son of Mago, of the house of Hanno

It took two weeks to recover sufficiently from our injuries and, during that time, we received word from Kix-Kohor that we were to go back to our work of producing bronze. Under the terms of our original agreement.

That made us laugh.

So he had tried making bronze. Had tried finding the secret ingredient.

And he had failed.

He needed us after all. And that gave us power—at least as long as our supply of tin held out. But we knew the terrible truth—that we had little remaining. Our time was short.

As we worked, I came to the realization that I could not involve Be'nach in our dangerous adventure. I told him that I had a new assignment for him: he must take the gems I gave him as payment for his services and become a spy. Only the kind of spy he would be was one who appeared normal in every way. And for the next ten years, he was to appear completely normal—not drawing attention to himself. To that end, I instructed him to pursue a normal profession. He had spoken in the past of wanting a farm and to tend a few animals, so I instructed him to do exactly that. Most important, I told him to not cause anyone to be suspicious of him. He should farm his land and tend his animals. No one must suspect him. I told him that I might come for him at any time—perhaps a year from now, perhaps a decade or more—and I would ask to know what he had learned. Such information was priceless to me, I told him. And he warmed to the task.

He promised that he would do as I had instructed, and I gave him enough in wealth to keep him secure for the remainder of his life. He left sad but excited for the opportunity to become a spy. It was the last time I saw him.

Kix-Kohor, for his part, did not come by much after that. Nor did he send his guards, nor his spies. I suppose he had hatched some plan of conquest that depended on our bronze. He must have known that the surest way to get more of it was to leave us to our own devices.

The one person we did see more of was Xen.

To my surprise, she seemed . . . calm. Not so much without care but without rancor. She arrived in the afternoon, nursed our wounds and brought us nourishment, and often spent the better part of the evening with us before leaving.

I searched for signs of hatred and bitterness but could not detect any. To be truthful, I was yet wary—unsure whether her new attitude reflected a change in heart or a renewed effort by Kix-Kohor to infiltrate our operation and learn our secrets. For the first time since my arrival, Xen seemed warm and friendly—a welcome change, even if scripted. Even so, I found myself enjoying the sound of her laughter and the flash of her smile.

We were allowed increased freedom and time outside of our hovel—supervised, of course. But it was good for us to stretch our legs and mingle with the people. The more time we spent among the villagers, the more aware we became of our celebrity status. Some were afraid of us and rushed into homes, peeking out through darkened doorways as we passed by.

It seems that the girls Xen had been tutoring had something of a crush on Glaucus and me. Glaucus insisted it was because of his animal magnetism, but I knew better. They were fascinated because we looked so different and exotic from anyone else—that and the common belief that we were more than mortal. For whatever reason, the girls blushed deeply every time we came near. They never approached us individually but in packs, nervously laughing and trying to appear uninterested. Once, a brave young girl approached, a gaggle of others behind her. Surprisingly bold, she came up to me, lifted her chin and said, "Malchus?"

I nodded.

But the look of bravery fled from her eyes and, trembling, she turned back to the safety of her friends. They ran away in a flock, laughing. Glaucus and I looked at each other curiously, and then I looked up and my eyes met another pair of eyes.

Xen.

And in her eyes, a most amused light. Struggling not to laugh, she turned her eyes away before returning them to mine. I smiled and shrugged my shoulders. Then she did laugh, shaking her head mischievously, and I think I knew heaven on that day.

How I loved to see her smile. And her eyes—filled with amusement, mischief, and scolding.

I could not stop thinking of her. Could not stop dreaming of her.

How can I possibly describe her? Xen was altogether one of those rare and remarkable creatures who seemed comfortable, content, and possessed of a genuine inner calm. So unlike any other woman I have ever known. She was not loud, nor did she seek attention. But she seemed to always be at the center of everything. She was not so much quiet as modest and reserved. She never raised her voice. Her movements were never uncontrolled, brash, or erratic, but reserved and elegant—she moved . . . effortlessly.

She never *tried* to be anything. She *was*.

She was the kind of remarkable soul who could not keep the light inside of her; it simply was too bright, too perfect to remain within.

The tiniest smile or the most insignificant laugh exposed that light, enfolding those around her and bringing them into her joy. I loved her in spite of my knowing that I could never hold her, never gaze into her eyes, never speak to her of what was in my heart.

In my days I have known many hard and troubled people whose souls are saturated with bitterness and brine. Like an overfilled bucket, they cannot help but slosh bile about wherever they go—no matter how careful they are to conceal it. And there are others who are self-consumed and become offended when any element of the world—be it nature, man, or event—does not conform to their expectations. Their only true love is themselves, and they are completely incapable of seeing others except as possible contributor or obstacle.

Though she had reason enough, there was no bitterness in Xen.

I think perhaps the best description of her was that, to the core of her being, she was *good*.

Even her rancor toward me—the man who had slain her grandfather and, as a consequence, had placed her deranged brother on the throne—gradually *seemed* to fade. And in her faintest smile, I discovered . . . heaven.

To prolong the length of her visits, I spoke to her of Hector, Romulus, and Caesar. She, in turn, told me the great stories of her culture. Of how her ancestors had traveled from far away across the waters and established cities, temples, and nations.

And so my days passed as though in a dream. And though my heart was heavy, I think perhaps I had never been happier than I was in the company of Xen.

"I will tell you of Na'ma and the serpent," she said to me one day. "Na'ma was a young maiden who, against the advice of her father, loved to wander into the forest. She believed that she could speak to the animals in such a way that they would understand her. But even more strange, she believed she could understand them."

"A valuable skill." I smiled, intoxicated with the sound of her voice.

"One day, Na'ma discovered a beautiful but large green-and-yellow snake that slithered close to her, its scales shining like the feathers of the Kukul bird.

"'You are a pretty snake,' she said.

"'Dance with me,' the serpent replied. And so Na'ma and the snake danced in the forest. The girl sang and the snake hissed and they danced away the hours of the day.

"The next day, Na'ma came to the forest and danced again with the snake. On the third day, after dancing and singing, the snake said to her, 'Will you swear to do what I ask?'

"Na'ma, without thinking, promised.

"'You must kill me,' the snake said.

"Na'ma refused, saying she could never harm such a beautiful creature.

"The snake reminded her of her promise and said, 'You must kill me and bury me here in this grove underneath the sun. And after you bury me, you must come to this place and attend to my grave. Bring me water, for I will thirst.'

"The girl refused again, saying that she had never harmed a creature in her life and would certainly not harm him.

"But the serpent demanded she honor her oath.

"And so the poor girl was trapped, for it was the law of her people that when an oath was made, they were bound to comply or face the wrath of Xaman Ek, the god of darkness."

Xen paused, pain in her eyes, as though she had become the girl and faced the dilemma herself. "Na'ma had no other choice. She complied with her promise and killed the serpent. She wept bitterly as she placed it in the ground. The last thing she wanted to do was to return to that spot—the spot where she had killed that wondrous creature. But she had made a promise and so, faithfully, she returned every day and tended to

179

the grave ensuring that the ground received water and that it was not overrun with weeds.

"In a little while, she noticed a strange plant emerging from where her friend had been buried. She almost pulled it, but something within her told her to wait and see.

"The plant continued to grow—a wondrous and beautiful plant—one she had never seen before. It grew in a stalk until it was taller than she was."

Xen looked up as though seeing the plant in front of her. She reached out as though caressing the plant and then she smiled.

"And that was how my people discovered maize, the staple of our lives. A plant that, from year to year, sustains life and saves us from hunger."

The tale was, of course, strange, but perhaps no stranger than some of the stories of my youth: Chronus eating his children; Atlas carrying the world; Jupiter turning into a bull and seducing Europa; Sisyphus and his stone. Perhaps that was the nature of religion—ever curious and mysterious.

"You think it strange?" Xen asked. "This story of Na'ma and the serpent?"

I knew enough to understand that she was asking a different question. What she really wanted to know was if I thought her religion was absurd.

"Sometimes the strange," I said at last, "is the greatest evidence of truth."

When she asked what I meant, I replied, "We assume that the gods think and act like we do. But that is impossible. If god is eternal, all-knowing, and all-powerful, then he must think differently from us. If everything he does and says makes perfect sense, then isn't that a sign that he is no more than a fiction created from the mind of a mortal man?"

"I see," she laughed. "So it is only when religion doesn't make sense that you can rely on the fact that it may be true."

We laughed together at that. How I loved the sound of her laughter. It was a sound of life and youth and hope. I found myself hungering to hear her voice, hear the sound of her mirth, more every day.

"There is something even more unbelievable than the story of Na'ma and the serpent," she continued. "Something my mother claims to have witnessed."

"Stranger than a talking serpent?"

"A hundred times so. But my mother says it truly happened. And so does everyone else who saw it."

"I'm eager to know it," I said.

"Before I was born, there was a legend—not of my people, but from a region to the north. The legend claimed that God's own Son would descend from the heavens and become mortal. He would be born in a distant land—a land their ancestors had once claimed as their own long ago."

"An easy prediction to make," I replied. "I have heard a dozen such prophecies in my time. Of course, such predications have the virtue of being vague enough that they can neither be proved nor disproved. This, of course, is an indispensable element for any respectable soothsayer—at least those who wish to keep their reputations intact."

"But the believers went beyond prophesying that the Son of God would be born. They said that, on the day the child was born, there would be no night."

"That is a mistake no soothsayer would ever make. A thing such as that is altogether too easy to prove or disprove. Unless they were talking metaphorically," I said.

"They claimed the sun would go down and yet there would be light."

"Brave, but foolish. Better had they predicted a famine or a surging flood. Better to say there would follow an infestation of snakes or that the stars would be clouded by smoke. These things all have at least a chance at becoming true—in fact, they all will inevitably become true if one waits long enough. There is no explaining away a night that is no night."

181

"But it happened." Her voice was calm and sure.

Was she testing my gullibility? Testing my belief in her? I scarcely knew what to say or how to react. What she was saying was impossible, and yet I could see no doubt in her eyes. She believed it.

"How do you know?" I said at last.

"I told you, my mother was alive and saw it herself. Ask any of the elders of this village—of any village. It happened; they will tell you. See if you can detect deception in their voice. See if you can find versions of the tale that contradict. They are all the same."

There had to be an explanation. "Perhaps it was merely a bright moon. Perhaps that is all."

"It was more than that. Ask anyone. They will tell you that light filled the sky and it was as bright as day." She looked intently at me. "Of course, there are some who deny that it happened, but they lie. There are too many who saw it and do not doubt what they saw. There are those who try to explain it away. They say it was caused by natural events. A new star, perhaps. One that burned so brightly that it rivaled the sun."

"And those who predicted it would happen, what became of them?"

"Eventually, the excitement of the event faded. Later, some proclaimed that the light was not a sign of the coming of the Son of God but, rather, an omen that predicted prosperity for those who believe in the old gods."

I smiled. How like the soothsayers who interpret every event as favorable in order to win influence with the wealthy and powerful. "I find it hard to believe that things could go on as they had. Not after something like that."

"Those who witnessed it say the world changed—at least for a time. I suppose their thoughts were filled with the wonder of it all, imagining that somewhere, in a faraway land, a child had been born—God in mortal form. It gave people a sense of awe and reverence. Some, however, were afraid. What if this Son of God were an angry being? What if he punished the wicked and exacted revenge on those who cheated the widow and ground the faces of the poor? If he were a Son of God, who is to say that he wouldn't reign over the earth with blood and terror?

"Nevertheless, for a time my people walked as though they lived in a hallowed time. They were fair in business, kind to their families, considerate. But, like all such paradises, it didn't last. After a while, the sign was forgotten or 'explained' and gradually the people returned to their old ways, cheating their neighbors and seeking after money and power."

I didn't reply but sat attentively at her side, happy beyond measure that I had a few moments to look at her face, into her eyes; I could smell the perfume of her hair.

"It didn't take long before things were as they were before—it was as though nothing remarkable had happened at all. A few continued in their persistent talk of signs and the Son of God, of course, but for the rest of the world, life returned to what it had always been."

"What of those who predicted the light. Surely, they must have been revered as seers?"

She shrugged sadly. "I can't say. They live in a land to the north. They are ancient enemies of my people; we have little to do with them. They do not trust my people nor do we trust them. We have always been at war—an enmity that has lasted for centuries, beyond memory and beyond time. Our people will be at war again soon—my brother will see to that. It would take a miracle to change the hatred between our people. Though perhaps not even that would be enough."

My instincts were to dismiss the tale as an embellished story filled with half-truths. But the look in her eyes told me that this line of reasoning would only offend her and so I let the subject drop.

After a long silence, I asked if perhaps she would like to hear one of my stories.

"Yes, I would like that very much," she replied.

"Then I will tell you the favorite story of my youth, and my favorite story today. It is the tale of the great hero Aeneas."

"Another tale of your legendary Aeneas?"

I had already told her of his exploits at the burning ruins of Troy: how he carried his father out of danger; how he returned to seek his wife only to discover that the Greeks had slain her; how, despite the hatred and spite of Juno, his brave band made their way across desperate and turbulent waters until they had landed near the city of Carthage, the city of my birth.

"There, Aeneas first saw the beautiful Dido, queen of Carthage," I said. "It was their destiny to meet. Their fate to fall in love. And for a time, they lived in perfect bliss immersed in the smell of perfumed hair, the sound of the sweet words of poetry and affection, and the feel of tender caresses."

"Please tell me it ended that way," Xen said. "Tell me that they spent their days in the comfort of each other's arms. Tell me that they grew old and gray and that, when they were bent with age, they held hands and walked together long into the dusk and that, when they looked into each other's eyes, they did not see gray hair and wrinkled skin but that they appeared more beautiful to each other with every passing day."

"Must every story have a happy ending?"

"Oh, yes."

"But life is not about happy endings. It's about suffering, disappointment, and loss."

"If there is a choice in the matter, there must be a happy ending. Wouldn't you give everything you hope for, everything you possess, for a happy ending, Mal-Kuz?"

She rarely spoke my name, and I must confess that when she did, it made me happy beyond my ability to describe. It is a vain thing—something worthy of a young lad—to love the sound of your own name. I am embarrassed to admit how much joy I felt whenever the syllables passed her lips.

"It's only that life rarely ends that way."

"What of Aeneas and Dido? They were in love. Surely they had a happy ending."

The look in her eyes—how can I describe it? It was not merely hope. It was something more. A need.

I felt so strange in that moment. This woman who was so confident and fearless, this woman who could tame wild animals and face tyrants—there was a helplessness in her at that moment. A desperation. A childlike need for reassurance and comfort.

"Yes," I lied. "They lived in each other's arms, each day falling more in love. And in all the history of the world there never were two people of whom it could be better said that they lived happily and joyfully until the end of their days."

She looked up at me, a mist passing over her eyes.

And, for a moment, I felt such tenderness toward her that I wondered if it were possible for a man to be happier than I was at that moment.

But I had to put the thought out of my mind as quickly as it came.

This was impossible.

Inevitably, like Aeneas, I would leave my love and depart from this place, never to return again. Inevitably, my path led me far away from Xen and Kix-Kohor and everything else in this exotic land.

My destiny was set.

I was Aeneas. Destined to set foot on my ship and launch into the sea never to return, never to hold the only woman I had ever loved.

I could never have her.

There would be no happy ending. Not for me. That was not my destiny.

I was not destined for a happy ending.

I would leave her.

Though it would break my heart, I would leave her.

NOTES

The Tale of Na'Ma: This story is a synthesis of New World myths.

Aeneas and Dido: Aeneas, the ancestor of the Romans and the hero of Virgil's epic poem, *The Aeneid,* fell in love with Dido, queen of Carthage, but was forced by fate and the gods to abandon her so he could settle in Italy. Dido, overcome by grief, built her own funeral pyre and threw herself onto the flames (Virgil, *Aeneid,* book 4).

Chapter 17

The Book of Malchus, son of Mago, of the house of Hanno

It was at this time that Kix-Kohor began to insert himself once again into our lives and into our operation. At first, he pretended that he wanted to know more of our language—I assume he thought knowing Latin might be the path of knowing our secret—so we taught him such useful phrases as, "I wet the bed nightly," which we explained was Latin for "Hello," and "I have the face of a goat," which was how we said "Good-bye."

He learned those two phrases and delighted us endlessly with his enthusiastic self-proclamations. However, he soon tired of Latin and began a different, more direct approach.

He desperately wanted our secret, but this time, he attempted what he thought was a sincere approach. Flattery.

Our supply of tin was almost exhausted and, frankly, I didn't see a reason to withhold it from him any longer. "However," I said, "before you can learn the secret of bronze, you must be initiated in the order of metallurgy."

"That is what I want," he replied.

And so we set up an initiatory ceremony at the temple in full view of his people. Glaucus and I solemnly brought Kix-Kohor out in a thin, almost transparent nightshirt and began.

We told him to face north, south, east, and west and wave his arms. Then wiggle his head. Then his feet. And then his whole body.

We told him he had to pray to the god of the jaguar and, as everyone knows, to do it properly, one must get on his hands and knees and prowl about like a ferocious jaguar.

Then came the rat.

And then the crow.

And, of course, the monkey.

It was as he was imitating the sounds and gestures of a yellow-tailed lizard that the laughter of his people began to turn from stifled snickers to outright guffaws and Kix-Kohor finally came to a realization of what was happening. His face reddened, he shouted to his people to disperse, and then he invited his guards to escort Glaucus and me home.

This trick is numbered among the many things I have done in my life that, in retrospect, was undoubtedly a stupid thing to do. But at the time it was a temptation I could not resist. Glaucus and I laughed not only at the moment but a thousand, thousand times later as we described again how he tilted his head just so, how he shook his backside, how all who witnessed it began to smile, then snicker, and then laugh as they saw their leader as the fool he was.

It was a childish indulgence, but I still can't help but feel a certain happiness every time I think of it.

Kix-Kohor eventually appeared hours after the ceremony, still shaking with rage. We had humiliated him in front of his people, and he made it known to us in no uncertain terms that he would play our game no longer.

He held an obsidian blade at Glaucus' throat and demanded the secret. I gladly showed him, and even let him make a batch for himself to verify that what we said was true.

"Before you start feeling too confident, Kix"—it annoyed him to no end when I called him Kix and so I took advantage of doing it often—"you won't get very far without tin. It is the rarest of elements here. You wouldn't even know where to look for it. You'll never find it without us and that is why you still need us alive."

He took some of the metal and looked at it curiously. "I will find it," he said at last.

"If you could find it, you would have already," I said. "A word of advice. Before you kill us, try to find it yourself. If you are successful, then we are not necessary. You know all you need to make bronze yourself. You will be a wealthy and powerful man. But if you cannot find tin . . . then there is yet a reason for us to rely on each other."

Kix-Kohor hefted the metal in his hands. "You are wrong about that, Malchus. It is time for a new agreement. Obey me and you may purchase for yourself another day of life. I warn you not to test me. From this moment forward you are slaves. If you wish to live, you will come to understand that."

He gave instructions to his men to strip our room of anything that could be used as a weapon and doubled the guard. If we ever had a chance at escaping, that chance was gone.

And because of that realization, there was little need for Glaucus and me to talk. There was no reason to discuss what we both knew to be true. We had to escape, and soon. To delay would surely mean torture or death.

These thoughts were confirmed later that evening when Xen appeared, worried and frantic. "You must leave," she whispered. "Tonight."

"Tonight?"

"Tomorrow is a holy day. My brother will address the people and, at the end of the day, he will sacrifice you to the gods. You must leave tonight."

"How?" I nodded my head toward the guards.

"I don't know. But if you stay here, you will die."

"But how can I leave you?" I said.

She looked as though she had been struck for a moment. She closed her eyes and then opened them, the old bitterness pouring out of her. She spat out the words, "If you think I have any interest in a man such as you—a man who murdered my grandfather and my friends—you are a greater fool than I suspected. If you are so stupid that you fail to understand your circumstances, then I pity you. Stay and die, I care not."

And she left. I was too stunned to react. To speak. I simply watched her walk away and leave us to our bloody fate.

I looked at Glaucus and he at me.

I opened my mouth but could not form words. It seemed as though something should be said—that we should make plans, that we should spring to action—but I could think of nothing except Xen's final words. I could see nothing but the hatred in her eyes. I could hear nothing but the bite in her voice.

Glaucus and I sat together as the darkness enfolded us, the only sounds coming from the shifting of the guards and their whispering voices.

Silence and darkness and time.

An hour must have passed before I heard Glaucus speak.

"Maybe I'm being sensitive," he said, "but I think it's time for us to leave."

Chapter 18

The Book of Malchus, son of Mago, of the house of Hanno

They called it the time of tents—a strange affair where families abandoned their homes and came together in a large, open area where they erected lean-tos made of sticks, bramble, cloth, and large leaves. Each of these "tents" faced toward where Kix-Kohor stood on the steps of the temple so he could be seen as he addressed his people. I could not imagine the reason behind this ceremony but assumed that, given that it was an annual event, its roots were either religious or political.

I still reeled from Xen's biting words. So she still hated me, still despised me. And, on top of that, we were about to be murdered at the hands of a psychopath. That Kix-Kohor would kill us in an instant, I had no doubt. He had to save face in front of his people.

We did not know how much time we had before the guards would take us to our executions, but we knew each second brought us closer to death.

We could not see a way to escape by stealth, so Glaucus and I had resigned ourselves to the unpleasant reality that we would have to overwhelm the guards—without weapons. It was either that or die.

So we waited for the moment when our chances were at their highest. And we waited and waited. And then fate once again took me by the throat and thrust me into an unforeseen path.

Fate sent me a demon.

He was tall, this demon. Although bald at the crown of his head, hair cascaded from the sides down past his shoulders in tangled masses. Every visible part of his skin—chest, back, arms, neck, and face—was covered in what appeared to be permanent, detailed black and red paint. Images of weapons, slaughter, terror. Eyes bulging from lifeless sockets. Beasts of unimaginable shape. Headless humans. Monstrous shapes. Terrible and dark.

The creature's teeth were filed to points and his lips were stained with blood. His eyes were yellow and dark. In one hand, he carried a club. An obsidian knife hung from his waist.

The demon approached, and I backed away.

"You. Come," the demon said.

It did not appear to be an invitation for dialogue. I continued to back away, looking for something that I could use to defend myself, but Kix-Kohor had stripped us of anything we could use as a weapon.

Glaucus picked up a stone and balanced it in his hand.

The demon opened his mouth in a hellish grin and laughed. As he laughed, six other demons entered the room, each of them armed with a club and a dagger.

Glaucus looked at me and shook his head.

"What? You can't possibly think this is my fault."

"We waited too long."

But that argument was pointless. We had to focus on escape, and I told him that.

The seven men advanced slowly.

"For the record," I said, "I want it known that I have never seen these . . . men in my life."

"They're not friends of mine either," Glaucus replied.

The lead demon motioned for his men to stop. Then he held up a leaf in front of his face. "As a leaf is to the forest," he said, letting the leaf drop in a lazy swing to the ground, "Kix-Kohor is to this land."

"I have absolutely no idea what he is talking about," Glaucus whispered in Latin.

"Quiet," I answered.

"I am a servant of the exalted leader Ch'ul-B'alam, who will one day rule this land and all who inhabit it. Before him, Kix-Kohor is an insect. A maggot."

I turned to Glaucus. "We're not dead, yet, so I suspect an offer is coming."

The demon smiled a broad grin and held his hands out to his sides. "The exalted Ch'ul-B'alam has learned of your skill and sorcery. Most fortunate of days, he has smiled upon you and invites you to join with him and partake of his glory."

"Sounds reasonable to me," Glaucus whispered.

"You will come with us now. You will join us. Ch'ul-B'alam, one of the Immortals, will soon rule this world. Wealth and power you cannot imagine will be yours. Your name will be forever remembered. Anything you desire shall be yours. When you die, you will ascend to the highest heaven and be worshipped throughout time."

"Tempting," Glaucus whispered in Latin.

"Any ideas?" I asked.

"There's only one part of the proposal I'm not completely clear on."

"How to make bronze without tin?" I asked.

"That's the part."

"Now would be the time for any ideas. Anything at all."

"I have nothing."

The demon, unable to understand us, looked back at his fellow minions and gripped the hilt of his club. As his muscles tightened, I realized that if we did not accept his offer, he would spill our blood. There were seven of them against Glaucus and me. They were heavily armed; there was little chance we would survive.

I turned to the demon. "We will accompany you."

"Of course we will," Glaucus said.

"Hurry," the demon grunted.

Where were Kix-Kohor's guards? How had these demons entered the village without being seen?

If we went with these men, we would disappear into the forest never to return. Xen!

I would never see her again.

But in my heart I knew it was only a matter of time before I left her forever anyway. What difference did it make if I left now or in a week's time?

What was I thinking? Was I insane? What would happen when we arrived at the exalted one's camp without tin? What excuse could we give for our inability to produce more bronze?

Suicide.

Why could not circumstances simply work in our favor? Why had we not slipped into the night and made our way peacefully to the ships? Why were the Fates so determined to play with us?

"Come. Now," the demon commanded.

"Do we fight here?" Glaucus asked.

We could not survive a fight with these demons.

"I have an idea," I said.

"I trust it's one that doesn't end with us as corpses," he muttered.

I raised myself up to my full height, picked up a bronze helm, and took a step toward the demon. "You ask me to work my magic. You ask me to make your leader immortal. I have it within my power to do so, but only if I have the instruments of my magic."

For the first time, the demon looked confused. "No time."

"Can a sailor cross the water without a ship? Can the musician play his song without a pipe?"

The demon paused and looked at his fellows. The look on his face suggested that what he really wanted to do was simply murder us right there. But he ordered his men to put away their weapons and agreed to carry whatever we needed.

Glaucus and I began loading our supplies into packs and bags.

"Load them up as much as you can. Make it heavy," I whispered.

"We don't need this," Glaucus said, stuffing several odd-shaped rocks into leather sacks.

"They don't know that."

Each bag we packed, we gave to one of the men until all seven of them were loaded down.

"You!" the demon hissed. "You must carry!"

"And offend the fragile void of ethereal smithing?" I said incredulously. "Put even one tool on our backs and the magic will leave us! We cannot carry these tools or even be near them unless it is during the mystery of holy transformation. To do otherwise would offend the powers of sorcery and would weaken our ability to call upon the source of power."

The demon did not believe me; I could sense it. But he allowed himself and his men to be strapped with the heavy weights of our supplies.

"Remember this," he said. "At the moment I discover you have lied, I will have your head."

I bowed and motioned to the demon to lead the way.

As soon as we stepped out into the sunlight, I discovered why Kix-Kohor's spies had not intervened. Four of them lay dead outside our workplace—two of them bleeding from the chest and back, the other two bleeding from the throat.

I could hear the distant sound of people chanting. Kix-Kohor must be leading them in some sort of ceremonial ritual. In truth, I rejoiced that we would leave this village behind. But Xen . . . To think that I would not have an opportunity to see her one last time, to explain why I must leave. To look into her eyes yet one more time.

But that opportunity had been stripped from me by the demon and his men.

"Hurry!" the demon shouted as he led us deep into the forest.

I was amazed at how quickly they could move, even weighted down as heavily as they were. Even so, it was difficult to keep up with them. For the first hour, they seemed to have limitless energy, and I wondered if indeed there was something of the demonic in them to give them such strength.

After an hour, however, their legs eventually tired and their breathing became heavy. Sweat poured from their skin and they began to thirst for water.

I gradually slowed and motioned to Glaucus to do the same.

This was it. Life and death hung in the balance.

Everything depended on timing. And a little luck.

Before they could rest and regain their strength, we had to seize the moment and escape. Slowly, they pulled ahead and, as they turned a corner, I nodded to Glaucus, who rolled his eyes and shook his head.

"At times like this, I'm glad of one thing," he whispered.

"What's that?"

"I'm faster than you."

NOTES

Time of Tents: Annual pilgrimage rites were widespread in many ancient cultures. The "Time of Tents" is an allusion to such a ritual and is related to the Book of Mormon descriptions of the Feast of Tabernacles in Mosiah 16 (see J. Tvedtnes, "King Benjamin and the Feast of Tabernacles," in *By Study and Also by Faith.* 2 vols. [Salt Lake City: Deseret Book and FARMS, 1990], 2:197–237).

"Demon" arms and armor: Numerous Mayan reliefs and depictions of warriors show strange weapons, animal skins, helmets, and decorations depicting mythical ideas and creatures. For numerous examples, see L. Schele, M. Miller, and J. Kerr, *The Blood of Kings* (1992).

Ch'ul-B'alam: The name is Mayan for "Holy Jaguar." Mayan royalty are often associated with jaguars in names and mythic qualities. See S. Martin and N. Grube, *Chronicle of the Maya Kings and Queens* (2000), for examples and illustrations.

Chapter 19

The Book of Malchus, son of Mago, of the house of Hanno

The problem with running in a forest is that it's extremely difficult to keep your bearings. And, although we sprinted as fast as we could, it was hard to know exactly where we were sprinting to.

What helped were the screams from behind. Blood-curdling screams. And I could imagine the demons discovering our treachery, their faces burning with rage, blood in their eyes.

"If you have ever run before, run now," I told Glaucus.

"I hope you know that if you fall behind," he replied, "I won't know it until I reach the ship."

"Wouldn't expect anything less," I said as I sprinted past him into the deep forest.

There was no point in attempting to cover our tracks. We could hear the demons' shouting behind us. They were in close pursuit, and our only hope was that we had fresher legs and, theoretically, could make sufficient ground before they caught us.

It seemed for a time that the demons would overtake us. But eventually, their shouts grew faint, and Glaucus and I, for the first time since our capture, began to hope that we could make our escape.

That was, until we got lost.

"How could you not know where we are?" Glaucus' exasperated voice broke the silence.

"May I point out that there are two of us who came this way?"

"It was your plan."

"No time for debate; the demons will be here soon."

"Forgive me for questioning your strategy of running in circles," Glaucus spat and faced to the left. "I think this is the way."

"No. Here."

"And because you're the captain, we go the way you say?"

I didn't wait for a response but sprinted off in the direction I hoped would lead us to a familiar landmark. Glaucus would follow; I knew that for a certainty. Even if it meant we were heading to our deaths.

We had come this far and had endured this much; certainly the Fates would not be so cruel as to end our lives. Not now. Not after all we had endured.

I had within me an inexplicable sense of destiny. A sense that I was meant to find the ship. That I was meant to make the return voyage. That I was meant to tell the tale of our strange adventure.

More than that, I believed that I was meant to be as wealthy as a king and live the life of a respected nobleman—perhaps even that of a senator of Rome.

But all that depended on us reaching our ship before the demons reached us. Nothing looked familiar. The trees and leaves surrounded us to the point where it was impossible to see anything but what was directly in front of us.

"I have a bad feeling about this," Glaucus panted.

"Don't fall behind."

We heard the demons again, their voices giving me a point that I could steer away from. As long as I could hear them, my fears of doubling back and encountering them lessened. However, my confidence in my instincts to find the ship were fading quickly.

Perhaps Glaucus had been right. Perhaps, with every step, we were heading away from the ship and toward some new danger. Toward a new Kix-Kohor. New demons. Some new tyrant by the name of Ch'ul-B'alam.

Danger was everywhere in this place. It was too deadly of a place for me. Too wild and unpredictable. If only I could find the ship, I swore that I would retire in some peaceful country villa and never depart.

Let the barbarians, traders, and thieves split the rest of the world between themselves. Let them kill each other and spill their blood to their gods and their greed. What I wanted more than anything else were quiet and servants and food and never having to face danger again.

I had had enough for one lifetime. It was time to retire.

But we were forever moving in an unknown direction. Where was my ship? Where were my men? Why could I not find a landmark or even a trail?

In truth, there was little time to look. I had to focus every thought on finding a path through the vegetation and not tripping and breaking a leg in the process.

Just as I was beginning to abandon hope that we would ever find our way out of our predicament, I heard shouting.

But it was not the demons hot on our heels; it was something else.

Faintly, through the distance, one voice shouted more clearly than the rest.

I looked at Glaucus and he groaned.

Together we said the words, "Kix-Kohor."

So we had been heading in the right direction. We had to be nearing the village. We had to be on the right track.

But then, Glaucus voiced the thought I had not wanted to admit to myself.

"Looks like now we'll be running from both."

He was right.

Demons and Kix-Kohor. And no matter which of them found us, it was surely death. Kix-Kohor undoubtedly assumed that we had killed the guards and escaped. Without a doubt, he had assembled a small army and was in pursuit. And their legs would be fresher than ours.

There was nothing to do but trust in Fate and run until we could run no farther.

We arrived in a small clearing and caught a glimpse of the mountain peak that marked the entrance to the ceremonial cave where our strange adventure in this new land had begun.

"I told you I knew where I was going."

"Yes," replied Glaucus. "But don't you think Kix-Kohor is heading there as well? To the place where we first met?"

He had a point, but that was the way to our ships.

"All the more reason to pick up the pace," I said and pushed on in the direction of the caves.

But the demons seemed to be gaining ground. Not far behind them, we could hear the shouts of Kix-Kohor and his men.

It was now a three-way race. Glaucus and I knew that our choice was between pushing ourselves beyond the point of exhaustion or being beheaded by the demons or Kix-Kohor, depending on who reached us first.

Our months of being confined in a small space producing bronze had not increased our stamina, and I could feel my energy dwindling fast. Every step drew what little breath I had from me. Every time my feet hit the ground, deep pain stabbed into my sides. My legs felt weak and scarcely able to hold up my weight.

I looked at Glaucus and discovered that he was faring little better.

But we were getting closer now. And if we could simply push through the final steps, we could be clear of this land and forever away.

"You told the men to be ready?" I said between breaths.

"At a moment's notice," he grunted.

We ran.

But the shouts behind us were growing louder.

We were losing ground.

We could not die here. We could not allow them to reach us. Not when we were so close. Not when escape seemed so very possible.

A voice shouted from behind us, and I looked back to see distant figures moving in our direction. They had spotted us.

I could not tell if the voice belonged to a demon or to one of Kix-Kohor's men, but it did not matter. Either option meant death.

"Run!" I shouted to Glaucus.

But neither one of us could move faster than a trot.

Glaucus stumbled and fell to his knees.

"I can't make it." His breath wheezed as though from a bellows riddled with holes. "You have to go on."

"And give you more to complain about?"

"I can't." His eyes were filled with fear and resignation. "Tell my father that I love him."

"Tell him yourself," I said as I picked him up and put my arm around his shoulder.

"I can't."

"I can understand why you want to kill yourself," I said as we began moving forward. "And I can certainly understand why you want to kill me." As we leaned on each other, the pain in my side seemed to diminish slightly, and new energy began to pulse through my legs. We crested a small hill and looked below us at the most beautiful sight I had ever seen. My two ships were resting quietly, anchored in the middle of the harbor. And my men were milling about, preparing dinner.

"What I can't understand," I whispered to Glaucus, "is why you would want to murder your shipmates because there they are and if we are caught and killed, they will be too."

If I shouted to warn my men of our coming, those behind us would hear my voice. Without a doubt, they would pick up their pace. But I had no choice; it was our only hope.

"Longinus! Sempis! Hurry!" I shouted at the top of my voice. "No time to delay!"

The men, astounded at our presence, heard the urgency in my voice and instantly flew into activity. They hurriedly threw things into a raft and prepared to push it into the water.

As I had anticipated, a triumphant shout sounded behind us.

We stumbled down the incline and into the clearing by the beach. Bless my men for their diligence; everything was at the ready for a quick departure. My men rushed toward us and helped us clear the final distance to the raft.

From behind, the demons came shouting as though suffering the pains of hell.

We pushed the raft into the waves, and my men began to apply their backs to the oars as the demons emerged from the forest.

Surprisingly, they did not turn their bows on us but, instead, turned their backs to us and prepared to face the new threat—Kix-Kohor and his men.

To this day I do not know what happened when the two groups met, for I was in my ship and, having lifted anchor and setting sail, we pushed out into the ocean. I focused on putting every ounce of wind into my sails in order to get us farther away from that dangerous land and that barbaric people.

I heard the war shouts behind me. Death yells. I could see bodies fall. But the end result of the fight I did not know, nor did I care. It mattered nothing to me if any of them survived.

The one thing that consumed my every effort was putting distance between me and the danger behind me.

At last, we were far enough away that it was impossible for any weapon to reach us. They could not pursue us.

Against all odds, we had made it! We had escaped.

Like Aeneas, I stood at the prow of my ship, the sails filling with wind as we launched once again into the great ocean before us.

Gradually, my thoughts turned to the task at hand—crossing that immense Oceanus. Would there be winds? Consuming beasts? Would the gods prevent our passage? Or were we destined to return safely with a cargo of precious jewels in our hold?

If only we could arrive once again to the safety of Rome, I promised that I would find a peaceful villa and retire to a life of ease and never think of the ocean again.

I had escaped the barbarians.

I had lived to face new dangers and new adventures.

I was Aeneas. I would live to see another day.

Chapter 20

In the plaza that widened before the Basilica Fausti, a solemn Bishop Aurelius stood before the crowd that had followed him from the temple of Caelestia.

As news spread of what had happened at the pagan temple, spectacle-seeking citizens abandoned their homes and attached themselves to the throng as Aurelius moved toward the population center of Carthage.

Before him in the plaza, a mound of manuscripts heaped waist-high fluttered in the warm desert breeze. The bishop carried a torch in his right hand, and he lifted his head toward heaven, a beatific smile on his face.

"This day," he shouted in a voice that penetrated the murmur of the crowd, "is one that will not be forgotten. A day of awakening. Of repentance!"

As he finished each sentence, responsive whispers tumbled from the crowd in waves like dry leaves stirred by a directing wind.

Never forget.

Awake.

Repent.

"Let this day be the day we choose once and for all. We will follow the path of rectitude."

Follow.

"Shall we tread the path of superstition, sin, and darkness? Or shall we turn once and for all from the evil of unholy men and embrace the light?"

Light.

"You have heard how blasphemers have thrown down the walls of Rome and defiled the City of God. Some have said that this is the wrath of Jupiter. This is a lie."

Lie—it is a lie!

"Jupiter, Juno, and every other ghost of false religion are fallen demons overthrown by Christ. You have as much to fear from these stone pillars you see before you as you do from pagan gods. The world emerges from the night of centuries of superstition and darkness into the light of a new dawn."

Dawn. A new dawn!

"Our only hope is to turn once and for all from the childishness of superstition and embrace the knowledge of the one and true church."

Aurelius lowered his hands and gestured to his sides at the mound of manuscripts, books, and sheets of parchments and papyrus splayed out before him.

"Will the very demons of Gehenna flourish unchecked amongst us?"

No!

"Shall we not stand for truth?"

Truth!

"Purge your lives! Purge this city of all uncleanness! Destroy the influence of old superstition! Let the light of a new age put to torch every earthly remnant of the fiery pit!"

A thunderous shout arose from the mass of people that surrounded him. Carpenters and cooks, laborers and lawyers raised their voices in a shrill howl that resounded through the streets of Carthage.

"Burn them all!"

Among those in the plaza stood Gunderic, the servant of Lucius the philosopher and sage. "Will he truly burn them?" Gunderic asked to no one in particular.

"With a certainty," a grizzled man standing next to him said.

"Galen, Virgil, Cicero?"

"Evil."

"Knowledge is evil?"

Aurelius, thriving on the theater of the moment, looked from face to face, a tender expression suffusing his features. Compassionate and warm, his voice was more of an embrace than a command. "I call upon you now. Scour your homes, your neighborhoods, your city. Tear down every image of false religion. Bring here every scrap of parchment stained with words of sin and superstition. Anything that carries with it the pollution of that pagan religion."

"Burn them!"

Aurelius slowly lowered the torch until it kissed the piles of parchment. Slowly and elegantly, the fire licked the pages, teasing them with flame before grasping and hungrily devouring the texts.

"Feed this purifying flame!" Aurelius shouted. "Run to your homes! To the libraries! To the schools! Let us build up a flame that will be visible to Rome itself!"

As though the command had unleashed them, hundreds of Carthaginians scattered to do as they had been admonished.

Gunderic, however, remained silent, his lips tight.

"Better to say nothing than to burn with Cicero," the grizzled man said, pointing to the bonfire.

"Can this go unchallenged?"

"If you have a family, think of them."

As the flames leapt higher, Aurelius moved from person to person, taking one listener by the shoulder, another by the neck. "I tell you this day," Aurelius said, "we make a stand for the one true God! The light of this fire will ascend to heaven! Let Rome itself take notice of what we do!

For this is what our Lord meant when He said, 'I came not to send peace, but a sword.' Brother against brother. Son against father."

The heat from the fire pushed away those who had nestled too close as tomes, scrolls, and scraps of parchment fell from eager hands into the gaping jaws of ravenous flame.

"This day, we fulfill that command. Shall we allow sin to inhabit this city?"

"No!"

"We will raise the cry of cleansing so loud and so clear that the entire world cannot fail to hear. Will we permit iniquity to pollute the body?"

"No!"

"What shall we do with them?"

"Put them to the flame!" the mob began shouting. "Burn the impure! The heretics! Burn them all!"

Aurelius, orange light glowing across his face, continued, "Pagan, impure! Jew, impure! Donatist, Gnostic, and Arian—all impure!"

"Burn them!"

They put our city—your very lives and the lives of your children—at risk. We have but one hope of protection from suffering the same fate as Rome. Purification!"

"Purification!"

"What good is salt that has lost its taste? It is good for nothing but to be cast out and trampled."

"Destroy the heretics!"

"Will we, who have been called by the Lamb of God, not be obedient to His command?"

"We will obey!"

"Repent! Purify your homes! Your hearts! Shall we not make Carthage a shrine of the faithful? Shall we not offer unto our God a people wherein no evil dwells?"

More books and manuscripts flew from outstretched hands and

skipped across the flames, sparking ash and fire until they, too, submerged into the expanding flood of consuming fire.

"Behold the power of truth!" Aurelius proclaimed joyfully. "The evil one cannot abide the strength of the righteous!"

Gunderic shook off the restraining hand of the old man and moved toward the priest.

"Don't be a fool," the man said, but Gunderic gave him no heed.

"You say Christ came to bring the sword?" Gunderic shouted.

But only a few heard him. Every eye was on the bishop who, immersed in a state of ecstasy, moved among the crowd, blessing people with his hands and taking them in his embrace. "The righteous shall tread underfoot all who are evil."

"What are you calling evil?" Gunderic shouted, pulling a scroll from the hands of a wild-eyed woman and another that had fallen short of the flames. "Are you all possessed of madness?" He pushed through the throng, snatching manuscripts from hands and cradling them to his chest. "Do you know what you are destroying?"

Like a man drunk from wine, the attention of the crowd began to slowly focus on the cause of disruption.

"Here is Plutarch!" Gunderic lifted a tome above his head. "Do you know what you destroy when you feed this to the flames?"

"Heresy!"

"You destroy Alexander, Lycurgus, Pericles!"

"Heathens!"

Gunderic lifted up another scroll. "Here is Livy. Do you realize that you put to the torch the history of your ancestors when you burn this?"

"Feed them to the flames!"

"Here is Tacitus. Pliny. Galen. Destroy these and you destroy your heritage. Your blood."

"They are impure!"

"To the flames!"

"You claim that Christ came to bring a sword. How little you understand the scriptures."

This, at last, caught Aurelius' attention. He turned imperiously toward the slave, anger in his eyes. Then gradually, he pushed his anger away, giving place to that look of compassion he had worked so long and assiduously to perfect.

"Burn him!" the mob shouted.

But the bishop smiled and gestured for silence. "You deny, then," he said to Gunderic, a glint of victory in his voice, "that the Savior said those words?"

The mob, smelling blood and eager to experience it, quieted. They formed a circle around the two, pushing them ever closer together.

"How little you understand," Gunderic said. There did not seem to be fear in his voice. He stood not defiant, but calm; not belligerent, but composed. "The sword will come," Gunderic said, "but not because of those who follow Christ. The powers of this world have always been at conflict with the saints of God. It is evil that will raise the sword against the peaceable followers of the Way."

Aurelius looked at Gunderic carefully, like someone trying to place a face. "I know you," he said at last. "You are Lucius' slave, are you not?"

"He is! It is Gunderic!" a voice from the mob called out.

Aurelius smiled at the crowd before returning his attention to Gunderic. "You call yourself Christian?"

"I do."

Aurelius nodded. "Tell us in your own words who Jesus Christ is."

"He is the Savior of all mankind. The Son of God. He lived a sinless life and provided Himself a sacrifice for sin."

"Is he the Father?"

"He is the Son."

Aurelius raised his eyebrows. "I ask again—and please take care of how you answer—is Jesus Christ the Father?"

"He is the Only Begotten of the Father."

Aurelius' lips spread in a triumphant smile. "I invite all here to listen carefully to this slave's words. Answer me directly, Gunderic, is Jesus Christ the same substance and essence as God the Father?"

Gunderic did not respond.

"He is Arian!" Aurelius shouted. "Heretic!"

Gunderic looked about at the growing rabble. "Tell me this. Who is it that argued so persuasively for this doctrine of three gods in one?"

Aurelius, sure of himself now, motioned for the crowd to quiet. "Many—not the least of which is the holy Bishop Athanasius."

"Yes, Athanasius. Do you not know of the years he spent in Egypt?"

"What of it?" Aurelius said, a hint of irritation in his voice.

"As a youth, I lived in Alexandria," Gunderic responded. "There, I heard of the Egyptian religion, how they claimed that the gods Isis, Horus, and Set were not three, but one and the same. But that was only the beginning. Amum, Ma'at, Khonso—these three are also one in Egyptian lore. Atum, Shu, Tefnut, Mahet—"

Color reddened Aurelius' cheeks as he interrupted. "Am I to understand that you equate the sacred doctrine of the Christian trinity with that of pagan Egypt?"

"You argue among yourselves about the nature of God, and you ask me, a slave, to instruct you?"

The bishop shook his head. "Dissension is heresy. The great Emperor Constantine presided over a council that established this once and for all."

"Yes. Constantine decided the issue. A Roman who was not even baptized."

"He was the servant of God and His instrument. He was established by God to bring the Church to the world. How little you know of the emperor. Do you not know that he was baptized a Christian before his death?"

"I know that he was baptized," Gunderic replied. "He was baptized by an Arian bishop, Eusebius."

A murmur rose from the crowd, and Aurelius' eyes darted from side to side. "Answer the question!" the bishop roared. "I adjure you on penalty of death. Are Jesus Christ and God the Father and the Holy Spirit consubstantial? Or are they separate beings?"

Gunderic looked at the flames and then at the fire raging in the eyes of the bishop of Carthage.

"Jesus was the Son of God, else to whom did He pray?" he said. "He addressed His Father in sermon and in prayer. On the cross He prayed to His Father, 'Why hast thou forsaken me?' If they are the same person, how could the Father forsake the Son? At His baptism, the voice of the Father sounded from heaven and the Holy Ghost appeared—the three of them present and separate all at one moment. Tell me then, how can they each be present in different form and yet be the same being?"

"You speak blasphemy," Aurelius shouted. "Be careful what you say or your end will be the same as the wicked who will be cleansed from the earth by fire at the last day."

Gunderic spoke to the crowd that surrounded the flames. "He speaks of that day when the Lord will return. But does he know when that day is? Do you know?"

"No man knows the day of his coming," Aurelius said.

"You speak well. The angels of heaven do not know. Jesus claimed that He Himself did not know—only the Father. If the Son does not know the hour of His coming, but only the Father, how can they be one and the same?"

"This man is speaking nothing new." Aurelius stabbed his hand as though he were carrying a sword and impaling the slave as he spoke. "Like an erratic wind, he cannot stay on one subject but flits about from topic to topic."

The redness in Aurelius' cheeks flared briefly and then diminished as a serene look came over him, replacing the scowl. He turned to the audience that surrounded him. "You have witnessed for yourselves. This slave is an Arian heretic. No better than the accursed Donatists—no better than the pagans, the Jews. Heretics are the reason Rome is fallen! And shall we allow this iniquity to endanger our own Carthage? Shall we allow this evil to walk uncontested among us? Shall we not prove our worthiness as disciples of the one true God and purge this evil from our midst?"

Burn him!

Burn the heretic!

And as the flames of the fire rose, so rose the passionate cries from those who surrounded the two central figures—the esteemed Bishop Aurelius, and Gunderic, the slave of the pagan philosopher Lucius Fidelis Crescentius.

NOTES

Basilica Fausti: Now called the Damous el-Karita, the Basilica Fausti was one of the main basilicas by the central square of Carthage.

Pagan gods as demons: Many early Christians believed that the pagan gods were demons who had deceived mankind into following them in place of God (see Deuteronomy 32:17; Psalm 106:37; 1 Corinthians 10:20–21; Revelation 9:20). Part of the Christian consecration rituals for converting a pagan temple into a Christian church was the exorcism of the demon-gods who inhabited the temple. (A. Kofsky, *Eusebius of Caesarea Against Paganism* [2002].)

Christian book burning: Early Christians had an ambivalent attitude about the value of classical culture. Some saw great value in the philosophy and literature of the pagans. Many others, however, viewed classical literature as fundamentally evil, leading people to apostasy and sin, and sought to destroy classical learning. Despite the latter view, many great books of antiquity were preserved by medieval Christian copyists.

Plutarch, Tacitus, and Pliny: Plutarch, Tacitus, and Pliny were all famous classical authors. Plutarch (d. A.D. 120), a Greek priest of Delphi, was a widely revered historian and moral philosopher, author of the *Parallel Lives,* and a large collection of philosophical essays called the *Moralia.* Plutarch also wrote about Alexander, Lycurgus, Pericles, and other historical figures. Tacitus (d. A.D. 117) is often regarded as the greatest Roman historian, and Pliny (who died in A.D. 79 from toxic fumes while observing the eruption of Mount Vesuvius) was a renowned Roman scientist and natural philosopher.

Followers of the Way: In Acts, early Christians consistently called themselves "followers of the Way" (Acts 9:2; 16:17; 18:25; 19:9, 23; 24:14, 22), meaning the "Way of the Lord," and Jesus as the "way, the truth and the life" (John 14:4).

Arian Christology: Arius (A.D. 250–336) was a Christian priest in Alexandria who argued that the Father and Son were not consubstantial (of the same essence, substance, or "being") or co-eternal. His teachings were condemned at the Council of Nicaea in A.D. 325 (in the famous Nicene Creed), he was banished, and his books were burned. Many Germanic tribes, such as the Goths, were converted to Arianism, which survived in North Africa, Spain, and Italy through the seventh century. (R. Hanson, *The Search for the Christian Doctrine of God: The Arian Controversy, 318–81* [1988]; R. Williams, *Arius: Heresy and Tradition,* rev. ed. [2001].)

Egyptian Triune gods: Many Egyptians believed in various forms of consubstantiality among the gods and between gods and kings. Egyptians also worshipped a Father-Mother-Son trinity of Osiris, Isis, and Horus (E. Hornung, *Conceptions of God in Ancient Egypt: The One and the Many* [1996]).

Constantine's deathbed baptism: Constantine, who ruled from A.D. 306 to 337, became a Christian by at least 312, but wasn't baptized until on his deathbed. He probably waited, not because of a lack of belief in Christianity, but because he wanted to be cleansed of his many sins—including murder—before dying (Eusebius, *Life of Constantine,* 4.62).

Eusebius of Nicomedia the Arian: Gunderic refers to Eusebius, the Arian bishop of Nicomedia (d. 341), not Eusebius of Caesarea (d. 339), who was Constantine's councillor and biographer.

Consubstantial: A key concept of the Nicene Creed, the Latin translation of the Greek word *homoousios* means that the Father and Son are of one substance of essence. The idea is that Christ is of the same divine "essence" as the Father, just like all humans share the same human "essence." It is a complicated doctrine that has been widely misunderstood throughout Christian history (L. Aryes, *Nicaea and Its Legacy* [2006]; R. MacMullen, *Voting About God in the Early Church* [2006]).

Chapter 21

The Book of Malchus, son of Mago, of the house of Hanno

Of the return voyage I will write but little. Two weeks after setting sail, we discovered a slow leak in our second ship and were forced to salvage all we could of her cargo before abandoning it to the depths of the ocean. This was a relief, actually, because we scarcely had enough men to pilot one ship, let alone two, even if it meant we were now gambling our lives on the integrity of the *Morning Star.*

The weather was surprisingly calm during the long journey home and, with the help of a strong current and a steady northeast wind, we made consistent if slow progress across that seemingly infinite body of water. Even though we had made the journey before, fear and despair blackened our days and saturated our nights. Each member of my little band fought a nearly impossible battle to banish that baleful word *lost* from mind and heart.

During the return, Glaucus expressed an interest in learning to pilot the ship, and I gladly taught him the secrets of guiding a ship by the stars, wind, and currents. We kept a detailed record of our course—for history's sake—knowing that few would believe our story of discovering a barbaric people in a faraway land. The voyage stretched into days and weeks, and I was required to reduce our rations of food and water, although we were able to replenish these to some degree by rain and the occasional fish that we caught in our nets.

The day we at last sighted land was one of thanksgiving and blessed relief. Our greatest desire was to step once again onto our homeland and kiss the soil, but, in a twist of irony, we arrived near the coast of Lusitania, Audax's domain. And so we resisted the temptation to disembark and instead sailed to the south, ever looking over our shoulders expecting to see the sails of my erstwhile enemy's ships in close pursuit.

Once we had skirted the Iberian Peninsula and rounded the straits of Hercules—perhaps only then—I felt a degree of security that I had not felt in more than a year.

At Rome, we disembarked and found a ready market for our gems and exotic, brightly colored feathers, though we sold them slowly so as not to glut the market. The goods returned more in gold than I had expected—making all of us wealthy beyond our dreams.

With my portion, I fulfilled my promise and purchased a villa in a pleasant and sun-dappled valley to the north and east of Rome and settled into a pleasant routine of wandering through scented vineyards, attending quaint festivals, and offering oblations and sacrifices at the temple of Juno. Although I was not certain the gods had anything to do with our safe return, I did not want to tempt the Fates, particularly after evading death as many times as I had. And so I visited the temples frequently, sacrificing to Juno, Jove, Diana, and Mars and contributing to the support of the priests and priestesses.

Glaucus, ever at my side, purchased a villa close to mine, and we lived for a time in the quiet of the countryside, enjoying the rustic charm of bleating sheep and cackling hens.

I was not entirely inactive during this period. My greatest fear was that an assassin's dagger—courtesy of my old enemy Audax—would find me in the dead of night, ending my idyllic existence. It bothered me to the extent that I knew I had to learn of his fate. When my spies returned with the news that Audax had disappeared at sea more than a year earlier, and that another man sat on the throne—a rival and enemy of Audax's who had cleansed the world of Audax's sons, daughters, and even his distant relatives—it was only then that I breathed easy.

With the disappearance of that last and final threat, I settled in to spend the remainder of my days living the life of a nobleman, sampling delicacies made by my excellent Etruscan cook, and enjoying the taste of wines from as far away as Gaul and Greece.

Unhappily, it was a life I could not endure.

I think Glaucus and I discovered at about the same time that we were not suited for a life of indolence. After a few weeks of paradisiacal lounging, our conversation gradually turned toward the tin trade and the profits that could still be made transporting tin from Britannia to the far reaches of the empire. We even discussed from time to time—mostly when we were influenced by the spirit of the wine—returning to that strange new world, this time with a fleet of ships filled with tin. After converting that metal to bronze and trading it for gems, we could return to Rome as rich as Augustus himself.

But this was all pretense—at least on my part. If I am honest, I must say that the one thing that consumed my thoughts was Xen. During the day, I would notice a girl's hair that caught the light like hers. An upturned nose that almost approached the perfection of hers. And during the night I looked up at the stars and the moon wondering if she were looking at the same constellations and thinking of me.

But although my thoughts were consumed with her, I did not speak of her. Nevertheless, when I spoke to Glaucus of gems and exotic feathers and wealth beyond imagination, what I really meant was Xen, Xen, and Xen.

If I thought that absence from her would bring forgetfulness, I was terribly wrong. Her dimpled half-smile, her slender hands, her contagious laugh—these I saw everywhere. They saturated my dreams.

I ached for her.

It was insane. Because of my wealth and status as an eligible bachelor,

I had been deluged by local noblemen offering their daughters to me as a wife. But the more I saw of them—their painted personalities, dabbed faces, marble smiles, and self-absorbed conversation—the more I abhorred them and the more I thought of that genuine creature of tender eyes, spontaneous energy, easy laugh, and gentle heart.

It was absurd that I should think of her—a woman of a barbarian race—when I was surrounded by the flower of civilized Rome. But perhaps it is part of our nature that we desire most that which we cannot possess.

After six months of living amongst the crickets and barking dogs, however, Glaucus and I had reached our capacity to endure the comforts of civilized life, and we resolved to venture back into the world of adventure and risk as traders of tin.

And so, we began once again—each of us a captain of his own vessel—making the trip to Britannia, filling our hulls with that precious tin, and launching back into the ocean. I cannot explain it, but the feel of a heavy keel biting into deep water and a stiff wind rippling through canvas sails provided a purpose and happiness that I had desperately needed.

Because the tin trade was a profitable one, there was a great deal of competition. Every trader went to Rome, of course. And because of that, the price of tin in the capital city was a pittance compared to its value in the outlying regions of the empire. As a consequence, Glaucus and I decided on a riskier course. We decided to take our cargo far to the east of Rome, to one of the far provinces of the empire yet still accessible on the eastern reaches of the Mediterranean. In those far provinces, tin was scarce and, therefore, in high demand.

And so we made our way to one of the ever-troublesome outposts of the empire, a desert region known for its endless rebellions: the province of Judea. The region was in desperate need of the metal due to the endless building of a great temple which had been started half a century earlier by the great builder Herod.

And so we sailed east into the Mediterranean Sea. It thrilled me to travel the very waters that Aeneas had sailed nine centuries earlier, but thoughts of Aeneas led me to thoughts of Dido and thoughts of Dido led me to thoughts of Xen. What had happened to her? Was she married? Alive?

Had her insane brother brought war and death to his people? Had Kix-Kohor survived the battle with the demons? Had Ch'ul-B'alam descended on the village and taken it as his?

These questions haunted me to the point that I had to force them out of my mind or else enter a state of madness. Yes, it was better to never think of her again—never to think of the maid with the deep eyes and the musical laugh. Never to allow the image of her face to enter my mind. Never to think of her name—that beautiful name, that melodic and soothing name.

Our journeys took us close to the port of Carthage, and as we continued into the Mediterranean and around the southern shore of Italy, we sailed past Crete and further east until the city of Tyre appeared on the horizon. Tyre, that ancient mother-city of the Phoenicians that had given birth to Dido, the founder of the city of Carthage.

Our destination, however, was further south. We were heading for the port of Caesarea, a relatively new destination built by the Jewish King Herod a few decades ago. He had built the harbor himself, creating an artificial but deep port protected by breakwaters. It was masterfully done and, as a result, it was the largest and safest port in the East, making it the new center of trade rivaling Alexandria itself. Caesarea had become an international city, inhabited and frequented by those of all nations—Egyptians, Greeks, Romans, Phoenicians, Persians, and Syrians.

The land as a whole was the home of a people who called themselves Jews—a strange and dogmatic group who, like every other nation Rome had conquered, had at one point considered themselves God's chosen people.

Unlike most other vassal states, however, in spite of more than a century of living under the enlightened rule of Rome, the Judeans still held to their antiquated religion and hung fast to the fantasy that God would yet lift them up above all nations—even over the Romans.

Perhaps the genius of the Roman Empire was that, once it had conquered a new land, it did not require the people to change their beliefs or even their forms of local government. All that was required was that the newly incorporated people remain loyal as vassals of Rome and that they collect and pay taxes to Rome. A small price to pay for the cultural and technological advances Rome brought with them in trade, architecture, water systems, engineering, roads, and security.

Time and again, history had verified that once a barbarian nation knelt before the eagles of a Roman commander—on that day, the nation began its road toward prosperity and civilization. In place of hovels and filth, cities emerged—well-ordered, sanitary, and comfortable cities. Fire pits gave way to amphitheaters where culture and cathartic discovery filled minds and enlarged souls. Filthy water gave way to clean, public baths. And societal chaos and villainy gave way to the rule of law.

Only a delusional, self-absorbed people who were caught up in the arrogance of misguided ethnocentricity would be so stubborn as to fight against it for so long. But such were the people of Judea.

It was a country whose national focus centered on a single building that stood at the heart of their ancient capital, Jerusalem. It was a temple to their one god—a god so small that he only cared about one minuscule pinprick in the great world.

It was hard to understand this god of the Jews. In some ways, he seemed similar to Jupiter, and these people had recorded accounts of his appearing to their ancestors. But what kind of god demands that people venerate him by circumcision and abstaining from pork? Perhaps most strange of all, the "Jupiter" of the Jews ordered the people to make no image of him.

The good news for Glaucus and myself, however, was that because this people were so myopically focused on rebuilding their temple, the demand for bronze was greater in this land than in nearly any other realm of the empire. They could not get enough. The Romans needed bronze for armor, weapons, statues, vases, and decorations. The Jews demanded an endless supply of it in order to fill their temple with precious vessels and furniture that would justify their own self-importance. They created objects of worship and ornamentation that would lift its reputation as one of the great temples in all the world. It was to help Roman and Jew (and to make a very healthy profit) that I had traveled to Caesarea with a cargo of precious tin.

Upon landing, we immediately found ourselves among several enthusiastic buyers, each outbidding the other for the contents of our ships. We had discovered a market that would make our tin trade extremely profitable, and I was determined to make decisions that favored long-term contracts over short-term profits.

In the end, we came to terms with a cordial man, Antilochus, a freed slave of the Roman procurator of that province, Pontius Pilate. Pilate had been selected by Emperor Tiberius himself to travel from Italy to Judea and oversee an army of three thousand men, maintain order, and collect taxes for the empire.

By the time of our arrival, Pilate had been in place only half a dozen years, but he had already alienated much of the local populace. His first mistake had been marching into Jerusalem at night with Roman standards, upon which hung bronze images of Tiberius. An innocent enough mistake. How was Pilate to know of the Jews' aversion to images of other "gods"? How was he to know that the Jews considered the images of Tiberius to be images of a foreign god?

It was, of course, a technicality. The previous two emperors—Julius Caesar and Augustus—both had been proclaimed immortal and divine, and it was assumed that the emperors who followed them would be equally imbued with the divine essence of the immortals of Olympus.

The Jews took offense at Pilate's brazen act of bringing images of Tiberius near their sacred temple. Vast numbers of Jews marched to Caesarea, gathering around the Procurator's palace and demanding that the images be withdrawn. When the Jews refused to leave, Pilate ordered a cohort of soldiers to advance upon them, threatening them with death if they did not disperse. In response, the Jews knelt, pulled open their robes to expose their necks, and shouted that they would rather die than permit the violation of their ancestral laws.

Such was the nature of the people Pilate was trying to govern.

Pilate eventually realized that this was not a battle worth fighting. He relented and removed the standards. After all, one of his greatest priorities was keeping the peace and, more importantly, keeping disgruntled gnats from traveling to Rome and annoying the imperial senate and the emperor. One of the surest ways for a procurator in a faraway land to forfeit his position was to have the serenity of Roman politicians disturbed by persistent and noisome complaints.

Tiberius, in particular, valued his privacy.

Pilate knew that the more out of sight he remained, the better for him. The longer he could retain his post, the greater the opportunity to skim his share of graft and taxes and the greater his chances that he could retire in comfort the remainder of his days.

The second mistake after the matter of the Roman standards—and the more grievous one—was the troublesome affair of the aqueduct.

Pilate's freed man explained these stories to me in endless detail. In short, the population of Jerusalem stood on the edge of a desert. Predictably, it had grown to the point where the number of thirsty throats had exceeded the city's capacity of water. At the same time, the purifications and cleansings at the temple created an ever-increasing demand for the precious liquid. During feast days, the city was flooded with Jews from near and far, and the need for water increased even more. For Pilate, the solution was simplicity itself. Rome had long since mastered the technology of building aqueducts—that wonder of the world that could transport water from miles away to a city center. He identified a source of water some twenty miles away to the south and began construction.

In his mind, bringing water to a city that had been experiencing constant scarcities would make him a national hero. He would be loved and revered. Rebellions would decrease, making his job as procurator simplicity itself.

But that is when he made the fatal error. It was customary practice of the Romans to insist that the local populace share the cost of constructing edifices built for the common weal. But since the Jews had no state treasury except for the temple money—funds dedicated to its construction, beautification, and maintenance—Pilate naturally took the money from that fund.

And, of course, custom and standard procedure entitled the procurator to keep some of the money for himself—money that compensated him for his benevolence.

Once again, Pilate had miscalculated the fervent zeal of the Jews. When they discovered that money consecrated to the temple had been appropriated by a Roman overseer, the Jews massed together, working themselves into a fever of rebellion.

Pilate, desiring to soften the situation, had his soldiers dressed in civilian clothes and armed with hidden clubs.

It seems every decision Pilate made in regards to the Jews was the worst decision possible. This was no exception. The crowds, resenting the threat of Roman discipline, increased their zeal. And, as zeal is wont to do, it fostered a frenzy among the people. Roman clubs appeared from between folds of clothing and, before the day was over, hundreds of Jews lay beaten or dead.

"Those who advised Pilate believed that such a show of force would bring order to the area," Antilochus said. "Unfortunately, that was not the case. Whereas before the Jews were disgruntled, now they were enraged."

"Surely their anger has softened," I said. "After a period of time, the people will see the benefits of the aqueduct."

"Unlikely. The people grow more agitated every day."

"Why doesn't Pilate merely repay the money to the temple and find another way to tax the people?"

"Unfortunately, most of the money Pilate collected has already been spent. To make matters worse, it has become a point of pride. The procurator will not, *cannot,* return the money."

Who knows what expenses a Roman procurator must incur? What villas must be purchased on the sunny slopes of Latinum? Who knows why Pilate had become so stubborn? Whatever the reason, it was clear the man had no intention of returning the money to the Jews.

The trader in me caught fire with this news. The profitability of this market was immense. If I could earn the trust of Pilate—better, if I could place the procurator in my debt—I could build a fleet of ships. I could perhaps become the greatest and wealthiest merchant in the empire.

I looked at the freed man out of the corner of my eyes. "What if money were to become available?" I said. "What if Pilate had sufficient funds to replace those taken from the Jewish temple? Pilate could keep the taxes he has collected, and thus retain his pride. While the Jews, at the same time, would have their sacred treasury restored."

"Are you saying you have an idea that could make that possible?"

I nodded.

"That would solve every problem."

"Then I must meet the procurator," I said.

And with that, Antilochus bowed his head and motioned for me to follow.

NOTES

Current and winds: In the late spring the winds in the Caribbean blow steadily eastward, allowing ships to catch the Gulf Stream current. Convoys taking advantage of the seasonal winds and currents became standard in colonial Spain.

Phoenicia and Tyre: Roughly the region of modern Lebanon; the Phoenicians were renowned as great merchants of the ancient world. Tyre was the largest and wealthiest of the Phoenician cities, noted in the Bible for its alliance with Solomon (1 Kings 5:1) and for prophetic condemnation of its greed and profligacy (Isaiah 23; Ezekiel 26–28). Phoenician craftsmen from Tyre served as engineers and artisans in building Solomon's Temple (1 Kings 7:13). (See G. Markoe, *The Phoenicians* [2000].)

Caesarea: Herod the Great constructed an artificial port at Caesarea to shift trade routes and wealth to his kingdom. The ruins of Caesarea can still be visited in Israel today. Paul was imprisoned and tried there before Festus and Agrippa (Acts 25). The city remained the largest and wealthiest in the Holy Land for half a millennium, until the silting of the harbor brought economic decline. In the third and fourth centuries, the city became a great center of Christian scholarship under Origen and Eusebius.

Roman anti-Semitism: Romans were often incredulous (and poorly informed) about Jewish beliefs and practices. (See P. Schafer, *Judeophobia: Attitudes Towards the Jews in the Ancient World* [1998]; J. Gager, *The Origins of Anti-Semitism: Attitudes Toward Judaism in Pagan and Christian Antiquity* [1985].)

Bronze for the temple: Josephus describes the large amounts of bronze used for building the temple, especially for the monumental gates (Josephus, *War of the Jews*, 5.201–6).

Pontius Pilate: Procurator of Roman Judea from A.D. 26–36. While universally known from the Gospels as the judge who condemned Jesus to death, little is known of Pilate's life. Christian traditions developed around him, especially the apocryphal *Acts of Pilate* (H. Bond, *Pontius Pilate in History and Interpretation* [2004]).

Incident of the standards: Josephus, *War of the Jews*, 2.9.2–3; *Antiquities of the Jews* 18.55–59.

Incident of the aqueduct: Josephus, *War of the Jews*, 2.175–77; *Antiquities of the Jews* 18.60–62.

Chapter 22

The Book of Malchus, son of Mago, of the house of Hanno

It was at the newly built palace in Caesarea where I first laid eyes on Pontius Pilate. He was a short, rotund man, likable, if slightly obsequious, who wore his hair in imitation of the Julians. I suspected he had ability as a ruler—he was intelligent and active—but every syllable he spoke seemed as though it had been scripted and planned. Pilate seemed to be a man obsessed with one goal—to leave this forsaken desert with enough wealth to provide a comfortable retirement for himself far away from Judea. Considering the rumor that Pilate had bribed Tiberius for the appointment in the first place, he was a man who desperately needed a great fortune, and the quicker he could acquire it, the better.

We discovered him in the midst of making preparations for a trip that would take him from his home in Caesarea to the capital city of Jerusalem. It was in the spring of the year, and Pilate was readying his household, along with one of his many cohorts, to oversee and provide order during one of the Jew's quaint religious celebrations—a holy day they called "Passover."

Pilate did not seem pleased to see us, for he looked at us with annoyance and flashed a look of anger at Antilochus. After a short, hushed conversation between the Roman and his servant, the procurator abruptly turned to us with a warm smile and invited us into his private chambers.

"I understand you have a proposition?" he said to me.

He was a man who moved to the heart of the matter quickly. A businessman. Good; I trusted men who did not cover their intentions with layers of pleasantries.

I explained that I possessed something that could make the procurator's worries disappear: Two ships heavy in the water with cargoes of tin.

He poured wine into three goblets, taking one for himself and offering the other two to myself and Glaucus.

"Go on," he said.

"I am a merchant," I said. "A *wealthy* merchant."

"Yes, yes."

"And as a wealthy merchant, I have discovered that although money does not always make problems disappear, it has the charm of allowing one to deal with them in style."

Pilate raised an eyebrow. He was impatient, this Roman procurator, unaccustomed to having bait dangled before his eyes. But I did not care. He desperately needed my help. I, on the other hand, had a number of options as to where to sell my cargo. It is amazing the power indifference plays in negotiations.

"The wealthiest merchants," I continued, "have one thing in common: they make problems go away."

"And the best leaders make annoyances go away." Pilate paced.

Was that a veiled threat?

"Your freedman tells me the Jews are at the point of revolution."

Another flash of anger. Another nearly uncontrollable outburst. I had to admire the man's self-control. It was obvious he was accustomed to command and he did not like having the positions reversed. "If you would be so kind to get to the point."

"The point is simple: I can make your problem go away."

"You, a tin merchant, can make an uprising by an annexed population go away?" He laughed.

I raised an eyebrow and laughed in return—something that surprised him, I think.

The man had no idea that he and I were about to become fast friends.

To sum up: Pilate was not a stupid man and he accepted my proposal. I would receive a long-term trading contract at premium prices, Pilate would have his money for the Jewish treasury, and the anger of the Jews would eventually subside. We came to terms on how much Pilate "owed" the temple, and I offered to loan him that amount. He would repay the loan through the profits he would realize from reselling my tin to the Jews. It was a plan that, in the long run, would benefit everyone—particularly Glaucus and me.

We spent two days in Caesarea working out the details and, during that time, Pilate took great pride in showing us about the palace and the city where he had chosen to live. It was far enough away from the major population of the Jews that it could be readily defended, yet close enough that he could deploy troops to anywhere in the province, north or south, as the need arose.

Pilate warmed when he spoke of Herod the Great, calling him a visionary builder, perhaps the greatest of the age. The Roman Senate may have appointed Herod as king, but what the Jews received was a man who knew what to do with stone and shovel. Masada, the impregnable fortress, he built. The palace at Herodium with its magnificent baths was a wonder of the age. His greatest achievement, however, without question was rebuilding the temple at Jerusalem. Surely, Herod believed that this would gain him favor in the eyes of his subjects.

"In spite of these great achievements, the Jews despised their king, you know," Pilate explained. "They never have taken kindly to outside authority and, though Herod himself was half-Jewish, the Jews hated him still. Of course, the fact that the man was cruel beyond belief did not help his cause."

"Every king is forced to make unpopular decisions," I said. "I, myself, have made decisions to save my ship. Decisions that others may have considered cruel." The image of Antonius kneeling before me in the storm with his box and lamp splayed before him flashed through my mind.

Pilate laughed. "Perhaps an example to illustrate. Some thirty years or so ago, a group of soothsayers predicted that a baby had been born who would become king of the Jews. Herod investigated, called in his scholars, and in a fit of paranoia, when he learned where this child was supposed to have been born, he sent his soldiers to massacre every male child under two years of age in the city."

"I see."

"That wasn't all," Pilate continued. "He also murdered some of his own sons out of fear they threatened his throne. When word of this reached the Roman Emperor Augustus, he said, 'It's better to be Herod's pig than Herod's son,' alluding to the fact that Jews won't eat pork, so Herod's pigs were safer than his sons."

"Why did Augustus tolerate Herod?"

"Here we come back to where we started. Herod, for all his faults, was the greatest builder in the East. Everything you see around you—this palace, the entire city of Caesarea—was his creation. When you travel to Jerusalem you will notice the pool of Siloam . . . a wonderful achievement. The water system of the country, he renovated. Herod, though he lived in an arid land, surrounded himself with sumptuous baths of hot, warm, and cold water. Great arenas for races, amphitheaters for plays. The port you sailed into was man-made—by Herod."

"Remarkable."

"Perhaps you will come with me to Jerusalem? There, you will see his greatest achievement of all—the great temple of the Jews. It really is a remarkable structure. Herod was no fool. He knew it was in his best interests to keep the people happy. He understood that the more content his people were the easier his work as a ruler would be. Not to mention his life would be less cluttered with the unpleasantness of assassination, rebellion, and riot. So he announced that he would rebuild the Jew's temple that had once crowned the city of Jerusalem. But Herod could never do anything in half measures. His temple, he decided, would be larger than the original. And he was determined to make it more sumptuous. If you travel with me, you can judge for yourself if Herod deserves the appellation 'Great.'"

I was fascinated by the history of this place and spent hours with Pilate discussing its history and mythology. To his delight I, in turn, spoke of Rome and the latest developments and gossip. Pilate was a man out of place; though his body was in Judea, his heart was in Rome. As such, he was curious to hear news. We informed him of the latest rumors from Rome and he, in exchange, regaled us of tales of the quaint customs of this strange land.

"The problem with the Jews, you know," Pilate told us one evening over a dinner of stewed lamb, "is that they are a people who, even after a hundred years, have not yet accepted the obvious fact that they are conquered. You cannot imagine the frustration I endure."

He went on for two hours about the factions and the cults—the Zealots, Sadducees, Pharisees, Scribes, Essenes, Herodians, Baptists, Galileans, and Hasmoneans—each condemning the other and each of them staking claim to the moral high ground of being ordained of God.

"They have this unfortunate belief in a future, mythical, world-conquering king they call the Messiah," he said. "A half-man half-god, descended from their hero-king David, who is supposed to cleanse the earth not only of all Romans but everyone else not of the Jewish faith."

"Has there been any evidence of this Messiah appearing?" I asked.

"Nearly every day for the last hundred years. It's all too common—one or another of them will rise up, saying 'I am the one.' Of course it always ends badly. Always. And it ends just as poorly for those silly enough to follow the self-proclaimed Messiah. Always with bloodshed."

"A hundred years?"

"Oh, yes. Before us, it was the Greeks who ruled here. And before them, the Persians. And always the same thing with the Jews. Messiah coming to purify the land. Terrible business. You'd think it would do some good to put a few of them to the sword or crucify them. You'd think that sort of thing would discourage rebellion. Not so. As soon as one Messiah is put into the ground, a new one rises up claiming to be the true Messiah. And then you have to start all over again."

"Why are they so hardheaded?" Glaucus asked. "They're allowed to keep their religion, are they not? They rule themselves."

"Stubbornness, pure and simple. I'm afraid the only solution is to flatten the city. Particularly their temple. They take such pride in it. Symbol of their special status with their God, you know. I fear in the end, however, Rome will have no other recourse but to destroy it. Every stone, I'm afraid, will have to fall. Only then will their spirit finally be broken. Only then will we be able to finish this silly, endless round of rebellion."

During the course of the evening, Pilate asked about gossip from Rome. I told him of the strange rumors surrounding Tiberius—his disappearance from the capital and his secretive and isolated residence on the island of Capri and the stories of too-bizarre-to-be-true depravities that seeped from his isolated palace and entertained all of Rome with their unbelievable degeneracy.

He was especially interested in the rumors that Tiberius had begun to speak of his own deification. The deification of an emperor was always a thought that brought terror to anyone of influence in Rome—it bode ill for anyone who did not fawn over the man and who refused to flatter him with unthinkable sycophancies.

The emperor was becoming increasingly paranoid as evidenced by his treatment of Sejanus, commander of his Praetorian Guard and executor of his imperial will. Tiberius had grown fearful to the point where he had Sejanus executed and his body thrown from the walls of Rome into the Tiber River.

These things both delighted and appalled Pilate. Perhaps he was secretly delighted that the emperor was losing his mind. Yet, at the same time, he must have understood with clarity that his own security was only as stable as the whim of an emperor who was tottering between sanity and madness.

· Pilate was an excellent conversationalist and his questions and anecdotes flooded one after the other filling up the evening. In truth, we formed a bond, he and I. It seemed the most natural of requests when we agreed to accompany him to Jerusalem to witness the Passover feast of the Jews.

"If you really want to understand this people, you must come."

"I'm surprised you would go yourself," I said.

"Afraid it can't be helped. There is always some uproar about one thing or another. It's like kneading dough: you push down in one area, another expands. Always some trouble or another that needs a firm hand. You really must come. You can stay in my Jerusalem garrison—named after Marc Antony, you know. It's comfortable enough and it overlooks their temple. A perfect vantage point for observing their festival. It is an opportunity to see something few Romans can ever say they have witnessed."

And so the following day we found ourselves traveling overland in the company of Pontius Pilate and a cohort of Roman soldiers on our way to Jerusalem, the holy city of the strange people who called themselves Jews; the people of promise; the chosen of God.

NOTES

Corruption: The Roman government was notoriously corrupt, a fact widely recognized by Roman historians and politicians themselves. This corruption significantly contributed to the eventual fall of the Roman Empire. The fictitious deal struck between Malchus and Pilate was one typical of the age. See R. MacMullen, *Corruption and the Decline of Rome* (1990).

Herod the Great: Herod ruled Judea from 37 to 4 B.C. and rose to power as a Roman strongman under the faltering Jewish Hasmonean kings. He was relentlessly loyal to his Roman patrons, who included Julius Caesar, Marc Antony, and Augustus. Rome rewarded his loyalty by making him king of the Jews and adding several nearby, largely gentile, provinces to his domain.

Herod's tyranny and paranoia are well documented and include the murder of his wife and several sons and the High Priest Aristobulus III. His most famous atrocity is the murder of the innocents of Bethlehem in an attempt to forestall the coming of the Messiah, the true king of Israel (Matthew 2:16–18). Fearing that none would mourn his passing, Herod ordered the aristocrats of his kingdom to be slaughtered after he died so that the entire country would mourn. The order was not carried out.

The best sources for Herod's life are Josephus' books, *Antiquities of the Jews* and *War of the Jews*. See also P. Richardson, *Herod: King of the Jews and Friend of Rome* (1999).

"Better to be Herod's Pig": This may have been a play on words. In Greek, it reads: It was preferable to be Herod's pig (*hus*) than his son (*huios*). The fact that the Jews did not eat pork and therefore did not kill them for meat adds additional irony to the statement.

Herod the builder: Herod was considered one of the greatest builders of his age, most notably building the temple of Jerusalem. However, he also built the tomb of Abraham in Hebron; the port and city of Caesarea; several pagan temples; the aqueduct of Jerusalem; the palace, walls, and fortresses of Jerusalem; and the fortresses of the Herodion and Masada (D. Roller, *The Building Program of Herod the Great* [1998]; P. Richardson, *Building Jewish in the Roman East* [2004]; and E. Netzer, *The Architecture of Herod, the Great Builder* [2008]).

The temple in Jerusalem was considered as one of the great buildings of its age, even by pagans. Although architecturally nothing remains of Herod's temple itself, it remains the best documented and described building of antiquity. In addition to the Bible, intertestamental sources are collected by R. Hayward, *The Jewish Temple: A Non-Biblical Sourcebook* (1996). The archaeological remains of the building are examined in detail by H. Shanks, *Jerusalem's Temple Mount: From Solomon to the Golden Dome* (2007). For a cultural history of the idea of the temple in Judaism, Christianity, and Islam, see W. Hamblin and D. Seely, *Solomon's Temple: Myth and History* (2007).

Jewish sects and factions: At the time of Jesus, Judaism was split into numerous sects and factions divided by social status, politics, and theology. Some of these divisions are reflected in the New Testament discussions of Pharisees, Sadducees, and Scribes, but this is just part of the story. See A. Saldarini and J. VanderKam, *Pharisees, Scribes and Sadducees in Palestinian Society* (2005); S. Cohen, *From the Maccabees to the Mishnah,* 2d ed. (2008); J. VanderKam, *An Introduction to Early Judaism* (2000).

Jewish Messianism: At the time of Christ, many Jews expected a Messiah to come, although their understanding of what the Messiah would be and do varied wildly. Most expected a new, mortal king who would defeat the Romans and establish a righteous kingdom of Israel as the dominant economic and political power of the world. (This world-conquering concept is probably reflected in Satan's offer to Jesus of "all the kingdoms of the world" [Matthew 4:8].) For many Jews, Christ's claim that his "kingdom is not of this world" (John 18:36) was thus evidence that he was not the Messiah they were expecting. For background, see J. Collins, *The Scepter and the Star* (1995) and J. Collins, *King and Messiah As Son of God* (2008).

Destruction of the temple: In A.D. 70, the Romans destroyed the temple during the revolt of the Jews (see Josephus, *The Jewish War* [1981], book 7). The temple's destruction was foretold by Jesus in Matthew 24.

Sejanus: Sejanus was the real ruler in Rome during the self-exile of Tiberius to his pleasure palace on Capri. Sejanus ruthlessly eliminated all potential rivals—including poisoning Tiberius' son—only to be executed in a coup by the Roman Senate. The details of his life can be found in Tactitus' *Annals,* books 4–6.

The Antonia Fortress: Named after Herod's patron Marc Antony, the Antonia Fortress was built by Herod the Great to solidify his control of Jerusalem. It was attached to the northwest corner of the Temple Mount plaza and served as a garrison to control access and activities on the Temple Mount. It played a major role in defense during the Roman siege of Jerusalem in A.D. 70, but was destroyed, leaving only marginal archaeological remains (see L. Ritmeyer, *The Quest* [2006]).

Chapter 23

Lucius ran his fingers over the scratches that had been cut into the hard bronze. Had he not discovered these plates himself, he never would have believed that such a thing was possible. Had he not pulled them from the broken shards of the altar with his own hands where they had lain hidden for centuries, he would have scoffed at the very idea.

Somehow, this Malchus was tied to his own family. Was it possible that this record was written by one of Lucius' own ancestors? Why else would the record have been placed in his family altar? He imagined for a moment what it must have been like to have known Malchus—to have *been* Malchus. Somewhere in the distant past, this trader of tin walked the earth, stood on the deck of his trading ship, faced storms and pirates, and traveled to exotic, undiscovered lands.

Had any of his courage and ambition been passed from generation to generation to his own time? Did he, a philosopher and teacher, have any of the boldness of this man?

He did not see it. Perhaps the blood had been thinned too much through the generations of fishermen, potters, and plowmen.

No matter. It gave him great pleasure to know that once there had been a man named Malchus, son of Mago, of the house of Hanno. And it gave him even greater pleasure to think that perhaps he, himself, had descended from such a man.

The discovery of this record, he knew, was an important one. These writings revealed a secret history, one that had long been forgotten. The account should be preserved and copied and made available to historians. Would anyone believe his story of how he had found the plates? Would they scoff at him? Perhaps they would claim that he had forged the plates himself and invented the story.

Lucius smiled. If his competitors did not already think him senile, they certainly would after he announced this discovery.

As he was contemplating what he would do with the plates and to whom he would show them, a wail startled him and he leapt to his feet.

He rushed out of the room and ran toward Gunderic's quarters. When he entered, he felt as though his heart had been ripped from his chest. The pitiful sight of a mother holding the lifeless form of her dead child hammered at his temples and robbed him of breath.

He did not know what to do. Shout? Curse the gods?

What gods?

Rail at the sky?

What could he do? What could anyone do to fight against the massive mercilessness of the cruelty of this life?

What power did anyone have over death, decay, and forgetfulness?

The child had been taken by some vile ague that physicians did not have the slightest clue how to remedy.

A young, innocent child.

What could he tell the grieving mother? That all would be well? That there was hope?

Could he do that? Unbearable. Impossible that one so young . . .

He lifted his head and felt the feelings of helplessness that sucked the energy from his soul and left him spent and helpless.

Lucius was famous for his eloquence; he had, in fact, made a small fortune for himself as a result of his command of the language, his tact and diplomacy. But what could he say that could ease the heartbreak of a mother who had lost the dearest thing in the world to her?

Could he bring back the child?

Terrible, cold, and cruel life.

Out of instinct, he cursed the gods for this barbarity when the counterfeit of their existence reminded him of the emptiness in the hollow of his soul.

In truth, it was better that there were no gods. The alternative—that all-powerful beings did exist who allowed this measure of suffering—was an even worse and more unbearable thought.

He looked up and met the eyes of the mother and saw there a mirror of his own grief, a reflection of his own pain, a reminder of that terrible day decades ago when he held the lifeless body of his dearest Livia and pleaded with the gods to breathe life back into her unmoving frame.

But the girl did not breathe again.

He had assured countless grieving souls that the souls of the dead yet lived in the underworld, but such an idea did not comfort him now. It burned. It enraged him.

He slowly collected himself and tried to speak, but nothing came.

And, for a moment, he felt as though he should do something to help the woman. Embrace her. Offer some measure of comfort, speak some lie intended to salve that bottomless wound.

But he could not do it.

"Where is Gunderic?"

"In the city," she said in a broken voice that gave sound to the visual image of grief. "To get medicine."

"What can I do?" he asked. "Whatever is within my power, I promise. No expense is too great. Only name it."

She shook her head and buried her head in the little girl's hair. "Only leave me alone with my daughter until my husband returns," she said.

Lucius nodded and backed slowly out of the room.

He needed to think. Needed to clear his head. Needed to find a way to understand, though such a thing was impossible.

His steps took him to the peristylium where he, once again, surveyed the destruction he had wrought the night before.

Broken stone and shattered marble. That was all that was left. If there was a part of him that regretted having torn down these images, the last vestige of guilt fled as he stood among the shards of broken stone. That he ever could have believed that pieces of carved rock had any power— was he ever that foolish? That he had defended these gods. That he had worshipped them! Was he so weak-minded that he could be persuaded to defend and worship fable? The product of some other man's imagination?

Some scholar he had turned out to be.

You claimed to seek truth, Lucius. And yet you defended—no, you worshipped—lies.

The empire was losing faith. Belief was waning. Could the gods exist in absence of those who adored them? Those who still worshipped the old gods grew older by the day, and as each of them died, there was one less voice to offer prayers and sing songs to the sons and daughters of Olympus.

The youth flocked to this new god, the god of Gunderic. The priests of the new god claimed divine intervention. Miracles. They claimed that their god, unlike the gods of the Romans, actually cared about his children.

It was all foolishness. A painful foolishness—as Gunderic would discover soon enough. Perhaps it was best that he did. Was it not better to embrace cold and bitter truth? Even when knowing it brought little warmth? No comfort? No joy?

He moved forward and heard a crunching sound as though he had stepped on crisp parchment. When he looked down, he discovered the skin of a snake beneath his foot, a testament of its former self.

The snake had shed his skin, left it behind, and had emerged renewed. Why couldn't mortals do the same? Why couldn't mortals, when confronted with age or illness, merely slough off their old skin and emerge as a new creature? Any creator, any god with even a measure of compassion, would certainly have provided for this possibility.

Why did the unspeakable cruelty of death have to torment those who inhabited this earth? Why could man not live forever? With those he loved and cherished? With those to whom he had given his heart, soul, and life? Why did it have to end this way, alone, shedding unending tears of grief, unbelief, anger, loss, and remorse?

But then, if he had an answer to that question, he could begin a religion of his own that would rival that of the Galilean and challenge Jupiter himself.

He resigned himself to the fact that it was another of the too many impossible questions that mortals could never understand and that attempting to answer it would only add to the weight of misery that was a man's lot from the moment he took his first breath to the moment of his last.

NOTES

Roman afterlife: Within the Roman Empire there were many different beliefs concerning death and the afterlife, ranging from atheistic oblivion to reincarnation (J. Davies, *Death, Burial and Rebirth in the Religions of Antiquity* [1999]; J. Toynbee, *Death and Burial in the Roman World* [1996]).

Chapter 24

The Book of Malchus, son of Mago, of the house of Hanno

Jerusalem. City of stone walls and olive trees, packed from heel to head with shoulders, hands, and feet. Scarcely room to move. Cries of merchant song pleading for passersby to look here!

Figs, fabrics, fish!

Rank odor of spilt blood seeped through layers of roasting flesh and wafts of strewn and rotting refuse. Colors of earth: brown through light yellow—no startling hues here—as though every blue, orange, green, and purple had been banished from this solitary place.

Jerusalem, above all else, was a city of earth, and it emerged deep from yellow rock and the remains of human living.

From the moment I entered the city I regretted my decision to come. Everywhere I walked, a dangerous piety permeated the place as though, at a moment's notice, the zeal of worshippers could ignite into a fire of revolution. There was anger here—below the surface, yes—but a writhing, unspoken burning. I don't know if I have ever felt less at ease than I did in that city of law and religion.

They called this feast day "Passover"—an ancient tradition of the Jews commemorating their supposed Exodus from the land of Egypt. According to their history, Passover has been observed, uninterrupted, for some fifteen centuries. If their reckoning can be believed, the first Passover occurred more than half a millennia before Homer penned his immortal words, "Sing, goddess, the wrath of Achilles."

Was it possible that this people had existed as a nation before Agamemnon had held a scepter and Priam had paced the walls of Troy?

The procurator had promised us an unforgettable sight and in this he delivered. After taking the pulse of the city, Pilate recommended that rather than stay in the Antonia Fortress with the garrison that we stay in the Praetorium, another of Herod's palaces that gave added meaning to the word *luxury,* on the west of the city. Pilate invited Glaucus and me to his palace for the evening meal and we were not disappointed in Pilate's refined palate. He insisted on our tasting every delicacy.

As the governor of this province, his schedule was filled from morning until night with the demands of his office. Consequently, Glaucus and I were able to spend our time exploring the city and getting to know the people who inhabited it.

Early the next morning, we walked on the southern wall of the Antonia Fortress, which provided a view of the unforgettable world of the Jews. Our first glimpse of the temple in daylight was surprising, even breathtaking. It was built of white marble and covered in places with heavy plates of gold. The stones used in construction were massive—what a wonder of engineering to have placed them here! The workmanship was exact and impressive. Herod, indeed, was a master builder. I wanted to enter the temple and see it from the inside, but I was quickly informed that no one but priests could enter the building. The most sacred part of the building, the Holy of Holies, could only be entered once a year and only then by the high priest.

From the wall we could see the sacrificial courtyard in front of the temple. Even at this hour, the sacrificial fires were burning as throngs of people brought doves, lambs, and even oxen to the priests to be slain and offered up to their god.

We descended from the wall into the outer courtyard of the complex where non-Jews were allowed to observe or worship. The outer court was divided by a low wall the Jews called the "soreg," a sort of boundary wall that served as a warning to those not of their faith. It was some four-and-a-half feet tall with gates at regular intervals that allowed the Jews access into the inner courtyard.

Along the outside of that wall, hundreds of merchants sat in shaded stalls where they sold animals for sacrifice, peddled souvenirs to travelers, and changed foreign coins for Jewish fare.

"You want a lamb?" a bearded, toothless man lisped at us in Greek.

"What is he saying?" Glaucus asked me.

"If you will be so kind," I smiled as I spoke, "as to remember the thousand times I have upbraided you for not paying attention to your language lessons. 'An effective merchant must master Greek,' I believe were my words to you. It is the universal language in this part of the empire, and without it, you are at a terrible disadvantage."

"A four-word question: What is he saying?"

"He's offering a lamb. Three shekels."

"That's nine denarii," Glaucus muttered. "For that amount, I assume the lamb will grow wool that can be spun into gold?"

"What do we want with a lamb?" I asked.

"So we can sacrifice it to the god of the Jews, of course."

"You want favor here?" the old man lisped. "Sacrifice brings luck. Prosperity. Fortune in love."

Perhaps the man was right. It wouldn't hurt to gain the favor of the god of this place—if such a god did exist. If he didn't, then what harm could come from it?

"The priests do all the work," the man continued. "They slay and skin the lamb for you. Even better, they take only a little of the meat. The rest is yours to keep for the festival feast!"

I handed the man some coins and instructed him to keep the meat for himself, as I had no use for it.

"Very generous, sir!"

Glaucus, true to form, was annoyed. "I suppose you'll be dropping a coin into the lap of every man who claims he serves a higher power?"

"Possibly," I said. What good would it do to argue?

"It's not the waste of the money that I object to," Glaucus continued. "But that you would trust this man to take the lamb in for you. My guess is that the poor creature will return here and be sold five more times to unsuspecting foreigners."

"The man looks honest enough to me," I said.

"This is the sort of face that you would describe as honest?" Glaucus replied. "You may have a good head for trading tin but, lucky for you, I am a better judge of character. Tell the man that I'll take the lamb to the priests myself."

Glaucus took the rope that had been placed around the neck of the lamb and pulled the recalcitrant creature toward the wall. He was about to penetrate the wall when I held his shoulder.

"You might reconsider before you enter there."

Glaucus looked over the faces of those inside and said, "It's only priests and pilgrims. Nothing to fear."

"Once again, Glaucus, your lack of application in language could cost you dearly."

He looked at me with a puzzled expression, and I pointed to the stone inscription by the gates. "It reads, 'No foreigner is allowed beyond this balustrade. Whoever is caught doing so will have only himself to blame for his ensuing death.'"

"Not exactly models of hospitality."

"Apparently," I said, "it is a closed affair. No outsiders welcome. On pain of death."

I handed the lamb to the old man and smiled apologetically. The man lifted an eyebrow and tilted his head toward Glaucus and I laughed.

I handed him a few more silver denarii and told him to put them in the donation box inside.

Again, the man laughed, "Never been here before, have you?"

I explained that I hadn't.

"That's obvious. Everyone knows you can't bring coins with images of Roman gods on them here to the temple. You have to change them into temple currency. What do you suppose all these do here?" He waved at the rows of merchants exchanging foreign coin for local fare.

Because of my generosity with the lamb, the man offered to handle the changing of the money, taking, of course, a liberal fee for his services. With one last smile, he took the lamb and entered the inner yard. We watched him bring it to a large gate where he handed it to a man dressed in white—a priest, we assumed.

We stayed awhile, fascinated by the work of the priests as they continued their work of slaughter. The animals were tied to posts where they were inspected. Some—the lucky ones perhaps—were rejected and removed. When an animal's time had come, it was led toward a shallow channel that had been cut into the stone. There, the priests held the animal over the trough and slit its throat. The blood spilled into the channel and was carried down by a slow stream of water that trickled under the temple and outside the city. The priests hung the carcasses on posts where they skinned and butchered the animals, allowing the remainder of the blood to drain away before other priests came and divided the meat.

As I watched, transfixed, other images came to mind. Men chanting in a clearing before a cave. An obsidian knife sliding across a dog's throat. The blood dripping from the bodies of the chanting men. How could these scenes be so similar? But was that scene so different from my own Carthage? From my own Rome? Bulls, pigs, doves—all sacrificed before the altars of Ceres, Janus, Jupiter, and Juno. Why did religion have such a fascination with blood?

"You are interested in the sacrifice?" the old man with the leathered and deep-wrinkled skin said. "Three are fed by it—God, the priests, and he who offers it. Everyone feasts well at Passover."

We watched as thousands of animals were ushered past the gates of the soreg and handed to the priests. Blood rivered down the trenches and the smell of the blood and the thickness of the flies sickened me.

They had developed quite a system, these priests. It was impressive, but no more so than any of a hundred other Roman temples that did the same on feast days and holidays.

Sounds of trumpets, prayers, and shouts filled the air. The Jews were a noisy lot, shouting words and singing hymns in their native tongue. They spoke a rough, guttural language impossible to understand. A surprising number of merchants and foreigners were educated enough to speak Greek, but it was rare to find a local who could engage in conversation in that language. They held onto their traditions and language with a fervor that simply perplexed every governor from Rome that had presided over this land. It was more than stubbornness; it was obstinacy mixed with ardor and conviction. They actually believed—no, they *knew*—that one day, this pinprick in the midst of an arid desert would triumph against the world.

It was at that moment that we heard a commotion not far from us. Glaucus and I turned to witness a most remarkable scene. A solitary man in simple dress had fashioned a whip of ropes and was moving from merchant to merchant, shouting and turning over tables filled with money, scattering coins as bodies scrambled to get out of the way. Before the man touched any of them, the merchants tumbled and scattered like sand before a storm.

Three men of authority—a priest and two temple guards—ran toward the man with the whip and tried to take hold of him, but the man stood before them and spoke a few words. I have never seen men wither so completely. I do not know what words he spoke, but I watched as the three men melted away into the crowd.

At this point several of the merchants discovered their courage and looked toward the Antonia Fortress, shouting for assistance from the garrison.

At first, I did not know if the man was a brigand or a rebel. What motives he could have had for disturbing the peace I had no idea. It certainly wasn't monetary for he did not stoop to collect a single coin.

There was something masterful about him. Even without understanding a word of what he said, I could sense in him a majesty and nobility that I had never seen in any man—not even in the greatest of Rome's senators, generals, or aristocracy. There was something in his eyes. Something in his bearing. But what it was, I could not tell.

The man did not stop until every moneychanger in the outer court of the temple had scrambled away and fled. Then, the man looked around him and his eyes met mine. For what seemed the longest time, he and I looked at each other. Did he smile? I could not tell but it seemed as though he had recognized me—knew my name, my history, my heart.

I looked away for a moment, and when I looked back, he had vanished.

By the time the soldiers had arrived on the scene, order had already been restored and the merchants had scrambled to recover their coin and give their report to the centurion.

I reflected on the countenance of that man. There was nothing about him physically that would command such respect. He was . . . ordinary. Average of height and build, he appeared as though he came from a modest home. What was it about him that caused those others to scatter when he arrived?

Perhaps it was his eyes. There was something in them. But what?

A certain serene confidence. Clarity. Authority. Power.

This was a man who could command a legion—an army! He was the sort of man others would follow. Were he in Rome, most certainly he would be a senator—perhaps even emperor. I thought throughout the rest

251

of the day on that peculiar man and the effect he had on me. All I could think of to describe him were four words: "Here is a man!"

After the excitement had faded, Glaucus insisted on visiting the market, and so we spent the afternoon haggling with tailors, craftsmen, and sculptors hoping to take home some reminder of our visit to this strange city. Since Jerusalem was a city of pilgrimage, many merchants made their living selling to visitors. Unfortunately, with our inexperience both in the language as well as with local markets, we paid twice what we should have, nevertheless I was not distressed by the fact.

"The cost of being a tourist," I said.

"Whatever happened to a fair and honest price?" Glaucus replied.

"Do you think a Jew would fare better in Rome?"

Toward the end of the day, Glaucus had tired of the place and he returned to our quarters. For me, the mysteries of the city beckoned, and I decided to stay for a time and see what else I could discover.

I noticed a ridge that overlooked the city to the east, and I decided to make my way toward it in the hopes of getting a better view of the layout of the city.

It was at dusk that I arrived at the crest of the hill. It was a beautiful and serene place, populated by olive trees and vineyards. From that vantage point, I could look out over the city. The sun dappled against the brown stone of the houses and the Antonia Fortress, but the major landmark of the city was the temple where the sacrificial fires still burned bright. Even from here, the smells of the slaughter and burning flesh lingered. The smoke from the fires obscured the temple, masking the brick and bustle of the city, but underneath the haze, I could see the chaos of too many people attempting to move through narrow streets in search of food, shelter, and fodder. The walls of the city were as wide as they would ever be, as the city's dimensions were framed by deep valleys that dropped sharply on the south and east.

It was an ordinary city. An ordinary, dusty, unremarkable piece of rock upon which, eons ago, some shepherd decided to build a hut. Other than the temple, nothing distinguished it from any other city. Nothing of note. It did not figure in any of the histories. Did not occupy conversation. Did not excite curiosity.

And yet there was something about this place and this people that made me wonder if I could discover the mystery of this city and uncover its secrets before it was time for us to leave.

It was in the midst of my contemplation that I noticed a group of people, perhaps twenty, nearby. They were sitting in a circle, surrounding a man—in rapt attention.

I was shocked when I recognized the man at the center of the circle. It was the man with the whip. The man whose majesty had overturned the merchants' tables and sent the aristocracy of the temple running.

I drew closer, hoping to get a better look at this remarkable figure.

The men and women were intent upon hearing his words, and I was able to move to the outer rim of the circle without being observed. I stepped quietly, so as not to draw attention.

I could not understand what he was saying, but I could not mistake the tone of his voice. Soft and certain. Calm and commanding.

Again, I noticed his eyes. Something about them. Something—but I couldn't put my finger on it. Within them was farseeing. A deep sadness. And an absolute . . . love.

That was it! The man *loved.*

I know not how else to say it. His eyes, posture, voice, gestures. There was a purity about him. A profound love in his eyes. A love so great that I, a stranger, though unable to understand his words, could feel it from where I stood.

Lost in my thoughts, I did not realize that the man had stopped speaking and that all eyes had turned to me. I blushed as I realized I had been discovered and probably spoken to. I stammered, searching for words to excuse myself. Finally, I confessed in Greek that I couldn't understand what they were saying. I apologized for intruding and made to leave.

But before I turned, I looked into those eyes, the eyes of the man who sat at the center of the circle. He looked at me with such compassion that I could feel it as though it were an intense flame. It seemed as though he knew me. More, that he understood and loved me.

I wanted to say something. Communicate. Hear what he was saying.

But I had clumsily intruded upon an obviously private gathering and was out of place.

"Blessed is he that believes, though he has not seen," the man said to me in Greek.

Stunned, I opened my mouth, but no words emerged. I wanted to speak, to ask the man who he was, to discuss religion, the world, travel, politics, philosophy. But this was not the time. Perhaps at another time—before I left the city—I would meet up with him once again and, perhaps then, we could enter into conversation.

A realization gradually entered into my consciousness that I was still standing before the group, mouth open and unspeaking. I was making a spectacle of myself and clumsily backed away from the circle.

There was nothing for me to do but to enter into the dusk of the night and silently make my way back toward the city of Jerusalem.

NOTES

Praetorium: The Praetorium was the Roman garrison and headquarters in Jerusalem—the place of the Praetor, or commander. Although often linked with the Antonia Fortress, the Jerusalem Praetorium was probably at the old palace of Herod, located to the south of the modern Citadel on the western wall of the Old City. If so, this is probably where Jesus was tried and presented before the people prior to his crucifixion. (S. Gibson, *The Final Days of Jesus: The Archaeological Evidence* [2009].)

Court of the Gentiles: Herod's temple plaza was divided into a number of different courtyards, each with a different function and differing degrees of sanctity. The outermost court was called the Court of the Gentiles, where Gentiles were allowed to observe and participate in Jewish temple sacrifices, reflecting the belief that the temple should be a "house of prayer for all peoples" (Isaiah 56:7; Mark 11:17). Gentiles often saw the Jewish Jehovah as a powerful local god of Judea and would worship Jehovah without rejecting Jupiter or the pagan gods, as does Malchus.

Broadly speaking, the ancient Court of the Gentiles contained an elevated platform in the center that was accessible by stairs paralleling the inner courts of the Israelites where the Gentiles were forbidden to enter. Paul was nearly killed on the Temple Mount because the Jews believed that he had brought a Gentile into the sacred precincts beyond the Court of the Gentiles (Acts 21:27–32).

Shekel and denarius: The denarius (plural, denarii) was a standard Roman silver coin during the time of Jesus. It was about the size of a quarter and weighed around 3.4 grams. It was considered an average day's wage for common workers (often translated as "penny" in the King James Version, Matthew 20:2; John 12:5).

The shekel was a standard Near Eastern weight and coin, ranging in weight from 9 to 17 grams. The Tyrian shekel weighed about 14 grams and was worth about three or four denarii. The law of Moses required that Jews coming to pilgrimage festivals bring a half shekel as "ransom" (Exodus 30:11–16), which is probably the temple tax referred to in Matthew 22:17–21.

Soreg inscription: There were about ten gates in the soreg, each marked by stone inscriptions in various languages forbidding the entrance of non-Jews on pain of death (Josephus, *War of the Jews*, 5.2). Fragments of two soreg inscriptions from the Herodian Temple Mount have been discovered.

Coins in the temple: Moneychangers were necessary because, according to Rabbinic interpretation, offerings to the temple could only be made with Tyrian shekels (*Mishnah Bekhoroth* 8:7; *Babylonian Talmud Kiddushin* 11a); other coins were unacceptable because of lower silver purity or because they presented images of foreign gods.

Sacrificing at the temple: Although foreign to modern sensibilities, the most prominent activity on the Temple Mount was the blood sacrifice required by the law of Moses. These included daily, weekly, monthly, and annual sacrifices (Exodus 23:14–17; Deuteronomy 16:16–17), as well as numerous freewill, purification, and sin offerings (Numbers 28–29; Ezekiel 46; 2 Chronicles 2:4; Nehemiah 10:33). Blood sacrifice took place in the Court of the Priests before the gates of the temple. Only priests could perform sacrifices or enter into this court, although Israelite males could observe from a nearby courtyard. No blood offerings were made within the Holy Place, where bread and incense were offered.

On annual pilgrimage feasts, such as Passover, thousands of animals were sacrificed each day by pilgrims, turning the temple into a huge slaughterhouse. Water resources were channeled into cisterns in the temple to wash the blood from the courtyards. Blood sacrifice ended among the Jews with the destruction of their temple by the Romans in A.D. 70 (G. Stroumsa, *The End of Sacrifice: Religious Transformations in Late Antiquity* [2008].) However, Samaritans on Mt. Gerizim in Palestine still offer blood sacrifice each Passover. (For the sacrificial system at the time of Jesus, see E. Sanders, *Judaism: Practice and Belief* [1992]).

Jesus and the moneychangers: The Synoptic Gospels describe Jesus driving away the moneychangers from the temple at the end of Jesus' ministry (Mark 11:15–18; Matthew 21:12–13; Luke 19:45–46), while John describes a similar incident at the beginning of his ministry (John 2:12–35). The moneychangers Jesus expelled were probably operating in the Court of the Gentiles, and were thus profaning the temple.

Pilgrims at Passover: In biblical times, Jews were required to come to Jerusalem and offer their Pascal lamb at the temple. The lamb was slaughtered by the priests, and then returned to the offerer to be eaten. By the time of Jesus, vast throngs of people made the pilgrimage each year to the temple; Josephus claimed that three million were at Jerusalem for Passover in A.D. 65 (*Jewish War* 2.280). However exaggerated, the city was clearly packed during Passover, requiring Jesus to stay at Bethany. (F. Colautti, *Passover in the Works of Josephus* [2002].)

Chapter 25

The Book of Malchus, son of Mago, of the house of Hanno

That night I dreamed of the unusual man and his words to me: "Blessed is he that believes, though he has not seen."

It was absurd. What should I believe? Was the man pretending to be some sort of prophet? An Apollo walking amongst this backwards people? Was he looking for a new convert to *his* god? The god of the Jews? Or was it merely a general observation—that I should believe for the sake of belief—that the sun will rise, that the tides will swell? It seemed that somewhere in his statement was something of importance, and yet I could not unravel it nor could I rid myself of this peculiarly disturbing feeling of loss. Exactly what that loss was, I could not identify.

Like many who develop a following, the man was certainly charismatic, though in a quiet rather than a bombastic sort of way. I had seen my share of bright-burning philosophers, soldiers, and politicians. But few of them had left an impression on me. Theatrics and persuasive speeches may work on the masses who seek for meaning in a vacuous existence, but such words had little effect on me. Let the actors strut their way about the stage, gathering accolades and acolytes. I would not applaud. I could acknowledge the brilliance of their performance, but I would never be so shallow as to swallow words that were merely well-rehearsed phrases designed only to advance someone's own power, influence, and comfort.

Yet this simple and poor Judean troubled me. Perhaps the one common denominator of all the charlatans I had ever known was that they hungered for praise and respect. Their purpose was to be adored and admired. Not this man. While others yearned for attention, he simply was who he was.

It was the difference between a stagnant puddle of discolored water and a crisp, pure, sylvan spring. Both were of the same essence yet the difference between the one and the other was so vast that comparisons between the two bordered on blasphemy.

I argued with myself that morning. Should I forget I ever saw the man, or should I look for him and try to discover more about him? It was absurd, thinking about it. The man was poor, without influence. Why did I care?

It was foolishness. Preposterous.

Eventually, the practical merchant in me realized it. I was not the sort of man to be swayed by another. I laughed at myself for having given the man more than a moment's thought.

After a generous breakfast, I determined to take Glaucus with me and spend the remainder of my time in Jerusalem visiting the sites of the city. This feast of the Passover was to occur this evening; perhaps we could observe that firsthand.

Of one thing I was certain: I was ready to leave the shores of this unsettling land. I wanted to put it behind me and get back on my ship, smell the salt of the ocean, and set sail once again toward the vast blue horizon. There, at least, the mysteries of the sea were understandable and manageable. Here, on the desert soil of Judea, everything seemed to shift with the wind and nothing seemed certain. I would take my chances on the deep blue of Neptune's expanse rather than roll the bones of chance in this land of perplexity.

And so about mid-morning, Glaucus and I walked to the walls of the

Antonia Fortress and looked out once again over the temple and city of Jerusalem.

But it took only a moment to realize that something was wrong.

The temple court was comparatively empty. And there was a certain stillness in the air, a tension like a lyre string pulled tight past the point of its resilience.

And, although we could hear the sounds of the crowd, there was something eerie and unsettling about the muffled sound. We made our rounds around the outer wall of the fortress and, as we turned west, we heard another sound.

A procession stretched from the western gate of the fortress. The streets were crowded with people clumped together into one mass, a body of thousands that appeared as one. Was this part of the Passover festival? A triumph in honor of a local hero?

"What is happening there?" I asked a nearby guard.

"Crucifixion," he said callously. "Ordered by Pilate himself. Only this morning."

"That seems unusual," I said. "Why would Pilate risk the wrath of the populace on one of their holiest of days?"

"It was the Jews themselves who demanded it."

"What was the man's crime?"

The guard shook his head and let out a breath. "Who knows? The way I hear it, some fool claimed he was a god. Poor as a flea he was, and claiming he was a king. Insane. Wasn't local from what I gather. Came from some province in the north."

A sickening feeling took hold of me and stripped me of breath. I struggled to speak. "Did you see the man?"

"From a distance. Normal sort. Nothing of interest in him at all. If he's a king, I'm a camel." The soldier laughed.

"Did you notice anything unusual about the man at all?"

"Nothing at all—unless you mean his eyes. Something about his eyes. Not sure what it was . . ."

I did not stay to hear the guard finish the sentence. I flew down the stairs and toward the gate of the fortress, Glaucus behind me.

"What has gotten into you?" he shouted.

I did not answer. I could not answer.

I do not know how I knew. But I had no doubt in my mind. The man who was being led to his death was the man I had met the day before. I felt compelled to see for myself. To know for myself.

I flew through the streets of Jerusalem, shouting to those milling in the streets before me, "Clear away! Move aside!"

Glaucus, had he been able to catch me, would certainly have tried to restrain me, but I dove into and through the crowd with an urgency that forced spaces between bodies and parted the ocean of bystanders.

I ran without thinking. Without knowing why I was running. I punished my legs and lungs and sprinted through the pain.

My steps led me past the wall of the city and pushed me through throngs of curious spectators until I beheld a scene that has burned in my mind since that hour to this.

Upon a small hill, I saw three crosses.

And upon them hung three men.

And, on the middle cross, was the man.

It was too late. Though still breathing, the man was already dead.

Was it possible that I could have saved him?

Perhaps if I had not slept through the morning. Perhaps if I had been at Pilate's side, I could have offered words of counsel that could have made a difference. Perhaps, had I not spent so much time feasting on sweetbread and poultry, I could have been present when Pilate condemned the man. Perhaps I could have threatened to back out of our deal. Threaten to use my influence at Rome to destroy Pilate.

I looked up at the sun and realized it was midday.

I stumbled forward, toward the scene of the murder—for I was convinced that is what I was witnessing. Murder.

At the top of the crucifix, a crude plaque had been attached. On it were words written in Greek, Latin, and what I assumed was the local language: Jesus of Nazareth, King of the Jews.

"Who put that there?" I asked a soldier.

"Pilate," he said.

If Pilate had caused the sign to be written, then Pilate was responsible for the murder.

I walked toward the cross. I could not help myself. I wanted to look into the man's eyes. To make sense of this. Why had this man been crucified? What had he done? I wanted to hear from his own mouth an explanation, an answer. But he did not look at me, only at a small group huddled at the foot of the cross.

This small group, composed mostly of women, spoke to him and he to them, though what he said I could not tell.

As I stood there, Glaucus arrived.

He did not speak. Did not move. But we stood, shoulder to shoulder, witnessing the bloody scene.

I do not have the words to describe the emotions that coursed through my soul on that day. Any words that I could compose would do so great an injustice to the reality of what I experienced that I will not attempt to draw them out.

What I do know is that the sky darkened and the earth rumbled as though attempting to shake from its surface all semblance of polluted human life.

I looked at the soldiers, those hardened men of Rome, whose eyes were filled with terrible fear.

"Surely, he was the Son of God," one of them said.

Not one of them wanted to stay there a moment longer than

necessary, and I watched as one of the soldiers broke the legs of the two men on either side of the king of the Jews.

The soldier approached the center crucifix and raised his club, but a centurion waved him off. "Already dead," he said, and he took his lance and thrust it into the man's side.

It was done.

The man was dead.

I looked at Glaucus and breathed as though my lungs were made of lead.

There was nothing to be done but leave those who loved the man to care for the dead body, wrap it in burial cloth, and set him forever in the tomb.

I took one last look at the lifeless form of the man who had impressed me so deeply. And then I turned my back on that hill and began the long, slow walk away from that terrible place and away from the terrible images that I knew had been burned into my mind.

Those images have remained with me through the years, and even now I can recall them with terrible clarity. They haunt me still and, when I think of that day, I cannot help but feel that overwhelming cloud of despair and grief that I felt on the day the king of the Jews was crucified.

NOTES

Roman rhetoric and sophistry: Rhetoric, the art of persuasion, was a fundamental part of ancient education. Aristotle wrote a book on the subject, as did Cicero, the greatest of the Roman orators. For many people—often identified with the Sophist movement—rhetoric became an end in itself, a willingness to advocate any position for the right fee. In the late antique world, rhetoric became highly stylized, melodramatic, and rather florid. (W. Dominik and J. Hall, *A Companion to Roman Rhetoric* [2010] and G. Kennedy, *The Art of Rhetoric in the Roman World* [2008].)

Place of the crucifixion: The exact location of Christ's crucifixion and burial is disputed. The two main contenders are the Church of the Holy Sepulchre and the Garden Tomb; a third option is that the site remains unknown. Although Protestants prefer the serenity of the Garden Tomb, most scholars accept the Church of the Holy Sepulchre as the more likely of the two. For the background to these two sites, see P. Walker, *The Weekend That Changed the World* (2000) and, for the archaeology of the Holy Sepulchre, S. Gibson, *The Final Days of Jesus: The Archaeological Evidence* [2009], 127–48. For LDS-related issues, see J. Chadwick, "Revisiting Golgotha and the Garden Tomb," in *Religious Educator* 4/1 (2003).

Crucifixion: Malchus describes how a pagan might have understood the events of the crucifixion (Matthew 27; Mark 15; Luke 23; John 19). For a description of the nature of crucifixion based on archaeological and historical evidence, see S. Gibson, *The Final Days of Jesus: The Archaeological Evidence* [2009], 107–25.

Sign above Jesus: "Jesus of Nazareth the King of the Jews" (John 19:19). Known in medieval Christian traditions as the *titulus crucis,* the sign is usually depicted in medieval art as a small placard above the crucified Jesus with the letters INRI—an anagram of the Latin: "*Iesus Nazarenus rex Iudaeorum.*" The *titulus* allegedly survives as a relic and can be seen in the Church of the Santa Croce in Jerusalem, where it was supposedly brought by Helena, the mother of Emperor Constantine. Carbon dating of the wood, however, dates the relic to the eleventh century A.D.

Chapter 26

Lucius lifted his eyes from the table and sighed. Would there be no end to surprises on this day? But, then again, should anything in the world remain the same on the day that the mightiest empire in the history of the world tottered and fell into barbarian control?

But this?

That an ancestor of his had been in Jerusalem?

Had met the Galilean?

Had witnessed his death?

Not that it mattered whether the stories of the Galilean were based on historical fact or fiction. It made no difference whatsoever. Indeed, it made sense that the man had indeed existed.

In fact, it was fitting that there had been, at one time, a reality from which the legend had grown. Like all myths, it had not appeared fully formed in an instant, like Minerva from the mind of Jove, but a piece at a time. A flair of embellishment here, a fragment of exaggeration there. Each stone of the legend laid by the hands of fervent apologists until an edifice took shape.

So, the Galilean had died after all. And in the manner the Galileans claimed.

He smiled to think of how the anti-Galileans would chafe at this revelation. Their first line of defense had been to claim that the man had never existed. With that barrier breached, they would undoubtedly fall back to the secondary argument that he had been justly executed for sedition and practicing magic. Their last defense—and this they held onto with great passion—was that the man was only "nearly" dead. That he had been taken down from the cross and nursed back to health by his disciples.

After reading Malchus' account, there could be no doubt about the certainty of the Galilean's death. A soldier had thrust a spear deep into the man's chest. If Malchus was a reliable witness—and what reason could he possibly have for telling a lie—there was no doubt about that.

But who was this Galilean in truth?

A charismatic, that is certain. But history was full of them—rare souls who, through the magnetism of their personality, draw the world to them. Even his own ancestor, Malchus, a Roman merchant—a man accustomed to deceptions, lies, and manipulations—even he felt there was something special about the man.

That explained the Galilean's followers. Perhaps it even explained their fervor.

It was surprising to think that an ancestor of his had intercepted this moment of history, had witnessed one of those rare events that tilted the world.

Lucius laughed softly at the thought of this Jesus. So, this was the god of the Christians—a god so impotent that he could not prevent his own crucifixion.

Perhaps, in the end, the great truth of this world was that all religion was composed of lies. But at least in the Roman lies, those who created them had the sense to imbue their deities with enough power and wrath to prevent mere mortals from nailing them to a piece of wood. Say what you will about the Roman pantheon, but if any one of the gods of Olympus had been handled in a similar way, the city that attempted to lay a hand on him would lie in ruins.

One more evidence of the madness of the world. And one more evidence as to how easily little things could become engorged by superstition and make oaks of slivers.

Had the origin of the Roman gods begun in a similar way? Had Apollo been born from the stories told of a rustic sculptor who awoke before dawn and played the lute until the sun ended its round? Had Diana been a woman who hunted with a bow? Had Alcmene claimed that her son, Hercules, had been fathered by Jove to mask the shame of an illicit affair?

What difference did it make?

It was all fiction.

How did the world become so toppled? How could it be that men would willingly die by the tens of thousands to defend their own particular fairy tale against that of another tribe?

Lucius was about to return to the plates when he heard the distant sound of wood striking wood. Someone was trying to get his attention.

Would the interruptions of this day never end?

Once again he covered the plates, hid them among the stacks in his study, and shuffled toward the sound.

When Lucius opened the door and looked out into the street, he saw that a mob had gathered outside his house. He couldn't help it; he laughed.

An indignant man in clerical robes stepped forward out of the crowd. "Do you believe that the presence of the holy bishop is a matter of humor?"

"Apparently, I do," Lucius replied.

"Insolence!" the man shouted, warming to the heat of righteous wrath.

But from behind him appeared another man. Aurelius.

Here. Again.

"You won't mind that I have come to speak with you?" Aurelius said.

"Twice in one day. I am honored. Please enter, but if you would be so kind as to invite your mob to march to the harbor, board a boat, cast off into the deepest part of the ocean, and then take an axe to the bottom, it would be most appreciated."

Aurelius motioned for the group that had followed him to move out of the way, and he entered Lucius' home.

Lucius showed the bishop into the atrium and invited him to sit. "You'll forgive me for laughing, Aurelius. Just before you arrived I was wondering if the day could possibly be filled with more surprises. And here you are at my doorstep . . . accompanied by a mob."

"This day has indeed been filled with surprises," Aurelius replied.

"And the purging? I trust that is coming along well?"

Aurelius smiled and shook his head. "You always had a sense of humor, Lucius. I will give you that."

"If we cannot laugh about a little anarchy, what's the point of living?"

Aurelius lifted the corners of his lips in an effort to hide a frown. "I have come in person because I do not wish our conversation to be overheard by others."

"Very well, you have accomplished your first objective."

Aurelius, alone with his former teacher, seemed to soften. With no one around him to impress, the façade seemed to drop. He sighed deeply and said, "The world is changing, Lucius. It is a very different place from when I sat at your feet years ago."

Lucius sat across from the bishop. "You and I are in complete harmony on that account."

"I wish to come directly to the point," the bishop said. "I have come to ask you if you have considered my request that you vacate the city."

"I have considered your delightful offer; unfortunately, I must refuse. I have, however, decided to propose an alternative: that you, with all the rest of your Galileans, leave immediately. Within a fortnight. You can form a procession if you like—I know how much you enjoy processions. Just line up and march out. I'm sure it will be a memorable sight. One that will be commemorated for centuries. You will be better for it; the city will be better for it. Indeed, the world may be better for it."

Aurelius smiled; he hadn't completely been circumcised of his sense of humor. But the smile gave way to an expression of seriousness. "I have your man," he said.

"I'm sorry?"

"Gunderic, I believe is his name. I have him."

"Very good for you. Now, be a good fellow and give him back."

"It's not as easy as that."

Lucius resisted the impulse to laugh. That was the way it was with these Galileans. When they opened their mouths, absurdities nearly always followed. "Do you really think you can arrest a man merely because he belongs to the household of someone you cannot baptize? It's really preposterous, Aurelius. I know the church is flexing its newly found muscle, but even so—"

"I'm afraid it's more serious than that, Lucius. He has been found guilty of blasphemy."

"Blasphemy? Absurd. He's a Galilean just like you."

"He is Arian. A heretic. And he has spoken blasphemy. I have hundreds of witnesses."

"Ah, blasphemy. Well, that obviously changes everything. We can't have anyone challenging your beliefs. Absolutely not. That would be unforgivable. Well then, I don't see what recourse you have. Certainly, you must decapitate him. Better yet, crucify him. That will send a message."

"The world is changing, Lucius."

"So you keep saying."

"The fact of the matter is that the man's life is in my hands."

The revelation that Gunderic was a Goth intruded into his consciousness. And the hatred returned. That he could be part of the race that sacked Rome. Was there no revenge for that? He considered allowing Aurelius to keep him—but only briefly. Gunderic had been loyal and devoted and, though he had the misfortune to be a Goth, was that sufficient reason for him to die? More, he had lost a child. And he had a wife to care for.

No, he could not allow harm to come to Gunderic. He may be descended of Goths, but he was Lucius' Goth and that seemed to make all the difference.

"Let me see if I understand." Lucius turned his attention to Aurelius. "Because Gunderic said something you disagree with, you now have the authority to take his life?"

Aurelius sat still, a sad smile spreading across his face.

"You are serious."

"Alaric has set his eyes on Carthage, Lucius. It is only a matter of time before he and his soldiers are at our gates. You refuse to believe that I am sincere, but I am convinced there is only one way to prevent disaster and that is to purge the city of all uncleanliness and ungodliness. Unfortunately, that includes all who believe in the old gods. It includes you."

"Of course it includes me. Not that I disagree, mind you. I am as unclean as perhaps anyone in the city—at least as devilish as a man of seventy can be. But, foolishly, I always taught my students that it is in differing opinions—in the clash of ideas—that the truth emerges."

"We do not need to search for the truth. We have the truth."

"And once again the discussion is ended."

"It is impossible for us to come to an agreement on the philosophical aspects of this argument, Lucius. Therefore, let us come to an agreement on the concrete matter of the fate of your servant."

"I will tell you what." Lucius ran a hand through his white hair. "Let Gunderic go and I will come in his place. Disembowel me, feed me to the lions, call lightning from heaven, whatever your rituals dictate. Make it a death to remember. I won't argue. After all, I'm the one you want. We both know that. Leave my servant alone and I will accompany you."

Of course Aurelius was too shrewd to publicly execute the respected Lucius Fidelis Crescentius. Aurelius could murder a common servant and few would notice. But make a martyr of an old man—a defender of the old gods, a man known throughout the continent for his faithfulness to the old order—that would not do. It would be a triumph for paganism. Lucius smiled. Imagine it—Lucius, the great disbeliever, becoming a martyr for the cause of Olympus.

As he thought of the irony, his mind wandered to an old story he had heard in his youth. It involved two sons of a rich man, both of whom were proud and ambitious. They competed against each other in everything they did but particularly in one aspect—they both hungered to inherit their father's vast wealth and extensive lands. After the father died, the two sons were surprised to discover their father's will stated that the two sons were to race their camels from Carthage to Utica and back. The catch was that the son whose camel came in second would inherit the entire fortune.

And so the sons set out, neither of them wanting to lose either the race or the fortune of the father. But they didn't know what to do since the only way to obtain the fortune was to allow the other brother to win the race—and neither one was willing to forfeit a fortune for the bragging rights of having won a camel race.

They arrived in Utica at the same time and were on their painfully slow return to Carthage when, at long last, they came to the home of a wise man whom they hoped could help them with their problem. The man thought about their predicament, then lifted up his head and spoke two words.

Upon hearing the words, the two sons looked at each other dumbfounded and then, as one, sprinted out of the man's house, mounted the camels, and raced as fast as they could back to Carthage.

That was what Lucius needed now. Wise words that could set the world straight again. Wise words that could make sense of a world that had become increasingly locked within impossibilities and incomprehensibleness.

"This is a simple matter, Lucius. Agree to leave Carthage within ninety days and I will return your servant to you," Aurelius said. "I'm afraid I will need your answer now—before I leave."

Why couldn't he come up with the words that could straighten out this confusion? Why couldn't he think?

"Are you listening?" Aurelius repeated.

Lucius shook himself from his reverie and looked into the bishop's eyes. "After all that has happened today, I realize that I failed as your teacher. I failed to teach you the difference between tyranny and the rule of law."

Aurelius shuffled his feet and wiped his hands against his thighs. "I have not come to discuss ethics with you, Lucius. I have come to tell you that the fate of your slave is in your hands."

"You are quite determined, aren't you?"

"Please don't underestimate me. My mission is to save this city. The fate of one insignificant man is nothing compared to the lives I am accountable for."

"You would actually murder an innocent man in order to force me to leave? And you would do it in the name of your god?"

"Cleanse. We do no murder."

"Of course. Forgive me. Murder in this sense demands a holier word."

"Your answer?"

Lucius considered his options. He could not fight this legally. Civil authority rested in the hands of this robed monster. And if Lucius tried, it would be too late. Gunderic would be dead by dawn.

But could he leave Carthage? Leave his villa? His life?

All that he was? All that he remembered?

Could he, an old man, survive such a transition?

Where could he go? East, perhaps. Persia? But where could he flee that would take him far enough away from the influence of these zealots?

And what message would it send if he cowered and fled? It would certainly demoralize those who followed in the paths of the old gods. And it would be a moral victory for the Galileans, Aurelius was counting on that.

Why couldn't he come up with the words of wisdom that could settle this once and for all?

But did it really matter?

Why should he fight for a principle that was, in the end, nothing more than a lie?

But was he doing Gunderic a favor by preserving his life? The poor slave did not even know that he had lost his only child. If Gunderic survived Aurelius and returned to the villa, it would be to discover the terrible truth. And that scar he would carry for the remainder of his life.

"Now, Lucius. I need an answer."

"Let us be clear, Aurelius. If I agree to leave Carthage, you will release Gunderic. And, in addition, you will grant me—and any others who wish to accompany me—safe passage from the city?"

"You have my word. Only that you must leave within ninety days. After that, you have no guarantee."

"You're very generous."

In the end, Lucius thought of the mother who held in her arms the lifeless body of her only child. Could he bring upon her the double sorrow of losing, not only her beloved child, but also her cherished husband all in one night?

No, he could not.

And what was holding him to this villa? This city?

Carthage was merely a shadow of what it once was. It was scarcely the same city he remembered from his youth. The city streets that had been filled with discourse and debate, philosophy and rhetoric, were now silent.

What was the point in thinking when robed monks and priests had all the answers?

Lucius had amassed a small fortune, but who would inherit it? He had no heirs. Gunderic had been branded a heretic—his future could not be here in this city. There was only one logical answer.

Why not use his money to finance an exodus?

Perhaps he could start a new city, far away from the persecutions of this fanatical group. Perhaps he could go far enough away that he could flourish, enjoy life away from this evil.

Would it be so terrible to leave this behind?

"Your answer?"

Lucius stood and waited for Aurelius to do the same.

If he could not think of any words of wisdom, then he would have to simply do the best he could. "Very well, Aurelius," he said. "I will take you at your word."

"You agree to my terms? All of them?"

"I do."

Aurelius bowed slightly and then furrowed his brow. "You understand my benevolence will only endure for ninety days."

"Yes, yes, I understand. After that time you will burn our bodies, fold the ashes into meal, and feed them to the pigs."

Aurelius chuckled quietly and headed to the door.

"I'll expect my servant's return within the hour."

Before the bishop reached for the door, he turned, a sad expression on his face. "I'm sorry that it came to this, Lucius," he said. "You were always one of my favorite teachers."

Lucius held open the door, allowing the bishop to pass through the portal and disappear into the night. He closed the door and the reality of what he had just agreed to descended upon him.

"Tomorrow there is time to think of what I will do," he said to himself as he walked back to his lararium. Today, he would return to his study, pull out the ancient record, and finish reading the account of his ancestor.

NOTES

The Anti-Christian Arguments: The arguments mentioned here are typical of those made by pagans against Christians. The three most detailed surviving ancient anti-Christian books are Celsus, *On the True Doctrine,* tr. J. Hoffmann (1987); Julian, *Against the Galileans,* tr. J. Hoffmann (2004); and Porphyry, *Against the Christians,* tr. J. Hoffmann (1994). The response to Celsus by Christian theologian Origen is found in *Origen: Contra Celsum,* tr. H. Chadwick (1980). For general background see R. Wilken, *The Christians As Romans Saw Them* (2003) and R. MacMullen, *Paganism and Christianity: 100–425* C.E. (1992).

Persecution of Arian Christians: As Christians rose to political power under the Imperial Church of Constantine, they became increasingly intolerant not only of pagans, but of non-orthodox Christians (see H. Drake, *Constantine and the Bishops: The Politics of Intolerance* [2000]).

The wise man's words: According to legend, the two words the wise man spoke were "switch camels."

Chapter 27

The Book of Malchus, son of Mago, of the house of Hanno

I never spoke with Pilate again. Frankly, I didn't want to speak with him; I didn't want to see him. It is enough to say that I arranged the remaining details of our transaction with Antilochus, Pilate's freedman. That done, Glaucus and I prepared to leave that land as quickly as we could.

What can I write concerning Jerusalem in the days following that fateful crucifixion? Numerous extravagant rumors arose on every side regarding the death of the man Pilate called "King of the Jews." One story that spread about the city was that the massive curtain that divided the innermost room of the Jews' temple, their most holy place, split asunder at the very moment the man died—surely a sign of their God's displeasure. The Jews worked almost too zealously to deny the rumor and punished anyone who spoke of it, which caused me to wonder if there wasn't a kernel of truth in it somewhere.

There were other, more bizarre rumors. Some claimed, and it was widely attested as true, that the dead rose from the grave and actually walked the city—a grisly thought.

But these mutterings were silenced as well. Apparently, excommunication from the faith was a powerful motivator of silence, and few men were willing to stand against the wrath of the senate and rulers of the land.

The most troubling story of all was that this "king" had risen from the dead. The leaders of the religion denied it vehemently, of course, but the tomb was indisputably empty—a fact anyone could see for himself. The Jews claimed the body had been stolen by the man's disciples in order to perpetuate the myth.

Interestingly enough, the Jews were the very ones who had demanded Pilate post a guard at the tomb to prevent exactly this sort of event from happening in the first place. How the body ended up missing from the tomb, I had no idea. But I must confess, I enjoyed watching the leaders of the Jews squirm as they attempted to battle each new rumor with increasing levels of panic and frustration.

One thing was certain: every man, woman, and child in the city spoke of little else. Even under threats from the priests, they spoke of it in hushed tones. What did it all mean? Could there be a grain of truth embedded somewhere within all the fantastic stories?

Frankly, I considered the rumors to be wishful thinking created by grief-stricken disciples who could not bear to have their beliefs destroyed along with the man who had given them hope. I may not have been an expert in matters of religion, but I did know that in all my experience, once a man is dead, nothing in the world can make him alive again. And the man on the cross was absolutely dead. I saw the body become limp. I observed his lifeless, unblinking eyes staring down, all the while a storm railed around him. And when the centurion thrust a spear into his side, the man did not so much as blink.

There was no question, none at all. The man was dead.

Nevertheless, Glaucus and I tied up our arrangements as quickly as possible so that we could depart from that strange land and launch once again into the comforting expanse of the sea.

In the days that followed our departure, I immersed myself in my business, pretending to forget about the experience in Jerusalem. But it had unsettled me. It troubled me to the point where it invaded my sleep and worried my days.

It began to manifest itself in numerous ways. What at first appeared to be a continuing curse of bad luck eventually revealed itself as a series of poor decisions on my part. Like the Persians of five centuries earlier, I sailed into a storm off the coast of Greece and lost one of my ships. When an opportunity to invest in an iron mine in the Pyrenees presented itself, I shoveled coin at it only to discover the advocate for the enterprise absconded with all my holdings, never to be heard from again.

Gradually, my façade of a man consumed with his work began to unravel, and every day I became more angry and morose, snapping at my crew and even at Glaucus. I became ever more reclusive, not wanting to speak to anyone and finding solace in limitless swallows of dogmatic wine that shouted out feeble arguments in defense of moderation.

After several weeks, the image of the crucified man gradually bled from my mind and the troubled waters of my soul began to quiet into sweet forgetfulness. But just as the horror of that image diminished, another emerged—a fragment of thought that slowly crystallized and thrust shards of dull aching into my mind.

Xen.

The thought of her filled my consciousness and invaded my dreams more with each passing day.

What was she doing? Was she well?

Had she married?

At night, I continued my habit of watching the sky, wondering if Xen might be looking at the same stars. Did she ever think of me? Had she been able to avoid the consequences of Kix-Kohor's actions or had madness completely taken him?

Through it all, my two great allies—wine and work—kept me from losing my sanity. Business was the one constant in my life. Glaucus and I made our way through the straits of Hercules and up the coast of Iberia until we arrived in the land of the Britons, where we filled the hulls of our vessels with precious tin before making the return voyage back to Caesarea.

We had no trouble from Pilate, who honored our prior agreement without incident. His freedman, Antilochus, perhaps anxious that we not speak of our previous arrangement, was generous and prompt with his payment.

In short, the days turned into months, and life began to once again put on the vestments of the normalcy that mercifully cloaks our lives with the comfort of routine predictability. But in spite of this, I was never at peace. And I was rarely, if ever, completely sober.

It was during the middle of a still night with the moon hovering just above the horizon that Glaucus finally confronted me.

"You're killing yourself," he said.

"Apparently not fast enough."

"Don't misunderstand; I have nothing against it. It's only that in case you were too drunk or too stupid to know it, I felt a responsibility to inform you."

If Glaucus had a gift, it was to perturb. I don't think anyone had the ability to get under my skin the way he did. But I was not in the mood for a fight that night. I was in the mood for forgetting.

"I am perfectly aware of what I am doing," I said. "And if you would be so kind to leave me to it, I would be most grateful."

But he refused. "What do you want?"

"Why must you always ask such irritating questions?"

"You're rich. Relatively young. You have wonderful friends. Let me rephrase that—you have *one* wonderful friend. And yet you sulk."

"I've worked hard to get to the point where I have the luxury of sulking whenever and however I want."

Of course, Glaucus was not the type of man who would leave me soaking in my own pity. Nor was he the kind of friend who would leave when I demanded it. The man was impossible to fight. He did not take offense when I insulted him. When I shouted at him to be silent, he remained at my side. Like a scorned pet that returns to its master's side despite being scolded or beaten, he stayed with me.

How could I remain angry with a man who so obviously loved me?

Of all the people in the world, he had nothing to gain from his friendship with me. He could have struck out on his own. Been successful without me.

And yet he stayed. Silent. Faithful. Patient.

"I know what you want. I can see it in your eyes," he said.

"I have no idea what you're talking about."

"Do you realize that you talk in your sleep?"

"I hope those conversations are more rewarding than when I'm awake."

"There are no conversations. Only a single word. Over and over. The same word. Every night."

If I was not angry before, I was now. I did not like feeling vulnerable. I did not like that Glaucus knew something about me that I did not know myself.

"Absurd."

"Would you like to know what word it is that you speak?"

"Not in the slightest."

"Xen."

It was possible. It seemed like every moment of my waking life I thought of her to some degree, no matter how hard I attempted to drown those thoughts with cask after cask of wine. At first, I convinced myself that it was more curiosity than obsession. But eventually rationalization and denial gave way to the truth. I, who had never loved any woman, was in love with the one woman I had no possibility of ever seeing again. Perhaps the fact that she was so completely unobtainable heightened my obsession. Obsessions, however, are rarely respecters of convenience and, consequently, I found my misery eclipsed only by my determination to numb my senses to the pain.

I thought constantly of the last time I saw her. I remembered her biting words, each one a blade that seared my flesh and left burning scars.

"If you think I have any interest in a man such as you," she had said with poison in her voice. "Stay and die, I care not."

Each time I rehearsed the words they drew flesh blood. They did not sting so much as burrow. And how I had suffered because of them. How I had burned—a slow, painful, burrowing grind.

But lately, I began to wonder. Had she meant what she said? Had she done what she did not out of hate but out of love? Had she said those things to save my life?

I told myself over and again that I was not a schoolboy caught up in the romance of a first crush. I knew there was a distinct possibility that I was painting the scene with colors of my own choosing.

But had there been something in her eyes that belied her anger and revealed a kinder emotion?

I could not be sure. But with the passing of time, I began to imagine that, indeed, there had been signs that betrayed the sincerity of her words. I began to believe that she had spoken those words because it was the only way she could save my life.

What fools we are to fantasy. What slaves we are to rationalization.

But the thought would not leave me, and I began to despise myself for leaving the woman who had saved my life. But what could be done about that now? It was only a memory.

My heart had been broken. But was I any different from every other man and woman in the history of the world? Was I unique?

No. I was merely a man who had made yet another poor decision and, as a result, would live with a wound that could not heal and a grief that could not be slaked.

"It is always the same word," Glaucus said again.

The conversation was becoming more distasteful by the syllable, and I expressed that sentiment to Glaucus.

"I have an idea—leave me in peace."

"I have a better idea," he said. He placed both hands on my shoulders and waited until my eyes met his. "Let's go back."

"What are you talking about?"

"Go back. There. To her."

Was he insane? Go back? We lost most of our crew the first time. The possibility of even finding the same place was so remote as to be a fool's errand. It was far more profitable to simply ply our trade here. Not to mention Kix-Kohor would certainly slit our throats if we ever set foot upon his land again.

"We did it once; we can do it again."

"Absurd," I replied, and rehearsed the list of reasons that had filled my brain like layers of thick sediment—impossible. Insane.

"I understand everything you have said. I know as well as you the risks of such a journey. Let's go back."

He spoke of the adventure, of the wealth to be made. If we took two or even three ships instead of one, we could barter with the king of the land. We could return home with holds filled with gems and have stories to tell that would last us until our mouths were too old to form syllables.

"Only think for a moment," he said. "You can return to Xen."

And once he had uttered these words, I knew I would go. I would do anything to see her once again, to hear her laugh, to look into her eyes. In spite of the risks, in spite of the odds against us, in spite of the fact that finding Xen meant finding Kix-Kohor, which more than likely could cost us our lives, I wanted more than breath itself to make the attempt once again.

"Yes," I said at last. "We will go."

Glaucus smiled and turned to look at the stars. We did not need to speak. Glaucus had discovered the source of my pain and, like a skilled physician, had applied the one remedy that would speak to the hunger deep within me. And, with three words, the course of our lives was once again forever and unalterably changed.

We would return.

And soon.

NOTES

Jewish "senate": A Roman perception of the Jewish Sanhedrin ("sitting together," "assembly," or "council"), which functioned as a legislature and court for the Jews. Jesus was tried by the Sanhedrin, the Greek term being translated as "council" in the KJV (Mark 14:53–65; Matthew 26:57–68; Luke 22:63–71; John 18:12–24).

Persian fleet: In 480 B.C., the Persian war fleet was caught in a great storm off the island of Euboea and many of the ships were destroyed. With the Persian fleet crippled, the Greeks won naval victories at the battles of Artemisium and Salamis, and hence victory in the Persian wars (see Herodotus, *Histories,* 8.8–18; B. Strauss, *The Battle of Salamis* [2004]).

Chapter 28

The Book of Malchus, son of Mago, of the house of Hanno

From that moment on, I became a man possessed with one passion—to once again cross the vast waters and arrive at the other side. I stopped drinking and immersed myself in the task like a man gripped with a white fever.

That we had made the voyage once, I knew, was perhaps something that bordered on the miraculous. To do it again—only a madman would attempt it.

But perhaps that was what I had become: a madman.

Once the decision had been made, I could think of nothing else. There were three keys: first, build the right type of vessels; second, stock them with the right provisions; and, third, find the right crews to man them.

We had already learned much from our first crossing about the kind of ship that would be required to make such a vast voyage, and I laid a fortune at the feet of the finest shipbuilder in Rome to construct two deep-keeled vessels worthy of the venture.

I had supposed that finding a crew would be my greatest difficulty. I was pleasantly surprised, however, that this was not the case. My reputation, aided from the stories of mysterious wealth gained from my first voyage, bolstered interest in the enterprise, and Glaucus and I found that we had the luxury of turning away two men for every one we selected.

But I remembered the faces of those men who accompanied me on that first fateful voyage. Eleven of them did not survive. So I chose men of courage. Men who would not become frightened by the prospect of such a voyage. I did not accept any who were newly married or who had children. As a consequence, my crews were comprised of young, fearless men willing to risk everything on one throw of the dice.

Glaucus was magnificent through it all, perhaps even as obsessed as I was. Whether it was because of a lust for wealth (his self-professed motive) or, as I suspected, merely out of his loyalty for me, I did not know, nor could I tell.

We never again spoke of the why, only of the how. And of that we spoke day and night.

I discovered during this process of preparation that, with enough money, even the thorniest of problems could be purchased and retired. And I also discovered that as I immersed myself in this work, my old energy returned, and I caught myself a time or two actually feeling a measure of joy.

We trained our crews relentlessly, preparing them physically and mentally for the voyage. We withheld from them specific information, explaining only that the voyage was perilous—that there was every likelihood that many who embarked on the ships would never return—but that there was a chance that those who did return would never have to work another day in their lives. I spent sleepless nights reviewing my journals of my prior journey, analyzing every detail, making calculations as to time and food. I made plans for every possible contingency: What if disease broke out? If the food spoiled? If a storm hit? If a leak in the hull appeared? If a monster from the deep rose up?

Every "what if" consumed my thoughts and I focused my every ounce of ability and energy anticipating and solving in advance every conceivable challenge.

At long last, the preparations were made and we set sail. It was a bright and clear morning with a hot sun and cloudless sky. At the point where the eastern horizon was only just visible, I explained to my men what we were attempting and gave them one final opportunity to abandon the enterprise. To my surprise, not one of the men turned back.

And so we set our sails toward the west and determined to risk our lives once again in search of that strange land.

I could fill volumes with the struggles of that voyage—the near mutinies, the superstitious fear, the windless days where it seemed we would forever stall and never move forward.

Many times, we spotted land. But it was not *the* land.

It was not the land of gems, or life, or Xen.

We disembarked twice for water and game, but we always set sail again, looking for those familiar landmarks that I could never forget. My greatest miscalculation was that this new world was vastly larger than I had supposed and, after sailing along the coast for the better part of three weeks, I began to despair of ever finding the site of our original landing.

But fortune favors the persistent and, after a month of searching, we discovered the mountain peak that had haunted my dreams and fired my thoughts.

Glaucus and I both knew it immediately. We had arrived.

Chapter 29

Lucius held his hand in front of him and willed it, unsuccessfully, not to tremble. How had the backs of his hands become so wrinkled? Spotted with brown? Frail? How had the skin become so thin? He noticed the red bruises on his arms. He merely had to lean against something and they appeared, purple and brown continents changing shape over the landscape of his skin.

He remembered the day so many years ago when, as a young man, he had looked at his own father's hands—blue veins slithering under the wrinkled skin, so close to the surface—and realized, with a certain horror, that his father, who had always seemed strong and invincible, was becoming old. The realization struck him with force. And he, at fourteen, felt a certain triumphant pride that he would never be that old. That his hands would never look so shriveled. That he would never become frail.

His father had died nearly four decades ago; he had been sixty years old when he ceased to breathe the air of this earth. And Lucius had already outlived his father by a decade. In truth, even at seventy years, he still thought of himself as a man in his thirties. But oh, what a change in the outer man. The transition from boy to man to frail and elderly. What would the youthful Lucius have thought had he the chance to glimpse what he would become? How horrified would he have been to see the man he was yet to be?

How had he, a young man, become trapped in this old and feeble frame? He was a captive in an ever-confining prison that he had carved out, a day at a time, for himself.

Lost in his thoughts, he scarcely perceived the sound of footsteps coming down the hall.

He recognized the walk. Gunderic.

One step slightly heavier than the other. There was little of elegance in his servant's walk. Each foot slapped at the ground, like a toddler learning to walk.

The poor man had no idea the measure of grief awaiting him in a few steps.

His heart was probably filled with joy and gratitude to his god for a miraculous release from the seemingly-fatal consequences of confronting Aurelius. More than likely, Gunderic clutched in his hands the medicine he had sought in the town. The medicine he hoped would provide a cure for his pale and fragile child.

How little he knew of how his life would change the second he entered that small room and discovered the precious soul he had fathered and loved and cared for, limp and lifeless, pressed to the bosom of his wife.

He was about to receive a wound that would never heal, one that would torture his mind day and night for the remainder of his life. Every day another drop of blood. Every hour another little sorrow. A sigh. An ache. A quick breath. A closing of the eyes. An imperceptible shake of the head.

He expected to hear a cry. He waited for it to fill the air. But there was only silence.

Every man deals with death in his own way.

Some rise in anger, striking at the wind.

Some whimper.

Some grow closer to their gods.

Others never forgive them.

As for himself?

He would take the journey that all who had lived before him had taken. But he would not do it with calm.

He would not do it with courtesy or resignation.

He would go. But with clamor.

But what could he do to console Gunderic? What could he do to take away the agony?

Could he say something? Provide comfort of some kind?

But then he remembered how he had resented those who had tried to comfort him after the death of his own Livia. As though any words could soften the pain he felt. As though he wanted any words to soften the pain. No, he wanted to grieve. He wanted to feel wrath and anger. He wanted to scream at the night and seek vengeance on the day.

The only advice he could give to Gunderic with certainty was that the pain may diminish but it would never go away.

He could tell him that although the pain seemed so severe that it would swallow him—slowly, with every passing day, the acrid, unbearable pain would lessen.

Time would soften sorrow.

But not in a day or a month or a year.

Slow-dripping time. The imperceptible drip of a particle of sand in the vast hourglass of time.

Until then, the pain would be consuming and unstoppable.

And, no matter the remedy, the burning would consume and torment.

But one day in the future—one blessed day—he would remember the way she smiled. The way she laughed. The way she had said that she loved him.

And on that day, he would smile. A painful smile, to be sure. One born of anger, hurt, and bitterness.

Even so, he would smile.

And eventually, another moment would come. And then another

until they grew a little more frequent. And finally the day would come when the gratitude for having known and loved her would outweigh the pain of his loss.

He wanted to tell Gunderic these things but thought better of it. There would be time later for advice. Now, however, was a sacred time—a time of deep sorrow and grief. And Lucius had enough sense not to clumsily interrupt.

Who knew? Perhaps Gunderic, as a true follower of the Galilean, would cause her to rise from the dead. Wasn't that the sort of thing the Galilean had developed a reputation for? If the Galilean did it, why shouldn't his believers do the same?

Should Gunderic appear with his daughter revived at his side, certainly then Lucius would consider the possibility that miracles existed, that there was something notable about this upstart religion. Let them lift a body from the emptiness of the grave and then he would believe.

But Lucius knew better. Once a man's eyes closed for the last time, there was no coming back. A brief lapse. A sleep. And then nothing. No time. No thought. No feeling.

Nothing. Endless nothing.

And Lucius could feel his time of nothing approaching. He no longer denied the reality of it. It could come upon him at any moment. But would that cause him to cower in fear? Would it drive him to depression and inaction?

The only way to fight against death was to *live*. To breathe fire. To never let the sword out of your hand. Slash at the darkness. Defy it. Laugh, insult, and challenge it.

This would be his course.

More, he had his future to think of.

Banished from his home, where would he go?

To the north, the land was overrun with Alaric and his hordes. To the east, the Galileans held an even-greater stranglehold on the people than they did here. To the west was endless water. But to the south? Perhaps there, he could find a new home. In the lands his ancestor Hanno had explored so many, many hundreds of years ago. A savage and strange country. But was that alien land any more feral than his own *civilized* Carthage?

Perhaps what he needed in his old age was a new adventure. Yes, that was it.

A worthy adventure, one that would kill him. That would be perfect. Better to meet his death at a charge rather than sitting in the comfort of his villa, hands folded and waiting meekly for the moment when he would vanish from existence.

So he feared death. What of that?

All the better to confront that fear.

Yes, he would use his fortune. He would use it to buy camels, food, guides.

And he would leave his beloved Carthage behind him. He would voyage into the unknown wilderness and discover a new land far away from here. From all that he knew. From all that he loved.

That was precisely the way he wanted to live the remainder of his days. Violently seeking a new world. Defiantly challenging his fears.

He would look death in the eyes and smile.

Come what may, he would not wait quietly for it.

"Come after me, thou terrible twilight," Lucius whispered. "Assuredly you will find me. But not here. Not here!"

NOTES

Miraculous healing: The belief in miracles was widespread in the ancient world, among both Christians and pagans, and miracles were believed to be an important sign of the divine authenticity of Christianity (W. Cotter, *Miracles in Greco-Roman Antiquity* [1999]; E. Eve, *The Healer from Nazareth: Jesus' Miracles in Historical Context* [2009]).

Chapter 30

The Book of Malchus, son of Mago, of the house of Hanno

Was I nervous? Certainly. But I must confess that I felt an ever-increasing sense of elation knowing that soon, very soon, I would see Xen once again. The questions I had been asking, the doubts, worries, and fears—all would be answered. I could feel my heart pounding inside my chest.

I took three men with me besides Glaucus and gave instructions to those remaining to set up camp and forage for food. It was important that we use stealth and that we confront Kix-Kohor on our terms and not his. My plan was to offer my services as a merchant. Let him make the bronze himself—I did not care. I would supply the precious tin in return for gems and other trade goods. It was a simple trade transaction. Since I was his only hope of creating more of the metal, I felt that my chances of survival were good enough that I was willing to risk my life in the gamble.

I believed that, in the end, his greed would overcome his hatred and even his insanity and that he would accept the offer.

And once he accepted the offer, I would find Xen and apologize for everything. I would spend the rest of my life making her life the perfect one she had imagined since she was a little girl.

We entered the forest and made our way toward the sacred cave, but it was not long before it became obvious that something was terribly wrong.

Our way was infinitely more difficult this time because of the inordinate number of dead trees that lay strewn about. It was as though some giant had picked up a corner of the earth and shook it like a blanket. Many of the trees stood akimbo, pointing at every altitude as though vainly searching for the North Star but falling forever short and perishing in the attempt.

We made our way over and around them, painstakingly making our way toward that secret cave where we first encountered Kix-Kohor and those savage men who had spread lifeblood upon their bodies and spilled it across the ground. But the cave was closed off, buried beneath massive stones that cut deep into the ground and lunged out of the mountainside. Already small lichen had begun to form on the southern exposures, evidence that whatever happened, had happened a while ago.

The landscape had been so completely altered that I began to wonder if we had lost our way. I scrambled over the rocks, seeking for an opening into the cavern. At last I discovered a crevice the size of a man's head that revealed an empty cavern below. I lit a torch, let it drop, and saw in the flickering death of the flame the unforgettable color of the walls, the bloody floor, and the stone altar.

I looked at Glaucus and he at me.

This closing of the cavern, this spilling of the trees, had not been caused by any man.

Earthquake.

And of a massive sort.

It was the only thing that could explain the dead trees and misplaced stones.

How widespread this catastrophe had been, I could not tell. But a sinking feeling began to weigh upon my heart by the minute and terror, such as I had not felt since I was a child, took hold of me.

"Xen," I said through my teeth as I set my feet in the direction of her village.

There are times when the knowledge of events arrives before the word, sight, or evidence. For me, this was one of those times.

Glaucus and the other men called out to me, shouting for me to slow my pace, warning me of a myriad of dangers, but I could not make my feet respond to any thought of slowing.

I ran until my lungs wanted to burst and the sweat of my body drenched my hair and bathed my skin. But I could not stop. I could not slow my pace. I had to reach the village. I had to know what had happened to my Xen.

The first sight of the village confirmed my greatest fears.

In the place of well-ordered structures, rubble. The beautiful symmetry of stone edifices were replaced with jagged stone, a symbol of destruction and chaos. Makeshift living quarters of sticks and leaves had been formed out of the remains; branches and bark spread over openings like fragile roofs. Rocks had been cleared away from broken passages.

The temple that once stood proudly in the center of the village was scarcely more than a jumble of broken stone.

At that moment I did not care if Kix-Kohor greeted me with an army. I had to find Xen.

I had to know what had happened to her.

I ran toward her home, only vaguely hearing the voices behind me.

Glaucus.

But he knew where I was heading. He would find me.

The palace she had lived in was broken and shattered. It had the appearance of a tomb.

She was not there.

In fact, little remained of the palace of Kix-Kohor. His dwelling, once the pride of the village, was now a den for rodents and snakes.

It was then that I noticed the smell. The stench of dying. The terrible, fading decay of rotting corpses.

I ran to a nearby man, his face vaguely familiar. "What happened here?" I demanded.

He shrugged, fear saturating his eyes. I must have appeared to him as a madman.

"Kix-Kohor—what happened to him?"

Slowly, a group of villagers began to surround us. I looked into their eyes, and each of them held within their expression immeasurable sorrow. Whatever had happened here, it had affected every one of them.

An ancient woman, wrinkled and shaking, stepped forward. "Kix-Kohor is no more," the old woman said. "Taken in the time of wrath. Along with my sons and my grandchildren. All of them perished in the time of the wrath of God."

I could see the solemn sorrow in her soul. I could sense the great sadness, the unspeakable depth of pain.

But I needed to know.

"Xen. The sister of Kix-Kohor," I said, with scarcely enough breath to speak the words. "Where is she?"

The elderly woman shook her head. "Better for her had she perished."

I took her by the hands. "She is alive?"

The woman looked to her right. I followed her gaze only to find a young boy who motioned for me to follow.

He led me to a small hut with adobe walls.

Can I possibly paint the landscape of feelings that went through my mind as I stood before that dark opening?

Dread. Fear. Desperation.

Perhaps more than any other thing, though, I felt hope. If she could be alive, then all else was possible. I could care for her and nurse her back to health—of that I had no doubt.

I stepped inside the darkness.

And heard a gasp.

"Xen?" I peered through the dark and saw a form huddled against the wall. "Xen, are you here? It is me. Malchus. I have returned."

"No," said a muffled voice.

"I am here."

"No. No. No," the voice repeated over and again.

I took a step toward her and heard a wounded cry. "Go away."

"I am so sorry. I should never have left you. I should have stayed. I should have been here," I said.

The voice seemed weaker now. Helpless. "Leave me."

It was her voice. I was certain of it. She was alive and she was here.

"Go away and never return."

"I know you are injured."

"I don't want you here."

"I have come to help."

"Please." The pleading in her voice revealed a depth of sorrow that penetrated my heart. "Leave me."

I slowly walked toward her, my eyes becoming accustomed to the dark. She was alone in this place of eternal night; perhaps she had been here for a long time. She had lain here in this lightless room, her face toward the wall, probably wanting nothing more than to die.

At her side was the gray dog that had always accompanied her, his chin resting upon her stomach.

She was crying. Sobbing. But silently.

"I am here, Xen."

"No."

I knelt by her side and tenderly placed a hand on her shoulder. "I am here."

She turned toward me, her face bathed with tears that glistened in the pale light against her skin. She had cut her hair short and it was matted and dirty.

I looked deeply into her eyes and saw in them a hidden sorrow that I could never comprehend.

She put a feverish hand to my face and held it there for a moment. She smiled a bitter and deep smile filled with such great pain that I could not hold back my own tears, and they fell upon her dirty hands and trickled over her stained fingers.

"You should never have returned," she said at last and pulled the old blanket away from her legs. "I am dying."

In the dim light I could see the story of what had happened. She had been caught in the earthquake. Perhaps in her home. Pinned by falling rock.

Her legs were misshapen and withered. Discolored and infected.

I picked up her little body. How light she was. Lighter than a child.

She buried her head in my shoulder as I carried her toward the light. She whimpered in the most heartbreaking tone and pleaded with me to leave her to die.

"No. No. No," she repeated over and over. "I do not want you here. Leave me to die."

"Whether you are going to die I do not know," I said. "What I do know is that if you are meant to die, it will not be here. Not in the dark. Not by yourself."

I would not allow it.

She would not die amidst this filth and stench.

And, if there was anything I could do about it, she would not die at all.

Chapter 31

The Book of Malchus, son of Mago, of the house of Hanno

It took only a moment for Glaucus and I to realize that our plans to become rich had turned to dust. The people had no money and what little they had they traded for food and shelter and other things that could sustain life, bring a portion of comfort, and delay death.

I dispatched Glaucus back to the ships with instructions to return with my men, and as soon as they arrived, we put our backs into the work. We spent our days removing rubble, constructing shelters, and building cisterns to hold clean water.

Xen refused my help; at least at first. She had resigned herself to die. She wanted to die—had been praying to die.

But our wills were entirely at odds. I willed her to live.

And my will would not be denied.

The people of this land had a great knowledge of salutary plants and herbs that were remarkably effective in treating maladies, but Xen had refused help and, since everyone in the village had their own private grief to grapple with, they had left her to fend for herself.

More than half of Xen's people had perished on that great day of the time of God's wrath. Every family had lost many of those they loved and the grief of tragedy yet burned in every heart, although it had been a year since the tragedy had occurred. I learned to my sorrow that Be'nach, my faithful apprentice, was numbered among those who had not survived.

Since so many of the people here were broken both in body and mind, the aid of my little band was of immense relief to them. We worked from earliest light until dark, extending ourselves to all who needed succor.

As a result of our life-saving service, we discovered that in a short time, we had become heroes in the village. The people treated us like royalty. They even pleaded with me to become their king—an honor I steadfastly refused. I had no intention of becoming the next Kix-Kohor. Besides (and perhaps especially), I knew there were other, more powerful, kings in the region—I had met their emissaries firsthand—and they would undoubtedly and inevitably seek to take my life and then subjugate the village. No, that was not the life for me.

For her part, Xen steadfastly refused to speak with me. She would scarcely acknowledge me. Nevertheless I prepared food for her and tended to her wounds. I saw to it that someone was at her side every minute of the day.

I went to see her several times a day and each time I approached, she turned her head to the side and would not look at me.

"Yes, I understand, you want to die," I said cheerfully. "But in the meantime, drink this."

"Yes, it's quite clear you wish to hurt me," I said with a smile. "In the meantime, take a swallow of this porridge."

And so it went until, one day, the corners of her mouth turned up into the hint of a smile and it seemed as though for a brief moment the sun and moon had become brighter and that their healing lights were bathing not one but two souls.

As far as the destruction was concerned, I could not discover much of its cause—only that it had come without warning. It shook the world, turned it upside down, and blanketed the land with a darkness so black that fire could not burn. The earth moved like waves of the ocean, toppling everything on its surface. For three days, the land remained in darkness and the air was filled with the lamentations of those who had lost husbands, children, mothers.

As it was in the village, so apparently, it was across all the land. Who could say how many people had perished? As many as were killed during the cataclysm, more died in the aftermath. Disease, pestilence, and starvation had taken the lives of hundreds in this village. They had only one source of water—a filthy and festering pool that held stagnant water with no outlet. Few of the villagers were healthy enough to begin the work of reconstruction and so buildings had remained toppled and broken, a symbol of the bodies that inhabited the land.

Only now, nearly a year later, were people beginning to recover. Of those lucky enough to have survived, many had broken limbs which had left them crippled, unable to work, walk, or will themselves through the day.

Through the industry of my men, we were able to provide clean water, shelter from the rains, and protection from wild animals that ventured into the village from time to time, scavenging for food.

A few of my men were excellent hunters and they provided meat; others began tilling the soil and growing all manner of food.

When I think of the selfless hours my men gave to the people of that village, tears brim over my eyelids, even to this day. Never have I seen a group work so hard and so selflessly and without pay or any hope of reward. And there was no reward—no reason to work from earliest light until late at night other than our desire to lift the burdens of someone in need—even if that someone was a complete stranger.

My estimation of my men grew daily. I rarely heard a complaint, although I knew that many of them were eager to return home. And, for a group who had joined a risky venture in the hopes of wealth, I was frankly astounded that so few of them grumbled about the loss of fortune.

Something quite unexpected happened during these weeks of toil: I noticed that my men were happy. In truth, I think that for some it was the first time in their lives that they had become so. And they were shocked to realize it. For my part, I, too, discovered that strange emotion growing within my own heart. I felt a terrible contentment. I say terrible because I had long ago given up any hope of ever experiencing that emotion again. Yet there I was, smiling like a simpleton and feeling within my breast the unmistakable signs of happiness.

At the end of the fourth week of steady labor, the village was beginning to take form. Seeds planted. Shelter provided. Each day we learned more of the healing virtues of local plants and herbs and within a short time, this broken and demoralized people began to lift themselves up. Others from the village joined in the effort until, soon, the entire village worked to help the rest. Even those who were disabled wanted to help. Some crafted pottery, others worked looms, and still others assisted with cooking and mending.

And it came to pass that we lived in peace and contentment.

But no matter how contented the people became, I felt great sorrow for Xen and for the many others whose lives had forever changed on the day the earth shook.

So many of them had given up hope. And all lived in terror that another earthquake might follow and finish what the first had started.

It was on a quiet evening, the stars brilliantly sparkling in a velvet sky, that Xen finally told me the story.

"It came in the morning," she said. "The ground shook so violently that I could not remain standing. No one could. And so many died in their homes, crushed by the walls of their homes."

"Your legs . . ." My voice trailed off.

Her lips tightened and she nodded slightly. "The next day when there should have been light, there was none. When the sun should have lifted into the sky, there was a dense dark—so thick we could not make fire. For three days, we could not see the sun or the moon or the stars. All was black. I wondered if we would ever see the sun again but, on the third day, light returned and with the sun, two neighbors heard my cries and moved the stones that had fallen on me. And that is how I was rescued from death. How many times since then have I wished that I had not cried out so they wouldn't have found me."

I imagined the despair she must have felt. Alone in that darkness, unable to move, unable to free herself. Wanting to die. I cursed myself for ever having left her side. I should have been with her. I should have been there to help.

She looked up at me. "And then we heard a voice. Everyone heard it. Everyone in every village, in every city."

"The same voice was heard by all?"

She nodded and told of how the voice had warned everyone everywhere to repent, that the evil one was laughing and his angels were rejoicing at the wickedness of the people. "It was only then," she continued, "after so much sorrow, that we understood the truth we had been trying to deny. *They* had been right."

"They?"

"The believers in the Son of God."

"I don't understand."

"The same ones who predicted the birth of the Son of God also predicted what would happen on the day of his death."

"I remember you told me once of a people who said that, on the day of the birth of the Son of God, night would not fall but day would extend throughout the night."

She nodded.

"And they also spoke of the earthquake?"

"They warned that there would come a time when this man—this Son of God—would be murdered by his own people. They said on that day, the skies would darken and the earth would shake and the whole world would feel the wrath of God."

"When?" I asked. "When did it happen?"

305

"Almost one year ago."

Her words struck at my heart and I found it difficult to breathe. I thought back to where I had been a year ago.

Jerusalem.

I was with Pilate in Jerusalem.

I was on the outskirts of that city, witnessing the murder of an innocent man who had been nailed to a cross.

Xen placed a hand to her forehead. "Why didn't we see? Why didn't we believe?"

Even now, I still thought of him. I remembered the moment he looked into my eyes and said, "Blessed is he that believes though he has not seen."

But I did not believe.

I was not the kind of man to believe simply because someone suggested that I should. I had seen too much gullibility in the world and too much fraud to be taken in by the pitch of some charismatic charlatan.

And yet, I reflected on that terrible day in Jerusalem—the storms, the lightning. The earth shook, rending the rocks and causing everyone to fear for their lives. The stories the people told of the strange events following. Could that be connected with what happened here?

Impossible.

For one, when the earth shook in Jerusalem, it was in the afternoon. When it shook here, it was at first light. So it couldn't have been at the same time. The hour wasn't right.

This thought gave me comfort.

But I could not let go of the feeling that perhaps there might be a connection between my experience and Xen's.

Was it possible?

"There is more," Xen said. "These believers also taught that after the Son of God would be killed by his own people—after he had been placed in his tomb—that he would rise from the dead. And that after he had risen, he would come here. Come to this land."

I found my heart lifting as she said these words. Was I so foolish as to think that the man I had seen could be the one? The Son of God?

Absurd. Jerusalem had no importance. It was an insignificant city on the edge of the Roman world so far away from the hub of civilization and learning that it took weeks to make the journey. If God were to send his Son into the world, surely it would not be to a rustic province in such a backward place. It would not be among a people so primitive and proud that they had not yet been fully assimilated into the empire.

But the thought haunted my mind and struck at my heart.

"Tell me," I said, fearing her response. "Did he appear? Did this Son of God appear? Did he come here like they said?"

She shook her head. "No."

"So the prophecies are false? The earthquake was merely a coincidence?"

"That is what many believe. Others say he will yet come."

I considered her words. Was it possible? Had I seen him on the day of his death? Had I witnessed the crucifixion of a God? Or was my mind playing tricks on me? Was it all a remarkable coincidence?

The thought would not leave me during the days that followed and I reflected often on the terrible image of the man being crucified. Why had this experience affected me so? There had been something about him. Something that I could not define.

But the more I considered it, the more I convinced myself that it was foolishness. A weakness of the human mind that assigns importance to events that happen to us merely because we witnessed them. That is all it was.

And I had convinced myself that this was the case. In fact, I had found peace with the whole idea until something happened that changed everything.

It began with shouting. A young man I had never seen before ran into the village, shouting as he ran. A sheen of perspiration coated his skin and trickled from his forehead and down his cheeks and nose.

"He is come!" the young man panted. "The Son of God!"

Everyone looked to me and waited for my reaction. But I was not in the mood for this superstition. In the end, all it did was create frenzy in the minds of those whose efforts should be focused on creating a better world rather than in dreaming about imaginary beings who inhabited imaginary places and promised imaginary glory to those who obeyed imaginary dogmas that only served to empower priests who benefited handsomely from the whole imaginary mess.

"I saw him with my own eyes," the young man said. "At the temple in the land of Yutal. Come and see!"

You could not fault the boy for his sincerity. That was the thing about fanatics. Their certainty was contagious.

"He has appeared. You must believe me. I saw him with my own eyes. You must hurry! Come with haste to Yutal, for he is there!"

I hated the silence that followed. The people, the boy, everyone looked to me. But what was there to say? I could not allow my people—yes, I called them my people, for although I had refused to be their king, I had begun to look on them as a father does his children—I could not allow my people to hope for something that would turn to dust. They were too fragile. Too vulnerable. And I was building something of substance here. I could not afford for the entire village to yearn after a fable. There was work to be done. There were houses to build and roads to repair.

I directed someone to bring the boy food and water and invited him to sit. "You say you saw a man," I said.

"He is no man. He descended from the sky."

"He flies, this man?"

"I saw what I saw."

"Tell me what this flying man looked like. Did he have feathers? A beak? Talons for feet?"

A few snickers told me my words were having the intended effect.

The boy shook his head. "He looked like a man."

"What kind of man? Was he young? Old? What color was his skin? Eyes? Was his hair white with age? Or was it black as ebony?"

The boy looked around and then pointed at me. "He looked . . . like you. Only younger."

I laughed. "Then we are finally arriving at something of interest. You say he looked like me?"

"More or less. Except . . ."

"Please go on," I said.

"He was younger. And there was something else." The boy hesitated.

I could see he did not want to reveal something. What was he hiding? "Something else?" I prompted.

"He had wounds in his hands, wrists, and feet."

The words struck me with such force that I felt my knees weakening.

"What do you mean, wounds? How did he come by them?"

"When he stretched forth his hands, they were there. I don't know how he got them. All I know is they were there. I touched them myself."

Was I dreaming? Was this some nightmare generated by my foolish obsession to know more about a man I had met only briefly? Was my mind playing tricks on me?

I glanced at Glaucus and saw the troubled look on his face. I lifted my eyebrows and he shook his head as though sharing my confusion.

"What else? What else did you notice about this man?" I demanded of the boy.

"Only what I have said." The boy took a step backward.

"What else did you see?"

When the boy looked at me, his eyes were filled with sadness. "There was something else."

"Yes?"

"He had a wound in his side."

"Could it have been caused by a spear?" I asked, emotion rising in my voice.

"I don't know," he stammered, attempting to remember. "Yes, I think so. It could have been caused by a spear."

I felt my knees weaken again and I looked frantically at Glaucus. The words had struck him as well. We had both witnessed that gruesome scene. The man Pilate had crucified, nails penetrating his hands, wrists, and feet. The thrust of a spear into his side. We had both watched that man die.

That the same man could be here now was insanity. Impossible. Mere fantasy.

What were the words written on the sign over the cross? The sign Pilate caused to be written? The sign that so annoyed the local priests?

King of the Jews.

But there had been another name. What was the man's name?

"There is one other thing," the boy said.

I looked at him, not having words to reply.

"The name. The Son of God told us his name." He looked from face to face and finally into my eyes. "He said his name was Jesus."

And perhaps it was at that moment that—for the first time in my life—I found certainty. A clarity I had never felt before in my life.

In that instant, I knew. I knew I would go to where the boy directed. I knew I would take my people there.

And when I arrived, I would come face to face with the man I had seen in Jerusalem a year ago. The same man I had watched perish on the cross, crucified outside of the walls of the ancient city of Jerusalem.

I would go. And I would see him again.

I would see the man called Jesus.

NOTES

Christ's arrival in the New World: The date of the great earthquake that coincided with the crucifixion of Jesus Christ was in the thirty and fourth year, in the first month, on the fourth day (3 Nephi 8:5). After the quake, darkness came over the land for the space of three days (3 Nephi 8:23) and the people in all the land heard the voice of Jesus Christ (3 Nephi 9). But nearly a year passed between the time of the earthquake and the appearance of Jesus Christ in the New World (see 3 Nephi 10:18).

Yutal: In the Mayan language, *yutal* means "fruited" or "fruitful." We are using it as a hypothetical translation of Bountiful (3 Nephi 11:1), the location of the theophany of Christ in 3 Nephi 9–28.

Chapter 32

One thought thundered through Lucius' mind.

Impossible.

Impossible!

It could not be.

He prided himself on his ability to think critically. On being able to dissect rhetoric, cut through persuasive babble, discover flaws in logic, and respond with acerbic intellect.

But after reading this? What now?

What should he do? Fall to his knees? Become one of them—a Galilean? Should he believe? Or dismiss this Malchus as an impostor and charlatan?

In spite of the violence of the previous night, Lucius knew deep within him that it had been years since he had believed in anything. On the day his Livia died, the roots of belief had been cut and the branches of faith had been turning brown and brittle, one leaf at a time, until there was no sap left within. Perhaps not even a hope.

How many years had he simply gone through the motions of pretending his faith? Defending a withering religion? Knowing but refusing to acknowledge that he was a well without water, a trumpet incapable of making a sound?

One thing he knew: everyone was selling something. Fish or philosophy, residences or religion. All of it sprang from the same source.

Find someone with passion in his voice and at the end of his fervor

313

you inevitably found the desire to make a sale. And the motive was always the same: personal gain.

That was human nature. That was fact.

But this Malchus? The man was perhaps his own flesh and blood—a merchant by trade, a man whose life was devoted to the art of making a sale—what was he selling?

Nothing that Lucius could discern. Malchus was merely carving his life one painstaking stroke at a time into sheets of bronze, making a record of what he had experienced and witnessed.

But what he suggested!

That the Galilean had risen from the dead? Impossible.

That this Galilean was, in truth, the Son of God? Unthinkable.

That Aurelius could be right? That was the most bitter thought of all.

Was it possible that Lucius had fought all his life against something that was, in fact, true?

Cruel irony that he should find this record in the twilight of his life, a final and resounding thunder proclaiming his life a fraud, a magnificent miscalculation.

Perhaps there was a god after all. Such perfectly formed irony could not be conceived by mortal hands.

He whom the gods hate, they destroy. Their revenge is infinite. Their animus, terrible.

And the greatest, most horrendous punishment Lucius could conceive would be to be forced to face the unspeakable truth that his entire life had been a blunder. That it had counted for nothing. That he had been wrong in nearly every thought. That nearly every decision he had made was a futility. That his confidence had been a sham.

If this Galilean had indeed come back from the dead, it was the greatest miracle in the history of mankind. Was it possible that Lucius' own ancestor had witnessed it? And, if so, what did it mean about death? About his death? About Livia's death? Was it possible there was something more than infinite nothingness? Was it possible there was such a thing as life after life?

He felt compelled to read more but couldn't force his eyes to focus on the words before him. If Malchus' convictions were true—if the Galilean was indeed the Son of God—what did that mean for him?

Would the world change?

Would he?

Could he ignore it? Marginalize it? Forget it? Or, heaven forbid, would he become one of those rabid, bleary-eyed souls who folded their hands, fashioned for themselves an expression of holy bliss, smiled at insults, whispered unintelligible supplications, looked terribly hurt whenever anyone scowled at them?

Lost in thought, he scarcely registered the sound coming from down the hall.

Soft singing. A chorus of voices, young and old. A sweet, mournful melody that perfumed the air with its sound.

Gunderic.

He had completely forgotten about his servant. What grief the man must be feeling now. What sorrow.

The events of the night had washed from him his bitterness of the revelation of his servant's connection to the hated Goths. All that remained was sorrow. Lucius raised himself from the table and decided that, as much as he wanted to avoid it, he had to speak with his servant. He had to say something, offer a word of comfort. Perhaps he could speak of his own grief—the death of Livia and his own journey to recover from that terrible wound. More than likely, he would stand before his servant and no words would come. But he had to try.

Why did they sing? Had the girl been raised from the dead? Had the power of the Galilean reached through the centuries and returned the child to life? If the girl lived again, then he could believe. He might even become one of them if such a thing happened.

The thoughts pounded in his skull as he stepped heavily toward the quarters of his servant. As he neared the room, the singing grew louder. People stood outside the doorway, each with a candle in hand.

Singing.

What were the words? He could not quite understand . . . new birth, veil, live again, rise in the resurrection . . .

The small group parted as he neared, allowing him to enter the room. Inside, he saw Gunderic on his knees in front of his unmoving and lifeless child, his cheeks bathed with tears. His voice choked, and yet he sang.

He sang!

What were the words?

Blessed name of Jesus Christ, lift the voice in praise of He who conquered death.

A song of gratitude? Of thanksgiving?

He looked into the faces around him. Great sorrow, yes. But something else.

Hope.

No, greater than hope.

Confidence. Calm surety.

What Lucius wouldn't give to have the knowledge that when he perished, he would not simply disappear once and forever, an ember disappearing in the growing dark, but instead that he would live again, a resurrected man in a youthful, perfect body. He would give all that he possessed to be able to once again take the hand of his beloved Livia, embrace her tightly in his arms, hear her laugh, and feel the softness of her cheek.

. . . Though removed from us a little space, one day we shall again embrace . . .

He slowly approached Gunderic and dropped to his knees, placing a hand on his servant's shoulders.

Gunderic turned to look at him and their eyes locked, sharing incomprehensible grief and understanding.

"I am . . . terribly, terribly sorry," Lucius said.

Gunderic smiled briefly through his tears.

"I am pleased you have so many here to share your burden."

Lucius reached for the hand of Gunderic's wife and pressed it in his. "Whatever you need, whatever the cost . . ."

And then he rose to his feet and looked about the room again.

The sounds of singing filled him with . . .

What was that feeling?

. . . *And though thy hand will close our eyes and silence breath, in Jesus Christ we all will conquer death* . . .

Calm.

In the midst of death, calm.

Lucius looked from face to face and saw a common grief, yet a common surety. A common calm.

Whatever the shortcomings of this religion, it gave them comfort.

More, it gave *him* comfort.

The power of such a belief!

How he wanted to believe it. No, how he needed to believe it.

And here, amidst the song and sorrowful smiles, here amidst the love and calm, perhaps for the first time in a very long time, he entertained the thought that death may not be the end after all. And as the thoughts swelled within his heart, he felt the wetness on his cheek and the rising swelling in his chest.

He turned quickly and left the room so that he could not be seen.

But as he walked to his library, the emotions overcame him at last and he wept unashamedly and without restraint.

Perhaps there *was* hope.

Perhaps darkness was not his fate.

Perhaps one day, he would once again look into his beloved Livia's eyes. And how glorious—how incomprehensibly joyous that would be.

If only it were true.

NOTES

Early Christian funerals: These funerals were notable in the late antique period for the Christians' belief in the resurrection of the dead. Although mourning was an integral part of funeral rituals, the expectation of a blessed afterlife, including the resurrection of slaves, was puzzling to pagan Romans. Singing psalms and hymns was common, as depicted here.

Chapter 33

The Book of Malchus, son of Mago, of the house of Hanno

The journey took the better part of a week. We departed at first light, leaving no one behind who wished to come. Those who were well enough to travel assisted the injured and sick. Some walked with the aid of staffs, others we placed upon beds of sticks and branches that we carried as we walked.

For the first time since my arrival, I saw a spark in Xen's eyes. She did not have to tell me she wanted to make the journey; I could tell that she yearned with all her heart to go. I gladly made a makeshift bed for her to lie on as Glaucus and I carried her toward Yutal.

It was a journey that caused in my people a certain fear. Yutal was the city of the enemy. And my people had a deep-rooted and abiding hatred of them. The conflict between Xen's people and theirs had lasted not generations, but centuries. Could such hatred be measured in heartbreak or death, certainly it would stand among the most terrible and severe since the beginning of the world.

A story too similar to the hundreds of others that has been replayed over and again—heroes and hierophants, tyrants and traitors—the same tired tale repeated endlessly until the earth refilled itself and overflowed with blood, horror, and sorrow.

Each faction had right on their side. Each army oppressed. Each with a thousand justifications for vengeance.

This great, overarching conflict had stretched through the centuries. It was longer even than Carthage's war with Rome. It had been an epic conflict on the scale of Rome's struggle with the Teuton barbarians or the titanic conflict between the Greeks and the Persians.

When I probed to discover the roots of this hatred, I discovered at its source the shards of a broken family. Long ago, two brothers fought. They separated, passing their hatred of each other to their children until it became an all-consuming civil war that had lasted nearly six centuries.

Like many other such conflicts, the root of this one was religion—something I could not readily understand. Religion had never settled into my heart. Since a youth, I had looked at it as something to endure—as one who accepts the heat of summer. Bearing one's back to it grudgingly and fatalistically. In the end, my relationship with deity was more of a non-aggression pact than a belief. I did little to offend the gods, hoping only for similar treatment in return.

But now, something had changed. Before, my belief had been little more than curiosity mingled with apathy. Now, it was something different. Was it knowledge?

I suppose that was it.

I knew.

When I first saw the man in Jerusalem, *I knew.* I do not know how, but I knew. And yet, I compelled myself to disbelieve. For true belief required action. Change. And I refused to change as a result of a chance encounter.

But now, *I knew* again.

And when I came face to face with the man, I would not be surprised. Seeing him in the flesh could not add to the knowledge I already possessed.

I focused on the task at hand: to get my people to the land of Yutal. It was a journey of only a few days but, with our crippled and ailing, the sun had risen, ascended, and touched the western horizon six times before we entered the city.

Yutal. At one time, it must have been a magnificent city. Larger than the city of my people by four or five times, it had the appearance of majesty and authority. Yet it, too, was broken. Jagged stone cut into the horizon and debris covered the ground, giving testimony that destruction had indeed descended on the whole land. Charred trees and ashes littered the landscape and the sides of buildings showed scarring of fire.

In spite of the destruction, the city bristled with activity, filled with a sudden influx of immigrants until the inhabitants spilled over its edges and into the surrounding land. All had come here, come to see the god who had descended from the sky and spoke from the heavens.

"Where is he?" I asked a group who were huddled together.

"Departed."

The finality in their inflection troubled me. "When will he return?"

They did not answer but the sorrow in their eyes made my heart sink.

But this could not be. Surely he would return. Surely, I had not traveled so long and so far not to see with my own eyes.

"Did he say where he was going?"

A crowd began to gather around my people. Was there anything more terrible in the world than understanding eyes? Compassionate eyes?

I looked at the faces of those who had followed me. Immeasurable sadness in their eyes. I looked into Xen's eyes and the sorrow within them broke my heart. For the first time since our decision to make the journey, I began to feel overcome by the weight of sadness.

None of us had the energy to go on. We found a clearing and rested our weary bodies and tried to accept the burden of disappointment. Soon strangers appeared with food and drink, and we accepted their hospitality gratefully.

Others offered shelter for as long as we wanted to stay in the city.

Men and women skilled in the healing arts appeared and tended to those who were sick and disabled.

There was something different about these people, I began to realize.

There was more than the mere look of compassion in their eyes. Where others offered pity, these offered succor. They extended themselves in service to us. Though they did not know us, they knelt at our sides and administered to our grief and pain.

"Why are you doing this?" I asked.

"It is his way," they said.

They spoke of how he had healed their sick. How the lame walked, the blind received their sight, the dead raised to life.

He was a man of miracles. A man of compassion. He had taught them to love others and minister to their needs.

And, once again, a terrible sadness came over me. If only I could have seen him. If only I could have told him how sorry I was that I had not come to his defense on that day so long ago. If only I had spoken with Pilate—I had his ear!

But I was too late. I had slept the morning away, unaware of what was happening in the city. I did not open my mouth.

I stood before my people and looked into their faces. They had offered their sweat and blood and sinew day and night to lift themselves up from the sorrow of the destruction. Their muscles and backs ached from their constant labors. And they never complained. They smiled and laughed as they worked, asking only to do as much as they could before the light of the sun evaporated into the darkness of night. How I loved my people.

Yes, I had remained silent that day—a wound I would bear for the remainder of my life—but I would not make that mistake again. I raised a hand and asked for the attention of my people.

"I have something to say to you this evening. A few days ago, a messenger arrived in our city saying that the Son of God had appeared to the people of this city. I am told he has departed. It is not known if he will return."

I looked into the eyes of my men. Men of the sea, who had been cut from the hardest, crudest stone. They, too, had become new men since arriving in this land. I had watched the sweat form on their backs as they broke stone, hauled timber, and hunted game—and all for strangers. I knew they had dedicated their strength and their might in relieving the distress of others.

"I grieve with you that he is not here. But we do not need to see to believe. Blessed is he who believes who has not seen. Look about you. That is all you need to do. Look into the eyes of those who are here. Look at their faces. They know."

An aged man stepped forward. "It is true. I witnessed it with my own eyes."

Dozens of others nodded their heads in silent witness.

"The people of this city have seen what we have not," I said. "With their hands, they have touched the hem of his garments and felt his embrace."

A young woman overcome with emotion said, "He reached forth his hands and I felt them. I touched the wounds in his hands."

I felt courage such as I had never felt before in my life. And certainty of such a nature that I burned from the inside until it felt as though a light shone around me. I spoke again, "We have come, hoping against hope to see what others have seen. I know you desperately wanted to see him. I wanted it for myself more than I have words to express."

I looked through the fading light for Glaucus, my dear friend. My dear brother. Toward the shadows in the back, I saw him. Our eyes locked, and I saw in him what I was feeling myself. I reached out and beckoned for him to approach.

"You are a good people. In all my days, I have not seen better. Your many sacrifices, your tireless toil for others, your tenderness and love—I have not seen its like. I know you are disappointed that you have not witnessed what these others have seen. But I stand before you this day with another witness."

Glaucus arrived at my side and I placed my arm around his shoulder. He fairly glowed with light. An indescribable joy and certainty descended upon me as I continued speaking.

"Those of this city have seen what we have not. But I stand before you today to speak of things that no one here knows. Glaucus understands, for he was with me. We stand before you as a second witness. We, too, have seen the Son of God."

Whispers shuttled through those of my people and from those around us. The sound of shuffling feet told me that others were arriving, filling the spaces to the sides and behind me.

"You say the Son of God lived in a land far away. That he healed the sick, lifted the hearts of the disconsolate, that he reached out to the poor and the despised of the world. You say that he was taken by evil men and crucified. That he perished on our behalf. Of this, Glaucus and I can testify. For we saw it with our own eyes. We were there on the day the Son of God was lifted up on the cross. We were there as he looked into the heavens and down upon his friends. We were there as life ebbed from his body. We were there when the spear was thrust into his side."

I looked at Glaucus and saw the same fire in his eyes that must have been in mine. I knew that he knew as surely as did I. He knew that the man we had seen on that day so long ago was the Son of God. The Savior of mankind.

"I have not been able to forget that day. To be honest, I did not fully know the significance of it until recently. Until I heard of a man who descended from the sky, wounds in his hands and feet. But I know now. I know with a surety that sight cannot amplify. He lives! He lives! I sorrow with you that we have not seen with our eyes, but I tell you the words that the Son of God spoke to me: Blessed is he that believes, though he has not seen."

I heard the sounds of footsteps and saw as people pushed in from all sides to hear my words. I looked into the eyes of my Xen. Tears bathed her cheeks and such a look of joy and faith glowed from her that I could not restrain my own tears.

"Can you not feel it? This is the witness, borne of God himself. And I know more surely than if he were standing beside me—this man, this Jesus, lived! He is the Son of the Father, our Savior, our God."

As I spoke these words, I heard the rustling of clothing from behind me, and I knew again without seeing, for my heart swelled with such force that I felt it might burst. My emotions rose to the point where I could scarcely speak.

And then I felt a hand upon my shoulder.

I turned.

And saw.

It was he.

The man who had purged the temple of moneychangers.

The man who had spoken to me of belief.

The man who had been lifted up on the cross.

I looked briefly into his eyes, wondering if he would remember. I wanted to fall to my knees before him but he acted too soon. He took me in his arms, and I embraced him and felt his arms encircle me.

And my heart and mind were filled with such overwhelming love that it enfolded and burned within me, bringing me such light and joy as I never thought possible to experience.

I stood before the Son of God. And though I was a wicked man, I felt pure and holy and clean.

In that moment, I knew with a surety that can never be shaken that this Jesus was my Savior, Redeemer, and King.

Before, I had wondered if my life would change once I saw with my own eyes and heard with my own ears.

Yes. Everything changed.

I became a different man. Forever different.

And the things I thought were important before, now seemed like a child's diversion.

From that moment on, I became a new man. A different man. A better, kinder, and happier man.

The entire world changed on the day that I felt the embrace of the man the world knew as Jesus the Christ, the Only Begotten of the Father.

NOTES

Rome's conflict with Carthage: This conflict lasted more than a century, from 265 to 146 B.C., and involved three major conflicts, most famously Hannibal's campaigns against Rome, before culminating in the destruction of Carthage. The course of these wars are recounted by Livy, *Hannibal's War* (2009) and Polybius, *The Rise of the Roman Empire* (1980). (See also A. Goldsworthy, *The Fall of Carthage: The Punic Wars, 265–146 B.C.* [2007].)

War with the Teutons: The struggle with the northern Germanic tribes lasted nearly two centuries, culminating with the fall of Rome and the capture of the western empire by the Germans. Lucius lives at the culmination of the Germanic conquests. (M. Kulikowski, *Rome's Gothic Wars: From the Third Century to Alaric* [2008].)

Greco-Persian Wars: Struggles between the Persians and Greeks lasted nearly two centuries, from the first Persian invasions of Greece in the early sixth century through Alexander's destruction of the Persian Empire from 336 to 329 B.C., and continued between Rome and Persia through the seventh century A.D.

Chapter 34

The Book of Malchus, son of Mago, of the house of Hanno

Thirty years have passed since that day—since the coming of the Son of God. Although much has happened since that time, I think often of that day.

I think of the man I was before and the man I have since become. I may have the same name and a similar outward appearance, but I am a man with a renewed countenance: his countenance.

I am a new creature.

To say that life forever changed on that day is too simple a statement. The words do not give proper emphasis.

White light piercing darkness.

Clarity chasing confusion.

No, I cannot adequately describe the transformation except to say that what was filthy and crude became pure and refined. Where the world was dim and chaotic, it became clear and bright.

The story of my life since that unforgettable day would fill volumes. But that is a tale of a different kind and for another time. However, for the purposes of this record, that day was both the end as well as the beginning.

On that day we all were healed. Some of physical wounds, but all of emotional and spiritual ones. We all felt the miracle as he touched us and we became whole.

I lifted my beloved Xen in my arms and carried her to him. He took her by the hand, smiled and spoke.

"Stand," he said.

And she stood.

She walked!

She leapt!

I swear to you that from that moment on, she could outrun me. And oh, how she loved to race! And what joy it gave me to watch her move and walk and dance.

I think that of the two of us, however, he gave to me the greater miracle. Where he gave new legs to Xen, to me he granted a new heart. In an instant, I became a better man. And every impulse of unkindness, every temptation to do wrong, evaporated like morning mist. From that day on I could not bear the thought of doing or thinking anything that would disappoint my Savior.

This was not a gift that lasted an hour or a day, but one that has stayed with me all my life. I have tasted the sweetness that comes from faith, hope, and charity. And, knowing the truth, knowing the difference between the fruit of good and evil, I turned my heart, might, and mind towards him who had saved me from my sins.

I became, for lack of a better word, holy.

Perhaps this sounds boastful. I do not mean it so. For the entire population—every man, woman, and child—became holy as well. And in the wake of holiness, joy greater than we could have anticipated. Such joy as to make the heart dance and the spirit sing.

Xen and I married soon after, and we were blessed with three beautiful children. Glaucus, I am pleased to relate, married as well; he and his wife had two sons.

After returning to our city, we set our backs to rebuilding it until it was greater than it had ever been before. Again, the people wanted me to be their ruler, but I refused. Glaucus refused as well. But ruling a city such as ours was not difficult work for the people were virtuous and every dispute ended in friendship, each person seeking the best interests of the other.

After the work of rebuilding the city, Glaucus and I began once again to do what we knew best. We formed a fleet of ships and began to trade up and down the coast. But we did not do it for money; worldly wealth had no allure for either of us. We provided supplies and nourishment to those farther away and, in the process, slaked our thirst for adventure.

Xen, despite my strong objections, would not leave my side. My cherished one would not listen to reason or pleading. And so she accompanied me on my many travels. My children, too, accompanied us so that, always, we were together.

Over the course of our years, we had many opportunities to tell our story to those who had not yet heard the remarkable news. And many entered the waters of baptism after hearing our witness.

And now, so many years later, I set my hand to record my story. My prayer is that these words will reach some descendant and that God will touch his heart so that he can understand what I know.

To those who might read these words, I cannot adequately describe what it is like to live in a world without greed, envy, or hatred. I cannot express the joy that consumes my daily walk.

There were no poor among us. For we all shared of our substance, and all worked to the best of their abilities in labors that benefited the whole.

In short, the span of our lives was bathed in peace, prosperity, and goodness. We loved our God. We loved each other. We lived our lives in peace, contentment, and fulfillment.

And though we were subject to the normal illnesses and disappointments of this mortal world, I do not think it too much of an exaggeration to claim that we lived in a paradise.

It has been nearly a year since I stepped away from my ships and returned home to live the remainder of my days with my beloved Xen, children, and grandchildren. And for all these years, Xen's legs have been strong and without pain. I am grateful beyond measure for that miracle. I, too, have had a similar miracle regarding my heart; it has never reverted back to the way it used to be. And for that I am filled with overflowing thanksgiving.

And so the years passed in peace, contentment, and prosperity. After many years, a few of my men—capable seamen who had accompanied me so many years ago—began to speak of returning to the old land. They desired to learn of the fate of their loved ones and see them once again before they died. They wanted to testify of what they had witnessed here and bring to others the joy they had experienced.

At first the success of such a mission seemed highly unlikely, given that only Glaucus and myself had ever piloted a ship across that great ocean. For my part, my life was here. My family was content. And I had neither the stamina nor desire to make the attempt. But, to my surprise, Glaucus and his sons warmed to the idea, and the more they thought of it, the more they wanted to make the journey. Though Glaucus, too, was growing old, he had made the voyage before. He knew the perils of the attempt. And, most important, he had the record of our previous attempts. He knew the way.

I gave him the benefit of my knowledge, of course. And I have, at the end of this record, described in as much detail as I can, the path I took to arrive at this land. Perhaps my record will inspire some other brave soul who will make the attempt and arrive one day on our shores. If so, know that you are welcome, for all who embrace the gentle Christ are brothers and sisters here.

And so Glaucus began the preparations for the journey. Two deep-hulled ships were fashioned from the finest hardwood. We stocked them with dried meats, grains, fruits, and water to last the voyage. We also provided him with gems and artifacts from our world that would not only give credibility to their words but that could also be traded, and thus supply them with the means to travel anywhere they desired and provide for their needs.

I assisted in building the ships, ensuring that they were seaworthy and capable of so great an attempt.

But there was one remaining task I needed to perform before the ships sailed.

The tin I had brought on my second voyage had been put to good use over the years. Of course, there was no need for weapons or armor. But oh, what tools I made! Knives for shaping wood, rings for my ships, biting plow blades that dug into soil and allowed us to plant and harvest crops. I guarded my supply of tin carefully, knowing how precious it was. But after all these years, the inventory had dwindled until I had only enough for a few remaining projects. I had to choose wisely and, as I thought of Glaucus' plan to return to our old world, I knew what I must do.

I fashioned thin plates of bronze. With a little work, I discovered a process where I could etch words onto the metal. It is a terribly slow ordeal but the importance of the work encouraged me, and I labored day and night writing the words you are reading now.

I do not know exactly why I feel compelled to do this. Perhaps it is the hope that the story of my life would not be lost. That the things I have witnessed and experienced would matter to some other soul. Perhaps even to one who is lost himself and seeking for a path to peace and happiness.

Perhaps my brother and his family who live in Carthage might read my story and find hope and comfort. Perhaps through my experience others might find faith.

How often I have laughed at myself for even making the attempt. As capable a sailor as Glaucus is, I know the perils of the voyage. The likelihood of these plates ending up at the bottom of an endless ocean is great.

Nevertheless, I have spent many hours in prayer beseeching my God that these records will not perish and have felt encouraged by the Spirit to continue, and so I have.

At last, I have arrived at the end of my story.

It is late at night as I etch these words, and my beloved Xen is at my side. She has ever been at my side. Of all the miracles I have witnessed, that is the greatest and most valuable of all.

How I cherish her. How she has enriched my life.

She has honored me beyond my power to describe in loving me. She is my joy and my consolation. She is my inspiration.

She is my life.

At first light Glaucus and his band will set sail toward the morning sun. I will hand to him this record with instructions to see it safely to my brother or his children in Carthage.

Faithful Glaucus—if anyone can accomplish such a task, it is he.

I am saddened that I will soon embrace my old friend for the last time. As the ships fill their sails with wind and fade into the distant deep, I already know the feeling of loss that will overcome me.

It is hard to say final good-byes to those who have entwined their lives with yours. Nevertheless, I trust in the Lord and believe that he will watch over my good friend and help him successfully navigate the great ocean.

To those who read these words, my greatest wish is that you know that once there was a man named Malchus, son of Mago, of the house of Hanno.

And though he was a common sailor, through the grace of Jesus Christ, he discovered truth. He discovered light. And perhaps most marvelous of all, he discovered love.

I pray that you will discover the same.

Amen.

332

Epilogue

The Writings of Lucius Fidelis Crescentius, son of Flavius, of the house of Hanno

How strange it is to etch characters upon this unforgiving metal. How remarkable that these plates were fashioned by Malchus himself. I wonder if he had any idea that nearly four centuries later, a member of the house of Hanno would read his words and add his own words to this record?

Marking letters on bronze is arduous work. Each stroke must be made with precision and force. It is a time-consuming task and, as a result, I have renewed respect for my beloved ancestor, Malchus. He has filled this book with plate after plate of writing.

I intend to take up only a little space. To add my postlude to his remarkable record.

All is ready for my departure. It is almost time.

I promised Aurelius that I would leave within ninety days, and at the break of dawn I will fulfill that promise. I have spent nearly my entire fortune in the building of two ships—deep-hulled ships that will carry more than one hundred souls away from this doomed city.

I say doomed because I leave it in the hands of Aurelius. If he does not destroy it, surely Alaric and his hordes will.

For me, I feel I have chosen the better part. I have chosen the path of high adventure.

In another hour, we shall set sail toward the setting sun and we will follow to the best of our abilities the instructions my ancient ancestor left in this record. We will attempt to seek that land of paradise where he lived.

I have shared the words of Malchus with my former slave, Gunderic; I say former because I have given to him and his wife their freedom. Gunderic has shared Malchus' testimony with others of his faith. They are all Arian Christians, of course, and therefore at risk of extinction at the hand of Aurelius and his Athanasian cult.

These friends of Gunderic seem, at least in embryo, reminiscent of the people Malchus described. They are kind. They seem sincere. Who is to say but that they will fit well into this new society and this new world?

Their obsession with religion is nearly more than I can stomach, but what is one small defect amidst so many virtues?

As for my part, I can't claim that having discovered and read the words of my ancestor has changed me in a dramatic way. If I am honest, all I can admit is that it has opened up possibilities that I had not considered before.

I have no reason to doubt the authenticity of Malchus' record or to question his sincerity.

His testimony is clear and compelling.

And yet, after a lifetime of learning and understanding the frailties of man, how can I not remain, at least in part, doubtful?

Perhaps doubt is too harsh a word. For I have considered things of late I never would have thought possible. Allow me to merely say that, although I may not be a believer, I am no longer a cynic either.

I am a believing doubter.

In spite of Malchus' record, I am not yet ready to call myself a Christian, although I do admit the possibility that there is more to life than perhaps I had supposed.

And this Jesus?

Perhaps.

I will not throw my soul into another delusion. Not yet at least.

No, I will wait for evidence.

I will attempt the voyage that my ancestor made. I will launch into the deep and challenge the great Oceanus. Though more than three hundred and fifty years have passed since Malchus wrote his final words on bronze, I yet hope to find the people he described. I have decided already that should we succeed in crossing the ocean and find at the end of our voyage a people living in peace and joy, each seeking the good of his neighbor, perhaps then, I will become as devout a believer as Gunderic.

What irony! Lucius Fidelis Crescentius, a Christian! Oh, how the Emperor Julian would laugh if we were to meet again!

As a philosopher, I want to believe that somewhere in the world, there are people who possess the truth. That somewhere there is a place without hunger. That somewhere there are people who seek not their own selfish interests but the good of others. A people who, when others suffer, accept that suffering as their own.

What a remarkable thing that would be! To be candid, I am eager to begin this great adventure. I will leave these plates with a great-nephew of mine. He is of a serious disposition and will guard them well. I have impressed upon him their value and have asked him to preserve them at all costs. Even hide them if he must, deep in some hidden cave out in the southern desert should Alaric advance on the city with his Goths. Perhaps these words will survive and some other future Lucius will one day find them and pass them on to those of his generation.

As I lay down this stylus and leave behind my old life, my beloved Carthage, and all that I have loved, I do so with the hope that I shall find at last what I have sought for my entire life: the knowledge that there is more to this mortality than merely what we see with our eyes and hear with our ears.

Yes, that is what I desire.

To at last believe.

To hope that when I close my eyes for the final time in this mortal sphere, I will open them again and behold a new and glorious land.

That one day I will once again take my beloved Livia in my arms. That we will laugh together and walk together and that I will shower her with endless kisses and speak to her of things that can encompass an eternity of living and love. And that she will never leave my side, never in all the time that remains forever and forever throughout endless eternity.

I would give all that I have and all that I am to have that faith, to have that hope. I would give everything to know that I am more than a mere speck of dust destined to forget and be forgotten.

Yes—and I will say it—I pray that I, too, will come to know that a man once lived who was the Son of God. A man who lived a perfect life, healed the sick, brought comfort to the weary, gave hope to the disconsolate, and broke once and forever the terrible bands of death. I pray with all the passion of my heart that there is such a thing as the hope of the resurrection.

Gunderic has come to tell me that all is ready.

They are waiting for me. It is time for me to say my farewells to my villa, my city. My old life.

The ship awaits. There is nothing left but to depart.

I am ready.

It is time.

About the Authors

NEIL K. NEWELL has written plays, screenplays, and novels, as well as more than one hundred articles in national publications. He has worked for many years for LDS Welfare Services and teaches creative writing at Brigham Young University.

WILLIAM J. HAMBLIN is a professor of history at BYU, specializing in the ancient and medieval Near East. He is the author of dozens of articles and several books, most recently *Solomon's Temple: Myth and History* (with David Seely). Hamblin has just returned from a year teaching at the BYU Jerusalem Center.

Learn more about the book and the authors at
www.thebookofmalchus.com